We
Never Asked
for Wings

ALSO BY VANESSA DIFFENBAUGH

The Language of Flowers

We
Never Asked
for Wings

Vanessa
Diffenbaugh

MANTLE

First published in the United States 2015 by Ballantine Books,
an imprint of Random House, a division of Random House LLC,
a Penguin Random House Company, New York

First published in the UK 2015 by Mantle
an imprint of Pan Macmillan
20 New Wharf Road, London N1 9RR
Associated companies throughout the world
www.panmacmillan.com

ISBN 978-1-4472-9450-4

Grateful acknowledgement is made to Jennifer K. Sweeney and Perugia Press
for permission to reprint an excerpt from 'In Flight' from *How to Live on Bread
and Music* by Jennifer K. Sweeny, copyright © 2009 by Jennifer K. Sweeney.
Reprinted by permission of the author and Perugia Press,
www.perugiapress.com, Florence, Massachusetts.

Feather illustration by Irina Krivoruchko @ istockphoto.com

Book design by Karin Batten.

Printed and bound by CPI Group (UK) Ltd, Croydon, CR0 4YY

Visit **www.panmacmillan.com** to read more about all our books
and to buy them. You will also find features, author interviews and
news of any author events, and you can sign up for e-newsletters
so that you're always first to hear about our new releases.

For Donovan, Tre'von,
Graciela, and Miles

And in memory of
Sharon Renee Higgins, 1991–2011

The Himalayan legend says
there are beautiful white birds
that live completely in flight.
They are born in the air,

must learn to fly before falling
and die also in their flying.
Maybe you have been born
into such a life

with the bottom dropping out.

—from "In Flight,"
Jennifer K. Sweeney

It wasn't too late to turn back. Driving through the fog at a quarter past midnight, Letty waited for the exit signs that appeared without warning, willing herself to swerve off the freeway and return the way she'd come. But at each split-second opportunity she wavered just a moment too long. The exits came and went, and she was left with nothing but a wall of fog and the tequila in her water bottle, pushing her forward—past San Jose and Los Banos and Coalinga and through the sour cloud of Harris Ranch, accelerating until even the short length of yellow line she'd been following for over two hundred miles transformed into a rush of white.

She'd left her children.

It wasn't premeditated, she told herself, as if this made it any less criminal. And it was true that it had happened quickly—too quickly for her to think, or to wake them up, or to take them with her. She'd come home to find her two children asleep in their beds in an empty apartment, a hastily scrawled letter on the kitchen table. Reading it, panic overwhelmed her, and Letty had done the only thing she could think of to do: she added her name to the bottom of the letter and ran out the door the way she'd come.

Her youngest, Luna, slept diagonally. Letty imagined her now, stretched across the bed they shared, searching for her mother in the darkness. Luna's hands would be cold, the covers a tangled mess on the floor. Across the room, in his small bed beneath the window, Alex would be snoring softly, or talking in his sleep—a scientific babble that only Letty had ever heard, and no one, including Alex, believed occurred.

"I'll be home before you wake up," Letty whispered, wanting it to be true.

But she kept driving, away from them.

At the base of the Tahachapi mountains, Letty dumped the remains of the tequila-water out the window and squinted into the night. Somewhere ahead of her, a Greyhound bus lurched toward the Mexican border, its pull as strong as a rope tied from the bumper to her beating heart. Once, she might have cut that rope and taken off running in the opposite direction. But that was a long time ago, now. A lifetime of mistakes had taught her what everyone around her already believed: that she couldn't do it; that alone, she wasn't enough, and so she'd long ago surrendered her life to the one person in the world capable of holding it all together.

She needed her mother.

One

1

The edge of the mattress dipped as Alex sat down. Luna was curled into a ball, doing that thing she did when she wanted someone to believe she was still asleep: eyes scrunched too tightly closed, lips pulled down at the corners because Alex had told her once that she smiled when she faked sleep, so now she overcorrected. Wisps of long black hair had escaped her braids and tangled around her gold earrings; a smudge of drool flaked white off her cheek. Checking to see who was there, she squinted at Alex through crusted eyelashes and then snapped her eyes shut again. Where she'd recently lost her two front teeth, her gums were swollen and red.

How could he possibly tell her?

She was only six. Only six and tiny too—even with their grandmother cooking constantly, there were weeks she lost weight instead of gaining it, and she didn't have any to lose. What would he feed her? He felt again the despair washing over him, as it had when he'd first woken up and read the letter; with puffed cheeks, he held his breath until it passed. *Everything is going to be fine,* he told himself. *Everything is going to be just fine.* He was fourteen years old, fifteen in a month. He'd been watching his grandmother long enough to know what to do. But it wouldn't be easy. Luna wasn't the kind of kid who just listened. Getting her to do anything took extensive negotiation, distraction, and occasionally—even with his grandmother—bribery.

Alex decided to skip straight to the bribery.

"Too bad Luna's not awake, because I'm about to have donuts for breakfast."

She pressed her face into the pillow to muffle a squeal and clamped her hands over her ears as if this might prevent their grandmother from hearing. It was breaking three rules, at least: (1) Stopping anywhere on the way to school, (2) Eating sugar before noon, and (3) Eating donuts, ever.

"Don't worry, she isn't here."

Luna peeled away from the pillow. Her brown eyes studied Alex, looking for clues as to how she should feel about this unfamiliar state of being. "Where is she?"

He forced himself to smile. "Mom took her to get Grandpa."

"They found him?"

Alex paused, then moved his head in a kind of circle, a motion that Luna would interpret as a yes but that was ambiguous enough to get Alex off if he was ever questioned for lying at the gates of heaven. He'd hidden his grandmother's letter behind the tip jar his mother kept in the kitchen cabinet, which he'd hoped would be full (she'd taken most of the money, though, leaving only three inches of coins at the bottom of the jar) and estimated the time it would take for them to return by the miles to Oro de Hidalgo and back, calculated at seventy miles an hour. Best case scenario: "They'll be back on Friday."

Luna was quiet, and for a minute Alex thought she was worrying, as he was, about how his mother would get his grandparents, Maria Elena and Enrique, back across the border—or whether they would get back at all. But then she asked what day it was.

"Tuesday."

She hummed the days of the week to the tune of "Clementine" and counted on her fingers. "Three days."

"Exactly. Three days of eating whatever we want and staying after school with our friends."

They didn't have any friends; Luna did not look convinced.

He squeezed her feet through the blankets, trying to think of something to comfort her. "We've been alone before, remember?"

She nodded, fear in her eyes for the first time, and he realized too late that it was the wrong thing to say. They'd both gotten stomachaches from the potatoes he'd half-baked, and she'd cried, inconsolably, the whole night through. That time, Maria Elena hadn't meant to leave them alone. She and Enrique had gone out of town and hired a babysitter, but the girl got sick and left, and even though they'd called Letty in a panic, she hadn't come home until six o'clock in the morning.

"I'm older now," he said and then, because he couldn't think of anything else to say: "Sprinkles?"

Luna studied him. "Are we really going to get donuts?"

"If you ever get out of bed, we are." She reached out, and he pulled her up and set her on the floor. "Need help?"

"Nana said I could wear my heart dress. She said she'd wash it."

"I don't know where it is."

"But she *said*."

It was exactly the kind of conversation that could spiral into hysteria; the recovery would take half the morning. "Hold on."

He looked in the closet, where his grandmother hung the clothes she'd ironed, and then in the kitchen sink, where she soaked things overnight; finally, he found it on the drying rack in the stairwell, stretched flat on top of a towel.

"It's wet," Luna said when he handed it to her.

"So wear it wet, or wear something dry."

"But I want to wear this. And I don't want it to be wet."

She held her dress by the sleeves and swung it around in a circle. The material flew just inches from his face. He reached out and grabbed it.

"Stop that. Come here." From her dresser he found leggings and a long-sleeved shirt, and dressed her in both before pulling the damp dress over her head. "You can't even tell it's wet."

Luna wrinkled her nose. "But why are we even going to school?" she asked. "Please, please, please, can we stay home and watch TV?"

"No way," Alex said. They were so different, he and his sister, that sometimes he couldn't believe they were even related. But then, Alex was different from just about everyone he'd ever met. While the other eighth graders in his class read banned magazines behind textbooks and painted their nails under their desks and avoided answering questions, Alex came to school every day armed with some strange fact to shock or impress his teacher. Most of these facts he got from his grandfather, the only person he knew who was like him. Enrique could recite the name of every bird that traveled the Pacific Flyway in alphabetical order, a skill he'd learned from his own father, and his grandfather before that. Alex had been able to do it for as long as he could remember.

Grabbing his clothes from the closet, he went to the bathroom to get dressed. Behind the locked door he pulled on the white shirt his grandmother had ironed. The kids at Cesar Chavez called him "Newsman" because of his shirts, but Alex knew he looked nothing like a television reporter. He was too skinny, for one, and his nose had grown before the rest of his face. But the real problem with Alex's appearance was his hair: a wavy, almost-blond mop he assumed he'd inherited from his father. Alex had never seen him, but in a shoe box under Letty's bed was a sealed envelope addressed to *Wes Riley, 536 Elm Street, Mission Hills, California*. When he'd searched the name on his school computer, Alex had found images of a man who looked almost exactly like him—blue eyes, milky skin, and a square jaw. In every photograph he wore scrubs and held a different dark-skinned baby. The captions read "Mumbai," "Malawi," "Guatemala City." He'd been given some kind of award in 2005, but the article about it was written in an African language Alex didn't recognize and couldn't understand.

But of all the information he'd gathered about his father, the address was the thing that most captivated him. It was just over the freeway. For years, Alex had imagined walking past the house, his father recognizing him from the window and rushing out. He'd never gotten far enough from Maria Elena's watchful eye to venture there alone, though, and he'd never summoned the courage to ask his mother about the man or the circumstances of his birth—mostly because he'd never summoned the courage to ask his mother about anything at all.

He brushed his teeth quickly as Luna pounded on the door.

"Alex! Let me in."

* * *

Maria Elena had packed their lunches for the week and stacked them on the top shelf of the refrigerator, all labeled. ALEX: TUESDAY, LUNA: TUESDAY, and behind those the Wednesdays, the Thursdays, and the Fridays. Below their lunches were the remnants of every meal their grandmother had made for the last two weeks, stored and dated and—Alex could imagine the smell without cracking open the lids—many edging toward decay. He pulled out the Tuesday lunches and stuffed them in their backpacks, checking to see that their tennis shoes were still at the bottoms of the bags, where they belonged.

From the bathroom, he heard the toilet flush and the faucet turn on and off, and then Luna stood in the doorway. Water dripped onto her forehead, from where she'd slicked the loose hair back into her braids. If her teacher ever noticed anything, she would notice that Luna's hair had not been rebraided that morning for the very first time all year. But Luna was the least of her teacher's problems—she probably wouldn't even look at her the entire day.

Fishing through the tip jar, Alex extracted a stack of quarters and stepped into his rain boots. He handed Luna hers: knee-high with pink polka dots. They were the one item of clothing necessary to survive life at the Landing, and the one thing his grandmother did not buy generic. Luna pulled them on.

"It's still there, did you see?"

"What is?"

She gestured for him to follow. In their grandparents' room, the bed was made as it always was, the quilt pulled tight and square, but he saw immediately that things were different. Only a nail remained where a small cross had hung over the bed; the top of his grandmother's dresser was empty of photographs and glistened with some kind of polish. Alex imagined her dusting while she packed. Luna pulled him across the room to where his grandfather's workbench sat under the window, his most recent project spread out exactly as he'd left it.

For six months, their grandfather had been focused on a single feather mosaic, a landscape of a rural village in Mexico, with small stucco houses tilting in imperfect rows and a shawl-wrapped woman looking up at a full moon. It was only the profile of the woman, and she was young, but Alex could tell it was his grandmother. It was always his grandmother. The feather work was so fine that from a few feet away it could be mistaken for an oil painting, each feather a single stroke, but instead the mosaic was created entirely of naturally occurring feathers stuck into a thin layer of campeche wax. The smell of wax hung heavy in the air, and it made him miss his grandfather intensely: the way he patted his thighs every time Alex stepped into the room, even after Alex grew too big to sit in his lap; the way he stopped everything to stand up and look outside, narrating the natural world for his grandson, who remembered every word he said.

Enrique had been gone for six weeks, returning to Mexico to be with his dying mother, and now Maria Elena and Letty were gone too. Alex moved to the window and looked out at the empty landscape.

They were completely alone.

More alone than seemed reasonable, given that they stood less than twenty miles south of San Francisco. Most of the time he didn't notice the isolation, or else he tried to think about only the good things: the birds, the view, the water. But every once in a while it hit him. Where was civilization? Outside, Mile Road stretched through the empty marsh, from Highway 101 to the edge of the bay, ending at the three squat buildings of Eden's Landing: Building A, painted an industrial peachy brown; Building B, half a shade darker of the same dull color; and Building C, closest to the water and painted a faded robin's-egg blue. A barbed-wire fence separated the Landing from the San Francisco International Airport to the north; nothing but a stretch of ever-shifting wetlands separated it from the bankrupt blight of Bayshore to the south. There were other towns nearby, nice ones like Hillsborough and Burlingame and San Mateo, but the expansion of the 101 freeway had cut off the Landing and Bayshore from the rest of the peninsula. Alex could see Mission Hills, the most affluent of the suburbs, directly across the freeway from where he stood—but it felt like a world away.

"He'll come back. Won't he?" Luna asked, interrupting his thoughts. She was studying her grandfather's mosaic. In a ring around the full moon the wax showed through, chocolate-colored and sticky; beside it, blue-black feathers poked from the top of a labeled envelope as if waiting for his return.

"Of course he will," Alex said.

But he wasn't sure.

Just before his grandfather left, Alex had complained that they didn't have even one piece of Enrique's work. He'd been sitting beside him at his workbench, as he did every day after school, separating the striped from the solid feathers of a marsh wren. Enrique had nodded solemnly but hadn't said anything, and now he was gone.

Perhaps he'd left the mosaic for them on purpose, Alex thought: a silent apology for his sudden flight.

It was late when they finally left the apartment. The sun was higher than it should have been, and Mrs. Starks was already sitting in her lawn chair in front of Building B, halfway through her second cigarette. She had the whole building to herself. The apartment on the top floor (the penthouse, she called it) was hers, as well as a boarded-up apartment on the first level that she referred to as her "shop"—full of old furniture she'd acquired as the buildings slowly emptied out. She was fixing it up, she'd told Alex once—the nice stuff, the antiques, the things people never should have left behind—and then she would sell it all and move away. She was going to be rich, she told him. It was her ticket out. But that was years ago, and still she sat there, day after day, smoking her cigarettes.

"There's my dirty girl," Mrs. Starks called when she saw Luna streaking across the empty parking lot. They were supposed to stay on the paths, but Luna never did. Stepping straight off the concrete into the marsh, she watched the mud creep up around the edges of her rain boot until it enveloped the rubber foot completely. Leaning over, she held on to the handles with both hands and pulled, releasing the boot with a loud sucking sound.

"Again!" Mrs. Starks barked, tapping her cigarette on the plastic arm of her lawn chair while Luna balanced on the other boot and then on both at the same time, sinking as if on a particularly slow escalator, halfway to her knees. Just before the mud could roll over the lips of her boots and soak her ankles, she jumped back onto the pavement.

"One more inch and it would have got you!"

It was like this every morning, until Maria Elena leaned out the window and put a stop to it. Sometimes Mrs. Puente from Building A joined in, and occasionally the Ramirez brothers too, though when they appeared, Alex didn't wait for their grandmother's scolding but pulled Luna straight down the path himself, no matter how she kicked or screamed.

"Good morning, Mrs. S," Alex said. Mrs. Starks looked at him curiously, surprised at the greeting, and then blew smoke out the side of her mouth.

"Well, good morning to you," she said, looking up at the window and then back to Alex. "You late?"

"We'll walk fast."

"Better get on with it, then," she said. She looked at the window a second time, nervous. Maria Elena didn't like them to talk to her and she knew it, but sometimes she stood out in the marsh after school, just past the point their grandmother could see, a sun hat pulled low over her long scraggly hair and her bare legs sagging out of short shorts, and held up a peppermint or a butterscotch she'd snagged from a waiting room. It was a little creepy, but Alex and Luna always took what she offered and ate it quickly, the hard sugar cracking against their teeth as they walked the last hundred yards home.

"Alex!"

Luna had waited too long; her right boot was filling. She reached up, waiting for him to help her out of the water. It was why he'd packed extra socks. Trying to hide his frustration, he grabbed her hand and pulled her forward, but she wriggled away, water sloshing from the top of her boot as she raced toward the shoreline.

Alex took off after her, following the well-worn web of trails that connected the Landing to the rest of Bayshore. He had trouble imagining it, but the Landing hadn't always been so empty. When the buildings were new, the apartments had swarmed with children. Someone was always lost; names being called echoed off the bay, the responses heard from unexpected windows or from somewhere within the marsh. The women didn't even mind the mud back then, his grandmother said, just chipped in for a dozen pairs of fisherman's boots, their dresses tied up in knots as they cut paths to the nearest strip mall. The entire salty peninsula had smelled like something frying. Alex had heard the stories so many times he almost missed it, this world he'd never even seen.

Luna made it to the water and climbed up the rock jetty that separated the wetlands from the bay. On soggy feet she jumped from one rock to the next, her arms spread like wings. Alex followed close behind, almost knocking her over when she stopped suddenly, crouching down and pulling something from a dark crevice between two rocks. She held it up.

A tail feather: eight to nine inches long, thick horizontal stripes alternating from medium to light gray. The very tip of the feather was bright white.

"What's it from?" she asked.

"A sharp-shinned hawk."

He took the feather from his sister's hand. Once, standing on the porch, Alex had asked his grandmother why they had stayed, when the buildings began to fall apart and all the other families moved out, when his mother was still young and the Landing had become dangerous, before it had become empty. She said nothing, just looked up into the sky, where a flock of western sandpipers appeared as if to answer his question. They had stayed for the birds. Unless it was to return to Mexico, his grandfather had refused to leave his perch beneath the Pacific Flyway, where directly outside his window millions of birds stopped each fall and spring to rest on their long migrations.

Alex tucked the feather into Luna's hair and jumped down off the rocks.

"Come on," he said, holding out his arms for her to jump. "I smell sugar."

2

The reunion hadn't gone as planned. When Letty finally intercepted her mother at a Greyhound station in North Hollywood, Maria Elena had been so surprised, and then angry, that she wouldn't get off the bus, wouldn't speak—wouldn't even look at her daughter. Desperate and exhausted—and just drunk enough not to understand the consequences—Letty heard herself lie to her mother. She hadn't left her children alone, she told her. She'd left them with Sara, her best friend from high school and one of the most responsible people either of them knew.

At this, Maria Elena dragged her suitcase from the bus to Letty's car and climbed into the passenger seat.

"Well, let's go, then," she said, adjusting her short hair and buckling the seat belt tightly across her stiff jacket. "It'll be faster this way."

Maria Elena wanted Letty to drive her to Oro de Hidalgo.

Stunned, Letty stood in the dark parking lot, trying to figure out what to do. If her children really were with Sara, there was no reason she couldn't drive her mother into Mexico to find her father—and if she told Maria Elena the truth, that she'd left them sleeping in their beds alone, her mother would send her home in a fury and disappear onto the bus and then across the border, maybe forever.

It was an impossible decision.

But Maria Elena had opened a map and was spewing directions from the front seat and Letty—willing to do anything to keep from turning around to face her children alone—got back in the car, flipped on the ignition, and started to drive.

Four hours later, they approached the U.S./Mexico border together. They were going the wrong direction for anyone to care, but still, Letty held her breath as they neared the heavy cement overpass. She had no idea what to expect on the other side. Letty had never been to Mexico. She had been born in the United States, which made her a legal citizen— but both Maria Elena and Enrique were undocumented. It wouldn't be easy to get them back into California, and this was assuming they could even find her father. Pushing these thoughts from her mind, Letty followed the slow line of cars through the immigration checkpoint and crossed to the other side.

The change was instant. South of San Diego, California felt wide open, great blue sky and speckled hills and planned communities cut into the empty space; but Tijuana was crowded: lines of cars and people and buildings with their second stories stacked not quite on top of their firsts, tufts of rebar sticking out the top like thick black hairs. Letty drove straight through the city, weaving in and out of traffic, until the buildings thinned to desert and they were alone on the narrow highway.

"Are you sure this is the right road?" Letty asked her mother.

"It's right," Maria Elena said, looking down at the map. She measured the distance with her thumb. "Straight ahead for a hundred miles."

Letty looked out the window, across the flat desert. It was almost morning. Any minute and miles away, Alex and Luna would wake up alone in an empty apartment and stumble out of bed to find Letty's signature scribbled across the bottom of Maria Elena's letter. The sky swirled electric pink, and all at once Letty was nauseous. What was she doing? She had to turn around and go home. But what good would that do? Alex and Luna didn't need her, they needed their grandmother. For nearly fifteen years Maria Elena had raised her grandchildren, rocking them through long, fussy nights, feeding them from glass bottles while Letty's breasts drained into the shower, teaching them to sit and stand and walk and talk. If Letty came home alone, her children would be devastated—if not terrified—and it was this thought that kept her fingers clutching the steering wheel, her foot heavy on the gas.

Beside her, Maria Elena startled. Letty followed her mother's gaze to a long, brightly painted fence, keeping nothing from nowhere on the side of the road. Casket-shaped boxes had been attached at intervals, numbers stenciled on the fronts in cheery colors—2002: 371, 2003: 390, all the way to the year 2012.

Border-crossing deaths.

"Don't look," Letty said quickly. Her stomach turning, she pulled her passport out of the glove compartment and jammed it down the front of her jeans, the corners poking sharp and comfortingly into her stomach. "Daddy's okay."

"He's not okay, or he would have come home," Maria Elena said. And then, after a long silence, she asked: "Why hasn't he even called?"

Letty had wondered the same thing. There hadn't been a phone line to their apartment building since a storm took down the pole five years before, but he could have called her cell, or her work, or left a message with the secretary at the kids' school.

"Maybe he forgot my number," she said. "Or ran out of money."

"Well, if he's alive I'll kill him. Making me leave my babies."

My babies. Letty felt the words hit her, a tiny jolt of validation. Alex and Luna really were her mother's babies, and she was the one who'd left them.

As she drove, Letty's mind wandered back to the beginning, when it had made sense for Maria Elena to claim them—or to claim Alex, at least. Letty had been a teenage mother, despondent and suffering from a heartbreak she'd tried hard to drink away. Bayshore was full of girls like her, and every night they went out, leaving their newborns at home and dancing their bodies back into shape. Maria Elena didn't complain. She'd wanted a big family but had only been able to have Letty, so it was a full year before she stopped her—hid her favorite high-heeled boots and broke her lipstick off at the base. Watching her mother's square frame block the only exit, Letty had expected a lecture on parenthood, but instead Maria Elena handed her an ironed shirt and a pressed skirt and told her to get a job. Enrique had hurt his back. They were a family of four now, with a grandmother and endless aunts, uncles, and cousins to support back in Mexico. Someone had to replace the income her father could no longer provide.

Listening, Letty felt a flicker of disappointment—Alex was her son, after all—but before she could even register the feeling it was replaced immediately by relief. She knew nothing about children; just being in the same room with her impossibly small, helpless son made her nervous. So she went out and got a job, and then another, and then a third, while Maria Elena stayed home. For fifteen years that had been their arrangement, and it would be their arrangement still, if Enrique hadn't gone home to see his dying mother and not come back.

Why couldn't he just have come home? Letty silently moaned. Maria Elena had taken care of everything before he left, buying his bus ticket to Morelia and handing over their entire life savings to a coyote named Benny to ensure Enrique's illicit passage back into the United States. She'd told Enrique exactly where and when to meet Benny—so many times that even Luna could repeat the information.

But something must have gone wrong. The day before, Benny had come back without her father. And he'd refused to return the money.

Letty slammed on the brakes.

Choked by the stiff seat belt, Maria Elena gasped. "What're you doing?"

What *was* she doing? Her father could be anywhere, and her kids were home alone. "Exactly," Letty said, suddenly furious. "What are we doing? Why are we here?"

"*I'm* here because my husband needs me," Maria Elena snapped. "I don't know why you're here."

Letty sunk low behind the wheel. *I'm here because I don't know how to take care of my children,* she thought, *and because it's unfair of you to expect me to, when you've expected nothing of me for fifteen years.*

But Letty held her tongue. After a long silence, she nodded slowly out the window, to the place the fence had been, but wasn't anymore.

"I'm here because I'm not going to let you become a number on that fence."

Outside the window, abandoned railroad tracks ended in a field of crooked cactus and Maria Elena sighed, surrendering to the long drive and to her daughter, fuming beside her.

They drove, and drove, and drove. When Letty couldn't drive anymore she pulled into a field of wheat and slept, suffering through a slide show of dreams in which she witnessed everything that could happen to two children left alone in an empty apartment: the slip of a bread knife, an electric shock, a three-story fall from a screenless window, or—horribly—the sharp knock of Child Protective Services on the door. *Don't open it,* she murmured, imagining suited-up social workers, imagining kidnappers. Overhead a second sunrise broke, but even awake the images kept coming: headfirst tumbles down the stairs, toes caught in the spokes of borrowed bicycles, and the worst: the bay, the beckoning blue water that lapped at their ankles turning suddenly deep, one going out after the other, two small bodies washed out to sea. Did they even know how to swim? She had no idea.

How had it happened, that one day she'd been an honor student, being told she could go to college, and the next she was lying on the ground a thousand miles from her children, a community college dropout with two DUIs, a mother who didn't even know if her own children could swim? The change had been gradual, but it felt like it had happened all at once, a tectonic shift, a free fall. The sky above her tilted back and forth and then back again, and she imagined the oxygen running off the edge of the earth like water until she was left, dizzy and panicking, to drown in a field of dry grass.

Maria Elena's face appeared suddenly against the blue sky. She looked older than Letty remembered. Her usually sprayed-to-perfection hair was pressed flat on one side, and age spots Letty had never noticed dotted her skin like fingerprints in the morning light.

"Ready to go?"

She couldn't go. She couldn't even stand up.

"I think we should turn around," Letty said. There was no way to rationalize it anymore. While her mother slept in the car, she'd finally tried to call Sara, only to find that her cell phone didn't work in Mexico.

"You're just tired." It was clear Maria Elena meant hungover, but she didn't say it. From inside a paper bag her mother withdrew a custard roll, the kind she made when anyone in the family had a fever. It was just like her, to have carried it all this way in her pocket, ready.

"Here," Maria Elena said, handing Letty the roll and pulling her to standing. "We're almost there. We'll find him, and we'll all turn around and go home together."

Letty tucked a loose hair behind her ear and tried to imagine what it would be like to find her father, at his childhood home or in the little town square, anxiously arranging his trip back north. Picturing his relief at seeing they had come for him, she felt a flicker of strength return.

They had to keep going. They were almost there.

But *almost there,* it turned out, meant another eight hours. Maria Elena sank deeper and deeper into the passenger seat, her body relaxing as they began to pass the landmarks of her youth—avocado orchards and lemon groves, cupola-topped churches and town squares. Every once in a while she would say something: *I wonder if Tia Juanita had her eyes fixed* or *I guess I'll finally meet Cristina's twins, although they must be all grown up by now.* Letty said nothing, just followed her mother's directions wordlessly, Highway 15 to 15D to 5, through Guadalajara and Ocotlán and La Barca, passing signs for Zamora and Zacapu and Morelia. And just as she was beginning to feel she couldn't drive a single mile farther, she saw it: a dusty road sign, tilting in the sandy earth.

ORO DE HIDALGO, it read, EXIT 19C.

The Espinosa family home was even bigger than her childhood imagination had allowed: three stories and stucco, with vines growing up the side walls and flowering around the attic windows. It had been magnificent once, but as she followed her mother up the path, she could see that it had fallen far from its original splendor. The yard was a tangle of overgrown grasses; a six-foot pile of garbage and broken furniture held up what was left of the rotting fence. Around the side of the house, the infamous swimming pool was nothing but a giant empty shell—the interior walls cracked and faded gray.

Maria Elena pushed open the heavy front door. Inside was just as Letty's father had described it: the wide marble staircase imported from Italy in the 1940s, framed on either side by gold railings leading up to the second-story landing. As a child, Letty hadn't been able to comprehend the elegance or the emptiness, and now here it was, spreading out all around her. She crossed the cement floor that had once been covered with plush carpet, fingered the powdery plaster encasing the fireplace, where a marble mantel had once hung. Through the dining room window she saw the lemon groves that had been sold off acre by acre, and she remembered her father's stories about the years the pool was filled, when boys would walk for hours from the neighboring villages to swim all day and sleep in the orchards at night, just to swim again in the morning. All this was before the war ended, before Letty's grandfather's unsold feather mosaics filled the attic rooms, long before the family had been forced to hawk everything in the house that wasn't bolted to the foundation. It was fickle, the art world, had been Enrique's only explanation: feathers had fallen out of fashion. And so he'd had no choice but to leave, the only child of a once prominent artist going north with his young bride, following friends who fought for work as day laborers in San Francisco. Enrique found a job on a landscape crew and made enough to support his family and still send money home—until his back gave out and Letty had to step up in his place. She had sent money back to Mexico for years, but not nearly enough, it seemed, to maintain such a grand estate.

Letty's thoughts were interrupted by a loud crash. Turning in the direction of the noise, she walked through the empty dining room, down a long hall, and into the kitchen.

And there he was: her father. He sat at the table amid a tumble of feathers—Kelly green and olive, forest and chartreuse. The jars into which he had been sorting the greens were lined up on the edge of the table, and one of them had fallen to the ground. Maria Elena kneeled beside him, gathering the glass with her bare hands.

"Are you okay?" Letty asked, addressing her father. "Where's Grandma?" It felt strange to call her Grandma, even though that's what she was to Letty. They'd never met.

Maria Elena looked up from the glass and shook her head solemnly. She nodded to the kitchen counter, where a water-spotted newspaper clipping lay. On it was a photograph of Letty's grandmother as a young woman, and a paragraph in Spanish about her life. An obituary, dated the week before.

"I'm sorry," Letty said, crossing the room to her father. There were feathers everywhere, on the table but also on the bench and floor, clusters of red and orange and yellow like pools of spilled paint. She placed her hand softly on his shoulder.

Enrique nodded, acknowledging her, but before he could speak, Maria Elena stood up, her hands full of glass. "He says he wants to stay."

It was too much to take in all at once: that her grandmother was dead; that her father was alive, and seemingly well; that he didn't want to come home. "What do you mean? He can't stay here all alone."

"Tell her," Maria Elena prodded.

Letty's father wouldn't look at her. Instead, he held Maria Elena's gaze. "You're my life," he said. "You're my everything."

Her mother studied him. Even at sixty-five he was handsome: his smooth skin cleanly shaven, his eyes as blue as the water in the pool must have been, and their draw just as strong. Dumping the glass into a waste bin, Maria Elena cleared a spot on the bench and sat down heavily beside him. Letty watched the unsettled feathers drift to the floor.

Finally, her mother turned to her. "He wants me to stay with him."

Letty stood in confused silence, trying to understand her mother's words, and all at once it hit her. Of course. Enrique hadn't missed his ride north—he'd stayed on purpose. For as long as she could remember, Enrique had wanted to move back to Mexico, and in the last few years, his pleas had become more urgent. Oro de Hidalgo was home. It was where his family had been for generations and where his extended family lived still. Of the twelve homes surrounding the tiny town square, Espinosas lived in eleven. *It's time,* he would say over his morning coffee, when he thought Letty was still asleep. Always Maria Elena would argue, citing Letty, citing her babies, but Enrique would argue back. *She's all grown,* he would say. *She doesn't need us anymore.*

He was wrong. Letty knew it and Maria Elena knew it, but the argument had persisted, and it seemed obvious now: drawn back by his mother's illness, he'd finally been given a reason to return to Mexico. And he wasn't leaving.

Well, he could stay if he wanted, Letty thought—but he couldn't keep Maria Elena. She hadn't driven halfway across a continent to turn back without her mother.

"You're not staying," she said, looking her mother in the eyes.

Maria Elena said nothing.

"They can visit," Enrique said. "We'll fill up the pool."

Maria Elena stared at the table. If she could survive it, Letty knew, her mother would cut her heart in two and send half back to California, to care for her daughter and grandchildren, and keep the other half here, to live out the remainder of her days with her husband. But she couldn't. She had to choose. The room spun, as Letty realized that for the first time her mother might not choose her.

"No, no, no," Letty said. "You can't leave me. I can't do anything without you."

"If you can't, it's my fault." Maria Elena looked at Enrique, her expression half accusation, half surrender. "Your father thinks I've ruined your life."

"You *are* my life," Letty said, realizing as she said it that her father had said the same thing only minutes before, and how much more pathetic the words sounded coming from the mouth of a thirty-three-year-old woman, aimed at her mother.

Enrique sighed, turning to Letty for the first time.

"Baby, baby, baby," he said softly. He'd called her "baby" until the moment she'd started to show, and then the nickname had fallen away. Hearing it now, her throat closed. She shut her eyes against the tears. "You made two beautiful, perfect children. They deserve their mother."

"Really? A bartender with no education and two DUIs. You think that's what they deserve?"

"Don't say that," Maria Elena said. "That's not you. That's never been you."

"It *is* me. They need *you*."

The room fell silent. Maria Elena looked at Enrique in that way that had always made Letty slightly ill, a look that didn't belong anywhere outside the walls of a church. He opened his arms, and Maria Elena leaned against his chest. Letty felt herself losing. Grasping, she flung about for anything that could change her mother's mind and landed on her children.

"They're all alone," she said. "Right now, at this very moment."

Maria Elena pulled away from Enrique.

"What are you saying? They're with Sara."

"They're not. I left them alone."

It was cruel, but it was all she had left. Maria Elena looked like her insides had been extracted and laid out on the table, a mass of color as tangled and exposed as the feathers. Her mother didn't deserve this. Not after all she'd done for her grandchildren and, for seventeen years before that, for Letty. Maria Elena had been a good mother. While the other kids at the Landing ate Cup O'Noodles in the stairwells and stayed out past midnight, their parents passed out drunk or too high to care, Letty ate *pozole* and hot tortillas at the kitchen table and never missed a bedtime. She'd had everything she'd ever needed. That she'd become a teenage mother and done nothing with her life was her own fault, and now it was Maria Elena who had to suffer the consequences.

She didn't deserve it, but still, Letty couldn't let her go. She looked directly into her mother's eyes. *"Please."*

Letty couldn't do it. Maria Elena knew she couldn't do it.

But her mother shook her head, anger and betrayal settling into heavy disappointment.

"You can do this," Maria Elena said finally. "Your father's right. You can." She looked across the empty kitchen as she said it, and Letty saw how much her mother wanted to believe her own words, and also how much she clearly did not.

Letty closed her dark, tired eyes and pressed two fingers into her aching eyelids. "I'm not going home without you."

Maria Elena shook her head. "Letty, please. You have your whole life ahead of you. You have to take it."

"I won't. I told you I won't and I won't."

"You will."

Letty pulled her eyelids back open and they stared at each other, two pairs of wide brown eyes locked, and all at once Maria Elena sprang up, clutching both of Letty's hands and half-dragging her across the kitchen, down the hall, to the front door. For a moment Letty thought she'd convinced her—that she would pull her mother into the car and they'd both drive home together. But instead, Maria Elena pushed her daughter outside.

Giving Letty one last angry, pleading look, she let go of her hands and slammed the door between them.

Alex and Luna would die without their grandparents. It was the only possible outcome, Letty thought, as she stood shell-shocked on the front stoop, in the same place a thousand wounded birds had breathed their final breath. She pounded the door. She popped a triangle of already shattered glass from a window and tried to climb through, but the space was too narrow. The glass pierced a row of holes across her palm, blood dripping onto the dirt as she walked around the side of the house and down into the bottom of the empty pool, collapsing into the cement cradle.

It was dark when she awoke. Decomposing leaves smeared her cheek, the smell of earth turning new, and she searched through glazed eyes for manzanitas, for arched willows, for the web of her father's hummingbird feeders—all the hallmarks of home—but instead she took in the cracked walls of the pool and the flat face of the enormous house and remembered. She wasn't at the Landing but in Mexico, two thousand miles away. Swaying and dizzy, she pulled herself out of the dry depths and staggered back around to the front porch. All the windows were dark.

She tried the front door. Still locked.

They weren't going to let her in.

"I'll forget to feed them," she whispered, a desperate, final attempt. Though she couldn't see her, she knew her mother was on the other side of the door, her back pressed against it, as close to her daughter as she could be in the moment before good-bye. "They'll starve to death. I'll go to work and they'll drown in the bay."

Something heavy creaked against the wood, the sound of her mother standing up.

I love you, she thought she heard, but it might have been: *Go home.*

3

Luna's hair was exactly half-brushed. Maria Elena's tight braids had lasted two days, but by Wednesday morning no amount of water could coax the loose hair flat against her scalp, so she'd pulled the rubber bands out and tried to pull a comb from top to bottom. Her thick hair knotted and the comb stuck just below her chin, and again at the back of her head, and in a wild snarl above her right ear. She left it that way. It looked terrible, but when Alex tried to help, she screamed and ran out of the bathroom, refusing to brush her teeth.

Now, in addition to worrying about his sister, he was starting to worry that someone would notice they had been left alone. Maria Elena would never allow Luna to go to school looking like that—but what choice did he have? Pulling on his boots, he dragged her out of the house before Mrs. Starks settled into her lawn chair and chased her all the way to her classroom, where he lifted her up onto a low row of cubbies and swapped her rain boots for tennis shoes.

"Are you going to come get me after school?" she asked.

He nodded. "Stay right here, okay?"

"Okay."

With open palms he tried to smooth her hair flat, but she pushed his hands away and jumped down, throwing open her classroom door. Alex inhaled sharply, watching as the door bounced open and then inched closed on a taut spring: closing, closing, closing, closed.

Finally. He exhaled, long and loud.

He'd always liked school, but it was different now; now, it was the only place he could breathe. For six and a half hours—from the time he dropped Luna off in her first-grade classroom to the time he picked her up—she was not his responsibility. She could scream or cry or whine or say she was hungry or thirsty or tired and he would have to do— nothing. Not one single thing. Yesterday he'd been able to forget they were even alone, sinking into math worksheets and spelling tests and an extra-credit report he was writing on native snakes of the San Francisco Bay, and it wasn't until after school, when he thought he'd lost her, that he'd been jolted back to reality. She'd come to find him at the same time he'd gone to find her, and they'd crossed paths in the crowded halls. After a frantic search he'd found her sobbing by the back fence. *I thought you'd left me,* she said, and he had to carry her crying all the way home, her rain boots dropping off her feet again and again until he finally gave up and carried Luna in one arm, her rain boots in the other.

But today, even the thought of Luna safe inside her classroom was not enough to ease the pressure on Alex's lungs. They were out of quarters and dimes and milk, and even if he'd been able to forget about food or money for one moment, there was no way he could forget the scalding three-inch-long burn on his forearm. The night before he'd tried to make eggs for dinner. All had gone fine until he took the frying pan off the stove and somehow ignited a dish towel, which burned a hole in his cotton sleeve, straight through to the skin. He'd barely slept from the pain. Underneath his shirt he'd wrapped the long blister with a wet paper towel, but it hadn't helped much.

Dreamily, he thought about skipping school and lying on his back by the bay, burnt arm floating on the water. But he wouldn't do it. He hadn't missed a day all year. Quickly, before he could give in to the imagined ecstasy of the cool water, he turned and walked to his classroom.

"Are you Alex?"

Behind his teacher's desk sat a substitute, a note in her hand. It was what his teacher always did, whenever she missed a day, because Alex was always there and always on time. He read her instructions and found the vocabulary tests under a pile of grammar worksheets at the back of the classroom.

"Couldn't you have just *pretended* you didn't know where they were?" Marcus Cooper grumbled from the front of the room. "Just this once."

He wasn't in the mood for Marcus. Alex gave him his test first and then passed them out to the rest of the class before walking to his own desk, where he found a present waiting for him. Spread out on his plastic chair was a bright pink spray of seaweed, shaped like a sprig of mistletoe, the tips opening like little hands: a gift from Yesenia. He looked up at her and smiled; she nodded and then turned to the vocabulary.

Yesenia had been in his class on and off since kindergarten, and although they'd never talked much, they had a silent connection. Barely four feet tall even with her thick-soled shoes, she often went missing from school for weeks or months at a time, returning in a wheelchair or with bandages on the backs of her legs. But she would know the answers on every test, no matter how long she'd been gone.

The seaweed was the continuation of a long string of unexplained, sciencey gifts she'd left in his seat: an iridescent dragonfly wing, a sticky chunk of honeycomb, the exoskeleton of a Jerusalem cricket. It wasn't every day. Maybe once a month at the most, but it was enough to make him think about her while he lay in bed at night. He wondered what was wrong with her body, what exactly they were trying to fix. She looked fine to him. Better than fine, really. There was the way she walked—a dip in her step, more than a limp—and her height, of course, but other than that she was—well, she could only be described as pretty. Perfect. Dark skin and dark eyes and dark lashes, and she'd grown this year, not up but out, her top half bigger than that of any other girl in class (unless it just looked big in comparison to the rest of her, which was possible). Recently, she'd dyed an inch-thick strip of her long dark hair a bright pinky red, the same color as the seaweed, and bought T-shirts to match.

He rolled the seaweed and put it in his front pocket so that just the tips showed, lacy and layered like a carnation, and turned to his test just as Yesenia finished hers. She flipped the paper over and started to draw. On his left, Washington Reed inched toward him, and as fast as he scrawled, Washington kept up. Alex slid his test as close to Yesenia's desk as possible and defined the last word—*embark*—while flipping his paper, so that at the very least he would deny Washington the final answer.

Test done, Alex settled in for the long wait. It was the same at school every day, too much time and too little to do and hardly anyone doing it anyway. Yesenia spent the hours drawing, and Alex worked in his notebooks, listing the things he'd seen on his walk to school—a black-bellied plover or an American coot or the footprints of a raccoon or weasel—and then, if the class computer was working, he would ask permission to look up the habitat, range, and breeding habits of each one. Most of the time it was enough to keep his mind occupied, but today there was the burn, which idleness seemed to make worse. Reaching under his sleeve, he pressed the blister gently and then harder, the liquid ballooning beneath the skin. Maybe he should pop it. Would it heal faster that way? With his nails he pinched until he broke the skin.

It hurt. A fierce stinging started where the liquid ran out of the small hole and then shot up the length of the burn, a pain so intense the room started to spin. He needed water. Something—anything—to cool it down. He shot up from his desk.

"Yes?"

Alex handed his test to the substitute.

"Should I get the math books?"

They didn't have math books, just occasional photocopied work-sheets, but she didn't know this.

"Oh, of course."

He was already to the door when Yesenia stood up. "I'll help."

She knew they didn't have math books, but Alex was so focused on the water he didn't stop to wonder what she was doing. At a full sprint he crossed the playground and climbed through the hole in the back fence, racing to the shore. Not even bothering to push up his sleeve, he submerged his entire arm into the muddy shallows. It was a long time before he caught his breath and looked up.

Yesenia sat on a rock beside him.

"Are you okay? You looked like you were going to pass out."

"It's just a little burn."

He pulled up his sleeve; she grimaced and turned away.

"What happened?"

Cooking dinner, the eggs, the fire: all of it led to the fact that they were alone. He picked up a rock with his good arm and threw it as far as he could manage.

"I was trying to make eggs," he said finally.

"Is your grandfather still missing?"

"How'd you know?"

"Everybody knows. In my building they say Benny never even planned to bring him back. Mrs. Avalos says she wouldn't trust him to transport a dead rat across the border."

Yesenia lived in the Courtyard Terrace apartments. They were well known as a drop-off point for newcomers, men and women and children smuggled into the United States from Mexico and Central America, so she knew Benny and every other coyote who worked Bayshore.

Alex had been to her apartment building only once, when a bus driver dropped her off after a field trip and asked Alex to walk her to the door. They'd gone through the parking lot and around the back of the building, and inside windows and open doors he'd seen mattresses lining living room floors, sleeping bags on couches, eight, nine, ten people sitting around tiny kitchen tables. Behind a partly open garage door he'd seen a mother and too many little kids to count, all lying on a bare mattress on the ground.

Yesenia's apartment was different. From outside he could see carpet as clean as Maria Elena's, and a vase of silk flowers on a coffee table. When she opened the door he was met by a particular smell: lime and bleach maybe, and something fried, and even though he'd never been there, it had reminded him of Mexico.

"Everyone thinks Benny just left him there?"

She nodded.

Alex shivered, suddenly cold, but sweating too. It was probably true. The question was whether or not Enrique wanted to be left behind. "What else do they say?"

"They say he's the best in the world."

"I thought you said they wouldn't trust him with a dead rat."

"Not Benny. Your grandfather."

Everyone knew about his grandfather's art. It had been the same in Mexico. If a bird died anywhere in the state of Michoacán—and later, in the Bay Area—it found its way to the Espinosa family's front stoop. It was why Enrique had never given up hope. There must be a market for his work, he said, if God had gathered all of North America to support it.

"He might be."

"Is it true you shoot birds for the feathers? Maritza says that's why you're always in such a hurry to leave after school."

Alex laughed. He should say yes; it was so much better a reputation than having to run home just because his grandmother demanded it. "No. People bring him the birds, or we find them. They're already dead, most of the time, or hurt and dying. My grandfather leaves a basket for them outside our door."

"And he plucks the feathers?"

"Yeah. And files them. He sorts everything by species and color and date."

"Sounds cool."

"It is."

She looked at him directly, and he was surprised by her confidence. "Can I see them?"

"Now?" Alex checked his watch and felt a moment of panic—they'd been gone too long already, and he hadn't even thought of what he would say when they returned empty-handed, Alex with a soaking wet sleeve.

Yesenia stood up and dusted off the back of her pants.

"No, not now," she said. "Friday?"

"Sure, Friday."

There was a chance his mother would be back on Friday. But knowing Letty, they would probably still be waiting, and alone.

4

She retraced her steps, 5 to 15D to 15, a map open on the passenger seat, where Maria Elena had been. As Letty drove she tried to imagine her children's faces when she walked through the door, but she'd spent so many years trying not to look at them that she couldn't picture them clearly. The fear in Alex's eyes she remembered, and the feeling of Luna's fingertips on the back of her neck when she crawled, late at night, into the bed they shared; but the features themselves were blurry. She couldn't quite imagine them. Instead, she tallied other details: Alex's straight-A report cards taped onto the ceiling above his bed, his white button-down shirts, Luna's long braids and the way she ate an ice cream cone, only the top half, while the bottom dripped in streaks down her arms.

She loved her children. It was there, under the fear, under the avoidance: a love lit with awe, so bright it hurt to look. They were perfect, in their own ways, and they looked perfect too. How was it possible—with the mud and dust of the Landing—that they were always so clean? It was something she should have asked her mother, the details of their bed and bath and school routines, but Maria Elena was hundreds of miles away already, probably cooking something for Letty's father in that big empty cave of a house. The thought of her parents there, speaking Spanish like newlyweds, made her angry all over again. They wouldn't even have had a home to go back to if she hadn't bankrolled it for so many years. And this was how they thanked her: abandoning her outright, without even a warning.

All night and all day she drove, staring out the window as cities stretched into deserts, deserts climbed into mountains. Light carved dusty villages out of the landscape, shacks made of corrugated metal and flapping tarps and walls of crushed cans, dark blue like the Jumex juice of her childhood. Hungry children and chickens scoured piles of garbage, and she thought about what the dishwashers at work told her: *en México ni hay nada que robar.* Nothing even to steal, they'd told her, and she'd thought she understood. But she hadn't. She'd understood poverty, seen violence and despair. But she hadn't known hunger. Even at her most desperate, most afraid—all the years the taxis and pizza boys and even the cops wouldn't answer a call from the Landing—she'd always known that just across the freeway there was another world, so close she could smell it, warm like spun sugar at the county fair, so close it seemed the wind could shift just an inch and it would be hers.

Which was worse? she wondered, as four, five, seven, twelve hours passed. Here, there was nothing even to steal. There, she had known, every moment, everything that could have been hers, and wasn't.

The sky grayed and then darkened. Shivering, she reached for her coffee, cold now, and checked her speed. The gasoline light flicked on. Letty startled. She'd filled up in Guadalajara (where she'd tried and failed, again, to reach Sara), and then stopped at a shabby taco stand by a small puddle of a lake, but the service station there had been out of gas. So she'd started up the mountain with half a tank. It had been a bad decision; a terrible decision, she realized now, as she scanned the vistas frantically for light. She had no idea where she was, and she had no more than forty miles before she'd be stranded alone on the side of a Mexican freeway in the middle of the night.

After ten minutes, her panic growing with every mile, she spotted a power line, and then a billboard, and not long after that, a gas station came up fast on the right. She pulled off the twisted highway into the dirt lot. The light over the single pump glowed orange and was speckled with the black carcasses of dead bugs. Underneath it a man sat alone in a folding chair. She saw the lit end of his cigarette first, and then the tattoo creeping out from underneath his white tank top and up the side of his neck. He looked her age, or maybe a few years older, his half-closed eyes evaluating her in a way that would have made her pull right back onto the road if she hadn't been so desperate. In neutral, she idled. Maybe two hundred yards farther, she could make out a small gathering of houses, a closed store. But there wasn't another gas station. She needed to fill up, and she needed to try Sara again. She had no choice but to stop.

The man stood up when she got out of the car and stamped out his cigarette. *"Cuánto?"*

She dug into her pockets. At the last gas station she'd exchanged money, but she was almost out again. Setting her remaining pesos on the hood of her car, she opened the gas cap.

"As much as it will take."

He stepped forward to take the money. The air that accompanied him smelled of gasoline and smoke, a lethal combination, and she was aware all at once of her black pants, too tight, and the low tank top she wore for the specific purpose of attracting attention behind the bar. He took her money and reached for the pump without ever taking his eyes off her.

She backed away. With her hand she made a sign like holding a phone to her ear. "I need to make a call."

Gas ticked into the tank. He set the nozzle to automatic and pointed to a pay phone, glassless and graffitied, in front of a bathroom.

"Can you make change?" She held a twenty-dollar bill into the space between them. Snatching it out of her hand, he pushed it into his jeans before withdrawing a handful of coins from the same dirty pocket. He held them out to her.

It wasn't an even exchange, not even close. "More."

He lifted one corner of his mouth in a half smile, his eyes on her face, her neck, and the thin strap of her tank top.

"Quieres más?"

The hand not holding the coins moved back to his jeans, closer to the button than the pocket this time. He was cheating her, but she was a woman alone in a foreign country in too-tight clothes and needed to call Sara, so she grabbed the coins out of his dirty hand and ran to the phone. Her heart racing, she fed the pesos into the machine so quickly they spit back out the bottom.

"Necesitas ayuda?" His voice was far away, but coming closer.

She pushed the coins in faster, acutely aware of her position inside the three metal walls of the phone booth. If he got near enough, he could block her exit, and she had no idea what she would do then. She doubted there was anyone close enough to hear her scream.

He was only coming to help, she told herself, but there was something about his swagger, the way he looked at her chest instead of her eyes, that told her he could just as easily be coming to hurt her. Without waiting to see which it was, she bolted out of the phone booth, sprinting in a wide arch around the light and jerking the pump out of her car with one hard yank. Gas spewed everywhere. The handle limp and leaking, she dropped it on the ground, jumped into the driver's seat, and peeled away.

She'd been right to run.

His sharp whistle, as he watched her struggle with the pump, was enough to let her know. She'd been stupid, and she'd been lucky, and not for the first time in her life. Her jeans were wet in a line where the gasoline had struck her, and as the car filled with fumes she was transported back to the Landing, to the very last time she'd ever been left alone with either of her children.

She drove faster, trying not to remember, but there it was: Maria Elena and Enrique walking out the door, Alex almost two years old, crying as he woke up from his nap. It was a Sunday. Maria Elena had asked Letty to babysit, so she and Enrique could go to a church meeting, and Letty had pulled him out of his crib and taken him immediately outside, where he was always happiest. They climbed rocks and tracked footprints. They waded with nets and buckets, and then they wandered back to the parking lot, where Tony Morales was working on his car. She'd never liked Tony, and she might have gone straight upstairs if she hadn't, just the night before, had an epic fight with Wes on the phone. He'd called to tell her he wouldn't be coming home from college for the summer, that his father had gotten him an internship.

Why don't you come to New York? he'd asked, which was impossible, of course, but when she'd told him that, he'd accused her of not caring about him anymore and being too afraid to tell him. Which was ridiculous.

That wasn't at all what she was afraid to tell him.

So there she'd stayed, lingering on the stoop, leaning over the open hood, half-flirting with Tony and half-watching Alex. He was down to his diaper, a heavy, sodden thing, and she kept trying to coax him to her with a shaker full of puffed cereal, but he wouldn't come, just continued through the maze of wrenches and tubes and rags littering the lot. He picked up something that looked like a giant pair of toenail clippers, then set it down and reached for a two-liter jug of orange soda.

Put that down, Letty said, but he didn't, and Letty didn't make him. He started to drink. It was only after Alex fell, and Tony had begun to scream, that Letty saw the iridescent puddle, leaking from the soda jug and pooling by Alex's diaper.

It wasn't soda; it was gasoline.

By the time she reached him he'd gone rigid. She searched for a pulse but found only salt water, dried in rings around his pudgy wrists and ankles, and she pictured him as he'd been just an hour before, hands and feet in the mud, yellow hair lit up in the sun as if it had been electrified. Behind her, Tony pounded 911 on his cell phone while Letty watched Alex's cheeks turn white, then purple. He needed oxygen. He needed oxygen, or he would die, but when she peeled back his lips she found his jaw locked shut, tiny rows of baby teeth blocking his windpipe. She didn't remember deciding to do it, remembered only reaching for the screwdriver, and the sound of Alex's teeth, breaking, and then the infinite minutes she spent breathing through the toothless gap and waiting for the ambulance to arrive. He'd lived, and recovered, and even forgotten, but it was the last day Maria Elena had ever left her to be a mother alone.

The clock on the dash read 2:00 A.M. It felt like she'd been driving forever. *I'm coming,* she wanted to scream, but she also wanted to give up, to curl up, to go to sleep. Why was she trying? It had been too long already, and suddenly she wasn't sure she was even moving. She checked the weight of her foot on the gas and looked for progress out the window, but the mountains were all the same, one after the next. Had she driven over this many mountains with her mother? She couldn't remember. It felt like an eternity since Maria Elena had been in the car beside her, not a single night. Up ahead a yellow sign warned of curving roads, and she moved one hand to her stomach, aching with hunger or fear—she'd never been able to tell the difference. If it was fear, good, it would keep her awake, and if it was hunger, too bad. She didn't deserve to eat and there was nowhere to buy food anyway. The children and the chickens crossed her mind, and she turned the radio on loud to drown out the desperate image.

Static blasted from the speakers.

She took her eyes off the road to adjust the dial.

Later, she would remember feeling a brief, powerful moment of peace just then, before she looked up and saw the sharp curve in the road and the headlights directly in her path, lighting the way forward.

5

Pus oozed from a wrinkled patch of scalded skin. Two days had passed, but if anything it looked worse: crusty and swollen and transitioning from white to a dull green around the edges. All the bandages in his grandmother's first aid kit were too small, so Alex left the burn uncovered beneath his shirts, patting it down with a tissue every few minutes, so the broken blister wouldn't soak through his sleeve. No one had noticed, but this morning it was starting to smell bad, and he worried one of his classmates might say something. Plus, he hurt all over, not only the arm with the burn but his head, and the back of his neck. Walking to school he'd started to shiver, though it was late May and sunny.

He might not have gone to school at all if it wasn't for Yesenia. They hadn't talked about it again, but today was Friday—the day she'd asked to come over to see the feathers. He couldn't risk skipping school for the first time all year and having Yesenia think he'd done it to avoid her, so he'd woken his sister up and, ignoring the pain, gotten them both ready and out the door as usual.

They had been shy in class all day, Yesenia's eyes meeting Alex's and then darting away, and when the final bell rang they both took their time packing up their things.

"Ready?" Alex asked when the classroom was empty.

They walked to the Landing in a line—first Luna, then Yesenia, and then Alex. Alex offered Yesenia his rain boots, but she refused, walking barefoot instead. Her heavy orthopedic shoes swung one in each hand, and he saw now just how thick the soles were, and uneven—a one-inch platform on the right shoe, a three-inch platform on the left. Her hips dipped with each step, her shorter leg straining to find the ground. But bare, her tiny feet were perfect. She'd painted her toenails purple, and the mud rising between her toes made Alex's heart pound.

The tide was way out; the exposed sludge had cracked. When he was a boy, whenever the water receded past the tip of the dock, he would point out the window and Enrique would grab a bucket, and together they would peer into the rivulets that formed at the bottoms of the cracks, catching the tiny crabs and fish and water striders swimming in circles, looking for a way out. Now a snowy egret had taken their place. It stood tall on its long legs, bright white and grand, its head bowed.

Yesenia slowed.

"Walk in front of me," she said. "I don't like people walking behind me, especially when I'm barefoot."

"Why not?"

"I just don't."

They switched places, walking in silence until they reached the empty parking lot. Luna ran up first, and Alex told Yesenia to wait while he went to get a towel to clean her feet. He caught his breath while she wiped away the mud. He felt even worse than he did when he'd woken that morning, his body aching all over, but he didn't want her to know. Smiling too widely in an attempt to disguise his pain, he led her up to the apartment.

"Where is everyone?" she asked.

He'd meant to come up with a story—his mom was at work, his grandma was at a church meeting, something—but he was suddenly so exhausted, and so relieved to not be alone anymore, that he had neither the strength nor the desire to lie. He let his sister answer truthfully.

"They went to get my grandpa."

"In Mexico?"

Alex nodded.

"When are they coming back?"

"My mom said today, but—" He paused, trying to think of a way to explain his mother that did not sound criminal: "She's usually late. It's better with them gone, though. My grandpa's protective of his feathers."

Alex retrieved a lollipop he'd reserved for exactly this purpose and bribed Luna onto the couch. He turned on the TV.

"Stay," he told his sister, and then turned to Yesenia. "They're in here."

Yesenia followed him into his grandparents' bedroom, where they stood over the almost-finished mosaic. Her eyes grew wide, and Alex could tell she felt about the piece the way he always had, that they were standing in the presence of something miraculous. It shouldn't be possible to create such detail with something as imprecise as the tip of a feather, yet his grandfather was able to, over and over again.

"You can see how he starts, here," Alex said, pointing to the ring of exposed wax around the moon. From the envelope of feathers on the workbench he pulled a deep blue feather, cut it half an inch from the top, and pressed it into the wax. It looked like a kindergartener had added the final stroke to the ceiling of the Sistine Chapel. He pulled it out again, turning to the black metal cabinet that stood beside his grandfather's workbench.

"He files them in here, so they aren't exposed to light."

Reaching for the second drawer from the top, he glanced reflexively over his shoulder—he'd never looked at his grandfather's feathers without him there. He flipped through the files until he found his favorite. It was labeled first with the color, using a system Enrique had inherited from his father: MINERAL RED 1033, and then with the bird species and date found: ALLEN'S HUMMINGBIRD, APRIL 2006. The feathers inside were Alex's favorite, and had been his grandfather's favorite too, for being exactly the same color as the setting sun. The red-throated birds passed by en route to Mexico every year, and Enrique encouraged their visits with a web of hummingbird feeders forever full of sticky sweet syrup.

As he extracted the envelope from its file, a blue Post-it note fluttered to the floor. He recognized his grandfather's handwriting immediately and bent to pick it up. It was only two lines, the small, neat printing centered on the paper.

For my Alex, it read. *Make wings.*

"Wings?" Yesenia asked, looking over his shoulder.

Alex understood what he meant: use them. They are yours now, the note said, to have and to hold and to analyze and to deconstruct. Enrique knew his grandson wasn't an artist: on the most recent occasion he'd attempted to teach Alex the family trade, the day had ended in a four-part experiment mixing campeche wax with various substances—beeswax, candle wax, white glue, maple syrup—and then heating them at different temperatures and for different lengths of time. But he knew also that his grandson worshipped the feathers as much as he did, just for different reasons: Enrique loved them for the masterpieces he could create; Alex loved them for the clues they held to the world around him.

Alex put the note back where he found it.

"It means they're mine now," he whispered. "It means he's not coming back."

In the living room, Luna chewed on the now lollipop-less stick and jumped up and down on the couch.

"Stop that," Alex said, yanking the stick from her mouth. "You'll choke."

His grandfather wasn't coming back, which meant his grandmother wouldn't either. He imagined his mother charging in alone to find Luna impaled on a lollipop stick and Alex delirious from fever. It was more than she could handle. It was more than Alex could handle.

"But there's nothing to do," Luna complained. "I've already seen this one."

Alex was about to snap at her to watch it again, whatever it was, but Yesenia raised her eyebrows and nodded to the recliner pressed up against the window. *You look like you could use a break,* her eyes said. Which was the understatement of the century.

"I'll play with you," Yesenia said, turning to Luna.

"You will?" She bounced off the couch and knocked right into Yesenia. "What do you want to play?"

"What do you have?"

"Yahtzee?"

Luna went to get the game, and Alex sank into a chair. He hadn't realized how tired he was, or how cold. With Yesenia in the house he felt like he could relax for just a moment, and he did, the sound of dice in leather shakers like a bedtime story in which all the kids were happy, and safe. Almost as soon as his eyes closed he fell asleep, and when he woke up hours later to Luna shrieking something about Park Place, he saw the coffee table had been pushed to the side of the room and a Monopoly board—along with every other game they owned—had been laid out in its place. It was dark out. Alex was sweating.

Yesenia looked up. His already hot face flushed. He was grateful to have her there, but embarrassed too. When he'd invited her over he'd imagined their fingers in the feathers, soft and maybe even touching, not Alex asleep in a chair and Yesenia playing endless games with his little sister.

"Are you hot?"

Alex shook his head. "Cold."

Yesenia disappeared and came back with the blanket from his bed. He pulled it up to his chin, and Luna crawled onto his lap, wrapping her arms around his neck.

"Are you okay?" Luna asked. "I don't like you like this."

"He's just a little sick," Yesenia said, running her fingers through the knot of hair over Luna's ear, untangling it strand by strand. She turned back to Alex. "Are you hungry? There are taquitos."

The heavy scent of hot oil hung in the air.

"You made them?"

"They were in the freezer. I just microwaved them."

The freezer—of course. For two days they'd eaten everything raw and cold, corn tortillas with butter and jam, and beans and black olives straight from the can, Alex too scared to light the stove. But his mother couldn't cook either, and his grandmother knew it. She'd probably left a dozen meals labeled with instructions in the freezer, but he hadn't thought to look.

He shook his head no, his temples pounding with the effort.

"Did you eat?"

Luna nodded.

He let his eyes close, just for a moment.

When he woke again his sister was asleep. He felt her thin weight on his legs, her toothpaste breath on his cheek. Something was pressed against his lips. He opened his mouth, tasted powdered grape. He chewed. They're back, he thought, but when he opened his eyes it was only Yesenia.

"I'm going home," she whispered.

"Will you come back?" His voice broke. It was Maria Elena he wanted, but Yesenia nodded and pressed both his eyes closed.

"I will. First thing in the morning."

Minutes later, or hours, Alex woke to a sharp knock on the door. Yesenia had forgotten something. He thought of her muddy feet— maybe she wanted to borrow his rain boots after all. He tried to get up, but his hot body was heavy, and he was just starting to drift off again when the knock returned, louder this time. It wasn't his body that was heavy, he realized then, it was Luna, still asleep on him. Wriggling out from under her, he lifted her up and set her on the couch. He wasn't cold anymore. Whatever Yesenia had given him had worked. He would thank her, he thought, opening the door.

But it wasn't Yesenia.

It was Sara, his mother's best friend. And seeing her there, he knew. His stomach sank. They were dead. All of them.

"I'm sorry," Sara said. The cell phone in her hand counted the seconds on a flat screen. Someone was on the other end of the line. The police station? The morgue?

"What happened?"

"It's your mother," Sara said, holding up the phone. "She's been in an accident."

6

The room smelled like too many bodies. In the dim moonlight she counted them, wrapped in blankets and sleeping bags, pillows scattered across the hard floor. Twenty-seven. Men, women, and children pressed so close together it was hard to tell who was snoring. That was how it was here. Ten beds per room, one nurse per floor; there were no visiting hours, only family, day and night, changing sheets and bedpans and carrying the old or injured to and from the bathroom.

Letty ached for Maria Elena, a pain more acute than any of her injuries, but from the moment the seventeen-member support squad found out that she was alone and no one was coming to care for her, Letty lacked for nothing. In fast, serious voices, pesos had been exchanged, plans made. It was a bring-your-own-food, bring-your-own-toilet-paper kind of a place, and within minutes she had been surrounded by trays of sliced mango, pineapple, pan dulce, and (because she was American) a small, wrinkled hot dog.

After she ate, an old woman washed Letty's hands with sanitizer and warm towels. She had tried to pay them back, but not a single person in the room would take her money. Just by virtue of being in the public hospital, Letty knew every single one of them was poor, and their refusal made her eyes fill, which just brought more sweets, more flowers, more hand-crocheted handkerchiefs, until she thought she might be buried alive in their generosity.

Twenty-four hours later she still felt the physical shock of what had happened to her, a dizzy tingling as she replayed over and over again the bloody ride to the hospital in the flatbed of a farmer's truck, convinced she was going to die right there underneath the starry sky. She could have died—she'd swerved to avoid the oncoming car and driven straight off the mountain road—but she'd fallen into a shallow ravine instead of careening off one of the many steep cliffs, and the dense shrubbery had cushioned her fall. At the hospital she'd needed ten stitches for a cut to her forehead, just above the hairline, and they'd given her a series of tests to rule out traumatic brain injury. Afterward she'd asked to use the phone.

It was the middle of the night, but Sara had answered, finally, accepting Letty's collect call and then driving straight to the Landing with Letty still on the phone. *I'm glad you're okay,* Alex said, relief and something more complicated in his voice, and then Luna, sleepy and uncensored: *Where's my nana?*

Letty asked her to put Alex back on the line.

I'm not telling Luna, he said when she told him his grandparents weren't coming back. So she asked for Sara—but already she could hear Luna in the background. *Tell me what? Tell me what?* Alex whispered something to her, and she sniffed once and then started to cry.

It was a tiny sound, that sniff, just a whimper, but it haunted her: the physical incarnation of everything she feared, proof that it wasn't her they wanted, that it didn't matter if she went home. All day she had heard her daughter in the chatter of the children stretched out on the neighboring beds, in the tears after poorly executed shots, in the excitement over a pending patient release.

Now, night had fallen, and her anxiety had gotten worse: every whimper of a sleeping stranger sounded like Luna crying out for her grandparents. Letty covered her ears, but she could still hear the gasping and snuffling all around her. She would never fall asleep. There wasn't enough air in the room to satisfy all the hungry, gaping mouths. Standing up, she felt her way along the wall—gingerly stepping between elbows and knees, noses and ankles—to the window at the far end of the room. It was open, but there was no breeze. Fresh air hovered stubbornly on the other side of the screen. Leaning into it, she pulled a breath through the dusty metallic mesh.

"Are you okay?"

Letty was startled to hear perfect English, without even a trace of an accent. She looked down the row of bodies. Only one pair of eyes was open: a girl wrapped in a red crocheted blanket, sitting against the cinder-block wall. She looked sixteen, seventeen at most. It wasn't the first time Letty had noticed her—she was the only one who'd been there as long as Letty had. It was why she had the coveted spot, underneath the only window.

"I'm okay."

"Are you sure?"

"I'm sure," she said, but she felt more light-headed than sure. "I just need some air."

"I'll take you outside, if you want."

Letty followed her through the maze of bodies. When they were outside, the girl unwrapped herself and draped her red blanket across Letty's shoulders.

"Thank you."

They walked to a bench and sat down, looking across the mostly empty parking lot and into the forest. Out of habit Letty looked for her own car, even though it was still in the ravine where she'd crashed it, and it would stay there, being scavenged for parts and scrap metal, until there was nothing left. She took a big gulp of air and thought about her children, asleep in Sara's loft. Safe. She didn't like having to ask so much of her friend, but what choice did she have? And anyway, Sara owed her. In high school it had been Sara who was a constant runaway. Letty had spent years tracking her down in San Francisco, sheltering her from her parents' violent fights and from a long chain of bad boyfriends. Sara always said Letty was the only reason she'd even survived high school, and when she'd gone off to college she'd remained fiercely loyal to her high school friend.

"How much longer will you be here?" the girl asked after a time.

"Six more days," Letty said. It was the soonest Sara could get a ticket. "What about you?"

"I don't know." The girl nodded toward the building. "My grandma's in the hospital, and our family's small."

"Where are your parents?"

"I lived in Los Angeles with my mom until she died."

It explained the girl's English, for which Letty was grateful. Maria Elena and Enrique had stopped speaking Spanish at home when Letty started school. She could still understand a lot of what was being said around her, but it took all her concentration to figure it out—and her head hurt too much for that now.

"I'm sorry about your mom," she said.

"It was ten years ago."

The girl had been tiny when she'd lost her mother. Luna's age. Letty's heart leapt, thinking how very close she'd come to leaving her own children motherless.

"Where's your family?" the girl asked Letty, changing the subject.

"I just left my parents in Oro de Hidalgo, near Morelia, but I was born and raised in California. My kids are still there."

"With their father?"

"No," Letty said, shaking her head slowly. "No father."

Singular: as if there had been only one. Because in Letty's mind, Luna's father was hardly a person at all, just a fuzzy moment she tried not to remember, and even when she was pressed—as Luna had done on more than one occasion—she couldn't recall much, and nothing at all she could tell her daughter. She remembered the bartenders she'd gone out with after closing one night, and the woozy feeling of too much to drink; she remembered the room spotting out in black and gray and thinking she should put on her pajamas, as if she could go to bed instead of watching the couples pairing off in twos or threes, not even bothering to look for a private room. Then—and this was the clearest memory—she remembered thinking how very glad she was that she was only watching the sloppy groping, at the very same moment she had a surreal, almost out-of-body realization that she wasn't watching at all. She was doing, or being done to, and she would have stopped it if the next thing she remembered hadn't been waking up alone in a filthy, unfamiliar apartment. When she'd found out she was pregnant she'd considered having an abortion, but she'd been such an absent mother with Alex, she couldn't help but think this was her mother's God, giving her a second chance.

"What happened to him?"

The question pulled Letty back to the only father that mattered. Alex's father, Wes. "He left. It was a long time ago—after high school."

They were quiet for a long time, the girl studying Letty and Letty studying her hands. Blood flaked from deep underneath her fingernails, trapped there from the hour she'd spent holding the cut on her forehead closed before they reached the hospital.

"Did you love him?" the girl asked.

Letty thought about denying it, but she couldn't. She'd loved Wes immediately. It had surprised her—she actively disliked blonds, and there was Wes in the front row of honors science, his shaggy yellow hair long enough to partly cover one eye, his hand stretched high in the air. She was a junior, finally confident in the extremely foreign universe of Mission Hills, and her first conversation with him had been an argument. *Why don't you do something that matters?* he'd asked, when she and Sara presented their project idea to the class. They had designed an experiment testing whether different colors of food dye affected the temperature at which sugar hardened. Wes was working on a water purification system for use in third-world countries.

Later, he told her that his father had tasked him to "use his powers for good," and Wes's powers were many: he'd been given more than his fair share of money, intelligence, and good looks. Letty might not have had exactly the same powers in exactly the same proportions, but Wes argued with her like she was squandering her talents, and though she fought him hard and loud, she was secretly flattered. Did he really think she had talents that could be squandered? His pencil pounded the desk in a way that could only mean he did, and his belief in her made her work harder, and her hard work impressed him, and soon they weren't fighting, they were dating.

She remembered the first time they'd gone out, to Half Moon Bay at low tide. He identified all the invertebrates by their scientific names and then took her to an Indian restaurant, where she pretended she'd eaten *palak paneer* and *aloo gobi* a million times before and that the dishes didn't slightly scare her, the neon yellow cauliflower and pureed spinach with something floating in it that Wes called cheese. But she felt better for having tried it, brave and cultured, and that was how it was between them. Wes pulled her into his world and acted like she belonged there, and she struggled to keep up.

The girl was quiet beside her, and when Letty looked at her, she realized she was waiting for an answer to a question that Letty hadn't heard. "What?"

"Was he angry?" she repeated. "Is that why he left? That's why my dad left my mom. He said she got pregnant on purpose."

"No," Letty said. "He wasn't angry." Then, after a long pause, she added: "He wasn't angry, because he didn't know."

The girl sat in silence, considering this, and Letty was surprised at her own honesty. Only Sara knew the truth, but it was easy to tell the truth here, to this girl she would never see again.

"How could he not know?"

It was the question Letty had asked herself every day for the past fifteen years. She rocked back and forth, squeezing her knees to her chest. Finally, she spoke.

"Because I never told him," she said simply. "He had bigger things to do. He was on his way to college, and I didn't want him to get stuck at home with a baby, hating me for it. I figured I'd tell him eventually."

The first Christmas after Wes left for New York had been the hardest. She was hugely pregnant and he'd wanted to see her, but Maria Elena had turned him away—believing (because Letty had told her so) that Wes had left her outright, caring more about college than about his own child. During summer vacation she'd refused to see him yet again, because she was still fat (and young and stupid and vain, she thought now), and then the second summer, when she'd promised herself and Sara she would tell him, he hadn't come home. Then Alex had almost died and it was off the table that she'd tell Wes, and have to explain Alex's broken teeth, and what she had done to him.

She told the girl all of this, every excuse and rationalization.

"But for some reason I still thought he'd come back someday," she finished. "When I think about it now I'm always surprised how long it's been—and that I'm still alone."

"You're not alone," the girl said. "You have your children. And they have you."

Letty sighed. She wanted it to be that simple. But they'd never had her, not really. Her absence had been equal parts genuine need—it wasn't easy to support a family of five, and then there were the constant requests from relatives she'd never met on the other side of the border— and genuine irresponsibility. When she wasn't working, she'd been asleep or hungover. What had she been thinking? There were so many moments she could have made a change. She remembered one vividly. It was just after Alex's third birthday. She'd gone out drinking after work, returning home just before sunrise to find her son asleep in her double bed. She'd been surprised—Maria Elena must have decided he was too old for his crib; or maybe he'd finally succeeded in climbing out. Changing quickly, Letty had crawled into bed beside him, wrapping her arms tight around his protruding stomach—and for one blissful minute she'd held him against her heart, his eyes and lips sealed shut, all the guilt and remorse of the past years fading away.

But just then, the morning sun shot through the window. Alex stirred awake, wide-eyed and beaming to find his mother there. *Go get a book,* Letty whispered, locking eyes with him and smiling conspiratorially. Alex wriggled off the bed and slipped into the living room, but when he reappeared a minute later, he was sitting high on his grandmother's hip. Maria Elena walked over to the bed and pulled up Letty's covers. *Better get some rest,* she whispered, glancing at the clock. It was five-thirty in the morning. In six hours, Letty would have to be back at work. The room started to spin, and she realized she was still drunk, and that she'd driven home drunk, and whispered to her son drunk, and that when she woke up to go back to work in six hours, she might still be drunk.

She nodded silently and turned away from her mother and her toothless son, closing her eyes against the shame.

You have your children. And they have you. In the quiet night, Letty made a mental list of all the things she would have to do in order to make these words ring true. No drinking and driving. No drugs. No going out after work. No sex with younger men—no sex, period. No sleeping late, no skipping meals, no leaving her children alone. No chasing her mother, no depending on her mother, no blaming her mother. The list went on and on and felt to Letty as if it included every single thing she'd ever done in her entire life.

A breeze blew across the garden. Next to her, the girl shivered. Letty lifted one corner of the red blanket to make room, and the girl scooted into the space she created. In the darkness their eyes met, and Letty looked at this teenage stranger, this young woman, almost grown now and still missing her mother. Would it be Letty in ten years, middle-aged and still mourning the loss of Maria Elena? Probably.

But she wouldn't let it be Luna.

Fifteen years after the birth of her first child, Letty was going home to be a mother.

7

Migrating birds reorient themselves at sunset. The exact reason is unknown, but at twilight, just when the sun drops beyond the horizon line, birds flying in the wrong direction correct their flight paths all at once. Given this, it made sense to Alex that his grandfather, at this exact moment in his life, would look around and adjust direction. It didn't make it easier, but it made it understandable, and the fact that his grandmother had stayed with him gave Alex a flicker of confidence in his mother, his leave-in-the-middle-of-the-night, car-crashing mother; a confidence she might not actually deserve. But Yesenia had agreed, when he'd called her early Saturday morning to tell her what had happened: his grandmother would never have left them if she didn't believe Letty could do it alone.

The real question was whether or not Letty *wanted* to do it, and it was a question Alex steadfastly ignored as they settled in with Sara, shopping for food and ibuprofen and waiting almost three hours at urgent care for a doctor to treat his burn. He was lucky—the infection hadn't spread to his blood. But the pus had to be drained and the abscess packed, a process so interesting it almost made the entire thing worth it. Alex imagined the look on Marcus's face when he told him, in detail, how he was saved from premature death by tube and scalpel and cotton.

Sunday morning, for the first time in four days, Alex woke up without a fever. The sky outside Sara's window was white with a strip of blue at the top. The Landing was out there somewhere, buried in the fog. It felt strange to wake up here, in the busy, blue-skied world. Below his window a man pushed a double stroller, managing a cup of coffee and a dog on a leash at the same time, while a troupe of women in fluorescent tank tops circled wide to avoid him. Alex closed the window against the unfamiliar chatter before changing his clothes and walking downstairs.

In the kitchen he found Sara, studying the contents of the refrigerator. Luna tapped impatiently at the breakfast bar. His sister looked hungry; Sara looked tired. She was the kind of pale—paper white skin, brittle blond hair—that looked constantly tired, but it was even worse now; the rings under her eyes were almost the exact same color gray as her eye shadow, giving her the appearance of a raccoon. She'd given up her bed for them, and though her metal-and-glass loft in the heart of downtown Mission Hills had been carefully (and expensively, it seemed to Alex) furnished, there wasn't anywhere else comfortable to sit, let alone sleep. The sofa in the living room was a hard, bench-like object, nearly the same color and texture as the granite countertops in the kitchen.

"How are you feeling?" Sara asked. She set an unopened gallon of milk onto the counter and pressed her palm against Alex's forehead.

"Much better."

"I'm glad."

A bit of the exhaustion lifted, and she hummed as she pulled two bowls out of the cupboard. Maybe she'd been worried, Alex thought, not tired. Sara had known Alex all his life, even if they hadn't seen her much. First she'd been away in college, and then in graduate school, but she always remembered his birthday with T-shirts and toys and books. When she moved back and became a professor at the community college, he thought they might see her more, but Letty had kept Sara mostly to herself.

Luna finished her cereal and pushed her bowl away, looking at Sara expectantly. Alex shook his head, remembering Sara's mistake. On the very first morning they'd been together, Sara had played Uno with Luna for three straight hours. Now, his sister expected to be entertained—every single second. Sara looked at the clock, and Alex knew exactly what she was doing. She was calculating the hours until Luna's bedtime, as he himself had done every day since his grandmother left.

"What are we going to do today?" Luna asked.

"I don't know." Sara poured two glasses of orange juice and looked at Alex, and then back at the clock. Letty's flight wasn't until Thursday—a full five days away.

"I have an idea," Luna said.

"Oh, yeah?" Sara asked. "What's your idea?"

"We could go to the fair."

The county fair had been in town for a week. Every day after school, Luna had spent hours describing the rides and carnival games and chocolate-dipped bananas to Alex, all of which she had heard about but never seen. It had been the same the year before, and the year before that, but no amount of begging or bargaining had convinced Maria Elena to take her.

Sara frowned, considering. "Alex?"

"I don't care."

It would take a half hour to get there, they would stay three or four hours, and then drive another half hour home. For ten dollars a ticket it was as close as they could get to a full day of entertainment.

"Well, get dressed, then," Sara said finally, ushering Luna up the stairs. "Let's get there before everyone else does."

They arrived just as the gates opened. Sara pulled them straight to the midway, hoping to beat the lines, but Luna tired of it almost immediately. She wasn't tall enough for anything but the baby rides, and when she lost at a dart-balloon game she burst into tears.

"But everyone loses!" Sara exclaimed. She pointed at the families walking away empty-handed from the other stalls, but it didn't work. Luna kept crying until Sara found a game with a guaranteed winner, a squirt-gun-racehorse contraption that cost five dollars a play. Sara

handed over fifteen dollars and they all sat down, Sara and Alex dutifully shooting anywhere but the target until Luna was declared the winner. The prize was a Hello Kitty key chain, and Luna clipped it gleefully
onto Sara's belt loop, pulling her toward the animals.

A girl in her class had told Luna she'd once seen a cow being born at
a fair, and though Alex knew for a fact that the girl had lived in Indiana
before moving to Bayshore and said so, Luna wouldn't listen. She
dragged Sara from building to building, through a gardening exhibit
with baskets of polished carrots and tomatoes and squash, past a row of
jam jars labeled with flavors like strawberry-rhubarb and black-currant
marmalade, and through a long, winding hall of amateur art: first-,
second-, and third-place ribbons identifying winners but not, in Alex's
opinion, quality. If his grandfather had ever entered his work in the fair,
he would have received Best in Show.

"Your mom won a ribbon once, did she tell you?" Sara asked as they
looked at the paintings.

"Nope."

"It was a requirement at Mission Hills, for second-year painting. She
was really good."

Alex knew the ribbon. It was in the box underneath her bed, with the
letter she'd never mailed to Wes Riley. He'd read the back countless
times: *Leticia Espinosa, Grade 11,* but he never knew where she'd gotten it.

"Wait," Alex said, pausing. "My mom went to Mission Hills?"

"She didn't tell you? Just for high school."

Of course Letty hadn't told Alex. She had never told him anything.
But when he thought about it, it made sense. It must have been where
she'd met Sara, and then Wes. Alex remembered a story Sara had told
him once, about an egg drop in their high school physics class. Just as
everyone else dropped their eggs out the first-floor windows, Letty appeared on the third-floor fire escape, two floors above the rest of the
class, having hopped a No Students sign to get there. Sara said Letty had
whooped as she let go, and that no one was surprised when hers was one
of the only eggs not to break, or when she earned the only A+ in the
class. Everything about the story had baffled Alex. He couldn't imagine

his mother earning top grades or *whooping* at anything, ever, but it somehow seemed possible now, knowing she'd been at Mission Hills. She must have been someone else entirely, to go to school there. He wondered how she'd gotten in.

Luna skipped back to grab Alex's hand, pulling him forward. "This is boring," she said. "Let's look somewhere else."

An hour later, Luna finally had to admit that Alex was right. There were no live births at the county fair. Most of the animals were on the auction block; Sara tried to pull her away before Luna could ask what would become of the perfect lambs and calves and swine, but she wasn't fast enough. Learning the truth, Luna started to cry. Again. And it wasn't even noon.

"Cotton candy?" Sara asked, her voice full of false cheer. Luna wiped her nose with the back of her hand and followed Sara to a food truck. Fortunately, the sweet blue gauze did its job: Luna stood, silent with wonder, transferring handful after handful of the spun sugar from the stick to her tongue.

When she was finished, Sara led her by one sticky hand to the final exhibition room: Rain Forest Wonderland.

Luna squealed the second she walked inside and bolted to an enormous glass pen, where a giant tortoise lazed against the far wall.

"You like turtles?" Sara asked. Alex cringed but didn't say anything. It was a tortoise, not a turtle.

Luna ignored her, hypnotized by the slow-moving creature. It blinked one wrinkled eye in her direction, and she kneeled. It took a step toward her, and she pressed her forehead against the glass.

"It's coming over!" Luna whispered fiercely.

Five minutes later, it took another step.

Alex sighed. They could be here awhile. He made a loop around the tent, reading the descriptions of spider monkeys and tarantulas and even holding a scorpion, and when he got back Luna and Sara were still watching. Luna sat on Sara's lap, her head tucked underneath Sara's chin as if she'd spent half her life that way. Watching her, Alex wondered if it was something particular to six-year-olds or particular to his sister, the ease with which she attached to anyone within arm's distance: first Yesenia, and now Sara. The very first night in her home, Luna had fallen asleep with her arms around Sara's neck, the tip of her blond ponytail in her mouth. It was the exact way she latched on to their grandmother every night when she put her to bed.

"Is it any closer?" Alex asked.

"Six steps," Luna whispered, her gaze never leaving the tortoise. If only Luna could pull her mother home with the same display of telepathic will, Alex thought, Letty would be here by now.

Sara wrestled a twenty-dollar bill out of her pocket and slid it across the floor to Alex.

"Better go eat," she said. "We're not going anywhere soon."

When he returned the second time, full of nachos and ice cream, neither of them had moved. If the tortoise had moved, he couldn't tell.

"Progress?" Alex asked, sitting down beside them.

"A little," Sara said, at the same time Luna said: "Yes."

They watched the tortoise take another step, and then Sara gestured around the room. "Anything I should go see?"

"Nah. Just some monkeys, and a bunch of kids screaming about how scorpions are evil. I tried to tell them that scorpion venom is being tested as a cure for MS, but they didn't listen."

Sara's eyes grew wide, and she looked like she was about to say something. But instead she pursed her lips, turning back to the tortoise.

"What?" Alex asked.

"Nothing."

He was about to ask again, but just then Luna squealed and clamped a hand over her mouth. Through parted fingers she whispered: "Alex! Look. Right now."

The tortoise had made it to the glass. He stood up and stretched his neck until he was as tall as Luna, then settled down onto his shell and stretched his front legs out. His hind legs lay flat behind him, his knees on the ground and the bottoms of his feet facing the ceiling. The pads of his feet were worn and white. Luna spread out on her stomach, only her head erect, mirroring his posture.

"I think he likes me," she said, laughing.

"He must," Sara said. "In turtle-steps I think he walked about a thousand miles to see you."

"Tortoise," Alex corrected, not able to contain himself a second time. "Not turtle. It's land-dwelling."

Sara looked at him with the expression he'd seen on her face just moments before, but again she just shook her head and looked at the ceiling.

"What?" Alex asked. "Why do you keep looking at me like that?"

"It's nothing," she said.

"Yes, it is. It's something."

"It's just—you sound like someone I used to know. He was always correcting our biology teacher, and spewing random facts that no one cared about. Not that I don't care what you're saying," she added, flustered.

It took a moment for Alex to realize what she was saying—Sara knew his father. And looking at Alex now, she was reminded of him. Wasn't that it? They all must have gone to school together in Mission Hills.

There was so much Alex wanted to know, but Sara looked as if she already regretted what she'd said.

"How else do I remind you of him?" he asked, careful not to use his name. But still, he hit a nerve. Sara hopped up.

"Who?" she asked, feigning confusion, and before he could answer she'd scooped up Luna and set her down on her feet.

"Come on," she said. "The *tortoise* has to go eat his dinner, and so do you."

She dragged Luna toward the door while Alex followed behind, studying the straight-backed walk of his mother's best friend, who somehow knew more about his life than he did. She wouldn't tell him, though. Whether she felt it wasn't her place or she'd made some kind of promise to Letty, one thing was certain: he'd learned everything he was going to learn from Sara.

The rest, he'd have to find out himself.

8

Letty was sober when her plane touched down in San Francisco. She'd spent the hours looking out the window, listening to the women next to her chatter about a business conference while consuming half a dozen glasses of red wine. Letty didn't have the money to order her own drink, but it still felt like a tiny victory, walking off the plane clearheaded and ready.

Without any luggage she raced past baggage claim and down the hall, slowing as she approached the exit. There, on the other side of the glass, were her children. She saw them before they saw her, and her heart pounded as she watched Sara and Alex in conversation, Luna with her entire face pressed against the security doors. No REENTRY stretched in yellow and black decals above her daughter's head. The accuracy of the statement was almost comical. When she walked through those doors, everything would be different. There would be no going back.

Letty stopped walking, overwhelmed, but just then Luna saw her and shrieked, the sound jolting a tired TSA officer to his feet. Her daughter ducked around the door and bolted past him. With one arm extended he started to say something, but then he stopped, thinking better of trying to stop a wild-eyed, wild-haired six-year-old girl's reunification with her mother. Letty kneeled down to meet her daughter's fierce tackle, lifting her up into her arms and carrying her back through the doors to Sara and Alex.

"Are you okay?" Luna asked, tapping the gauzy bandage on Letty's temple and then continuing before she could answer: "Alex almost died, did you know?"

"What?" Letty's already racing heart jumped into her throat, and she reached out to check Alex's forehead, but he stepped back, away from her.

"It was just a little burn," he said. He rolled up his sleeve to show her a patch of gauze taped to his forearm.

"But you told me you could have died!" Luna protested.

"I said if it turned into a blood infection I could have died, which it didn't. You need to listen."

Letty raised her eyebrows at Sara, who smiled. "Welcome home."

"Thanks." She set Luna on the floor and gave Sara a hug, squeezing her tight.

"Thank you for taking care of them," she said. "And for buying my plane ticket. I seriously don't know what I would have done without you."

"It's okay. You know that."

Letty turned to Alex. He was taller than she remembered, and stood awkwardly in his new height. His sleeves were too short, and the front of his shirt had come untucked, falling over his belt. Sometime, between now and when she'd last looked, Alex had grown up. She leaned toward him, but when he didn't reach for her, she settled for a pat on the shoulder.

"It's good to see you."

"You too."

She turned back to Luna, the harder, but simpler of her two children—but she was no longer wrapped around her waist.

"Luna?"

After a moment of panic Letty found her in front of a glass café case. "Can I have a chocolate muffin?" she begged. "Please?"

Letty pulled her last three dollars from her pocket, a collection of wrinkled bills and coins splayed out on the counter.

"Chocolate muffins for everyone," Letty declared magnanimously, but when the barista counted out the money it was enough for only one muffin, which Luna weaseled out onto the curb and wouldn't share.

Sara drove them back to the Landing and stayed just long enough to do the dishes and make the beds before giving everyone a hug good-bye. Luna gave her a whole-body hug, and it took effort for Sara to peel her away and escape out the front door.

Letty followed behind. "You don't have to go, you know. There's no one here to chase you out with a spatula."

Sara smiled. It was a joke they traded regularly, referring to the time they'd been caught watching a horror movie—one that had been expressly forbidden by Maria Elena. Letty had thought she was asleep, but at the first gunshot Maria Elena had burst out of her room in a floor-length nightgown, waving a spatula above her head.

"I would, but I have a night class to teach. And I've got to go cram for it. I didn't have much time to prepare this week."

"Welcome to the rest of my life."

"Yep." Sara smiled, raising an eyebrow. "Welcome to the rest of your life."

Letty swallowed hard, and Sara reached out and gave her hand a quick squeeze. She took a step toward the stairs and then seemed to change her mind, turning back around. "Hey, I know you probably don't want to discuss this, but I think you need to talk to Alex. I think he knows."

"Knows what?"

"About Wes."

"How could he know?"

"I don't know. Kids just know things. He'll be fifteen this summer—it's not a surprise he's asking questions."

Letty sighed and leaned against the railing, looking down at the parking lot below. "But what should I tell him?"

"I don't know. His father's name. That he's a doctor. It doesn't have to be much."

"I don't know much. I haven't heard from him in over ten years."

"So tell him that. Just tell him something. I can see it's hurting him, not knowing."

"Well, it won't be the first time I've hurt him."

"Stop."

The word sealed Letty's lips before she could start, strong and swift like a hand cranking closed a leaky faucet. Sara would not let her go there. For all her criticism, for all the hundreds of times they'd fought over Letty's decision not to tell Wes, Sara had never blamed Letty for the day in the parking lot with Alex. When Letty had called, hysterical, she'd flown home from college immediately and spent a week in the hospital room, holding Letty's hand. Now, she pulled Letty to her. Sara was taller by a good four inches, and Letty pressed her face into the space between her neck and shoulder.

"I'm scared," she whispered.

"I know you are. But it's time."

"Past time," Letty admitted, and Sara didn't argue, just gently turned her face, so that she could look into her eyes.

"This isn't *all* your fault," she said. "Remember? You tried."

She was talking about Luna. Luna was supposed to have been Letty's second chance, her new beginning. And it was true that Letty had tried. She'd stopped drinking and taken vitamins and quit all her jobs except one, bartending at Flannigan's, where she could make three times the minimum wage in tips. She'd even saved enough to buy a new crib with soft pink bedding, which Maria Elena had promptly assembled in her own bedroom. It would be easier, she'd claimed, with Letty working nights, and Letty didn't argue, not then and not when Maria Elena dumped the milk she'd pumped (tainted, her mother assumed, not trusting her) and started feeding the baby formula. It felt selfish to complain, when Alex was growing up healthy and happy, when her children were getting everything they needed, when her mother could so clearly do everything better than she could. But still it gnawed at Letty, and the guilt pushed her further away. Sundays, her only days off, she spent mostly with Sara, where for a few weightless hours she could pretend at a different life, one that did not include two children who needed her and a mother who did not.

"I didn't try hard enough."

"Maybe not," Sara said. "But it isn't too late."

Letty thought of what her mother had said, just days ago, before throwing her out of her father's childhood home: *You have your whole life ahead of you.*

"I hope not," Letty said, letting go of Sara. "I'll call you tomorrow."

She stood on the porch until Sara's car disappeared, and then took a deep breath and walked inside. Alex and Luna were in the kitchen. Alex stood on a stool, getting the dinner plates from the highest shelf, where Maria Elena insisted they be kept; Luna counted silverware onto the table. As was her job whenever she was home for dinner, Letty filled a pitcher with water and set a glass at each place setting, and then they all sat down for dinner together.

There was a long, awkward moment. Alex and Luna sat at the table like hungry birds, waiting to be fed, and all at once Letty realized. They were waiting for *her* to feed them.

She sprang up from the table.

Okay, she thought, *this is it.* Her chance to show her children (and herself) that they were all going to be just fine. She could make dinner and do the dishes and get them ready for bed. One, two, three: done. It wasn't impossible. Not even hard, really. Grabbing the ruffled apron Maria Elena kept on a hook, she tied it on and flung the refrigerator open. Foul air poured from within. She slammed the door shut. Better left for tomorrow, she thought, and scanned the cabinets for something she could make.

"She left meals in the freezer," Alex said, coming to her rescue.

Clear glass casserole dishes were stacked on the left; gallon Ziplocs of soup, tamales, and taquitos were piled on the right. She pulled out a plastic bag of what looked like chicken soup and read the directions written on the front with permanent marker. *1. Thaw in warm water. 2. Transfer to glass. 3. Microwave.*

Thawing would take hours. Who had time for that? She skipped to the next instruction, but when she unzipped the bag and tried to dump it into a mixing bowl, the frozen block of soup wouldn't budge. Resealing the bag, she stuck it into the microwave and set it to cook for five minutes, and just as she finished washing and drying three soup bowls, a noise like a small bomb exploded from inside the microwave.

"Damn!"

She covered her mouth at Luna's horrified expression. The microwave door beeped angrily when she opened it. Soup dripped from the ceiling and door and dribbled from the shredded plastic, pooling on the glass plate. She salvaged as much of the soup as she could and set the bowls on the table.

"It's fine," she said with a smile, picking up a spoon.

Alex took a bite. He immediately spit out a chunk of ice, concealing it in a napkin.

"I don't like it," Luna said.

"You didn't even try it," Letty said. She took a huge, half-frozen, half-burning-hot spoonful, biting into a long strip of plastic bag. She pulled it out of her mouth, held it up, and laughed. "Come on. What could you possibly not like about *this*?"

"Gross." Alex smiled for the first time since she returned.

Letty checked her watch. It was getting late; there was no time to try again with one of her mother's other meals.

"I think it's time for the emergency reserves," she said, standing up to clear their plates. She dumped them with a clatter in the sink. "Your nana doesn't know everything in this kitchen."

They looked doubtful but watched as she cleaned the microwave and then pulled a sleeve of popcorn from a paper grocery bag folded flat and tucked into the broom closet. While it was popping she grabbed a box of chocolates from somewhere within their bedroom.

"Dinner is served," she said grandly. Luna squealed as Letty filled a mixing bowl with steaming popcorn and plopped the box of chocolates onto the table.

They ate quickly, shoveling huge handfuls of popcorn into their mouths. Alex's eyes darted to the door, as if worried their grandmother would march in and put a stop to it. When the popcorn was gone Luna crawled, chocolate-smeared, under the table and into Letty's lap. She tilted her head back and smiled with both eyes closed. Luna's lashes were curly, just like hers, and Letty sighed, leaning over to kiss her daughter's salty lips. Luna was so forgiving. Letty didn't deserve it, but she was buoyed by it: all she had to do was try, and they would figure it out together, how to be a family, just the three of them. She sighed, wishing she didn't have to cut their reunion short. But she didn't have a choice.

Picking Luna up and setting her on the bench beside her, Letty stood. "I have to go to work."

Judging by the looks on their faces, it was like she'd said she had to go to the moon—or back to Mexico.

"I'm sorry. But I've missed more than a week already. I can't miss another shift." She paused, waiting for them to say something, and when they didn't she turned to Luna: "I'll get you ready for bed, and then you can watch TV. Alex will just have to tuck you in when you're tired. Or fall asleep on the couch, I don't care."

Maria Elena never let them sleep on the couch, not even for a nap, and there was something about the suggestion that seemed to terrify her daughter. The color drained from her face. Letty reached out to hug her, but she wriggled away and pressed herself flat against the wall.

"What?" Letty said, growing exasperated. "Alex can take care of you for a few hours, you know he can. You were just home alone for a week and you were fine."

But looking at them, she knew they had not been fine. Alex was still taking antibiotics for his skin infection and Luna had lost weight, and those were only the things she knew about. There could have been dozens of other near misses and nightmares between when she left them and when she finally got in touch with Sara. The buoyancy she'd felt just minutes before was replaced by a heavy weight. She didn't want to leave them, but what else could she do? Sara was the only friend she trusted, and she had just been with Letty's kids for days and bought her a plane ticket home. Letty couldn't ask Sara to come back barely an hour after she'd left, especially not when she had a class to teach. Besides, if they didn't get used to it they would all starve, and her parents in Mexico would starve too.

"Fine," she said, turning away. The longer she lingered, the longer she negotiated with her daughter's pleading eyes, the harder it would be to walk out the door. "Sleep under the table. I'm already late."

In her bedroom, she hurried into jeans and a fresh black tank top, scouring a pile of laundry for a clean apron and settling on a dirty one. Avoiding the mirror, she pulled her heavy hair into a high bun. When she walked out, Luna stood by the front door, her rain boots on, skinny knees bare below short shorts.

"I'm coming with you."

"You can't come with me. I work in a bar."

Luna tugged on one gold hoop earring, the way she did unconsciously in the middle of the night, whimpering from a bad dream. "You work at the airport."

"I work at a bar, in the airport," Letty corrected.

"I'm coming."

Letty sighed and reached out her arms, and Luna fell against her stomach. "I don't want to go. Really. But we have to eat. If I don't work, we don't eat." She tilted her daughter's face up. "Okay? You'll stay for me?"

Luna shook her head no. Her eyes filled, and she started to cry, big gasping sobs. Was she mad? Scared? Or did she just want her way? Letty vaguely remembered a tantrum of similar proportions about a missing yellow sweater, but maybe she was remembering wrong. Really she had no idea, and was struck again by the knowledge that she didn't know her children at all. Alex stood in the doorway watching, and when Letty turned to him for help he shrugged his shoulders. He didn't know either.

Letty walked down three flights of stairs with her daughter hanging around her waist. In Building B, crazy Mrs. Starks paced inside her apartment. Letty could see her silhouetted against the blue light of the television. Her gaze dropped to the apartment below, where Mr. and Mrs. Ramos used to live. Mrs. Ramos, with the embroidered curtains and embroidered tablecloths and embroidered napkins and embroidered everything, with whom Maria Elena could always leave Letty in a pinch. But the Ramoses had been gone for more than a decade now, and no one had moved in to replace them. There was nowhere at all to leave Luna.

From the lit window on the third story, Letty saw Alex watching. He would take care of his sister. With a swift twist Letty broke free of Luna and started to run.

"Go home," she shouted over her shoulder, but Luna sprinted after her, her short legs spinning in circles. Looking back, Letty could see the sharp bones of her daughter's rib cage heaving in and out, the veins of her clenched fists bulging in desperation. *You'll understand when you're older,* Letty wanted to yell back, but maybe she wouldn't, because Letty could barely understand herself. All she knew was that she needed to work. To do anything else was to risk losing what she had left, her job and her home and her children. Blood beat in her temples. She couldn't imagine how Luna was keeping up on her tiny, thin legs, but every time Letty glanced back there she was, gravel flying behind her in a wild spray.

Letty ran faster than she ever had. Her only chance was to get to the frontage road that ran along the freeway and turn before Luna could see her. Not knowing the way, she would stop running and let Alex carry her home.

But just then Letty heard a shriek. Spinning around, she saw Luna flat on her stomach, bloody hands lifted up.

She stopped in her tracks and ran back to where her daughter lay.

"What are we going to do?" Letty wailed desperately, idiotically, as if she were the bleeding six-year-old splayed across the road and not the mother standing over her. Luna didn't answer. Her eyes were shut tight, and she sucked in her lower lip, snot and silent tears running down her face.

Letty rolled her onto her back and then pulled her into a sitting position. "Oh, my God, can you even stand?" she asked, and when Luna stood, blood from both knees dripping into her rain boots, Letty asked: "Can you run?"

Luna hobbled, and then jogged, and then ran.

Reaching for her hand, Letty pulled her forward, and together they sprinted, their faces matching masks of fear, all the way to the terminal and into the airport bar.

9

There was blood in the gravel where Luna fell. Alex waited until they were out of sight before sprinting down the stairs, around the site of the accident, and all the way to the freeway. Without pausing he climbed the steps of the pedestrian bridge and continued, over the freeway and up the steep sidewalk into Mission Hills. Glancing over his shoulder, he could see his dark apartment at the end of Mile Road. He ran and ran and ran away from it, even as his heart pounded in his ears and he gasped for breath. He couldn't stop. His mother couldn't do it alone. When Sara saw his face she would know, and she would come back. She had to.

Alex paused at each corner, comparing the names of the streets to the map he'd internalized from a lifetime of sitting at bus stops. Every street in Mission Hills was named after a tree, and he passed them one at a time as he worked his way toward Sara's condo: Sycamore, Ash, Cherry, Elm. *Elm.*

All at once, he stopped running. Hands on his knees, chest heaving, he remembered the envelope beneath his mother's bed.

Wes Riley, 536 Elm Street, Mission Hills, California.

This was it. All his life he'd been waiting for the chance to see his father's house, and now, with his grandparents gone and his mother and sister at work—this was the time. It seemed impossible his father could still live there—every photo on the Internet showed him with a different country as backdrop—but maybe Wes's parents did. And maybe they would help.

He meant to keep running, but he was tired and, all of a sudden, nervous. As he got closer, his steps slowed, until he stood unmoving at the corner of the five hundred block. It was dark already; he tried to make out the addresses, but the numbers were too far away. It could be any one of the oversize houses on the block, all immaculate, all with neat rows of flowers and bushes trimmed square under wide windows.

Crossing to the even-numbered side of the street, he walked from house to house, pausing in front of every quiet face: 512. 520. 524. Then, on a giant white house, in the place where all the other numbers had been, a sign: WELCOME TO THE RILEYS'.

The sign itself was almost too much for Alex. With one swift blow it destroyed every late-night fantasy he'd ever had about his father. They were poor, he'd decided, living in the only rotten house in Mission Hills, without even a crust of bread to share, or else his grandparents were evil, and had threatened Wes if he so much as wrote a letter to his son. These were his favorite fantasies, when he imagined his father didn't want to leave but was forced to by circumstances beyond his control. But a bright white house with a WELCOME sign—they were neither poor nor evil; they couldn't be.

Alex took in other details: a blue door, an iron balcony, wooden beams supporting a tile roof. The front window was arched, the high walls stucco. In a pot under the WELCOME sign a bright red bundle of flowers had been overwatered; dirt spilled in a line down the side of the pot and onto the cement porch.

He could tell by the dark windows and the empty driveway that no one was home, so he walked up onto the front porch to peek inside. It was dangerous—they could be back any minute—but he'd waited all his life for this moment, and he wanted to see everything. Behind the glass he took in a polished wood table surrounded by glossy black chairs, and through an arch he made out the outlines of a kitchen, white floor and white tile and white appliances, everything as stark and bright as the exterior except for a round, bright green table. The table was stacked with what looked like dirty breakfast dishes, an open box of cereal beside them. Alex had an urge to close it—*It's your stale cereal to eat,* he heard his grandmother say, as she'd said for months and years, until he'd remembered to close the box on his own and she didn't have to say it anymore.

At the far end of the porch, a wooden swing hung from the eaves. He walked over and reached out, setting it gently in motion. His mother had sat here. He was sure of it. He imagined her walking to Wes's house after school, her backpack heavy with books, and sitting here hand in hand with his father, watching the world go by. A *New York Times* sat open on the swing now, and he picked it up before setting it down quickly, exactly as he'd found it. No one could know he'd been here.

Just then he heard a noise behind him. A car on the road, slowing down, and before he could even worry about whether or not it could be his grandparents, he felt a pair of headlights slice his midsection, a car turning in to the driveway.

They were home.

He raced across the porch and was halfway down the front path when a door opened and slammed shut. Alex stopped in his tracks and turned to look.

But it wasn't his grandparents.

It was his father.

He recognized him immediately, the light from the streetlamp reflecting off his dark blond hair. He wore a loose set of pale blue scrubs, a highlighter tucked into the front pocket. He waited for Alex to speak, and when he didn't, he walked around the car and paused.

"Can I help you?"

Yes! A voice in Alex's head screamed. *Please. Help us.* But instead he shoved his hands in his pockets and backed away. He was looking at the man who'd left his mother, the man who'd spent fifteen years no more than a mile away but had never once come to visit, the man who'd held babies all over the world and had never held his own son. He could ask him to help, but it wouldn't do any good. He'd made his decision a long time ago.

"No," Alex said. "Sorry. Wrong house."

Wes stood still, looking at him, and before he could say another word, Alex turned and ran.

Two

1

There was a honeymoon. After the abandonment, after the popcorn and chocolate and chase down Mile Road, after Letty begged her job back with Luna bleeding on a barstool beside her, they behaved, all of them. Letty switched to the lunch shift when school let out for the summer, and Luna went to work with her every day, sitting obediently in an oversize chair in the terminal with an empty suitcase beside her and a purse in her lap, props intended to make it look like her mother had left her there for just a moment to use the restroom. Letty worked with her eyes glued to the chair, her attention divided between her customers and her daughter.

At home, Alex took over the microwaving of Maria Elena's food, setting the table each evening the way his grandmother had taught him and reporting out long days in strained sentences: he'd patrolled the cracked wetlands, throwing stranded minnows back into the bay; he'd refilled his grandfather's bird feeders; he'd met some girl named Yesenia on the rock that they'd determined to be exactly halfway between their apartments. After dinner, they sat in a line on the couch watching television, speaking in soft, careful tones and asking questions instead of making demands (Letty: *Do you want to put on your pajamas?* Luna: *Do you want to help me?*). They were afraid to be together, but they were afraid to be apart too. Even with an empty bedroom they still slept three to a room: Alex in the twin bed pushed up against the window and Luna in the full bed on the opposite wall, her sweaty cheek sealed to her mother's, arms tight around her neck.

It lasted exactly a month. On the day after they'd eaten the very last of Maria Elena's meals, when there was nothing left in the freezer but a bag of ice, Letty looked up from making change at the register to find Luna crouched behind the bar, her long hair stuck to a bottle of simple syrup.

"What are you doing?" she hissed, swiping her daughter's hair away from the row of bottles and glancing around to make sure her manager wasn't on the floor. "You can't be back here."

"But I'm bored."

"So keep coloring."

"I already finished the book. I want a new one."

Switching to the lunch shift had cut Letty's earnings in half, and over the past four weeks she'd spent the majority of what she made at the airport gift shop. She bought coloring books and puzzles and stuffed animals, anything to keep Luna in her chair. But now the food in the freezer was gone. She needed to start buying more than milk and cereal and chips and Kool-Aid, plus there was the letter she'd received from her mother just the day before, pages and pages of everything she forgot to tell her (*Luna breaks out in hives when she eats blueberries! The dollar store on Rollins sells produce on Wednesdays!*), followed by a postscript: *The address is on the envelope, just in case you can.* Send money, she meant, though she didn't even have the decency to ask outright. Letty wanted to ignore her letter out of spite, but she couldn't bear the thought of her parents walking through that big, empty house hungry, and so she'd already started dividing her tips in her apron pocket. "I can't buy you another one," she said to Luna, turning her daughter toward the end of the bar. "Color the backgrounds?"

"I already did."

"Add patterns? Hearts? Stars? Tear out all the pages and make paper airplanes?" Luna shook her head: no, no, no, no. "Well, figure it out, then. You have two more hours."

She led Luna across the rubber mat toward the door, but before they were halfway there two women entered Flannigan's, wheeling suitcases. She pushed Luna down, so the women couldn't see her behind the bar.

"Hey, there," Letty said casually, one hand on top of Luna's wriggling head, the other reaching for bar napkins. "Have a seat anywhere you'd like."

Go, she mouthed to her daughter as the women hung long overcoats over the backs of two stools, but Luna stuck out her lip and wouldn't budge. There was nothing to do but drag her out. Better her customers saw than her manager, who had promised he'd fire her the first time he saw Luna getting in her way. Letty grabbed her daughter underneath the armpits and carried her protesting into the hall. The chair where she'd spent most of the past month was smeared in dried glitter glue and marker. Letty dropped her into it.

"You can't tell me this entire thing is full," she said, picking up the book. She'd bought it only that morning. Flipping through, she found two pages Luna had missed in the middle. "See? Here. Color."

Spinning around, she jogged back to her place.

"Can I get you ladies something to drink?"

The women were in their sixties, well groomed, one with a short gray bob and no makeup, the other with dyed blond hair and an oversize orange purse, which she placed on the bar beside her. They asked for two Cokes without taking their eyes off Luna. She had flipped over onto her back, twig legs sticking straight up the back of the chair, her hair flowing off the cushion and all the way down to the floor. With one hand she held the book in the air, and with the other she scribbled pink marker onto the page.

"She's beautiful," said the blonde.

"Thanks." Filling two glasses, Letty set them on the napkins. "Eating lunch today?"

They nodded. She turned to get the menus, and when she spun back around Luna stood in the doorway, holding up the colored pages.

"Sit down, please," Letty said, in her best imitation of a patient mother. "I'll be right there." And then, to the women: "Sorry about that. Babysitter canceled. Anything look good to you?"

The woman with the gray bob had taken a sip of her drink and puckered her lips, forcing herself to swallow. "I don't think this is Coke."

"No?" Letty picked up the glass and smelled it. She was right; it wasn't Coke. For ten years nothing had changed at Flannigan's, and then the week she was gone, management had decided to put iced tea in the soda gun. She still hadn't gotten used to it. "You're right. Sorry about that."

Taking a step closer, Luna shook the coloring book. The noise flapped through the empty restaurant.

"One minute," she said to her daughter, her voice significantly less patient this time. "I'm sorry. Let me swap those out for you."

Flinging the dishwasher open, she pulled out two tumblers and shoveled them through the ice bin in the way that was expressly forbidden. The glasses could break, rendering the ice unusable, but they didn't, and her manager didn't see. Double-checking the gun to make sure her finger was on the Coke, she filled both glasses and pushed them across the bar before dragging Luna back out into the hall.

"You *have* to stop doing that," she whispered, her anger barely contained. "Sit down." She picked up the book again, praying for more blank pages, something, anything, to keep her daughter occupied at least until the restaurant was empty again, and found what she was looking for: a section of the book had been glued together by some kind of butterscotch dribble from the candy the TSA officers were always handing Luna—eight or ten pages at least.

Merciful God, she thought and almost laughed aloud, she sounded so much like her mother. She unstuck the pages and slammed the book down, victorious.

"Now *stay.*"

Luna didn't look enthusiastic but didn't protest; Letty ran back to the bar. The ladies hadn't touched their drinks.

"Coke?"

"Maybe."

The blond woman pointed to lipstick marks on the glass. With sudden horror, Letty remembered: she hadn't yet run the dishwasher. She'd served them in dirty glasses. Biting back tears, she whisked the glasses away and dumped them into the sink.

"Maybe the Cokes just weren't meant to be," she said, trying to smile. "What do you think? Something stronger? It's already midnight in London."

They looked at each other, surprised. "How did you know we were going to London?"

She'd seen a pocket-size travel guide in the orange purse when the blond woman had reached inside to check her phone. But Letty didn't like to give away her secrets. She'd spent ten years trying to figure out where people were going or where they'd come from based on accents and dress and baggage and any other clues she could scavenge.

She gestured to their long coats. "It was either that, or you are the first tourists in history to believe the hype about summers in San Francisco."

They laughed. "Sure. Give us something stronger. You choose."

Letty made them Bloody Marys, counting slowly as she poured vodka into a shaker and then adding the rest of the ingredients, topping off the glasses with celery and green olives and umbrellas. The drinks were so full and the towers of celery and umbrellas so extravagant it took all her skill to carry them to the bar without spilling.

"Wow," the gray bob said when Letty placed one in front of her. "Now, that's a drink."

"On the house," Letty said.

The women raised their glasses. The Bloody Marys were a little too brown—too much Worcestershire, probably—and just as she handed them over, Letty remembered she'd forgotten the salt.

But they were free.

Clinking their glasses, the women sipped, and then grimaced, but they did not complain.

Forty-five minutes later the women had finished lunch and sped off to their gate, tipping generously enough to almost cover the cost of the drinks Letty had bought them. She loaded the glasses into the dishwasher and turned it on, glancing up just in time to see Luna dart from her chair and disappear. Letty abandoned the wet rag on the counter and ran into the hall. Luna stood with her back pressed against the doorway, peeking around the corner as if preparing another surprise appearance behind the bar.

"Uh-uh. Not happening. Back in your chair."

"But there's nothing to do," Luna complained. "Why won't you buy me a new coloring book?"

Letty reached deep into her apron pocket and pulled out a pathetic collection of wrinkled dollar bills. "Because you can't eat a coloring book."

"I'm not hungry."

"You aren't hungry now, because you just had lunch."

"I won't be hungry later," she said, drawing an X across her heart with one finger. "I promise."

"Oh, Luna." Letty knew it was a lot to ask a six-year-old to sit in a chair for a six-hour shift, but what else could she do? Luna refused to stay home with Alex. Sara was teaching, and all Letty's restaurant friends were probably still asleep, not that she trusted any of them to watch Luna anyway. There was barely enough money to buy food; she could never afford to hire a babysitter. "Listen. We'll go to the dollar store this weekend and buy you more things to do. But right now you have to sit here. If you can't you're going to have to stay with Alex tomorrow, no matter how much you fight me."

"No," Luna said, crossing her arms and pushing herself into Letty's stomach. "No, no, no, no, no. You can't leave me."

I'll never leave you, Letty wanted to say, but she'd given up her right to ever say that again when she left them sleeping in their beds and drove to Mexico.

"Then sit down."

"I won't."

Luna started to cry. Letty held her tight, her grasp half comfort, half muffle, but Luna would not be quieted. She pulled her face away and took big, gasping breaths. Tears streamed down her face. Businessmen talking on cell phones crossed the hall to get as far away from them as possible, while heavily burdened mothers stopped their own complaining children to ask if they could help.

"She's fine," Letty muttered, embarrassed by the scene they were making.

Hearing this, Luna pulled herself away and stomped over to her chair, climbing up onto the seat and then onto the back, balancing taller than the potted palm beside her.

"*I am not fine!*" she screamed, a spectacle that caused the entire hallway to stop and stare.

An eerie quiet fell over the terminal.

"You're the worst mom ever," she whispered into the sudden silence. "My nana would buy me a coloring book. I want my nana."

"So do I," Letty spit, to which Luna began to cry again, and the crowd turned in on itself, chatting loudly about nothing, trying not to watch. Blood rushed pink to Letty's cheeks, and she felt like ripping off her apron right there and giving up. She couldn't do it. She *knew* she couldn't do it and she'd *told* her mother she couldn't do it. Maria Elena's blank stare and empty encouragement popped into her mind, replaced almost immediately by the expression on the London-bound ladies' faces at the dirty-brown Bloody Mary bribes she'd thrust at them. She couldn't do anything right.

As she stood there, trying to figure out how she could walk away from it all, Letty felt it—someone was watching her. A shadow moved from the back of the restaurant, drawing closer, and all at once the fantasy of fleeing faded. She couldn't leave, and she couldn't lose her job. In the time it took to turn around, she saw exactly how her life would be if she lost this job: hungry kids, no apartment, no hope. Her manager had already warned her more than once. Luna couldn't come into the bar, couldn't get in her way, couldn't distract her. And now he'd found them both in the hall, Luna wailing, while a band of passersby watched it all.

But when she turned around, she was relieved to find that it wasn't her manager after all. It was Rick Moya, the bartender hired to fill her evening shifts. He was early. As she exhaled, her panic turned to morti-

fication. Of all the people to be witnessing this spectacle, she wished it
didn't have to be Rick. There was something about him she just didn't
like. He had the kind of groomed good looks she assumed to be un-
trustworthy: dark hair kept short, square jaw cleanly shaven, black-
rimmed glasses, and expensive-looking dark jeans. But even more than
his appearance, there was the fact that he'd been brought on to work her
shifts. Every night he closed up and drove home with what she still
thought of as *her* tips.

"I'm guessing now would not be the time to offer to buy her a coloring book?" he asked. High on the back of the chair, Luna resumed her
wailing. "Breaking every parenting rule?"

Letty sighed. "Do I look like I know any parenting rules?"

Rick walked over to Luna, and Letty watched as he attempted to
coax her down from the back of the chair. Whatever he was saying
seemed to be working. Luna nodded and stuck out a snot-smeared
hand; he took it and shook hard before leading her away, down the hall
and around a corner. When they reappeared ten minutes later, Luna
carried a licorice rope longer than she was and Rick held a stack of coloring books that looked like it might keep her busy for the rest of her
life.

"What'd you make her shake on?" Letty asked.

"Her firstborn."

"You can have it," Letty said, but she stopped rolling silverware into
linen tubes, waiting for him to answer in earnest.

"That she would stop crying," he said. "And that she would apologize to you."

Letty didn't see that happening. "Well, thanks," she said. "What are
you doing here, anyway?"

"I work here."

"You aren't on the schedule until four. Don't think I'm splitting tips
this hour. I need the money."

He looked out into the hall, and Letty followed his gaze. Luna had
popped off her shoes and was scratching her cheek with a crayon. The
collar on her white polo was crusted brown; her tears had dried in
muddy lines on her face, as if she hadn't been bathed in a week, even

though she'd had a bath just the night before. Letty didn't need to tell him she needed the money. It was obvious.

"It's cool. I'm not on the clock."

"So why are you here?"

"Just setting up."

From a stuffed backpack he pulled a small blackboard, a pencil box full of chalk, and tiny brown bottles labeled in a delicate script: SMOKED ORANGE, BERGAMOT, SOUR CHERRY, PASTICHE. He lined the small bottles up and then pulled out two bigger bottles, unlabeled, one filled with a clear liquid and the other with a bright pink syrup.

"What else you got in there?"

She was joking, but he kept them coming, more bottles and then a stack of books: *The Savoy Cocktail Book, The Bon Vivant's Companion, The Art of Mixology.* It felt like watching a magician pull objects out of a hat.

"Seriously? Does management know you're doing this?"

"No. But as long as they're making money, they don't care."

"But why?"

"I don't want to be stuck here forever."

He frowned as soon as he said it, turning red.

"Like me," Letty said. "You don't want to be stuck here forever like me."

Rick shook his head and looked into the hall. Still in her chair, Luna had tied one end of the licorice to her ankle and had the other end in her mouth. Every time she took a bite, the rope pulled her leg another inch off the chair.

"It's a fine place to work. But there's a brave new world of bartending out there. People want their drinks like their technology. All new. And there's serious money to be made."

"Not here."

"Nope, not here. But I had to start somewhere."

He wasn't that young. Her age or a little younger, and she wondered what he'd been doing before this. Not everything about Rick added up. Just below his collar, where he kept his shirt unbuttoned (one button too far, in Letty's opinion), a tattoo stretched from one collarbone to the other, something scripty in Latin that Letty thought out of character with his otherwise young-Republican look. And where did he learn how to bargain with a six-year-old? But before she had time to ask, a middle-aged man in a business suit took a seat at the counter. Letty placed a napkin in front of him.

"What can I get for you this afternoon?"

He scanned the row of alcohol spotlighted behind the bar and squinted as if trying to read something too far away to decipher. Letty followed his gaze and saw him watching Rick write the word SPECIALS across the top of the board and beneath that SAZERAC, BLOOD & SAND, and RANGOON GIMLET. She'd never heard of any of them.

"Those look different."

Letty glared at Rick, who attempted, too late, to turn the chalkboard away from the bar. "I'm sorry. The specials aren't available until four."

The man checked his watch. "I've got way too much time before my next flight," he said, pulling out a laptop and opening it on the bar. "I'll wait."

Yanking back the bar napkin, Letty scowled. He hadn't planned to split her tips for the last hour; he'd planned to steal her tips. She wanted to protest, but she was exhausted by Luna's outburst. Untying her apron, she tossed it toward the laundry bag, where it landed in a crumpled pile on the rubber floor.

"All you," she said, clocking out. "Have fun."

She turned to find her purse and caught sight of the bartending books stacked on the counter. Rick was deep in conversation with the businessman about the merits of the "craft" movement. Without thinking, Letty pulled the top book off the stack and stuffed it into her bag before walking out of Flannigan's.

"Come on," she called.

Luna jumped off the chair and raced after Letty, a trail of licorice following them through the crowded terminal.

2

Four weeks of observation and Alex had learned the following things about his father: (1) He subscribed to the *San Francisco Chronicle* and *The New York Times*. (2) His housecleaner came on Tuesdays and brought her own supplies. And (3) He left for work at seven and got home between six and six-thirty, usually carrying takeout. Alex watched all this from the corner, sometimes with Yesenia, sometimes following behind as his father walked a letter to the mailbox or bought a half gallon of milk at the corner store, always careful not to be seen. Never did he see any sign of another human being—no wife, no kids, not even the grandparents Alex had expected to see.

It was becoming obsessive, this daily tracking of a man he'd never met. Halfway through the summer, while his mother and sister slept in the bed across the room, he promised himself he wouldn't go again, but by noon the following day there he was, dragging Yesenia back across the freeway.

The walk was hard for her. On the wire-caged pedestrian bridge they paused, looking through a mended hole in the fence at the speeding cars below. The same faded silk roses had been tied to the spot for all the years Alex had been alive. He fingered the dusty petals as Yesenia sat down and rested against the low cement wall.

"You okay?"

"I'm okay." She always said she was okay, no matter how her heart beat, no matter how long it took her to catch her breath. For a long time Alex believed she was embarrassed, or too shy to tell him the truth, but lately he'd started to think she really was okay; even though it looked hard to Alex, it was just normal life for Yesenia.

When she was ready she stood up and they continued over the bridge and up the hill, settling into their usual place on the corner.

"What are you looking for?" Yesenia asked.

She'd asked him this before, but he didn't have an answer. He just felt compelled to watch, to do everything he could to learn about his father, about himself. Everything, that was, except speak to him. Alex shrugged his shoulders.

"Why don't you just say something to him?" she prodded.

"Because I can't."

"Why not?"

He tried to find the words to describe how much it had hurt when his father looked him right in the eye without the slightest glimmer of recognition. "Because he doesn't want to know me. He chose that."

"You don't know the whole story. You don't really know anything." She paused and squinted at the big white house, opened her mouth as if she was about to say more, and then closed it.

"What do you mean?" Alex asked, prompting her. When she didn't respond he reached out and touched her chin, lifting it until she looked at him. Sunlight filled her eyes honey-yellow; her skin glowed dark, darker even in contrast to the neon pink bathing suit she wore underneath her white tank top. If she hadn't been sitting next to him, he wouldn't have believed she was real. Every morning all summer he'd woken up fearing it was all a dream; that there was no Yesenia, that she wouldn't meet him where she said she would, and he waited on their rock with the same anticipation he'd felt as a little boy when he would run to his grandfather's bedroom every morning and Enrique would lift him up to the window and together they'd wait for whatever rare bird they were expecting to appear at the feeders below. Yesenia, though—Yesenia was more beautiful than every one of those birds.

"What?" he asked again.

"Just that," she said finally. "You don't know the story. Sometimes you think you know the story, and you don't." A car turned down Elm, driving so slowly that Alex and Yesenia stopped talking, but it pulled into the next-door neighbor's driveway. "Do you remember what I told you? That my mom left a bad relationship in Guerrero, and it wasn't until she got to California that she realized she was pregnant?"

Alex nodded. "It's not true?"

Yesenia shook her head. "I never believed her. And last week I found my birth certificate. I've been looking for ages, whenever my mom is at work."

Carmen was always working. It was one of the first things Alex had asked, embarrassed, when he'd seen Yesenia back at school after the night she fed him grape-flavored Tylenol and put him and his sister to bed: *wasn't your mom worried about you?* But Carmen hadn't even known she'd been out late. She cleaned houses during the day and medical buildings at night, and in the few hours between she cooked dinner and watched American soap operas in an attempt to learn English. Except for five o'clock, when they ate dinner together, she was hardly ever home.

"Where was it?"

"Under a loose corner of carpet in her bedroom. Yesenia Lopez-Vazquez. Mother: Carmen Lopez-Vazquez, born 11:30 A.M., March 16. Nuevo Rosita. Mexico."

They sat in silence, thinking about everything written and unwritten, and what it all meant for Yesenia.

"No father."

She shook her head no. "But I expected that. What I didn't expect was to find out I was born in Mexico. I put it right back, so my mom doesn't know I know."

Yesenia was not a U.S. citizen. All her life she'd been here illegally, and she hadn't even known it. Alex didn't know what to say, but before he could think of something, Yesenia stretched and stood up. "Speaking of my mom. I should go home soon. She's making you dinner."

Alex hadn't met Carmen. His stomach leapt at the thought. "She's making *me* dinner?"

"Don't you want to come over?"

"Of course I do."

She grabbed his hand and pulled him up, but instead of turning home, Alex walked across the street and sat on the front porch swing, as he did almost every day, for just a minute, before walking home. Yesenia sat beside him.

"You know you have to say something to him, or stop doing this. It's going to make you crazy."

He couldn't argue; he was already starting to feel crazy. But before he could say anything, a brown mail truck pulled up. The driver hopped out the open door.

"Package for Wes Riley."

"I can sign," Alex said, jumping up. To see his father's name on the electronic board gave him a quiet thrill. He reached for the signature pad.

Alex Riley, he wrote slowly, trying to call up an image of the boy he'd be if his father had stayed, if he'd given him his name and his home and his family and his love. But nothing came to mind. Alex Riley simply didn't exist.

And in the eyes of his father, Alex Espinosa didn't either.

Three hours later, Alex stood at Yesenia's door. He'd gone home and taken a shower, washing his hair and ironing his clothes and putting on so much deodorant that he feared his arms wouldn't lay flat against his sides. He checked his watch as he rang the doorbell. He was a little early. But girls liked that, didn't they? He had no idea what girls liked, but before he could change his mind and disappear down the stairs, Yesenia opened the door.

She had flowers in her hair. Fake flowers, but still, Alex broke into a smile when he saw the yellow orchids tied haphazardly to her ponytail, the wire stem sticking out like an antenna.

"Hey."

"Hey."

They'd said good-bye only a few hours before, but standing there, clean and in slightly different clothes (Yesenia with the flowers, Alex with a shirt more pressed than wrinkled), Alex felt suddenly shy. Yesenia stepped to the side but did not invite him in, and he stood there, wondering what to do, when Carmen appeared in the hallway behind her daughter. She had the same dark hair, but instead of messy and striped red, she wore it slicked back in a tight bun. The bun, along with glasses and an embroidered apron, made her look older, even though her face was almost as soft and smooth as her daughter's. He guessed she was young—younger than his own mother, even.

Squeezing Yesenia's shoulder, she said something softly to her in Spanish. *"Sí, Mamá,"* Yesenia replied, and Carmen smiled. Squeezing her daughter a second time, she said, *"Pues, presentámelo,"* and extended her hand to shake.

"Alex, this is my mom, Carmen," Yesenia said. "Mom, this is Alex."

"It's nice to meet you, Alex," Carmen said, putting the emphasis on the second half of his name.

"It's nice to meet you too. Thank you for inviting me to dinner."

From far away he felt his grandmother smile at his manners. Carmen stepped aside. *"Pásale, pásale,"* she said, waving him down a dark corridor. Through a door on the left he saw the kitchen, peach tiled counters and something fishy steaming in a soup pot that made his stomach turn. Carmen stirred the pot while Yesenia pulled him past the door.

The living room was dark, with thick woven curtains hung across the only window. Yesenia pulled them apart, revealing a beige-carpeted rectangle similar to his own apartment, with the couch against the longest wall, the TV across from it, and a coffee table in between. A row of photographs lined the wall over the couch—school portraits in identical gold frames, Yesenia in kindergarten through eighth grade, hair long and then short with bangs and then long again. He remembered her at every age, but it was weird to see her like this, her development on display.

From the coffee table he picked up a book: *Top 50 Math Skills for GED Success.*

"My mom just passed last week."

"Wow."

"It's why I invited you over, kind of, to celebrate."

"I should have brought something," he said, glad she hadn't told him. The pressure of having to figure out what to bring to celebrate the mother of his almost-girlfriend passing the GED would have kept him up at night.

"It's okay, she doesn't like much fuss."

From the kitchen, Carmen called them. She'd set the table with a turquoise cloth and clear plastic cover, paper napkins, and a cluster of tall, saint-wrapped glass candles. They washed their hands at the kitchen sink and Carmen said something in Spanish that Alex didn't understand.

"She wants to know if you pray," Yesenia said as they sat down.

"My grandmother did, when she lived with us."

He bowed his head, but not before he saw Carmen flash a conspiratorial grin at her daughter.

"We usually just eat, if that's okay with you."

Alex looked from Yesenia to Carmen and back again. There was more to the story, but they weren't saying, and he saw for a moment how it was between them every night, mother and daughter at the kitchen table together.

Carmen took his bowl and brought it back filled to the brim with soup: potatoes, onions, carrots, a whole green pepper, and a chunk of white fish, still wearing its silver scales.

"I hope it's okay," Yesenia said. "My mom was worried you wouldn't like fish."

He didn't—Maria Elena had stopped cooking it years before because it was the only thing he wouldn't happily eat—but of course he wouldn't say that now. Instead he broke a chunk off with his spoon and nodded with what he hoped was the right amount of vigor to be believable. He took a big bite.

Carmen watched him eat with satisfaction, her own soup untouched in front of her. When he'd swallowed and wiped his mouth, she asked where he was from.

"I was born here," he said. "But my family is from Michoacán."

"Yesenia was born here too." Yesenia's eyes flickered to Alex's, and for only a moment it filled him with happiness—being on the right side of a secret this time—before he realized just what this secret meant to Yesenia and her mother. This home—the photos on the walls and soup on the table and fresh flowers in the windowsill; this life—Yesenia's school and surgeries, Carmen's work and studies, everything they'd built here together—it could all be taken from them at any moment. Alex couldn't imagine what it would be like to live knowing that, and he understood why Carmen wanted so much to believe the story of her daughter's birth that she'd created.

Turning back to Carmen, he congratulated her on passing her test. She looked to her daughter, who translated.

"Yes," she said, beaming. "Thank you."

While they ate, Yesenia told him how her mother had done it: the eight years she'd studied, the community center where she took English and math, the three failed attempts before she passed. This fall she would quit her day job and enroll in Cañada College's medical assistant program, Yesenia said. She would keep working nights and go to school during the day.

"It usually takes eighteen months, but it might take my mom longer, because we have to pay full tuition. She can't apply for financial aid, because . . . well."

Carmen was undocumented, she meant, but Yesenia skipped over this detail and went on to describe the classes her mother would take, Carmen interrupting every few minutes to correct her. Alex listened, struck by the ease with which they wove in and out of languages, finishing each other's sentences and talking about themselves as a single unit. *This is what a family looks like,* he thought, and for the first time in his life he realized his wasn't one. It wasn't that he didn't have a father, or that his mother worked all the time, or that his grandmother was too strict: it was that they didn't share a life, not any of them. They didn't share a vision of the future, not like Yesenia and her mother did. All his grandfather ever wanted was to move back to Mexico; all his grandmother wanted was to keep them safe, no matter the cost. His mother—

well, he had no idea what she wanted, he realized then: no idea what she thought about all day, what she was working toward, or if she was working toward anything at all.

Yesenia and her mother had gone quiet, and when Yesenia spoke again, Alex realized it was to repeat a question.

"The soup?" she asked.

He took another bite and chewed slowly, pretending to linger over the flavor. When he swallowed, he looked up at her and smiled.

"I love it," he said.

And strangely, he did.

It was dark when they headed back across the marsh. Carmen and Yesenia had taught him *burro castigado* after dinner, a card game that Alex didn't know and that he'd lost, badly, and when Carmen left for work Yesenia said she'd walk Alex halfway home.

"My mom likes you," she said as they crossed the parking lot outside her apartment building.

"Do you think so?"

"Yeah. I knew she would. She likes people that dress nice."

"I like her too. I think it's cool she's—you know. She's an adult but it's like she's still trying to go somewhere, like we are. If that makes sense."

"Yeah, it does. She's only twenty-eight."

Alex did the math in his head. She'd had Yesenia at fourteen. "My mom's thirty-three."

They walked in silence for a time, each thinking the same, separate thoughts.

"Do you think about it?" Yesenia asked finally, and Alex knew exactly what she meant. Their lives weren't planned, weren't desired; he wondered if Carmen had had a decision to make in Mexico, or if there hadn't been any other options for her there.

"Sometimes."

They were halfway across the marsh, and Alex couldn't remember when they'd stopped walking. It was dark all around. Facing the water, they couldn't see anything, not even light reflected off its surface, just a great expanse of nothing.

When Alex turned to Yesenia, she stepped closer to him, her head tilted up to his. "So," she said softly. "Are you ever going to kiss me?"

He nodded, slowly and then with more determination, and she was almost all the way to him, tilted on the tops of her toes, before he closed his eyes and bent down to meet her. Their lips touched—four stiff straight lines brushing against one another.

She pulled away and studied him closely.

"Hmm," she said, and he feared he'd been a great disappointment, but then she pinched his lips and cheeks, loosening him up, and leaned in again. His lips tingled where she'd pinched them. Wrapping his hands around her back, he kissed her harder, her lips parting. Beneath them, he felt the muddy earth give way, his shoes sinking inches into the path, and suddenly, as he stood there with her, the mud felt incredibly sexy—the wetness of it all, the suction—and he wanted to take off his shoes and be barefoot, wanted to take off her shirt, wanted her to keep kissing him that way and any way she wanted for as long as she wanted. But just as he began to hope they might stay locked that way for the rest of their lives, she broke away and started running, with that dip in her step but fast, not to her house and not to his but to the water. On the dock she unlaced her heavy shoes and stretched her bare arms to the sky and he chased after her, scrambling over the rock levee and the short strip of pebbly sand. At the end of the pier he caught her, grabbed her, kissed her again, and when he let go she tipped backward, a shriek, arms flailing; a splash.

And then silence. Alex thought about jumping in after her, but he couldn't swim very well, didn't know how deep the water would be, and so he just stood there in shock, watching the place where she'd disappeared.

She didn't come up for a long time, long enough for the rings of her entry upon the surface of the water to smooth over, to become still and then fall into the rippling pattern of the waves, and when she finally did she gasped and started to laugh.

"Did I scare you?"

Alex shook his head slowly, dropping to his knees. *Scared* was not the right word. Alex had died when she went under, brought back to life only by her reappearance. He reached one arm out, and she took it, and he pulled her, wet and salty, out of the water.

3

Flakes of dried mint floated on top of a pee-yellow drink. She was pretty sure they weren't supposed to do that. Taking a sip, Letty inhaled a fleck and coughed out a mouthful of what tasted like pure acid. Luna whimpered as a spray of liquid landed on her cheek. She was asleep. Hours earlier, Luna had given up halfway through a Happy Meal and laid her head down on the table, refusing the bits of meat and bun Letty tried to push into her mouth and falling asleep right there. Letty should have moved her, but she was too exhausted and afraid Luna would wake up, so instead she covered her with a blanket and left her at her seat.

Reaching across the mess of a table—empty McDonald's bags, an open jar of applesauce, the mint, a yellow plastic lemon, half a dozen dissected green olives—Letty grabbed an open bottle of rum. It was ten o'clock. Alex was still out, somewhere. Across the dark field, past the red lights of the runways, Rick was still at Flannigan's, surrounded by his bottles and his fancy specials, making conversation with her customers. Thursday meant Joel would be waiting for the red-eye to New York; Manny would be just flying back from three days in Houston. The bar would be full, and in all likelihood, her regulars would have stopped asking about her. Rick had taken over, stealing her relationships and her tips, and she was stuck at home with a sleeping six-year-old and a mess of bad drinks, sipping rum straight from the bottle.

In the quiet, Letty heard Alex's footsteps on the stairs. He threw the door open and tripped out of his muddy boots, bounding straight to the kitchen sink, where he flipped on the faucet and dunked his head into the water. At first Letty thought he must be thirsty, but then she saw he wasn't drinking, just smiling, the water running over his half-open mouth. It took her a moment to figure it out: he was making sure he was awake, not dreaming. She remembered feeling the same way as a teenager, returning from making out with Wes in the marsh, rolling over on top of him on the deserted pier. She should never have let Alex go out alone with Yesenia—not that he'd asked her permission.

"You okay?" she asked. "Have fun?"

Shaking the water out of his hair, he looked at her as if she'd just asked Neil Armstrong if he'd had fun, walking on the moon.

"It was amazing."

"I hope not too amazing."

"Mom," Alex groaned. "I just turned fifteen."

"Exactly." She felt a pang of guilt, remembering his birthday. She'd bought him a chocolate cupcake at the airport, but Luna had licked all the frosting off on the walk home. "So what did you eat?"

He turned off the running water. "Her mom made some kind of fish soup. It was actually pretty good." He slicked back his hair and dried his hands on the dish towel she'd used to mop up runaway olive juice. Lifting it to his nose, he smelled the towel and noticed the mess on the table. "What're you doing?"

"Nothing."

"Nothing?" He picked up the glass applesauce jar and spun it around in his hands. "You and Luna feast on olives and lemon juice for dinner, with expired applesauce for dessert?"

"Expired?"

"It's the only reason we didn't eat it when you were gone."

He stopped speaking abruptly and looked away. They had an unspoken agreement not to talk about Letty's disappearance. If he had to mention it at all he said, *When we were at Sara's*, a euphemism that sounded a lot less like child abandonment than the truth did.

She took the jar out of his hands. USE BY DECEMBER 31. Her stomach turned, though whether it was the rotten applesauce or the lemon juice or the rum or any of the other ingredients she'd sampled, she couldn't be sure.

"It was for a drink," she sighed, handing him the book she'd borrowed from Rick: *The Art of Mixology: Creative Cocktails Inspired by the Classics.*

"Cool."

"It should have been. Until this happened."

"What were you trying to make?"

"Mojito y Más," she said, gesturing to the lemon-mint mess. "And a 'riff' on a None but the Brave. But it didn't work out. Obviously."

Alex leaned over the open book. *"Fresh muddled apples,"* he read. *"Pimento dram."* Looking up, he scanned the table again, where an entire jar full of green olives lay on the cutting board. Their red hearts had been extracted and now floated in a sweating glass on top of the applesauce.

"Wrong kind of pimento," he said.

"What do you mean?"

Alex pulled open a drawer next to the oven and rummaged through a pile of plastic bags until he found one with the same two words written on it in black marker. "Pimento dram. Allspice. It was confused by the early Spanish explorers with a kind of pepper, which is why it shares a name with the peppers inside Spanish olives."

Letty snatched the bag away from him, studying her mother's writing. "And you are an expert on the history of the pimento for what reason?"

He shrugged. "I read about it."

"You read about it," she said, unbelieving. "Where?"

"In the encyclopedia."

The fine hairs pricked up on her arms. The only person she'd ever known to read the encyclopedia was Wes. She dumped her failed experiments down the drain one at a time, avoiding eye contact with her son. "I didn't know the encyclopedia still existed."

"It does. At least L through R does. Those are the only volumes we have at school."

Letty stacked the empty glasses in the sink and turned back to the table.

"So I could quiz you on lemons or rabbits, but you wouldn't know anything about, say, salamanders."

"In theory," he said, and she raised her eyebrows, waiting for him to explain. "I got *Amphibians and Reptiles of the United States and Canada* for my eighth birthday. So the salamander isn't a good example. But it's the right idea."

She rolled her eyes to the water-stained ceiling, awed by her encyclopedia-reading, fact-reciting son.

He flipped back to the mojito recipe. "So you want to make this? I think we could find the ingredients."

"What do you mean, find them?"

Alex looked at his sleeping sister and disappeared into his bedroom, returning a moment later with a heavy black flashlight. He grabbed the book.

"I'll be right back."

Before she could stop him—or even decide if she should—Letty heard his footsteps retreating down the stairs, and a moment later he appeared in the marsh below the kitchen window. She watched him cut straight toward the water. The slant of yellow light bounced on the path as he jogged. She went out onto the porch and called his name. The sound echoed, and after a silence she heard: *Just a sec!* Or *I'm coming!* Or *I found it!* But whatever it was he wasn't afraid. He was happy. It might be wrong that she'd let him out at night alone to run straight for the water, and it might be worse that she was letting him play head chef in the creation of an alcoholic beverage, but the truth was they'd exchanged no more than two dozen words in the month since she'd returned, and all of them had been awkward. For the first time since Maria Elena had left—or, if she was honest, for the first time since the ambulance had whisked his stiff little body down Mile Road all those years before, they were, suddenly and miraculously, partners in something besides fear.

She returned to the kitchen for the bottle of rum and a blanket, setting up in the stairwell to watch for his return. The way the dry brown grass smelled in summer, it reminded her of everything good about the Landing, back when she was a little girl and the buildings were still safe and crowded and she traveled with the other kids in a pack, stomping through the hollows. She took a long breath and an even longer drag on the bottle of rum, pulling in the antidote for her surging emotions.

When Alex finally returned he was shirtless, carrying his white cotton button-down like a knapsack, the arms tied in a knot. She took another quick sip from the bottle while he climbed the stairs two at a time, his boots pounding so loudly she worried he'd wake his sister. At the top of the stairs he untied the shirt and emptied a tangled collection of weeds, a handful of strawberries, and a fat lime onto the blanket.

"Find what you were looking for?"

"Yep. Do we have soda water?"

She went to get it and a few other supplies: ice and sugar and a wooden spoon and a pair of jam jars, while he went to put on a shirt. When he returned he carried a set of glass beakers, rattling on a metal tray. He set them on the blanket.

"Where'd you get the berries?"

"From the old sandbox. The lime too."

Mrs. Puente had converted the sandless wooden box into a garden a decade earlier, and her reputation had kept everyone away from it. "You aren't afraid of her?"

"She likes me," Alex said, handing Letty a bundle of tangled greenery.

"What's this?"

"Mint. It grows like crazy down by the water." He plucked a leaf and rubbed it between two fingers, breaking it up and releasing a strong smell. "It's easy to identify. And it doesn't have any poisonous look-alikes, like parsley and garlic do."

Was there anything her son didn't know? Watching him measure in glass beakers brought to mind Wes in their high school chemistry class, and she suddenly missed him. Perhaps Sara was right. Maybe it *was* time for her to tell Alex something about his father. It was wrong that she hadn't. She knew that, and had known it for a very long time. But she couldn't do it now—she didn't want to share this moment with anyone, not even the memory of Wes.

"I thought we should try different ratios of soda to rum," he said. From right to left he poured light to heavy, and then filled them to the top with soda water. Looking at the book, he asked: "What's it mean to muddle?"

Letty showed him, squeezing the lime and dropping a handful of mint into a jam jar and mashing it with the wooden spoon. She added sugar and handed the jar to Alex to mix while she sliced strawberries into a second jar. Filling it with ice, she scooped a portion of the muddled mint and filled the glass with the lightest-pour beaker.

She stirred and took a sip.

"Wow."

Alex smiled. "Good?"

She took a second, longer sip. It was amazing. Sweet and sour and exotic somehow, even though Alex had gathered all the ingredients from their own backyard.

She handed the drink to him.

"You try. Just a taste."

He looked around the empty stairwell. A moth buzzed on the yellow porch light. Taking the jar, he smelled it and then tilted a negligible amount into his mouth. He grimaced.

"You don't like it?" She wanted him not only to taste it but to love it, to understand the perfection of the drink they'd made together. Hearing the disappointment in her voice, he tried again, digging out a mouthful of strawberries with a spoon to chase the alcohol.

"It's pretty good," he agreed, finally. "Simple syrup would have been better than sugar, though. Ice causes water molecules to slow down, which is why most of the sugar is still sitting undissolved at the bottom of the glass."

"Oh, my God, would you just drink!" Letty laughed, mixing a second glass and thrusting it into his hand. He grinned and drank the entire cocktail as quickly as he could. When he was done, he slammed the empty jar down on the blanket.

"See, it's good, right? Tell me you like it."

He shuddered, and then smiled. "I like the strawberries."

She laughed.

"Well, that's a start," she said and mixed another drink.

Three beakers later, they were both officially drunk. Letty had heard about the kiss (So sweet! So innocent!) and about Yesenia's play-fall off the pier, and about Alex's near-death experience while watching.

"You can't act like you care so much," she said.

"That's bullshit," Alex said and then clapped a hand over his mouth. "Why would I act like I don't care if I do?"

"I'm just saying."

"You're just saying nothing," Alex slurred. "Nothing, nothing, nothing." He shook the ice in his empty glass and looked up into the stars.

"So what's she like?"

"She's beautiful. And perfect. Well, not actually perfect. See, she has these shoes."

"Shoes?"

"Her legs. It's not important. Just don't stare when you meet her. Because OH, MY GOD, she's beautiful. Beautiful!" He yelled "Beautiful" out over the empty parking lot, listening to it echo back: *Beautiful! Beautiful! Beautiful!*

Letty pressed her hand over his mouth. "Shhhhh," she whispered. "You wake your sister, you're the one putting her back to sleep."

Alex pushed her away, and her knee knocked against the beakers.

"Hey, hey, hey," he said, growing suddenly serious. "Hands off the science kit."

He moved it off the blanket, arranging each measuring glass in a line on the metal tray. Of the eight in the set, only two were full. Watching him with his precious instruments, she felt a gut-punch of guilt. What was she doing? She was a terrible mother. A terrible, terrible mother. She'd somehow gotten her smart, kind, handsome son drunk, and he was a stupid, blubbering drunk, though she was worse. She didn't deserve him, or Luna. She should sober up and turn herself in somewhere. She wasn't fit to be a parent.

Turning back to Alex, she sighed heavily, imagining giving him up, the acute pain of separation filling her chest. He studied the chemistry set, slowly picking up the beakers and setting them back down, as if pondering a mysterious substance that only he could see.

"You okay?" she asked, moving a loose curl of hair away from his eyes.

"Grandpa and I used to make sugar water in these, for the hummingbirds," he said quietly.

"You miss him."

Alex nodded. "He said he'd get me an acid/base kit for my birthday, and we'd test every corner of the bay together."

His birthday had come and gone, and his grandparents had sent nothing but a card.

"I'll get you one, as soon as I can," she said.

She knew exactly what he was talking about, from her days in Mr. Everett's honors science class at Mission Hills. For two years she'd sat in his classroom, surrounded by every book and instrument invented to dissect and study the secrets of the universe. She imagined Alex sitting there, in the room where she and Wes had met, encouraged to ask questions and answer them. Mr. Everett would see his passion and talent immediately, and would take him on field trips to labs and science museums all over the Bay Area.

But it wasn't possible. The busing program she'd been part of had shut down years before, and all of Bayshore and the Landing were districted to Bayshore High. She'd never been to Bayshore High, so all she knew about it was what she'd read in the headlines. Sixteen gang members had been arrested on campus recently, and just days before school let out a loaded gun had fired from inside a backpack. It wasn't where Alex belonged. It wasn't where anyone belonged, really.

A good mother would get him out of there. If Maria Elena was still there she would find a way, Letty was sure of it, even if she had to break the law to do it.

And then she had an idea.

"Wait," she said quietly, the plan starting to take shape. They couldn't move out of the Landing—not yet. She barely had enough money for milk. But she didn't need to actually *move* to Mission Hills; she just needed to be able to claim an address on the other side of the freeway. And that was something she could do.

"What?" Alex asked, looking at her with curiosity as she sat perfectly still, thinking it through. It would be good for Luna too. She was tiny and underweight, a condition her pediatrician had labeled "failure to thrive." Luna's stomach hurt constantly, and when the doctor had asked if she was worried about anything, she had been quick to reply: *school.*

Rocking slightly, Alex pinched his cheek, his nose, and his tongue. "What?" he asked for the second time.

"You're going to high school in Mission Hills."

She would use Sara's address to enroll him, and he wouldn't waste the opportunity like she did.

"What?" Alex sat up straight, his body shocked sober, and Letty took the last two beakers, not even bothering to mix them with the strawberries and mint. She handed one to Alex and kept one for herself, holding it up in the air between them.

"Cheers."

Letty clinked beakers with her son, then shot the last of the rum and soda as Alex jumped to his feet and ran to the bathroom, slamming the door behind him.

4

The noise of the airplanes vibrated in Alex's skull. He'd woken up in that room almost every single day of his life, and yet nothing, ever, had sounded as loud as the engines did that morning. With extreme effort he sat up, peering out the window at the planes passing overhead, every ninety seconds a new one. Usually he would count the exact time between takeoffs, but today the ticking of the seconds only emphasized the blood pulsing painfully in his temples. His head hurt. His stomach hurt worse. Turning away from the light, he closed his eyes and groped around the window frame until he found the cord to the roller blind. A quick tug, and the relief of darkness pressed gently against his eyelids. He flopped back onto his pillow and pulled the blanket over his head.

What had happened to him? He remembered collecting mint at the water, and sitting on a blanket in the stairwell with his mother, and he remembered the rattling glass of his beakers on their metal tray. There was a lime. And strawberries. And there was an echo, and someone shouting something over and over again—but it must have been him shouting, because he remembered the salty hand of his mother clamping down on his mouth and thinking about Yesenia, and feeling weird that he was thinking about her then, with his mother's hand on his face and her alcohol breath so close to his nose.

He'd gotten drunk with his mother.

It was too horrifying to think about. Burrowing farther under the covers, he heard his sister walk into the room.

"Alex?"

"Go away," he moaned.

"Mom told me to tell you the bus comes at eleven oh eight and we're going to be on it."

"What time is it?"

"I don't know. But get up. We've already been to Mission Hills and back this morning."

At the mention of Mission Hills, his mother's final words of the night popped into his mind, the ones that may or may not have caused him to get sick all over the bathroom floor: *You're going to high school in Mission Hills.* Or so she had said, in a moment of drunken inspiration. He doubted she even remembered it now.

Luna climbed up onto the bed, stepping on his covered knees and hanging on the cord until the blind shot up, bouncing off the top of the window frame.

"We brought you something."

She plopped a grease-spotted paper bag on the bedspread. He peered inside and saw a blueberry muffin. His stomach lurched. He didn't want to eat ever again.

"You can have it," he told his sister.

Luna tore a chunk off the top and stuck it in her mouth, chewing and licking the squashed blueberries off her fingers.

"Where are we going, anyway?"

"To Sara's," Luna said with her mouth full. She jumped down off the bed and paused at the door, waiting for Alex to get up. "Come on. Mom says now."

He groaned and kicked the covers off the bed, which satisfied his sister enough to leave him alone. As much as he didn't want to get out of bed, he wanted less to fight with his mother. He didn't even want to look at her. Sitting up, he found a pair of pants, pulling on one leg and then the other. The effort caused him to sweat, and he was afraid he would be sick again, but he didn't think there could possibly be anything left in his stomach.

Why were they going to Sara's, and why did it have to be right now? It was the first time they'd been to her house since Letty had come home, and it made him feel sicker, remembering that first night in her apartment. If Alex didn't know his mother so well, he would have thought she'd woken up determined to make good on her proclamation of the night before. But that couldn't be it—at least Alex didn't think so. It was true Letty had surprised him more than once in the weeks since school let out. She'd promised Luna she'd let her come to work with her every day and she had; she'd nearly kept up Maria Elena's immaculate standards of housecleaning. And the day before she'd made oatmeal for breakfast. None of this, of course, was as hard as enrolling them illegally at Mission Hills; it was foolish for him to even consider it.

But what would he do if she did? All he knew about Mission Hills was that they won the state science fair every year (last year it had been on the front page of the paper, a seventeen-year-old creating an early-detection system for pancreatic cancer using dipstick technology), and that all freshmen took a trip to Washington, D.C., every spring (he'd never even been on an airplane—which was ironic, given his view of the runway). These two things combined were enough to make Alex feel like saying no would be the equivalent of taking a match to his grand-father's feather collection on purpose—endless possibilities extin-guished. But could he really leave Yesenia to face Bayshore alone? Bayshore students were more likely to be in the obituaries section of the paper than the awards section. Luckily, he thought as he pulled on his socks, it was not a decision he would ever have to make.

Taking a deep breath, he walked out of his bedroom to face his mother. Letty stood by the kitchen sink, a glass of water and two Tyle-nol in her hand. She didn't look at him when he entered the room, just thrust the water and medicine toward him and turned to the door.

"Come on," she said. "We're leaving."

An hour later they sat in Sara's kitchen, a ten-page lease agreement spread out on the counter. They'd tried to distract Luna with a bowl of flour-water and some food coloring ("make Play-Doh"), but five min-

utes later, she was a sticky mess and climbing up and down the bar-
stools, trying to see what they were doing.

"Don't touch anything," Letty said, putting her daughter back on the
floor and handing her a whisk. Luna dropped the utensil with a disin-
terested clank and climbed back up next to Letty.

"But where am I going to sleep?"

Letty had tried to keep her out of the conversation, but after the five
hundredth question, she'd explained what was happening. She was
signing a lease, pretending to rent Sara's apartment in order to get Alex
and Luna into school in Mission Hills.

"I already told you, we aren't really going to live here, but if anyone
asks, you have to *say* you live here."

Luna frowned, still not understanding.

"What's your address?" Letty quizzed.

"100 Mile Road, Apartment 31C."

"No. 770 Sycamore, Apartment 3."

"But you said we aren't really going to live here."

"Oh, Luna! Never mind."

Letty looked in the refrigerator for something to distract her daughter and, finding nothing, set her on the counter by the sink. She turned
the faucet on and pulled one hand and then the other under the running water, but the blue-brown flour glop was everywhere: wrists to
forearms to elbows, knees to shins to the bottoms of her feet. Changing
strategies, Letty plugged the sink and squirted in dish soap, stripping
Luna down to her underwear while the sink filled and then setting her
inside. The sink was enormous and undivided, and though Luna was
much too old for a sink bath, she wasn't too big. She laughed, delighted,
as Letty pulled out the hose and sprayed down her back and shoulders.
When the water had risen to her rib cage, Letty shut off the spray and
left her daughter in the bubbles.

Alex watched all this happen from his seat at the counter, looking
over Sara's shoulder as she completed the terms of the agreement seemingly at random: lease term, deposit, references. She put Maria Elena
down, making up a phone number beside her name, and then paused
at the blank space, where she was supposed to write the rent.

"What do you think this place would rent for?" she asked Letty.

"I don't know," Letty said, refilling the glass of water on the counter in front of Alex. "Drink. Maybe a thousand dollars a month?"

"No way. You can't even rent a parking space around here for that much."

She wrote down a number that made Alex squirm in his seat. His mother could never pay that. His mother could never even *pretend* to pay that. All morning, on the walk to the bus stop and on the bumpy, nauseous ride across Mission Hills, he'd practiced what he would say if his mother mentioned changing schools (variations on *no thanks*), and now he was sitting right next to Sara, watching it happen and saying nothing.

"That's probably not enough to be believable," Sara said, scratching out the absurdly high number she'd written and writing one that was even higher.

Alex felt his nausea pivot to panic. He was a rule follower, even when it didn't matter. And this mattered. If anyone found out, his mother could go to jail.

"They're going to know," he blurted. "There's no way we can pay that."

"Who's going to know?" Letty asked. "If you're there, they'll assume you're supposed to be there."

Letty looked to Sara for confirmation.

She nodded. "No one's going to question you."

But what if they did? Alex was a terrible liar.

"It's only for a few months anyway—as soon as we can, we're moving over here." Letty turned back to the lease and initialed by the smoking policy. "Hey—do you think Mr. Everett still teaches there?"

"I know he does. I ran into him just a few months ago. Honors science, zero period."

"Remember when Wes thought he disproved gravity?" Letty laughed. "And then Mr. E fixed the scale."

"He taught Wes?" Alex asked.

Letty stopped writing mid-signature, and Alex wished he could pull the words right back into his mouth. Obsessed as he'd become, he'd forgotten his mother was completely unaware of his new knowledge. He searched her face, looking for signs of anger, betrayal, surprise—but he found none. Instead, she looked him square in the eyes and nodded. "Both of us, and now you." She finished her signature with a wild flare. "Get ready to get up early," she added. "His class starts at six fifty-five."

Just then, from the forgotten bubble bath across the kitchen, a spray of water arched toward them, hitting Alex on the shoulder and splashing all over the counter.

"Luna!" Letty swiped at the lease, but it was too late. The ten pages stuck together, completely soaked through.

Alex went straight from Mission Hills to Yesenia's house. Carmen's car was gone; it was after dinner already. Nervous, he climbed the stairs to her apartment and found her leaning out the open doorframe.

"There you are," Yesenia said. "I went to your house earlier. Don't tell me you were over there again."

Alex had promised Yesenia he would stop spending entire days in front of his father's house, and for the first time he could tell her honestly that he hadn't. Between the line at the DMV, where Letty changed the address on her license, and the line at the school-district office, it had taken all day to enroll them in school.

"I wasn't. I was at the school-district office. In Mission Hills."

"You're moving?"

"No. But my mom got me into Mission Hills High."

She smiled. Immediately: without one split second of pause, so that Alex knew without a doubt that she was happy for him and not just pretending to be happy. He leaned in and kissed her, pulling away quickly when he heard a noise, but it was just a little girl on a scooter, racing down the halls. He kissed her again.

"How can you be happy?" he asked, when he finally pulled away. "We won't be together."

"Because you need to get out of here. Only ten percent of kids from Bayshore High go to college."

"How do you know that?"

"Because my mom told me. In the context of, you better be one of the ten percent."

"That sounds like something my grandma would have said."

They were quiet, Alex thinking about his grandparents, Yesenia squeezing his hand. "You should go to Mission Hills, Alex," she said finally. "Your mom is right."

Yesenia knew everything there was to know about Letty, and knew that *your mom is right* was a sentence that had probably never, in the entire history of the universe, been uttered in reference to his mother. Last night's drunkenness flashed through his mind. It wasn't right, but in her own strange way, he knew she was trying.

"Okay. I'll go to Mission Hills." His chest pounded with sudden excitement, finally allowing it to sink in. He shouted down into the parking lot: "I'm going to Mission Hills!"

"Calm down, Superman," Yesenia said, pulling on his shirttails, where they had popped free of his belt. "You're not going anywhere looking like *that*."

Alex looked down at his clothes: the same khakis and white button-down he'd worn every day for all of middle school. Or maybe longer. "What's wrong with the way I look?"

"You look great, if your goal is to impress your girlfriend's mother. But you already did that." Grinning, she dip-skipped down the hall and returned with a white envelope labeled ROPA. Clothes.

"We're going shopping."

"I'm not letting you spend your money on me."

"Do *you* have money?"

Alex dug his hands into his pockets, a reflex, though he knew perfectly well what he would find. Nothing. "No."

"So don't argue. It's not like I've grown this year. Or that I have any chance of fitting in."

Alex asked where they were going, but Yesenia didn't answer, just pulled him through the parking lot to the bus stop. They sat on the bench in silence as two, three, four buses passed. Finally the 67, Mission Heights, turned toward them. Yesenia jumped up.

Alex had never been to the Heights. He'd heard about it: an elite, woodsy neighborhood in Mission Hills, set into the ridge that separated downtown from the Pacific Ocean. They rode through town until the houses became estates, spread out, with sloping lawns and knotted trees between them. The neighborhood had its own downtown, just one cobblestone street with a handful of shops, and they climbed off at the bus stop in front of a bakery. The pastries in the window looked too fancy to eat.

"Where are we going?"

"Stop asking questions," Yesenia said. "Just follow me."

Past the bakery and two restaurants there was a secondhand shop. The sign announced it benefited the American Cancer Society. Under a bright red SALE banner in the window, six handbags hung off a silver bar in rainbow order: red, orange, yellow, green, blue, purple. The purple bag, closest to where Alex was standing, had been marked down to three hundred dollars from six.

"Are you serious?" Alex asked. "We should have gone to Walmart."

"We aren't shopping here."

She took his hand and led him to the alley behind the building. Tall stacks of boxes stood by the garbage cans, labeled SALVATION ARMY PICKUP. Alex was confused.

"A secondhand shop that donates to a secondhand shop?"

"They only keep the super-designer stuff, and they get rid of everything else. Which is also mostly designer stuff."

She pulled down a box and opened it, sorting out the women's and children's clothing and starting a pile of anything she thought might fit Alex.

"How do you know about this place?"

"One of the nurses at the hospital. My mom's been dressing me from this alley all my life."

Alex looked at what she was wearing: the hot pink bathing suit she'd worn all summer, cut-off jean shorts that Alex had assumed were old, or hand-me-down, but now realized had an intricately stitched pattern over the back pockets, and a white-on-white embroidered tank top that was so flowing it was probably made of real silk. He'd never noticed, because it wasn't the kind of thing he noticed, but now that he really looked, he realized she did dress a little differently than the other girls in class.

Alex lifted a second box off the top of a tall pile and started going through it. He was drawn to a pale green dress shirt that still had its tags, but Yesenia pulled it out of his hands and replaced it with a plain black T-shirt and worn-looking jeans.

"Put this on."

"Here?"

"I won't look."

She turned around. He was wearing boxer shorts and she wasn't even looking, but still he could barely zip up his jeans for the thrill of changing in an alley, his girlfriend an arm's distance away. He pretended it took a lot longer than it did to put on his shirt, to give his body time to calm down.

"Okay."

She turned back around, squinting her eyes as she assessed him. Stepping forward, she beckoned for him to lean over, and she tried to press his hair flat and to the side. He felt it flop back, exactly as it was before.

"I think that's as good as we can do."

"I'll take that as a *You look amazing.*"

"Basically." She grinned, turning back to her piles, picking up the stack she'd sorted for him. It was enough to fill his entire closet.

"We didn't even need your money," Alex said, taking the clothes she handed him.

"Oh, we're not done." Yesenia led him back out of the alley and to the bus stop.

"Seriously? Where to next?"

"To the place where normal teenagers hang out on a Saturday night."

"Where's that?"

Yesenia smiled. "The mall."

5

It was phenomenally easy, bartending without a tantruming child in the hallway. For the first few hours Letty looked up every two minutes—as she'd grown used to doing—and each time she saw the empty chair, the weight she'd been carrying around all summer lightened a little, and a little more. Luna was at school. All morning and for most of the afternoon she was safe, and cared for—and maybe even happy. When Letty had dropped her off that morning at her new school in Mission Hills, Luna was all eyes: ogling the playground, throwing fistfuls of fresh wood chips into the air, flopping down on her back on the fresh-cut grass—and that was all before she'd even gone inside her classroom.

She'd been assigned Room 10, Miss Noelle: a desk, homework folder, and pencil box full of school supplies were all labeled with her name. Luna had pulled out the safety scissors and snapped at the air with wonder while Letty turned away, embarrassed. Her daughter acted like she'd never seen scissors before. She had seen scissors, of course. She and Maria Elena had cut snowflakes to decorate the apartment windows every Christmas. But it was true she'd probably never seen a pair at school. Cesar Chavez didn't have a labeled pencil box full of school supplies for every kid. Half the time, they didn't even have pencils.

Letty had expected her daughter to be afraid, or at least nervous, but

Luna didn't flinch when she went to say good-bye, just kissed her mother squarely on the lips and marched away. *Remember to go to the after-school program,* she'd called, but Luna waved her away like all the other kids, and Letty's heart raced with the unexpected accomplishment. Finally she had done something right, and the thrill of it quieted the voice inside her head berating her for all her other failures: for getting Alex drunk, for not telling him about his father—even now, when she knew he knew. She'd answered his question and said not a word more, and neither one of them had mentioned it again.

After the lunch rush, she cleared dishes and rolled silverware and cut limes and refilled ketchup bottles faster than she ever had before, hoping to have time to finish Rick's book before his shift started. When she'd completed her side work, she pulled the book out of her bag, opened to the final chapter ("Exotic Syrups and Infusions"), and was deep inside a scientific explanation of crème de violette when a voice in her ear made her jump.

"I've been looking for that."

Rick stood next to her, eyeing the book. He was early.

Letty stiffened. "I was going to give it back."

"Uh-huh," he said. He raised his eyebrows to say he didn't believe her.

"I was." She closed the book. The spine was strawberry-smeared. Seeing it, she felt a crush of guilt, remembering Alex again, and she reached for a rag, attempting to wipe it clean.

"Keep it."

"It'll come off. It's just strawberry."

"It's not that. I've read it so many times I think I've memorized it."

"Are you sure?" He nodded, and she slipped the book inside her bag. When she turned back, Rick was writing the specials on the chalkboard. She grabbed it out of his hands. "Not until four o'clock."

"What am I supposed to do, then?" He pointed to the empty chair, where Luna usually sat. "I thought I had a date to ride the escalator."

Letty smiled in spite of herself. For weeks he'd been coming early to run around the terminal with Luna.

"School started."

"Already? Where does she go?"

"Willow Oaks," Letty said and, remembering the morning, added: "She loves it."

"I thought you lived at the Landing?"

With extreme deliberation, Letty reached for a rag and wiped the counter in slow, steady strokes, the motion in opposition to her racing pulse. Her children had been in school less than one day, and already someone was asking. "How do you know where I live?"

Rick turned red, and before he could answer she changed the subject, kicking at the backpack he'd set on the ground.

"What're you making today, anyway?"

He kneeled and unzipped the bag, pulling out a plastic Ziploc of lumpy brown sugar cubes and a dark bottle of orange bitters.

"An old-fashioned. You know how to make one?"

"Sure."

They locked eyes, and even though he didn't say anything, she felt as if he was questioning her. She *did* know how to make an old-fashioned, but the muddled glass of fluorescent red cherries and orange syrup was probably not the same cocktail to which Rick was referring.

"Fine," Letty said. "Show me." Deep inside her reluctance, Letty felt a glimmer of curiosity, a desire for knowledge she hadn't felt since high school. In the weeks since she and Alex had mixed drinks in beakers, she'd entertained flights of fantasy—her bar filling up, businessmen leaving fat tips on company cards, even moving across the freeway and finding an apartment in Mission Hills, her pockets full of hard-earned cash.

Rick bustled from one end of the bar to the other, gathering all the ingredients and spreading them out before her.

"The key is in the quantities," he said. "You use the sugar to measure the bitters. And don't let anyone tell you it's okay to free-pour, ever. Measure everything."

He got out a jigger (a "Japanese jigger," he corrected her, showing her the measuring lines on the inside of the instrument) and then placed a sugar cube on a paper napkin, using the eyedropper to squeeze orange bitters onto the sugar one drop at a time.

"See?" he said when the sugar cube started to leak onto the napkin.

"Complete saturation." He dropped it into a glass and handed it to Letty to muddle. Watching her pound the bottom, he took it back and started to stir it himself, pressing the dissolving sugar granules hard against the sides of the glass. When he was satisfied, he measured rye and poured just an ounce, then added a swath of orange peel and two cubes of ice, stirring before adding the second ounce. He stirred again—for what seemed to Letty to be an excessively long time—and then cut a final sliver of orange peel and spritzed it over the top.

"Try?"

Letty took a sip, swishing it around in her mouth, tasting the individual flavors of sugar and orange and rye.

"It's good, right?"

He waited for her reaction like a six-year-old holding up a perfectly tied shoe, and as much as she wanted to, she couldn't deny him the praise. It was amazing. She took another sip.

"Really good."

Setting the glass down, she rummaged around inside his backpack until she found another book. He'd brought only one this time. It was tattered and dog-eared and ancient: *The Savoy Cocktail Book,* the cover announced in gilded gold.

"Is this where you get your secrets?"

"One of the places."

"What is it?"

"Old recipes. In certain circles, that book's the bible."

She flipped it open, intrigued, scanning the introduction until she got to a line that jolted her.

"Wine was created for the solace of man, as a slight compensation, we are told, for the creation of woman—" Letty stopped. "What *is* this book?"

Rick frowned and snapped the book shut. "I don't remember that part. It was written in 1930, so it might be a little outdated."

"I guess so," Letty said. "Although you could find significantly more offensive statements in the actual Bible—don't tell my mother I said that."

"She's Catholic?" Rick guessed.

"Yeah."

"My mom too. She was brought up in the Metropolitan Cathedral in Mexico City, confirmed by the bishop himself. Cross her and she'll report you to the pope."

Letty shook her head. "Our mothers would get along."

"Does she live here?"

"Until this May. She and my father moved back to Mexico. What about yours?"

"She's in Mission Heights. She's always threatening to move home, but my dad was born and raised here and she'd never leave him, and he'd never live in Mexico."

Could Rick have been raised in Mission Heights? It begged the question, and not for the first time—what was he doing working here?

She would have asked, but just then a man with a small suitcase and a trim white beard sat down at the bar. He nodded to the drink they'd made, the orange and bitters and sugar cubes still spread out all around it.

"What're you making?"

"That's an old-fashioned."

"Sounds good to me."

Rick looked over her shoulder as Letty took her time, finding an old-fashioned glass and filling a second glass with ice, then placing a sugar cube on a napkin. With both of them watching, it took a few tries for her to figure out the eyedropper, and when she did, the bitters came out all in a rush. The sugar cube dissolved onto the napkin in a lumpy pile.

"Start over," Rick said. He whisked the wet napkin into the trash and handed her a new one.

"You've got yourself quite a teacher there," the man said, watching her work.

"Self-appointed," Letty said.

The man laughed, and she managed to ask where he was going (Seattle) and what he would be doing there (work) while concentrating hard on following the steps Rick had demonstrated.

"I don't usually drink this early," the man said when Letty finally handed him his cocktail. In Letty's experience, this was something only the heaviest drinkers said. She was right. He finished the old-fashioned in one long, slow pull, asking for a second before he'd even set the glass back down on the bar. Letty moved with more confidence this time, and faster, but when she transitioned from the muddling to the pouring, Rick picked up the glass and made her muddle some more.

"That's the stuff," the man said, pausing this time, halfway through his drink. "Self-appointed or not, I'd listen to that guy."

Rick bowed his head, an overdramatic display of humility at which Letty rolled her eyes, but her annoyance evaporated when the man withdrew forty dollars from his wallet and left it on the bar, telling her to keep the change.

"See?" Rick said. "There's money to be made."

She made change and added eighteen dollars to her earnings, her best tip of the day by far. She pulled out the rest of her money and counted it up, swapping the small bills for twenties and some change: $86.71. It wasn't much compared to the night shift, but it was more than she'd made working midday in a long, long time.

Rick watched her straighten the bills and put them in her wallet.

"There's no way I'm splitting this with you," she said. "Sorry. I'm saving for something."

"Saving for what?"

She looked at him hard. His olive skin was faintly freckled, and she wondered what he'd looked like as a little boy. "How old are you, anyway?"

"Twenty-nine."

Letty squinted at him. Mistaking her expression for disbelief, he pulled out his driver's license. *Ricardo Lorenzo Moya*. The picture was ten years old at least, his hair longer and curly, his eyes somehow aggressively confident and insecure at the same time.

"I'm not carding you," she said, pushing the license away, and then: "But just so you know, I do live at the Landing. Which means that until I save enough money to move across the freeway, I'm officially a criminal."

"I guess that depends on how you define *criminal*."

"Not really. I enrolled my kids in Mission Hills illegally, with a phony lease."

"Is it still breaking the law if the law isn't just?"

"What are you, a lawyer?"

"No, an MBA student. Well, not anymore." He frowned, and Letty guessed from his expression the end of his student tenure had not been because of graduation. He changed the subject. "So why don't you move?"

She rolled her eyes to the ceiling. "When I walk into Mission Hills, they don't exactly roll out the red carpet."

"You've got a steady job and eighty dollars, at least. It's not nothing."

"Says the man whose parents live in Mission Heights." *Who knows nothing about having nothing,* she thought.

He shrugged. "Whatever you think."

"Whatever I think?" It was her worst quality: she could go from zero to sixty in five seconds flat, and she felt it happening now, her face reddening, the blood beating in her temples. She hid her clenched fists in her apron pockets. She *was* trying. She'd worked five days a week all summer with a six-year-old in the hall. Rick had watched her. He, of all people, should understand what she was up against.

"Whatever I think?" she repeated, but he said nothing, just turned on the faucet and began to rinse out the sink with a calm thoroughness she found maddening. "Hey. Don't act like I'm not even trying."

"Well, are you?"

"Of course I am," she said. Over the last month, after winning the war over the airport gift shop, she'd managed to save five hundred dollars—and that was *after* sending money to her parents. But it wasn't anywhere near enough to rent an apartment in Mission Hills. At least she didn't think it was—it was true she hadn't yet tried.

She threw her apron in the dirty laundry bin, all of a sudden anxious to leave. "I'm out of here."

Rick spun away from the sink and stepped into her path. "Hey, I'm sorry," he said. And then, abruptly: "Let me take you out sometime."

"What?"

His eyes were glued to the rubber mat upon which they both stood, and he'd spoken so quickly and so quietly, she wasn't sure she'd heard him right. After a silence he repeated himself, louder this time: "Let me take you out."

"Are you serious?"

Rick had seen her and Luna at their worst. He knew she lived at the Landing and that she was, as of today, officially a criminal. *She* certainly wouldn't want to take herself out.

"I like you," he said finally, looking up and straight into her eyes. "You're a little defensive, not to mention a thief"—grinning, he spun her around, pulling *The Savoy Cocktail Book* from where she'd stashed it in her bag when she thought he wasn't looking—"but I still like you."

Letty laughed. "You've seen my life. There's not a lot of room in it right now. You can have dinner with me and Luna, or you can take me to McDonald's on my lunch break."

She'd meant it as a joke, but Rick smiled. "Done."

And without meaning to, she heard herself agree to meet him at Gate 37 on Friday at noon.

Letty took a detour on the way to Luna's school, walking quickly down the frontage road toward the Landing and speeding over the pedestrian bridge. She knew exactly where she was going. If she had even the slightest chance of renting an apartment in Mission Hills proper, it would be in one of the high-rise buildings on the other side of the freeway from Mile Road. The apartments had an uninterrupted view of the Landing, and occasionally as teenagers, she and Sara had turned on the light in her bedroom and flashed an SOS with their breasts—so it was ironic that she would go there now, looking for a way out. But it was her best chance. For ten years, NOW RENTING signs had hung from the buildings, because really, who would want to live there, with the Bay Area's busiest freeway in the backyard? Letty wouldn't mind, though, not if it meant her kids wouldn't have to lie about where they lived.

The young man in the rental office didn't look much older than Alex, his red hair mostly covered with a baseball cap. He stared at his phone when she walked into the room. A sign on a desk said PLEASE RING BELL FOR SERVICE. She rang it.

"Yeah?"

"Do you have any apartments for rent?"

"What are you looking for?"

"What do you have?"

Seeing that she wasn't going to be turned away by bad customer service, he shoved his phone into his pocket, rattling off the prices for one-, two-, and three-bedroom apartments.

"One-bedroom," Letty said. Hearing the price, her heart filled with hope. She didn't have enough money yet, but it was within her reach. Another week or two, and she could imagine walking in and paying the first month's rent in cash. Especially if she had a few more days like she'd had today.

He stood up and grabbed a key off the wall. Letty followed him in an elevator to the third floor and down a long hall. The dark corridor smelled faintly of beer and reminded Letty of the one time she'd visited Sara in college. He unlocked a door at the end.

The apartment was as dark as the hall, even after he flipped on the dim yellow light. Stepping inside, she found a square room opening up into a small kitchen. The only window in the room was over the sink. Light seeped around the edges of the drawn blind. Letty crossed the room and pulled the blind, pushing the window open. The freeway was shockingly close, and on the third floor she was at eye level with the drivers: she watched a woman check her phone as she flew past, another apply makeup. She felt her jaw shake as a semitruck rattled by.

"You won't even notice it after a day or two."

"Is that because I'll get used to it, or because I'll go deaf?"

He shrugged. It didn't matter to him how she got used to it, or if she did at all. It was what he was paid to say. But the price was right, and she could picture them there, leaving all the trappings of her mother's rules behind and moving over with nothing but what fit in the back of Sara's car. Alex would walk Luna to school and then keep walking, and they would really belong there. No lies.

"I'll take it," Letty said. "Can you hold it until next week? I can pay then."

"You have to fill out an application."

Because there is such a high demand for the apartment next to the slow lane, Letty thought. But she followed him back to the office and sat down at the desk, filling out the long application as quickly as she could.

"I'll need first month's rent and a cleaning deposit, but we can waive the deposit if you have good credit."

It was better than she thought. She'd heard some apartments required first and last, and some even had an application fee. First month she could do. She passed him her application and her driver's license. He took it and typed something into the computer. Checking the application, he typed the same thing again.

"Are you sure this is right?"

He pointed to the line where she'd written her Social Security number. She double-checked it.

"That's right."

Typing it a third time, he waited, and then he shook his head. "You don't have any credit."

"What do you mean I don't have any credit?"

"I mean you don't have any credit. Do you have a credit card? A car loan? A lease or utility bill in your name?"

Letty shook her head: no, no, no.

"What about your phone?"

"It's a pay-as-you-go." Every month she used her tips to buy more minutes.

He handed her back her application.

"You don't have any credit, I can't rent to you."

"But I'll pay cash." There was a note of desperation in her voice that she regretted. She took her time digging her wallet out of her bag and opening it up. "See?"

A wrinkled stack of twenty-dollar bills sat like a dirty offering between them. He looked from the bills to Letty, interested in her for the first time. His watery eyes traveled from her face down her neck. She crossed her arms over her chest.

"I'm a bartender."

He nodded slowly, unbelieving.

"I make plenty of money to pay the rent on time. And we both know there isn't anyone who wants to live in that apartment. It probably hasn't been rented since the place was built."

He moved his seat closer to the desk and leaned in. *"Believe me,"* he said, his eyes trolling her body. "If I could rent the apartment to you, I would. But no credit, no lease. Those are the rules."

Letty stood up. As she exhaled, all hope left her body. She would grow old and die in the Landing; it was stupid of her to even think it could be any other way, and stupid of Rick to suggest it.

There were rules, and those rules, as always, kept Letty out.

On the bus to Luna's school, Letty slouched underneath a heavy sadness. They weren't going anywhere, that much was clear, and as she rode her mind wandered to the big, sunny, open-to-the-elements estate in Oro del Hidalgo, where she'd left her parents. She missed them. For the first time it wasn't out of desperation or panic—she was okay, and her children were okay. But what did they have here? New schools based on documented lies and an old apartment they could never escape. It wasn't enough to call a life.

She'd done what her parents had wanted. She'd stepped up. Her children were fed and clothed and had gotten to school on time. So wasn't that enough? Did she also have to live out the rest of her life in a country where she wasn't wanted, a country even her parents had abandoned? An alternative started to form in her mind. They didn't have to stay. She could pack their suitcases full of new clothes and books and toys and buy three bus tickets south, and when they arrived in Mexico, clean and groomed and eager, with money in their pockets, she could tell her parents she wanted Alex and Luna to learn Spanish, and to grow up with family. Could they really argue with that?

Pulling up to the stop across the street from the school, the bus blew its doors open. When Letty stepped off, Luna let go of her teacher's hand and sprinted down the sidewalk. A smile beamed from her lips. Encircled in her daughter's arms, Letty felt an involuntary smile twitch at the corners of her mouth.

"I love my new school," Luna sighed into her mother's stomach.

"Oh, yeah?" Letty asked. She swallowed hard, trying to bury her overwhelming desire to run away from it all. "Tell me about it."

"Well," Luna said slowly and then, grinning, exclaimed: "I got to blue!" Letty had no idea what that meant, but Luna explained. Blue was the top level of their classroom behavior chart, a rare accomplishment that resulted in a trip to the prize box. "And I chose this."

Shoving a hand deep into the pocket of her corduroy dress, she pulled out a half-eaten, lint-covered lollipop, and before Letty could stop her, she shoved the sharp sliver of candy between her mother's protesting lips.

Turning an involuntary gag into a not-quite-believable laugh, Letty sucked the cottony, sweat-salty layer off the lollipop, until a shock of cherry revealed itself.

"I saved it for you," Luna said, her eyes wide and hopeful, awaiting her mother's approval, and Letty felt the heavy sadness melt away like the candy inside her mouth. "Do you like it?"

"I love it," Letty said, kissing Luna's cherry lips and wondering how a half-eaten lollipop could somehow taste like a reason to stay.

6

Alex's new shoes squeaked on the polished linoleum. In his hand he held a slip of paper with the number of an assigned locker—676—and a combination—10–20–7—which he'd already memorized. He took a deep breath, his lungs filling with sweet air. The girls who moved past him in clusters smelled strongly of citrus, or peaches, or maybe it was cotton candy—and the boys radiated something slightly less sweet but equally intoxicating. He was already excited, and the smell went directly to his head, turning his anticipation into a giddiness that he knew could only end in embarrassment. So he curled both lips inside his mouth and bit down hard, thinking *pain pain pain* to combat the *joy joy joy* he felt from being there on the first day of school, en route to zero period, honors science, with Mr. Everett.

Ten times that morning his mother had made him repeat Sara's address, just in case anyone asked, but no one would. With Yesenia's help, he looked like he belonged there. Gone were his khakis and white button-downs, replaced by jeans and a graphic T-shirt and the Nikes she'd bought him with her entire school clothes allowance. The remaining few dollars she'd spent on a scattering of buttons to decorate his backpack. His favorite, a cherry red circle with the word *Jenius,* had an arrow that she'd angled right to his head, but he also liked one with two rows of birds sitting on telephone wires, which made him think of his grandfather. He'd pinned only one button onto the strap of his back-pack where he could see it, a reminder he fingered as he walked: PEOPLE SAY I'M INDIFFERENT BUT I DON'T CARE.

The science wing was in the front of the school, a row of labs on one side of the breezeway with classrooms on the other. Mr. Everett's door was open. It was still early—the clock above the teacher's desk read 6:45—and only one student sat folded into a small desk at the front of the room. He immediately stood up, a gesture of such excessive polite-ness that Alex thought he was mocking him. But the boy smiled, a skinny grin on a lightly pocked face, and held out his hand.

"Jeremy Coker," he said.

Alex took his hand and gripped it as hard as his grandmother had taught him, shaking it so enthusiastically he could almost imagine Ye-senia's frown of disapproval. She'd told him to act cool.

"Sorry," he said. "I'm Alex. Alex Espinosa."

"Nice to meet you. You new here?" Jeremy asked.

"I'm a freshman."

He bit down on his upper lip as soon as he'd said it. The simple (and still truthful) answer would have been: yes. Yes, yes, yes! It was all he'd needed to say, but instead he'd admitted to being the lowest form of high school life, a monad with no link to the complex social structures of the world around him.

Jeremy turned to the teacher. "Hey, Mr. E—since when do you let freshmen into this class?"

Alex had been so focused on trying—and failing—to make a good impression, that he hadn't yet noticed Mr. Everett. He stood at the front of the classroom, brown hair silver-streaked and shaggy, an olive polo shirt untucked over slacks, and boots muddy enough for Alex to won-der if he'd spent the morning patrolling the Landing. His beard gave his face a friendly look, and the binoculars around his neck reminded Alex of a birder. Alex liked him immediately. He took a step forward, and Alex thought he might be coming to shake his hand too, that perhaps it was a requisite of Mr. Everett's zero period and one that he would have to learn to do more casually, but as he got closer he saw that his teacher was trying to read the button on the strap of his backpack. Alex moved one hand quickly to cover it.

Mr. Everett met his eyes. "Alex Espinosa?"

He nodded. "Yes, sir. You taught my mother."

The first thing Letty had done after enrolling Alex at Mission Hills was to call Mr. Everett directly and ask him to request Alex in his honors science class.

"I did indeed."

Jeremy gawked. "What? Mr. E, you aren't *that* old."

"It's a fact. A smart woman, Letty Espinosa."

Was she? It was the first time anyone had ever said that to him, and Alex wondered if it could be true. He'd always assumed he'd gotten his brains from his father, or maybe his grandfather—an insult to his mother, he realized now. He retreated to the back of the classroom and found a seat.

He'd never sat at the back of any class, and as the room filled, he saw that it had its advantages: he could take furious notes without being teased, he could stare at his classmates without them noticing, and (although he wouldn't on the first day, he'd promised himself this) he could even raise his hand and pull it down as he was called on, so that by the time the other students turned around to look it would seem as if he'd been called on without volunteering himself. But as the students filtered in, Alex began to understand just how different life at Mission Hills would be. Every student was on time. A girl in the front row pulled out a fat, worn book titled *Nano: The Emerging Science of Nanotechnology* and opened it to an earmarked page close to the end; the two boys next to him were discussing *Atlas Shrugged* and *The Fountainhead*, which they'd both read over the summer (seemingly for pleasure) and whose merits they fiercely disagreed about. For the first time in his life, Alex wouldn't be the only kid in class who knew the answer. In fact, he might be the only one who didn't.

When the bell rang, Alex counted the students in class: sixteen. In his previous life he hadn't even known sixteen kids who could wake up before 7:00 A.M., let alone get to class with their books open, and smelling good too. Not that Alex blamed them—why rush to get to school, just to see another substitute or a photocopied worksheet? Everything was different here, and the class hadn't even started yet.

"Good morning," Mr. Everett said, standing up. "And a very early one."

There was a collection of nods and muffled yawns as the class agreed with him.

"It's nice to see you all. I'd tell you I had a fabulous summer, but you know I was just counting down the days until school started." He was being facetious—wasn't he? Alex was terrible at understanding humor. But he knew one thing for sure: whether or not he'd had a good summer, Mr. Everett was genuinely glad to see them.

"Those of you who've taken my class before know what's coming. I've been giving the same speech on the first day of school every year for almost twenty years." Mr. Everett caught Alex's eye when he said this, and Alex knew he was thinking about Letty, sitting through what must have been one of the first of these speeches. "So if you know what I'm going to say before I say it, please chime in. After I'm done I'll take roll for the first and only time this year, and then we'll get to work. So: first things first. This class is an elective—which means? Rachel."

Rachel looked up from a hardbound notebook that lay open on her desk. "Which means you're here because you want to be here."

"Exactly. Which means I expect you to act like you want to be here: every day, on time, acting and thinking like a scientist. I have a zero-tolerance policy for sulkers, as I also do for hoarders. Hoarding of information, that is. You learn it, you share it. Which brings me to my next point."

He paused and looked around the classroom, giving the students time to catch up or interrupt, Alex wasn't sure which. To Alex's right, a girl with a dark tan and a bright yellow tank top nodded as if keeping time with Mr. Everett's words. She'd twisted her curly brown hair into a loose braid, and it fell over her shoulder and settled on top of her desk. The girls in the class were almost as distracting as the science, all beautiful. He thought of Yesenia and felt guilty.

The girl, who'd scrawled *Julianna Skye* on the top of her notebook, finally spoke up: "Competition."

"Thank you. Competition." Mr. Everett nodded. "There is none here. There's no bell curve, no grade race. Everyone in my class gets an A. You're graded on one thing, and one thing only: your love of science. And for those of you who are new and/or haven't yet caught the science bug, here's a foolproof method to a straight A in my class: if you don't feel it, fake it. Pretend to love it, hard, and one day you'll start to love it for real and you won't notice the day you stopped pretending. So that's it: come to class and love science—or pretend to love science—and you get an A. There will be no Bs, and no A pluses—so don't ask." He looked pointedly around the room, pausing to lift his eyebrows at a thin blond girl in the front row, who Alex thought had probably already asked.

"Okay." He hesitated here, and all around the room students dug into their backpacks, pulling out stacks of science books, each one different from the next. Alex wondered if he'd missed something—if there was some kind of summer project, a letter sent to Sara's, maybe, that she hadn't forwarded. "Hold on, now. We're almost there. This usually doesn't come up until December, but I've started addressing it up front, to preempt. Help me out, Jeremy, will you?"

Jeremy closed the book he'd opened midway through the grades lecture. "Sure," he said. "The question is: how can you say there's no competition, when this class exists for the sole purpose of entering—and winning—the state science fair?"

It was a good question, Alex thought. He waited for Mr. Everett to answer.

"So here's how it goes. We'll have an in-class competition in December. This won't be for the best results—it will be for the best project idea. Three of you will win, and everyone in the class will be assigned to one of those three project teams. Everyone competes in the state contest."

There was a silence while the class took in this information, and then Jeremy added, in the voice of an overenthusiastic game-show host: "And the money goes to . . ."

"The project lead," Mr. Everett said. "If a team wins a scholarship at the state competition, the money goes to the lead scientist on the project. Now, let's get started."

Alex was less focused on the money than on the title: *lead scientist*. He liked the idea of having a team of students—all of them older than he was—working to solve a puzzle he'd designed, but looking around, and then listening to roll, Alex knew he had a lot of catching up to do.

In the front of the room, Miraya Ahmed—first on the class list—was talking about executive function disorder, something that Alex had never heard of, but on which, from the sound of it, Miraya was an expert. As Mr. Everett went down the roll, each student spoke about his or her scientific interests, and Alex listened gap-mouthed as Nathan Allen described his idea to use the wasted heat energy of a motor to power a car and Rachel Burke talked about her interest in the effects of processing style on standardized test scores and Sophia Joyce Chen outlined her plan to treat hypercholesterolemic rats with something called HMG-CoA reductase inhibitors.

Alex should have been planning what to say, but he was so busy listening that he didn't even think for a moment about his own scientific interests. When Mr. Everett called his name, he sat in stunned silence. The class turned to look at him, and for the first time in his entire school career, he felt his face turn red, wishing that his teacher hadn't called on him. Everyone waited. He had to say something.

"I love science," he managed.

The class laughed. It wasn't a mean laugh, but an amused one, and he remembered then what Mr. Everett had said about loving science. The class thought it was a joke. He looked to the front of the room, hoping Mr. Everett didn't think he was trying to be funny. The teacher didn't look amused, but he didn't look mad either.

Alex took a deep breath. "I love birds too." He thought hard, trying to pull up some kind of elaborate language that would impress them, but all he could think of was the birds of the bay. He recited them in alphabetical order, as his grandfather would have done. "Acorn woodpecker, Allen's hummingbird, American avocet, American goldfinch, ash-throated flycatcher, barn swallow. Bewick's wren, black turnstone, black-bellied plover, burrowing owl—you know."

"I do know," Mr. Everett said, raising his binoculars and pointing them at him. "I like birds too."

He dropped the binoculars and turned to the class.

"So that's it, right? You all laughed, but Alex hit it—he loves science and he loves birds. And he clearly contains a knowledge base that most of us don't have. So that's what I want you all to think about, before you get started on any of these projects. What do you love, and what do you know? And then, what are you curious about? Everyone in the class has a unique story, unique interests—and these are what should drive your inquiries. So if you're having trouble figuring out your area of interest, spend some time thinking about what you know, and what you love, and what makes you different. The more different you are, the better."

Alex smiled. Proof, as if he had needed it: he was born to be a scientist.

Alex had promised Yesenia he'd meet her at the water as soon as school let out. But in his sixth-period English class, Mrs. Davis asked if anyone could stay late to help assign books for the year, and out of habit his hand shot up in the air. It took more than an hour to tag class sets of tattered novels, and then, even though he'd told himself he wouldn't, he detoured past Wes's house and looked in every window, for the first time feeling bold enough to walk up the driveway and into the backyard. Now—if Yesenia was still there—they'd have only a few minutes before she had to go home to dinner.

His shadow was long when he finally saw Yesenia sitting at the end of the pier in her bathing suit, crumpled clothes and heavy black shoes in a pile beside her. His generic deodorant had failed him. Alex squeezed his arms tight to his sides and sat down.

"Hey," he said quietly.

"Hey," she answered, turning over a flat rock in her hand. She threw it into the water.

It had been only twenty-four hours since they'd seen each other, but Alex felt suddenly shy. He'd lived a whole life in a single day, and he worried he'd changed, and she would see it.

"You look nice."

"Thanks."

He scooted as close to her as he dared, given the failed deodorant.

"So how was it?" she asked.

"I missed you," he said, avoiding the question. It felt like a trespass to tell her the truth: that it had been the best day of his life. But it was true that he'd missed her. "What about Bayshore?"

"I survived."

"Survived?"

She shrugged, not eager to elaborate.

"Why do you say that?"

"I don't know. It was different. Last year, as long as I stayed quiet, no one said anything to me. But now, with all these new kids . . ."

Her voice trailed off, and she looked out at the water.

"What did they say?" Alex asked, fear gathering in his chest.

She looked away from him and changed the subject. "Did you keep your promise?"

He lowered his eyebrows, remembering: he'd promised her he wouldn't raise his hand on the first day. It hadn't been as easy as he'd thought.

"Almost," he said. "Not exactly."

Yesenia laughed. "It's no use." She wiggled closer to him on the pier. "You'll never be normal."

"Thanks. I think."

"It was a compliment."

"Then thank you."

She shook her head, water spraying in salty pellets on his face and lips, and turned to him. "So what about zero period? Were you the only freshman?"

He nodded. "I liked it. He said the more different you are, the better."

"Well, that's good for you. What did you do?"

"Just took roll, and talked a little. He asked us to think about what we have that no one else has."

"That's easy."

She was right. Alex thought about the heavy drawers of feathers, all organized by color and species and date, and then his grandfather's note: *make wings*. It was almost as if he'd left them there for this exact purpose, as if he'd known Alex would have the opportunity to use them, to design a project that could help him win, and that that win would take him somewhere far from the life they'd shared. He just wished his grandfather were there to help him; it was overwhelming to think about doing it alone.

"So," Yesenia said, pulling both her feet out of the water and turning to Alex, smiling impishly. He was sitting cross-legged and she climbed onto his lap, wrapping both legs around him. "What do you have that no one else has?"

She was so small that even when she sat on his lap he had to bend down to look her in the eyes. "You?" he asked hopefully.

Her lips were wet. As she stretched tall to kiss him, she wrapped her arms around his waist, and he did the same, moving his hands lightly over her bare back, down her sides, and over her legs. He hesitated and then reached out and held each of her feet in his hands.

She gave a small shudder and pulled away, looking at the place where he had been holding her.

"Is this okay?"

"Yeah."

She held still as he ran his fingers from big toe to heel on each per-fectly formed foot, the skin white and wrinkled from the water.

"What happened?"

Yesenia placed her hands over his. "I don't know. My mom won't talk about it."

It surprised Alex—from his dinner with Carmen, he couldn't imag-ine anything she and her daughter didn't share. "Was it a birth defect?"

He regretted it as soon as he said it, but she didn't react to the words.

"I don't think so. I always thought it was, but a few years ago in the grocery store we saw a baby, a tiny baby, with casts on both legs, and a face that looked like something heavy had fallen on it—all black and blue. My mom just turned around and left. I waited for over an hour, but she never came back. I had to walk all the way home by myself, and then there she was, in the kitchen, pretending like nothing had happened."

It made Alex feel sick, to think of Yesenia as a baby, to think that someone might have hurt her.

She leaned toward him, closing his eyes with her fingertips.

"Don't think about it," she whispered, and then she kissed him hard and kept kissing.

7

Letty dumped a non-virgin virgin Bloody Mary down the drain. She hadn't made this many mistakes since the first week she'd brought Luna to work. Why had she ever agreed to meet Rick for lunch? He probably wouldn't even show up. Playing it out a little further in his head—movie nights with Luna wedged between them, taking Letty to meet his parents in their ritzy home in Mission Heights with her two disheveled children in tow—it wasn't going to happen. Letty told herself she wouldn't be disappointed when she walked casually by the McDonald's at noon. Being stood up would merely be a disaster averted. That morning she'd even dressed in her oldest jeans and a black blouse with bleach spots, so that when he showed up to work at four with some thin excuse, he'd be able to see that she'd expected nothing less.

At five minutes to noon she washed her hands, called the manager to cover her lunch break, and walked out of Flannigan's. Speed-walking past McDonald's, she threw a glance inside and was surprised to see him already waiting, his eyes on the door. He jumped up just as Letty squeezed into a plastic booth.

"I'll have a number two," she said. "With Coke."

"You didn't actually think we were going to eat here, did you?"

"Why not? Don't tell me you're one of those food snobs."

"I guess you could say that."

"So where are we going?"

Rick held up a brown paper bag. "Follow me."

He led her to the end of the terminal, down an escalator, and through a long corridor where the express planes lined up, waiting for their five o'clock flights, to a second escalator she'd never noticed. The moving staircase lifted her into a round room, all windows, with low black benches pressed up against the walls. There was only one door. It might have been a gate once, an entrance for the kind of double-decker jumbo jets they'd stopped flying with the recession, but now the door was locked and the room was just a lookout. The view stretched all the way to San Francisco.

"How did you find this place?" she asked. "I thought I knew every inch of this airport."

"I did a little research," he said, "when I found out I was limited to Terminal Two."

He'd done well. She turned away from the majestic view of the city and walked to the south-facing window. Just on the other side of the hurricane fence, the three buildings of the Landing teetered at the edge of the bay.

"I tried to move," she said, as Rick pulled paper boxes out of the bag he carried. "You were wrong."

"Yeah? What happened?"

"I didn't pass the credit check."

"Why? Do you have bad credit?"

"I don't have bad credit. I just don't have *any* credit." She thought about the promise she'd made Alex: *We'll move over the freeway, just as soon as I can afford it,* and how, in her disappointment, she'd briefly flirted with the idea of moving to Mexico with her children. "I have no idea how long it takes to build up credit. Alex will probably be out of school by the time I manage to do it."

Rick placed real silverware, two champagne glasses, and two take-out containers on a bench between them. With his thumb he popped a miniature bottle of prosecco and filled both glasses halfway.

"Do they like their new schools?"

"They love them. And Luna's always hated school."

Handing her a glass, he lifted his own until they clinked. "It's worth it, then. You're doing the right thing."

She tipped the glass and drank it all at once. When it was gone, she looked at the empty bottle longingly.

"I thought about bringing another, but I wouldn't have ever forgiven myself if you got fired for being drunk on the job."

"Good call."

He knew more than anyone how much she needed to work, and management was strict about drinking.

She opened the container he'd placed before her: fat butterfly shrimp, dripping in what looked like butter and chili, on top of a bed of lettuce. Thinly sliced avocado and jalapeños fanned around the edges.

"Wow," she said, her mouth full. She wasn't sure if it was the hit of champagne (exactly enough, she thought now: all the happiness without the impaired judgment) or the fact that she hadn't eaten breakfast, but it was the best thing she'd ever tasted. "What is this?"

"Al mojo de ajo," he said, his accent so beautiful it made Letty wish she spoke more Spanish. "From Avila's. I used to work there."

"Really? Why don't you anymore?" Avila's was the most popular upscale Mexican restaurant on the peninsula. To say it was a step down for Rick to be working at Flannigan's was to make the understatement of the century.

"It's a long story."

Letty checked her watch. "I've got twenty-five minutes. Talk fast."

Rick swallowed a bite of avocado and wiped his mouth on a napkin. "My dad owns it. I started working there when I was thirteen."

"What?" Letty's surprise was tempered only by her complete focus on the food. Her mouth was full of shrimp and three different kinds of salsa, and she willed her eyes not to roll back in her head from pure ecstasy. She took another bite and nodded as she tracked with his story: the family business his father had every intention of passing over to Rick, his oldest child, but not until he earned it, starting as a dishwasher and working his way through every job—prep cook to line cook to host to runner. He paid for college with his salary as sous-chef.

"So what did you do wrong?"

"My dad wanted me out of the kitchen. He didn't want me to spend the rest of my life smelling like grease and working past midnight. He told me I'd never find a wife, and he'd never expand his business. So he told me to go to business school."

"And you went."

"And I hated it. I love restaurants because I love food, not because I love profit margins and supply curves and tax accounting."

When he dropped out, he said, his father fired him. Letty listened to the end of the story while swiping the remains of the garlic sauce off the bottom of the paper box with her thumb.

"So why are you working at Flannigan's?" she asked when he finished. It was the only part of the story that still didn't make sense. With all those years at Avila's, he could have gotten a job at a much nicer place; it wasn't true what he'd said when they first met, that he had to start somewhere.

"My dad told all his restaurant friends not to hire me. I think he thought if I couldn't get another job, I'd come around. I pretty much just took this job to spite him."

"So you don't talk anymore?"

"Oh, no, we talk all the time. He's my father, and we love each other. This is just a test."

"A test of what?"

Rick was quiet for a minute, as he looked out the window. Men in orange vests waved planes into gates, their arms like windmills. "He's testing my passion. Seeing what I'm willing to sacrifice. Because it isn't an easy life—especially if you want a family." He looked away from her when he said this, embarrassed, as if he was suggesting he wanted a family with her.

"What does your mom think about the family feud?"

"She stays out of it. She's got enough going on."

"What does she do?

"She's got ten kids. Four still at home."

"Ten kids?" Letty said in shock, although it explained the licorice rope and his facility at bribery. Rick was the oldest of ten. "I can't even handle two."

"You have siblings?"

Letty shook her head no. "I'm it. All of my parents' disappointments, rolled up into one neat little package." She dabbed at her jeans, where oil from the dressing had soaked through the cardboard box.

"You act like working at Flannigan's puts you on par with drug addicts and child molesters. It's not that bad."

"You work nights," Letty argued. "At least you make decent money."

"Decent. Enough to pay for my books."

"I thought you dropped out of school?"

"Out of the MBA program. But I'm in my first semester at the California Culinary Academy."

"Ha!" Letty grinned at the accuracy of her intuition. "So you really are a food snob."

"Well, it looks like you enjoyed my food snobbery," Rick countered, taking the box she'd all but licked clean and walking it to the trash can with the rest of the boxes and bags.

As Letty watched she thought of something: "So how did you get those, if you don't work there anymore?"

"I still know everyone in the kitchen. I go to the back door and they'll make me anything I want. I'm like that dog in *Lady and the Tramp*."

"You mean the Tramp?"

"Exactly. The Tramp. You liked it?"

"It was great. But I could eat another."

"You're still hungry?"

His face fell, and she stood up, twirling around in her tight jeans.

"You don't get this figure on a diet of shrimp and lettuce." He started to apologize, but she thought of something and pulled him onto the escalator. "Now *you* follow *me*."

They retraced their steps to the little plastic table in the dining area of McDonald's, where they'd met only a half an hour before.

"Wait here," she said and returned a minute later with a small sundae. In the seat across from him she took a big bite, and then, loading up the spoon with equal parts vanilla ice cream and hot fudge, she held it out to him. He looked at her skeptically.

"You've never had one, or you wouldn't be looking at me like that."

"I haven't."

"Well, trust me. These things are good."

"You know, their ice cream isn't even made from milk? It's some kind of oil-and-water thing that doesn't melt. If you leave it out in the sun it separates."

She forced a spoonful of sundae through his protesting lips. "Who in their right mind would ever let this melt?"

He stopped talking and swished the vanilla and chocolate in his mouth, his eyes glazed over with pleasure. He swallowed. "Point taken."

She shared the rest of her sundae bite for bite. After the final, extra-fudgy spoonful, Rick shivered involuntarily. "Thank you for enlightening me on the virtues of the McDonald's sundae."

Letty laughed. "Thanks for lunch."

There was an awkward pause, where a kiss might have been, if it had been a real date, in a real restaurant, with a drop-off on a front porch instead of a race back to work. Letty threw away the plastic dish and returned to say good-bye.

"Hey," Rick said suddenly. "I don't want to meddle, but I'm sure I could find you a place to rent over the freeway. All my parents' friends have guesthouses. And a lot of them don't even live in the main houses."

It wasn't a world Letty understood, with main houses and guesthouses and neither one occupied, but if Rick wanted to take her there, she was happy to have him do it.

"Meddle away," she said, standing up to go. "I need all the help I can get."

8

For the rest of the afternoon Letty reverted to her old ways, abandoning her list of specials and pulling drinks straight from the frozen margarita machine. She was too distracted for the kind of calculated precision Rick had taught her, and she wanted only to move behind the bar like she used to, without thinking, so that she could think about Rick. Ricardo Lorenzo Moya. She replayed every moment of their lunch together, every exchange, every bite of food, from the expression on his face when she force-fed him ice cream to the still-hungry look in his eyes when he said good-bye. Her thoughts were so crowded that she forgot to beg leftovers from the kitchen staff, and for the first time since her return from Mexico, she left the bar empty-handed.

Now, she stood with Luna, staring into an empty refrigerator. She wished Alex had a cell phone so she could tell him to stop at the store. Once Luna was home, it was impossible to convince her to get back on the bus, not for any amount of bribery.

Letty closed the refrigerator door and tried the freezer. Something sand-colored caught her eye, buried in ice in the back corner. She chipped at the snow pack with a knife until a tamale popped loose. If she was lucky, there might be another, or even two more, and she wouldn't have to worry about dinner for Alex either.

Plopping the tamale onto a plate, she walked to the microwave, but Luna grabbed it out of her hands. "I like them like that."

"There is no possible way you like them like that."

"I do."

Luna pulled it off the plate, peeled back the corn husks, and started sucking the hard masa. Letty watched, appalled, as her daughter wrapped the tamale in a paper towel and wandered to the sofa. She was filthy. They'd taken a shortcut home from the bus stop, and Luna had gotten carried away, splashing muddy water up and down the backs of her legs, all the way into her hair. Letty should have made her shower, or at least change her pants, but all the furniture in the room had aged ten years in just the few months since Maria Elena left; a little more mud wouldn't matter now. Luna curled up on the white cushions, and Letty turned on the television, searching for something that would buy her a half hour of peace.

She'd just found a show and returned to her task of excavating the tamales when Luna called out from the living room: "Mom? Someone's here."

Wiping her fingers on her apron, she closed the freezer and walked to the door. A row of dead bolts separated her from whatever stood on the other side, one for every decade they'd lived at the Landing. Letty's frozen fingers were slow and slippery, and when she finally succeeded in opening the door, she almost shut it right back again.

Wes stood on the other side.

All at once, there was no air. She reached for the doorframe and steadied herself against it, trying to look casual while praying her legs wouldn't buckle.

"Hey."

She could barely hear her own voice over the sound of her beating heart. Behind her, Luna pressed the TV volume up until the entire room was filled with the sound.

"Luna!" Letty spun around. "What are you doing? Way too loud."

Luna pressed MUTE, and in the silence that followed, Letty saw her life through Wes's eyes: Letty in a bar apron, still in her parents' apartment, yelling at a dirty girl on a dirty couch eating a frozen tamale like a Popsicle. All the times she'd fantasized about Wes's return, it had never been like this. In her imagination she was graduating from college or wearing a business suit, and her children were clean and polite and smiling. Only Wes had lived up to his part of the fantasy, which made it even worse. He stood before her looking better than she'd let herself remember, or perhaps more handsome than he'd ever been. His blond hair was darker but still sun-streaked, his shoulders broad underneath the thin cotton of hospital scrubs. He was a man now, with a hint of stubble and creases around his eyes.

"What are you doing here?" she asked.

"What are *you* doing here?" he asked.

"What do you mean what am I doing here? I live here."

"You never left?"

"So you just dropped by to make me feel like a loser?" Letty raised one hand in exasperation. With the other she held on to the door, as if she might shut it again at any moment.

"Sorry. No. I—" He paused, looking past her to Luna and then into the kitchen, before lowering his voice and continuing. "There's this boy—he's been hanging around my house for weeks, and yesterday I followed him home, and he came here, to your old apartment. And the more I thought about it— Well, I had to come see."

"See what?"

"Do I really have to ask?" When Letty said nothing, Wes leaned into her ear and whispered. "Do I have a child?"

Letty glanced back to where Luna sat watching, all eyes.

"She's not yours." Pushing past him, she stepped out onto the landing and walked to the end of the open-air hallway, where not even a month before she and Alex had gotten drunk, and almost sixteen years before that, Wes had snuck up three flights of stairs with a bottle of wine and they'd toasted and cried over his 6:00 A.M. flight to New York City, where he would be starting his freshman year at Columbia. She hadn't known she was pregnant, then or for a good three months after, and when she'd finally realized, she'd spent the rest of her pregnancy worrying about the effects of that drunken night on the baby.

Wes joined her, and for a long, quiet moment she thought that was the end of it, that he had asked and she had answered, and while she hadn't lied she hadn't told the truth either.

"She's not mine," Wes said finally. "That's not a no."

Letty swallowed hard. She couldn't look at him. A jet rumbled into the silence, turning in a wide arc and pointing north. Wes's hands clutched the iron rail, his fingers hairy where they'd once been smooth. She thought of all the places those fingers had touched her and, heat in her face, turned away. "It's not a no."

"How could you not tell me?"

"I was going to tell you. But I got scared, and then you didn't come home that summer—"

"And then fourteen years passed?" Wes put his hand on her shoulder, forcing her to look him in the eye.

"It wasn't exactly like that." She turned away.

"It *was* exactly like that."

"You have no idea what it was like," Letty snapped. "I did the best I could."

"I'm not saying you didn't. I'm just saying you should have told me."

"Well, I didn't."

Wes sighed. He wasn't a fighter. He could argue and debate for hours, but the second Letty got angry he would back off and let her win. In high school she'd found it infuriating but was grateful for it at the same time, and she felt the same way now.

"I wonder how he found you," she said.

"I don't know. But he did. One day last spring—or maybe it was summer, I don't remember—I got home from work, and there was this kid looking in my front window."

"What happened?"

"Nothing. I asked him if I could help him, and he ran. I didn't think anything of it, until I noticed him following me to the store a few weeks later. He looked strangely familiar, even though I was sure I'd never seen him before, and then I suddenly remembered what you said, the last time I called."

It had been just a week after Alex's release from the hospital. A social worker had been assigned to investigate possible neglect, and Letty's panic attacks had come like contractions, every one more intense than the one before. Maria Elena had answered his call and held the phone up to Letty's ear. She had no recollection of why he'd called or what he'd said, but she remembered what she'd said: *You have to leave us alone.* She'd tried to self-correct, following quickly with *Please don't call me again.* And he hadn't, but all these years later, he remembered her slip. *Leave us alone,* she'd said, and what she'd meant was *Save us.* But over the phone line he'd heard only her words, not their meaning, and he had done as she'd asked.

She sighed. "He looks so much like you."

"Of course he does," Wes said, and for a second Letty thought he was going to detour into a genetics lesson, but instead he just shook his head and said: "I can't believe you let me just go off to college."

It was terrible, what she'd done. But she could still feel the terror she'd felt then, and the shame. All those years at Mission Hills, the things they'd said about the girls from Bayshore. How hard she'd worked not to be like them. And then she'd gotten pregnant.

"What was I supposed to do? You know what everyone would have said if you'd stayed."

They would have said she'd come to Mission Hills just to trap him with a baby. Wes had been warned about this when they'd started dating: by his friends, by his teachers, even by his own parents. Then, he'd defended her. But now, looking at her through disappointed eyes, Letty suspected he thought maybe he shouldn't have.

Finally he spoke, shaking his head slowly. "But *I* wouldn't have said that. You know I wouldn't have." It was right there, the love she'd felt all those years ago, her heart stuffed full. She turned away from it, but he moved closer, so she could feel his breath on her forehead when he spoke next. "I would have stayed."

"I know you would have," she whispered. "You would have given up everything, and stayed because you had to stay. And I didn't want that for you. Or for me."

She hadn't wanted people to say she'd trapped him, but she hadn't wanted him to feel trapped either. She'd wanted him to go away and come back of his own free will, and she'd wanted him to find her happy, and successful. In her fantasies she'd imagined transferring to UC Berkeley and putting Alex in preschool, and when Wes came back, a college graduate, she'd imagined him loving her fiercely for everything she'd done and for everything she'd allowed him to do. But instead of going to class she'd gone out every night, and then she'd had to get a job, and then another, and nothing had turned out the way she'd planned.

Wes took a step back toward the door, and Letty watched him look around. It hadn't changed much in all the years he'd been gone. The same couch, shabby now, the same square TV. The only difference was that her parents were gone.

"What did you tell your mom?"

Letty's eyes flitted to the bookshelf on the other side of the room, where she'd stuffed the last ten letters Maria Elena had sent, unopened. She wanted to read them, but it was too much, the endless advice and reminders, proof of everything she was doing wrong. So instead they piled up, unread, and she sent back short notes with as much money as she could spare.

Wes was still waiting for her to respond. Looking back to him, she answered his question honestly: "That you broke up with me when you found out."

"Are you serious?" The whispered moment of connection was gone as quickly as it had come, replaced by anger. Wes had loved Maria Elena, and Maria Elena had loved Wes. It had broken her mother's heart when Letty told her Wes had left her pregnant. "Where is she?"

He paced in front of the door as if he wanted to go find her, right then, and set the record straight.

"She moved back to Mexico. I'll write to her. I'll tell her the truth."

"No," he said. "I will."

Just then, Letty saw a flash of light on curly hair, and they both turned, watching a gangly, backpacked boy race through the parking lot below them.

"That's him," Wes said, half question, half statement.

Letty nodded. "Yep. That's Alex."

9

Alex wasn't sure what he'd imagined. Tears maybe, or excuses, or long-winded explanations, but throughout the days and weeks and months he'd secretly tracked his father, he'd never once pictured a stiff introduction, a silent drive, and now this: sitting across from his father at a tiny table at Zen Sushi, a bamboo-and-white-light-wrapped restaurant in downtown Mission Hills.

Alex stole glances at his father as he studied the menu, words like *unagi* and *udon* and *yuzu ponzu,* all mysterious to him. Up close Wes's blond hair was gray at the temples, his blue eyes flecked with hazel.

"Do you know what you want?" Wes asked him.

Alex returned his attention to the menu, then gave up and shook his head no. "You can order for me. I don't really know sushi."

"Are you sure?"

He nodded, and when the server came Wes rattled off a list of rolls so long Alex thought it would take them until closing to finish eating. The ordering done, they looked around the restaurant, and then reached for the water pitcher in the center of the table at the same time.

"Sorry."

"No, I'm sorry."

Wes poured two glasses, and they each drank in silence. Wes set his down. "So, how are you?"

"I'm fine. How are you?"

"I'm fine."

Wes took another sip of water. Alex did the same. A clock on the wall ticked off the seconds.

"It's strange to finally meet you," Wes said. "I guess I don't really know where to start."

There was a long silence, while Alex waited for his father to say something, anything else. But he didn't. Alex tried to help: "You could just ask me about my day or something."

"How was your day?"

Alex laughed, a nervous release, and thought about his day. It had been fine until he'd popped his head into Mr. Everett's class after school, to thank him for a book on bird migration, and been rewarded with an office chair and a class list. His teacher hadn't taken roll in a month, and had just been chastised by the school secretary. "It was okay. I had to stay late to help Mr. Everett with attendance."

"Mr. E!" Wes smiled at the memory. "I loved him. Although I'm not sure he loved me. I think I might have been the reason he outlawed competition in his honors class."

Alex smiled, remembering Mr. Everett's lecture on the first day of school. "I think he likes everyone."

They were quiet again. Alex studied the fish tank at the back of the restaurant. A thin film of algae clung to the glass walls. He wondered if the fish were for eating or for decoration; the thought made him feel slightly ill.

Wes waited until Alex looked back at him, and then he asked: "Did your mom tell you why I left?"

Alex shook his head no.

"Didn't you ask her?"

"We don't exactly have that kind of relationship," Alex said and then instantly regretted it. He didn't want Wes to think his mom hadn't done a good job. "I mean—I didn't want to make her feel bad. I asked my grandpa once, though."

Alex remembered the conversation vividly, sitting in his grandfather's lap at the window, watching the hummingbirds hover at their feeders below.

"What did he say?"

"He didn't answer, exactly. But he taught me about reverse migration." Alex waited to see if Wes knew what he was talking about, and when he shook his head no, he explained. "It's when little birds—not the big ones, who learn migration routes from their parents, but the little ones, who have the routes genetically programmed right into them—it's when something goes wrong, and the routes are programmed a hundred and eighty degrees in the opposite direction. So, for example, birds that are supposed to winter in Southeast Asia end up in western Europe."

"What happens to them?"

"Most of the time they die, but sometimes they survive, and reorient the next winter." Alex paused, waiting for Wes to refill his glass. "I think it was his way of saying you might come back, someday."

"If I didn't turn up dead in Finland first."

"Exactly."

They smiled, eyes locking for just a moment before Wes looked away. "I'm sorry it took me so long."

"It's okay. I'm sorry I stalked you."

"I'm glad you did. But I hope you aren't aiming for a career in the CIA. You aren't exactly the picture of stealth."

There was another long pause. Alex picked up his chopsticks and pulled them from the paper packaging, but he didn't know how to hold them, so he slipped them back in the wrapper.

"So where are my grandparents?" he asked, and Wes lowered his eyes.

"They died in a car accident a year ago."

Alex knew he should say something, that the tragedy was much worse for Wes than it was for him, but all he could think was that he was a year too late. He would never meet them.

"It was the reason I came back," Wes continued. "I was working in Uganda at the time. I only meant to stick around here for a few weeks, to take care of everything. But then I met someone at the Stanford Center for Global Health, and I ended up joining their team."

"And now you're here to stay?"

Wes shifted in his seat uncomfortably, and Alex knew that, whatever he said, the answer was no. "We've applied for a research grant through the World Health Organization, which would require some work in the field. But we probably won't get it."

Alex didn't believe him—from everything he knew about his father, he didn't seem like the kind of person who would be denied a grant. The server set their food on the table, a dozen varieties of rolls on a long platter, but Alex had lost his appetite. He wanted to leave right then, to tell Yesenia. He'd found his father, and now he might lose him again.

And then, all at once, he remembered. Yesenia. He'd been going to see her when he had noticed his father's car in the lot, and detoured home, and then forgotten Yesenia altogether. It was a good excuse—his father reappearing after a lifetime absence—but Alex hated excuses, and Yesenia did too. He'd left her waiting.

He stabbed his avocado rolls with a fork, eating them as quickly as he could and then waiting an excruciating eternity for his father to finish. If his father noticed his impatience he didn't show it, talking on and on about his work and asking questions about Letty—Did she go to college? Had she ever been married? Where did she work?—before paying the bill and driving him home. There was a quiet standoff then, Wes idling in his car waiting for Alex to go inside, Alex standing with his hand on the doorknob waiting for his father to leave so that he could run the other direction. It was just after eight and dark out. In his father's mind it was probably dangerous. Finally, Alex opened the front door of Building C and waited in the stairwell until the sound of his father's engine faded down Mile Road; then he opened the door again and started to run.

Yesenia wouldn't be at the water. It was way too late for that. As he ran he tried to picture what she was doing now, watching TV on the couch or doing homework in her room, but when he got to her apartment he looked up to see her windows as dark as the night sky. Carmen would be at work already. Inside, Yesenia was either asleep or punishing him, pretending not to be home.

"Yesenia?"

He called her name once and then raced around the building and up the stairs, knocking on the door and calling her name again. When he heard footsteps his heart pounded, but as they came closer he realized they were on the stairs, a troupe of boys in school uniforms passing. He looked around, trying to think of a way inside. If her apartment hadn't been three stories up he would have found a way to crawl through the window Romeo-style; if he'd known where her mother worked he would have gone there and asked to borrow the key. As it was, all he could do was knock, and he did so with one ear against the door, knocking and waiting, knocking and waiting. But an hour passed, and still she didn't come.

She didn't want to see him; that much was clear. There was nothing to do but go home. He didn't want to go home, though, didn't want to face his mother, who'd probably waited up for him and would grill him about every aspect of his father's life, and so instead he wandered for a while: through what was left of downtown Bayshore—a Western Union and a boarded-up bank and a liquor store—around Cesar Chavez, and down to the shoreline, scooping up rocks and throwing them into the bay one at a time.

So this is what it feels like to be the bad guy, he thought and realized then it was the first time he could ever remember being in this position. He'd spent his whole life living up to everyone else's rules, no matter how crazy or impossible they were; until now, he had never let anyone down. But now he had, and it was Yesenia, the person who deserved it the least. He imagined her curled up under her covers, blankets muffling the sound of the knocking she was determined to ignore.

But just then, this image was replaced by another: Yesenia sitting on the end of the pier, her body wrapped in a blanket whiter than the moon, her face pressed into her knees so that only her hair, tied up high in a ponytail, showed above the cloth.

Alex started to sprint. When he reached her, he kneeled down, placing one hand on the soft curve of her back, where her spine should have been straight but wasn't.

"I'm so, so, so sorry," he said. "Didn't you go home for dinner?"

Yesenia shook her head no.

"Your mom'll be worried."

Yesenia moved her shoulders up and down, as if to imply that this did not bother her, when in fact Alex knew with certainty that it did, and he told her as much. She sat up then, turning to him. "I can't go home."

Something had happened to her face.

Her right cheek was swollen, so big that it almost shut one eye. There were scratches too, on her jaw and on her neck, pale pink marks just visible in the soft light reflecting off the water. Whether her lips were purple because they were bruised or because she was freezing, Alex couldn't tell.

His stomach swimming, he tried to think of something to say. Finally: "What happened?"

"I got in a fight," she said. But the way she explained it, it didn't sound like much of a fight. Yesenia was drawing after school, waiting for the bus, when a girl threw her sketchbook into the street. She'd tried to get it, but she wasn't fast enough, and the girls had laughed as she'd stumbled and another girl had picked it up and thrown it farther, and when she'd reached it the second time, both girls had pushed her down and what had happened after that she didn't need to explain because it was all over her face.

When she was quiet again, Alex asked: "Is this the first time?"

Yesenia said nothing, and Alex's heart sank. Clearly it wasn't. How could he not have known?

"Does your mom know?" he asked.

"I can't tell her. You know her English, and she's afraid if she goes to the school someone will ask for her papers. I didn't want her to worry."

It wasn't right. She'd been hurting, and hurting alone. He understood why she didn't tell Carmen: after all her mother had worked for, Yesenia wouldn't want to put her in a position of having to choose—to protect her daughter or protect the life she'd built for them. But what he didn't understand was this: "Why didn't you tell me?"

Yesenia looked out at the water for a long time before turning to him. "You were just so happy. Why would you ever want to be with someone miserable?"

Alex touched her swollen cheek. "I want to be with you, however you are."

Lowering himself onto his back, he looked up at the sky, and she curled into him, her knees against his hip and her head on his chest. Wrapping his arms around her, he held her still, and when she started to shake, cold or crying or both, he covered her with the blanket and held her tighter. For the first time since they'd started school he regretted his decision deeply, regretted leaving her to face Bayshore High when he could have been there beside her. He'd never seen her as weak because she wasn't—but she was vulnerable, and he had left her alone.

Yesenia's body grew quiet. She tipped her face up toward his. "Kiss me?"

Dipping down, he kissed her frozen lips, and when he started to cry she held him as tight as he'd held her, and they stayed that way all night and into the early morning, when Carmen came and carried Yesenia home.

Three

1

Wes was back. Without warning he'd burst into their lives, show-ing up on her doorstep and shaking Alex's hand and taking him out to dinner. *I would have stayed.* His words echoed in Letty's mind, and it had taken an entire bottle of wine to wash away the image of what her life might have been like if he had; so much wine, in fact, that she'd woken up sick at four in the morning to a second shock: Alex hadn't come home. She was about to call the police when the front door opened and he stumbled through, his eyes bloodshot and his hair full of dirt. He'd been out all night with Yesenia.

It was too much.

Wes, Alex, Yesenia—everything. Standing across from her son in the predawn darkness, Letty felt the walls begin to pulse. She grasped the edge of the sofa as Alex swayed past, on his way to bed. His motion upset the air; she felt it blow against her face, cool and fresh, and she tried to breathe it in, to steady herself—but then Alex disappeared into the bedroom, and it felt as if all the oxygen disappeared with him.

She collapsed onto the couch. What had he been doing, out all night? Letty could imagine all too well, and the thought made the room spin, a woozy pressure building. Everything she had tried to do, it was all too little too late. The new school—the lies it had taken to get him there—none of it mattered. Their family history was set on repeat, and her

156

VANESSA DIFFENBAUGH

uncertain attempts to chart a new course were no match for destiny. Even Maria Elena had been no match. Stomach lurching, Letty turned her face to the couch cushion, pressing her forehead against the filthy material. She should set an alarm, she thought, but she couldn't move. And what did it matter if they missed a day of school, or even a week? It wouldn't change anything.

But just as she was about to surrender to sleep, Luna cried out. The sound echoed in the silent apartment, growing louder. *Go to her,* Letty silently pleaded to Alex, but there were no footsteps, no whispered comforts—only Luna's cries, tunneling through the unbreathable air.

She had to get up. Pulling herself to standing, Letty felt her way back to the bedroom. Luna had lost her blankets; her skin was cold to the touch. Finding them, she tucked the corners tight around her daughter's shoulders and then sat down next to Luna, rubbing her back until she grew calm. On the other side of the room, Alex sat on his bed facing the window, watching the morning's first flights line up on the runway. The collar of his shirt quivered with every careful breath, until he too lay down on his bed and fell asleep in front of the rising sun.

Letty lay down. Wriggling close, she felt her daughter's heartbeat against her own, the rhythm like a jolt, recharging her. She couldn't surrender. At any other point in her life she would have succumbed to failure, but there was no one to pass her kids off to now, no one to cook dinner or pack lunches or feed her custard rolls while she lay flat on her back and watched the ceiling breathe. It didn't matter that her world had turned upside down. Her kids were still cold, and tired, and soon they would wake up, and they would be hungry.

After a time, she got up and changed in the darkness. In the kitchen she emptied the refrigerator quietly, looking for something to cook. There was cheese, and stale tortillas, and in the cupboard she found a can of green chiles and a jar of salsa. She looked up *chilaquiles* in one of her mother's cookbooks. There were dozens of recipes, calling for everything from chopped onions and roasted tomatillos to fresh Oaxacan cheese. But she didn't have any of those things, so she set about trying to make the dish the way she remembered her mother making it, frying strips of tortillas in oil and adding chiles and salsa and cheese. It was a big gooey mess when she was done with it, nothing like the perfectly layered concoction Maria Elena made, but it smelled good at least.

She had just set three big bowls on the table when Luna bolted into the room. In her wide, searching eyes, Letty could see that she thought her nana had come home, but instead of crying, Luna pulled out a chair and sat down in front of her breakfast.

"Edible?" Letty asked, as Luna spooned great bites of chile-cheese tortilla strips into her mouth. She'd filled a bowl for herself, but she was unsure if her queasy stomach could handle anything more than soda water.

"Mmmm-hmmm," Luna said, her mouth full.

From the bedroom they heard a crash, and then a curse, and then the door to the bathroom slam shut. Letty had let them sleep in—Alex would miss zero period, and maybe first period too. When he walked into the kitchen a minute later, he'd gotten dressed and washed his face, but it hadn't helped much. A streak of mud ran from his temple to his chin.

"Why didn't you wake me up?"

"Because you were out until four o'clock in the morning!" She pulled out a chair and motioned for him to sit. "I made you breakfast."

"I don't have time."

"You're already late. Eat your breakfast."

Alex scowled but sat down. He picked up his spoon and used it to push the tortillas around in the bowl, excavating a long string of burnt cheese.

"Aren't you hungry?"

He shrugged. Letty studied him closely. It was more than just the dirt and exhaustion. He looked terrible, his eyebrows and jaw and shoulders all tense. She'd rehearsed what she would say to him over breakfast (*Don't you think for one second I'll welcome a grandbaby at thirty-three years old. I'm no Maria Elena*), but looking at him now, she couldn't bring herself to say it. He might have stayed out a good seven hours longer than he should have, but he had also just met his father for the first time, and he was clearly upset. She sat down at the table and poured him a glass of Kool-Aid.

"Are you okay?" She waited for him to look up, but he didn't, just set down his fork and used his fingers to stack the tortillas, the way Maria Elena would have made them. But he still didn't take a bite. "Alex?"

He nodded, looking out the window, away from her.

"You don't have to be okay, you know. It's a big deal." And then, when he still said nothing: "You can be mad at me."

"Why would I be mad at you?"

He turned to her, confusion in his eyes, and she saw right then: Wes hadn't told him. She had no idea how he'd explained his complete absence from his son's life, but she knew Wes hadn't told him the truth. Across the table, Luna finished her bowl and reached for Alex's, but he grabbed it back and took a bite. Letty watched him push the food around in his mouth and attempt to swallow, hoping he would offer up more information about his evening. When it became clear that he wouldn't, she prodded. "So what did you think of him?"

Alex shrugged. "He was kind of awkward."

Letty couldn't help but laugh at the observation coming from Alex, who was so much like his father.

"But he's smart," Alex continued. "Did you know he went to Haiti after the earthquake? He was one of the first doctors to arrive."

Letty snorted. "It doesn't surprise me. He was always trying to save the world."

"Well, *I* liked him," Luna said, and Letty turned to her in surprise. She hadn't even been introduced to Wes. "I wanted to go too, but Mom said no."

"You wouldn't have liked it," Alex said. "We had sushi."

"What's sushi?"

"Raw fish."

"Gross!"

She popped up and dropped her dish into the sink. On the kitchen counter, Letty's cell phone began to ring. Luna handed it to her and then climbed into her lap. Letty recognized the area code from when Wes lived in New York. Just the number made her stomach flip, the way it had done every time the phone rang the year after he'd gone to college.

"Aren't you going to answer it?" Alex asked impatiently.

She was absolutely not going to answer it. Wes's anger, the night before, had been tempered by shock. There was no way he'd spent all night thinking about Alex and that anger hadn't turned to fury. She didn't want him yelling at her now, in front of her children—or ever, if she was honest.

"No."

Alex grabbed the phone out of her hands, and for a second she thought he was going to answer it, but instead he slid it across the table, away from them, and blurted out: "Are we still moving to Mission Hills?"

Luna scurried along the table to retrieve the phone, handing it to her mother a second time. Letty looked at Alex, confused. "Why?"

"I just want to know."

"I'm working on it. I opened a bank account yesterday."

"Will it be soon?"

"I hope so."

He lifted another scrap of tortilla, chewed it, and swallowed. It looked like it took every bit of strength for him to force the food down his throat, and then for him to say what he said next, a quiet, desperate plea: "When we do, can Yesenia and Carmen come live with us?"

"What?" Letty said, caught off guard. "Of course they can't."

The muscles in Alex's jaw bulged, and he spoke through clenched teeth. "Why not?"

It was so absurd—both that he was asking and also his apparent focus on Yesenia, the morning after his father had walked back into his life. But Alex was serious, his eyes round and unblinking. Letty thought about all the reasons they could never come live with them, including the fact that she'd be lucky to afford a one-bedroom apartment and the even more pressing fact that she would do everything she could to keep Alex from spending too much time with his girlfriend. Not wanting to argue, though, she said only the most obvious: "I've never even met them. Among many, many, many other reasons."

"Could she use our address at least?"

"We're moving so we can stop lying, not start telling new lies! What's going on with you, anyway?"

The phone in her hand rang again, but it wasn't Wes this time—it was Rick. Just a few days before she'd been a single mom alone in the world, and now her phone wouldn't stop ringing, two men wanting different things from her: Rick, a relationship; Wes, an explanation. She opened the phone and snapped it shut, hanging up on him, and then turned back to Alex, but it was too late. He'd pushed his chair away and stood up. The conversation was over.

"I have to go," he said, grabbing his backpack from a hook by the door. "Don't wait up."

"Excuse me?"

His backpack was heavy. The straps dug into his shoulder blades, and he took it off, adjusting the contents before swinging it on again. "I said don't wait up. I'm going to Yesenia's after school."

"You just saw her."

"So I'm going to see her again."

Luna leaned back—a trust fall with no warning—and Letty lurched forward to grab her before she fell on her head. Alex stood waiting for her response, obstinate and insecure all at once. He wanted her permission, even though he wouldn't ask for it. And as much as Letty wanted to give it to him, give him anything he wanted, forever and ever, to make up for all the things she hadn't given him, she couldn't do it. She couldn't bear the thought of him out there in the world alone, making the same mistakes she'd made.

She'd been only sixteen the first time she had sex with Wes. He snuck over in the middle of the night with a flashlight and a blanket and pulled her up the hill, onto the roof of his neighborhood church. The flat metal roof had stored the sunlight; she remembered even now exactly what it felt like pressed against her back, the heat internal, like skin. She'd felt safe, close to Wes and close to God, and afterward she'd prayed fiercely that the sun would never rise, so that they could stay there, naked and tangled and happy, for the rest of their lives.

Her son was still looking at her, waiting for an answer. She shook her head no. It wasn't going to happen, not on her watch.

"What?"

"No. You can't go. I want you home for dinner."

He pulled the straps on his backpack as tight as they would go, so that she was sure he'd cut off all blood flow to his arms and shoulders.

"Why not?"

"Because you're too young."

Alex looked down at his shoes, glossy black high-tops that Yesenia had picked out. His laces were triple-knotted.

"Listen," she said, softening her voice. "I'm not trying to be mean. I'm just trying to look out for you."

"Is that what you were doing when you got me drunk?" He looked up from his laces, daring her to protest. "Or when you left us alone in our beds and drove to Mexico?"

"Alex!" Luna hissed. She twisted around in Letty's lap and wrapped her arms and legs around her mother's torso.

"It's true. She can't just show up one day and decide to be a mom."

Luna clung to her mother, a shield against his attack. "She didn't."

Alex was quiet, watching them both, and just when Letty thought he would go, he said: "You're right. She didn't decide to be a mom. She was forced to. She probably wishes every day she'd stayed in Mexico."

His words hit Letty hard. Luna started to cry—a loud, heartbroken wail—and Letty squeezed her tight, pressing her nose into her daughter's hair. Even all these months later, Luna still smelled like Maria Elena, and as she inhaled, she was filled with an unexpected strength.

"I'm sorry," she said finally. "But I'm not letting you stay out all night every night with your girlfriend. It's not happening."

Alex turned around and walked out the kitchen door. After he'd crossed the living room he paused, turning back to face her.

"You don't need to worry," he said quietly. "I'm not going to turn out like you."

"That's right, you're not."

It was one thing they could agree on, at least.

Wes called again while she was taking Luna to school, and then, while she was walking to work, he called a third time. She should answer it, she knew, but she hadn't had time to think. All morning, as she'd readied herself for work and Luna for school, Letty had told herself: *I need time to think.* Just one hour alone in a dark room to figure out how to talk to Alex about first love, and then one more to work out how to explain why she'd never told his father about his existence. Wes might not have told him yet, but there was no doubt in her mind that he would, and she wanted to be ready with her own side of the story when that happened. But she didn't have a quiet hour; she didn't even have a quiet minute.

It felt like just yesterday that she'd made her first old-fashioned, and already the rhythm of her job had shifted. From the time she clocked in at 10:00 A.M., the bar was rarely empty. Rick was right. People were looking for a place to get a decent drink, and an airport was one of the few places it wasn't unusual to have a roomful of businessmen drinking martinis at 11:00 A.M., having just disembarked from a flight from Frankfurt or Barcelona or Baghdad. What had surprised her, though, was just how quickly word had gotten around. Letty credited the specials board, where she wrote the names of drinks like the Silver Bullet, Bijou, Rattlesnake, and Corpse Reviver #2 pulled straight from *The Savoy Cocktail Book* and with her own additions (mint and sage and fennel, all fresh), and also the empty-restaurant phenomenon: an empty restaurant stays empty, a full restaurant stays full.

Ernie Thompson—the man who'd drunk her first old-fashioned— was partly to thank for keeping her bar full. He drank as much as he traveled. High up in tech, he flew once a week at least, and often with his entire team—fifteen men who could hold their liquor just as well as Ernie. Usually they came and went without warning, but today he'd called ahead. His team was flying to Austin, but before their flight they were meeting a group from Singapore. There would be over twenty of them, he'd said, at two o'clock, and asked if she could make a round (or two or three, Letty translated, knowing Ernie) of something with mint. He loved the wild mint she plucked from the bay on her way to work, which Rick had taught her to smack against the side of the glass before garnishing, a strangely aggressive act that released a sweet and delicate odor.

After some thought, she had settled on the Southside Fizz, and she spent the entire morning prepping: squeezing limes and trimming mint and tasting gins, and then setting a long table with waters and bar napkins. When Ernie arrived she set to work (*Heads up!* she heard Rick remind her) measuring and shaking and pouring, all the while answering questions about the history of the drink (Southside Sportsmen's Club, Long Island) and the origins of the gin (local to San Francisco, hints of citrus and botanicals). As soon as the others arrived, they sat down and got to work, and Letty considered it a success when the entire table requested another round without asking to see the drinks menu.

She'd just finished saying good-bye and thanking Ernie when she looked up to see Rick. She didn't expect him to be there. He wasn't on the schedule that day, and he was dressed in street clothes, jeans and a gray polo shirt, the frayed collar open wide. She wished he hadn't come—too much had happened, and she didn't have the energy to explain—but even as she wished it she found her sight glued involuntarily to the tattoo on his collarbone, its pull magnetic. Her heart beat hard in her throat as she moved to clear the table.

"You have a party?" he asked.

"Ernie again," she said. "And some businessmen from Singapore."

"Nice."

"Yep." She peeked inside the black folder at the credit card slip. He'd left her $125—the biggest tip of her life. She carried a tray of dirty glasses to the bar, and Rick followed behind, plates stacked in his arms.

"I tried to call you."

He was silent, waiting for an explanation for his unreturned voice mail. She hadn't even listened to it. Rick had been the last thing on her mind that morning, and as much as she wanted to start right where they'd left off—Letty force-feeding him hot fudge and feeling the nervous excitement of a beginning—too much had changed. "Sorry," she said finally. "I just— I had to get the kids to school."

The mountain of dirty glasses was a welcome distraction. Turning all her attention to loading the dishwasher, she filled the rack and then sank below the bar, pretending to look for the dish soap even though it was sitting on the floor right in front of her. With the machine full and set to wash, she wiped her way down the bar, Rick moving from stool to stool to stool as she went, so that when she finally looked up it was once again into his eyes. "Hey—are you okay?"

She sighed. She was not okay. But before she could figure out how to tell him that, the phone rang. There was no one else to answer it. Turning away from Rick, she grabbed the handset mounted to the wall.

"Flannigan's."

"It's me." She recognized his voice immediately. Older, deeper, angrier—and with none of the longing or the loneliness of those first calls from college—but still the same. She glanced over her shoulder, to where Rick waited.

"You can't call here," she said. "I'm working."

"What was I supposed to do? You don't answer your cell."

Alex must have told him where she worked. Letty wound the long cord around her finger, waiting for him to continue. She wished Rick would get up, get a glass of water or go to the bathroom or something, anything, so that he wasn't just sitting there, his eyes on the back of her neck.

Wes waited for her to answer.

"I don't know what you should do," she said into the phone. And then, against her better judgment, in an attempt to get him off the line, she added: "You know where I live."

At this, she heard Rick clear his throat, and when she looked at him his eyebrows were pinched together in question. *Who is it?* he mouthed, but she shook her head and turned away.

"I don't want to talk in front of the kids," Wes said. "And we need to talk."

"What do you want me to say?" she asked, exasperated. "I said I was sorry."

"Oh, my God, Letty, how can you even say that?" His voice was so loud that Letty was afraid Rick would hear. She half-covered the receiver with her hand as he continued. "I have a son. It's not an 'I'm sorry' kind of moment. It's a big fucking deal."

"I'm not saying it isn't."

She glanced back to where Rick had been sitting, but he was gone, and just then she felt his hands on her shoulders, the heat of his body like a wall behind her. She leaned into it, listening to Wes struggle on the other end of the line. When he finally spoke, his voice was childlike, confused.

"What am I supposed to do now?" he asked. "It's not like I can just take my son out to dinner and then drop him off and go back to my life. This changes everything."

"I know it does." Letty sighed, long and loud into the phone. He was angry, furious, and yet he was coming to her for advice, for approval. It reminded her of Alex, and she felt awash in tenderness toward him then, for his muddled pain, every bit of it caused by her own poor choices.

"Listen," she said. "I don't know what you should do. Really. If I did I would tell you."

They were silent, Wes on one end, Letty on the other, Rick silent behind her.

"You have to tell me something. You can't just not talk to me."

"I'm talking, aren't I?"

"But you aren't saying anything."

He wanted her to decide how he should move forward with his son. As much as she wanted to help him, it wasn't her decision to make.

"Talk to Alex," she said. "If you want to be a father, ask him if he wants one. He'll tell you the truth." A crowd of noisy college students walked down the hall in front of the restaurant. Letty held up the phone to amplify the passing commotion. "Sorry, Wes, we're slammed. I'll call you later."

Before he could protest, she said good-bye, returning the phone to its hook on the wall.

"What was all that?" Rick asked. Letty reached for a dirty rag and wiped down the already-clean bar. She was shaking. Rick watched the sloppy, quivering circles and then moved closer, reaching out to cover both her hands with his. He held them until they were still, only her heart pounding. "Are you okay?"

A nod was all she could manage. More and she might melt into a puddle on the clean bar. She could tell by his expression that he wanted to know what was going on, but just when she thought he would press her for information, he pulled away. Reaching behind her back, he untied the knot on her apron. Her shift was over.

"Go clock out," he said. "I have somewhere to take you."

Fifteen minutes later, Letty sat in the passenger seat of Rick's Highlander, her body relaxing into the curves of the road as they climbed farther and farther into the woods. Windows down, she felt the fresh air fill her, and she remembered immediately what she liked best about Mission Hills: the trees. Unlike the flat grassy marshes of Bayshore or the crisscrossing cement arms of the San Francisco airport, the trees here told the time of year. Flashes of red and gold surrounded them in the near-bare branches.

"Don't get your hopes up," Rick said as they turned onto a long, wooded drive. "It's not the first house you see."

The first house she saw was bright white, set back among the trees. It was beautiful, but not the kind of beauty she was used to seeing in the Heights. All over the peninsula, small, modest homes were being bowled over and built up with tech money, but out here, where there was land, it was even more extreme: architects designed sprawling Italian "villas" or garish Mediterranean compounds with stucco walls and miles of tile roof. This house was different. It looked like one of the first wealthy businessmen—Letty imagined a railroad man, or a gold rusher—had built a summer home, and the original house remained untouched. It was a simple Victorian, with a double-peaked roof and a widow's walk between the peaks—the view from there would be amazing—and a wide staircase leading up to the porch. The front door was set between two arched windows. Through one, Letty could see wood floors and white walls, but no furniture anywhere. A moving truck was parked in the circular gravel drive in front of the house.

"Are they moving in or moving out?" Letty asked.

"Neither. They had to empty out the first floor to replace the hardwood. Water damage."

"From what?"

"It's a second home. They hadn't been here in six months, and when they came back they found a leak in the refrigerator. The floors, the molding—everything was ruined. I can't even imagine how much it'll cost to repair."

Letty knew nothing about second homes—or first homes, for that matter. She couldn't imagine letting a place this beautiful sit empty.

"It's good timing for you," Rick said. "When I asked my mom if she knew anyone with a guest cottage for rent, she said they had just decided to look for a caretaker."

"What does that mean, a caretaker?" She hoped it had nothing to do with a hammer. None of Enrique's attempts to teach her maintenance had gone well.

"It just means walking through the house every few days, checking for leaks. Bringing in packages, that kind of thing. In exchange for extremely low rent."

"Is 'extremely low' the same to you as it is to me?"

"A couple hundred dollars a month?"

"Wow."

Rick parked behind the house and got out of the car. Manicured box shrubs outlined a path through a rose garden, flowers blooming in every color and variety. Beyond the garden, a wide stretch of grass separated the roses from a small cottage. It had been built to mirror the main house, but it was almost dollhouse size, with a tiny double-peaked roof and a wraparound porch. Over one side of the porch a pomegranate tree leaned, heavy with cracked fruit.

"This is it?" Letty asked, her heart skipping with excitement.

"This is it." He fit the key in the lock and pushed the door open.

The cottage was even smaller inside than it looked. The living room was just big enough for two overstuffed chairs and a coffee table, arranged around a built-in window seat. The walls around the picture window were lined with shelves and cubbies and little drawers, all built from dark, weathered wood; it reminded her of an old-fashioned card catalog, or the inside of a toolbox. When she opened one of the drawers she saw that her second guess was correct—they were full of nails, bolts, screws, and screwdrivers, all separated by size and variety.

Far from the rest of her life, Letty felt her stress ease, and she allowed herself to be led from room to room, Rick's hand on her lower back. Three steps down a short hall and she stood in the first bedroom, two twin beds and a desk under a window. Through an open bathroom door she could see a second bedroom on the other side. She and Luna would have to share a room, but Luna wouldn't mind—she'd probably prefer it, and by the time she wanted her own room Letty would have both enough money and enough credit to move anywhere she wanted. If she wanted. She'd been in the house only five minutes, and already she wasn't sure if she would ever want to leave. She loved the dark wood, the windows that framed living portraits of the forest, the drawers full of tools that she could replace one at a time with trinkets and toys and photographs and memories, her life filed away in little drawers where she would never lose it again.

"What do you think?"

Rick sat down on one of the twin beds, bouncing like a little boy.

"I love it."

"It's a little small."

"It's teeny. But perfect."

"You think so?" Rick asked. He smiled as wide as if he'd built the cottage himself and presented it to her as a gift.

"I do. If they'll have me, I'll take it."

"Oh, they'll have you." Color rose to Rick's cheeks. He hadn't meant it to sound sexual, but it had come out that way, and the bedroom felt suddenly too small, the tightly made beds suggestive. She grabbed his hand and dragged him through the house and onto the front porch, but outside she realized she didn't want to leave.

Letty sat down on the top step, and Rick sat beside her, so close their hips touched. She felt her body warm where they connected.

"So," he asked quietly, and for the third time that day: "Are you okay?"

"I'm better now," she said. She wanted to leave it at that, but it was unfair of her not to tell him, especially now that he'd gone so far out of his way to help her and her kids. She thought about where she should start, but everything that had happened—the knock on the door, Alex's late night, the phone call at the bar—it all felt far away here, a soap opera life that belonged to a different Letty. Not the Letty she was in this moment, sitting on a dollhouse-size front porch with a handsome, tattooed man, watching the warm afternoon light cast tangled shadows in the rose garden. It couldn't be her life; except it was. She had to tell him about it.

Rick looked at her, waiting.

"Wes came back," she said. Then, realizing that meant nothing to him, she added: "Alex's dad. He just showed up last night, out of the blue."

"After how long?"

Letty counted the time in her head. "Sixteen years."

"I thought Alex was only fifteen."

"He is," she said. Rick was quiet beside her, and Letty studied the skin on the side of his face, so smooth he must have shaved after lunch, before he'd come to see her.

"So, are you worried about him?"

The concern in Rick's voice was genuine, and Letty realized what he must have been thinking. A man who left his son and returned after sixteen years—he couldn't be up to anything good. But of course it wasn't like that.

"No, no, I'm not worried," she said. "He's a good guy."

She was about to add that he was a doctor, and that before he'd moved back he'd volunteered with children all over the world, but the look on Rick's face stopped her. As much as he didn't want Letty to be in danger, she could see from his expression that he also did not want Wes to be a *good guy*. He looked hurt, and a little blindsided. She tried to think of a way to take it back, to wipe clean the expression on his face, but she couldn't think of anything to say, and in a fluster of regret, Letty leaned forward and kissed him hard on the lips.

Rick pulled away, startled, his eyes wide with surprise.

"Sorry," she said.

He shook his head softly, a bewildered smile edging up the corners of his mouth. "Don't be," he whispered. Running his finger along her lips, he quieted her and then, pulling her closer, he leaned in and kissed her again.

2

Across the dark field, planes waited in a quiet line at their gates; except for the occasional barking of the Canada geese traveling south, the night was silent, the Landing as empty as it had been all of Alex's life. He missed his grandparents. After the fight with his mother, he'd started using their bedroom, thinking the smell of the wax and his grandmother's perfume might help him sleep, but it had the opposite effect. The smell of Maria Elena brought on a guilt so intense he awoke hourly, sheets soaked with sweat, the words he'd spit at his mother hanging in the air like the smells of her now-constant cooking, a permanent fixture.

It wasn't how his grandmother had raised him.

She'd raised him to avoid sugar and to always be early and to shake hands hard, not to talk back or question authority or stay out all night with his girlfriend. That he would even tell his mother not to wait up was proof of how far he'd fallen from the standards his grandmother had set, and the fact that he could parrot the teenage attitude he'd always despised shook him to his very core. He was not the kind of kid who flung accusations or said things that were purposefully hurtful. But that was exactly what he had done. The fact that his mother didn't collapse under the weight of his words didn't ease his guilt—if anything, it made him feel worse. She probably thought she deserved every word he'd said.

At four o'clock he couldn't lie in bed any longer. The red-eye flights had started to land, the roar a predictable rhythm. He'd never get back to sleep now anyway. Feeling around in the dark, he found the jeans with the hole in the knee that Yesenia liked best and a T-shirt that didn't smell. The kitchen was quiet as he packed his bag. Alex was surprised— all week his mother had been up almost as early as he had—but she was still asleep as he pulled on his boots and slipped outside.

He wanted to go see Yesenia, but he knew he shouldn't. Carmen would just be getting home from work, and anyway, his worry was starting to annoy Yesenia. She was fine, she said, and under a thick layer of makeup she looked fine, looked like someday she would be able to forget it had all happened. But Alex knew he never could. He couldn't sit in honors science and raise his hand and act interested in cancer gene variations and immunization patterns when, across the freeway, Yesenia was being singled out, intimidated, even hurt. It changed everything.

Crossing the freeway, he started the long walk to school. It was still dark out, too early for even Mr. Everett to be in the classroom, so when he got to Elm Street he took a detour. He hadn't seen his father since the night they had dinner. He didn't know if Wes had called again, but he hadn't been to the house, and Alex was starting to wonder if that was it—a brief, awkward dinner before they all went back to their independent lives. But when he crossed the street and looked up, Alex was surprised to see the downstairs lights on. Wes sat in the kitchen window, drinking coffee and staring outside. He was waiting for him. Before Alex could decide whether or not he wanted to be seen, Wes popped up and disappeared, reappearing a moment later on the front porch. He wore plaid flannel pajama pants and a baggy T-shirt. His feet were bare.

"Off to school?"

Alex nodded, neither of them acknowledging that it was just five o'clock in the morning, too early for even the most serious student to be headed to class.

Wes jingled a key ring. "Want a ride?"

"Sure."

He opened the passenger door first and then walked around, and they sat in silence as he backed out of the driveway. At the end of the street he stopped, looking back and forth and back and forth again. The street was empty, but he didn't move. Alex rolled down his window and smelled the early-morning air.

"Can't sleep?" Wes asked.

"No."

"Me neither."

Wes stared straight ahead, no longer even pretending to drive, and Alex studied his profile, disheveled hair partly covering one eye, smooth skin freckled across his temple. What would it be like to be Wes, a busy man with an important research job and a sudden son? It couldn't be easy. Shaking his head, Alex tried to expel the thought. He'd spent his entire life worrying about his mother, and now there was Yesenia. He didn't have mental space for another.

Wes turned on the radio, a blast of local news and then a jazz station. His thumbs tapped the steering wheel. "You know what's keeping me up?" he asked. Alex shook his head no. "I can't figure out why you aren't mad at me."

Alex considered his question. It would be the normal teenage response to so many of the things he had experienced lately: his mother's abandonment, his grandfather's decision to move home, Wes's surprise knock on the door. He flipped the sun visor down and looked at himself in the small mirror, trying to see a flicker of irritation, resentment, fury, anything. But he saw only himself, wide-eyed and worried. His entire life he'd wished for his father's return; now, he wanted only for him to stay.

He flipped the visor back up. "I'm just not."

"But why not?"

Alex was quiet. He didn't have an answer.

Wes studied him, looking for one. After a time, he continued. "I don't know why you aren't mad, because I don't *know* you. And as much as I tell myself that life is long and I shouldn't rush it, I just keep thinking that: *I don't know you,* and even if I get to know you now, I'll never know you as a little boy, or as a baby." His voice broke, and he stopped talking suddenly. With the car in park he revved the engine, a noisy expression of all he couldn't say, then shifted into gear, speeding through stop signs and around corners until he pulled up to the curb in front of the school.

After a long time, he said: "I'm sorry. Really, really sorry."

Alex looked out the window. The campus was still dark except for bright lights over the pool; the swimmers were there even earlier than the scientists.

Pulling his backpack from the floor to his lap, Alex opened the door. "It's okay," he said finally. "I'm glad you're here now."

Wes took a deep breath. "I am here," he said, all the speed and anguish of his earlier monologue replaced by a tiny, quiet peace. "If you want me here, I'm here."

Alex nodded, and even though they weren't looking at each other, he knew Wes could see it: the small consent. His father was here to stay. Whatever he'd said about international travel and research, he was here now, if Alex wanted him to be. And he did.

Alex stood up and put his backpack on. "Thanks for the ride."

"Anytime," Wes said and then, leaning over the passenger seat so he could see him, added: "And listen. I remember being fifteen. It's not all about hanging out with your dad on a Saturday night. You don't have to worry about offending me if you've got other things going on."

"You've met my mother," Alex said, frowning as he thought about Letty's recent ban on all things Yesenia. "I've got absolutely nothing else going on."

Wes smiled. "Then I'll pick you up on Saturday. We'll go paint the town red."

It was just an expression, but Alex imagined them, in matching plaid pajamas, lugging around a bucket of red paint. Waving good-bye, he turned toward the now lit science wing, backpack suddenly light.

Mr. Everett jumped up when Alex entered the classroom. Even with the slow drive and wrong turns, Alex was the first to arrive that morning, and Mr. Everett locked the door behind him and pulled a chair up to his desk. He motioned for Alex to sit down.

"Just the person I wanted to see."

"Should I be worried?"

"I am."

Alex swallowed hard, preparing for the lecture he should have known was coming. Their project ideas were due in three weeks, and he hadn't even started. He'd planned to dive in this week, but with everything that had happened, it was all he could do just to sit through class every day without falling asleep.

"I was going to start, I just—" He unzipped his backpack, rustling around for some kind of proof of his intention, but there was nothing. He hadn't brought a single book.

"I'm not worried about your project. I'm worried about you."

Had the change in him been that obvious? It was the problem with being always positive, always eager, he realized now: everyone noticed when you weren't.

His teacher waited until he'd dropped his backpack and looked up. "Listen. You can't let it get to you."

Alex startled. How did he know? Had his mother called the school? But she didn't even know; at least he didn't think she did. Confused, he tried to think of another explanation and waited for Mr. Everett to explain. Finally, he did.

"I know the competition is intense," he said. "No matter how I rant against it, it's always this way, every year. But you can't let it get to you. Jeremy's got a bigger ego than you do, but not a bigger brain—don't let him make you feel like he does. And Miraya—she has a great idea, but she won't be able to pull it off. She's involved in too many other things and doesn't have the patience or the time for the kind of data collection her project demands."

Alex nodded, filling with understanding and relief: Mr. Everett was talking about the competition, not Yesenia. His teacher thought he'd shut down under the pressure. It was good. Not true, but good because it was believable.

"It's hard," he said, not meeting his teacher's eyes. Alex was talking about something else entirely. Before Yesenia, he'd gotten a thrill from the intensity of the class, enjoyed both the high stakes and the pressure. It was only because she'd been hurt that he found it hard to care; it had nothing to do with anyone else's ego or ideas.

"So ask for help, then. When I tell you all on the first day of class to act like scientists, that doesn't mean you have to do everything on your own. In fact, you shouldn't. The best scientists know how to collaborate." He paused, but when Alex said nothing, he kept going. "Let's brainstorm. Think about what you have to work with."

"What do you mean?"

"I mean: tell me what you know, what you love, what you're interested in. And we'll go from there. Tell me about the birds."

Alex didn't want to talk about it, not any of it. But he could tell from his teacher's expression that, until he talked, he wasn't going anywhere.

"It was my grandfather," he said finally. "He's a feather worker, or at least he used to be. He left last year."

"What's a feather worker?"

Alex was surprised that Mr. Everett didn't know about the feathers, since he'd had his mother as a student. But then Letty had never been as interested in the feathers as he was—she probably had never told her teacher about them. "It's a kind of artist. He makes mosaics out of natural bird feathers. No dye. He left me his feathers when he moved home."

"How are they organized?"

"By color, date, and species. He's been collecting them for over thirty years."

Mr. Everett let out a low whistle.

"Well, there's your project," he said. "The first thing you need to do is make a list of everything you can learn from a feather. You'll be surprised, I think, when you look into it."

Mr. Everett studied him, waiting for confirmation that the conversation they'd had would end in Alex returning to some semblance of the student he'd first met. It was against his principles to give such direct advice. Alex had heard him say more than once that coming up with the right questions was even more important than coming up with the right answers. But Alex had needed direction and he'd given it to him; Alex was grateful.

"Okay," he said. "Thanks."

Mr. Everett nodded. "Good. Now get to work and leave me alone before Miss Faye comes in and yells at me for not taking attendance again. I'm trying to catch up."

"Do you need any help?"

"You know I won't turn down an offer of free data entry."

Mr. Everett smiled and opened a desk drawer, pulling out a packet of Pop Rocks. "Here. The chemical reaction is scientifically proven to make you more productive."

"Really?"

"No—but sugar always helps, don't you think? And these have the added benefit of keeping you awake."

Alex took a handful of the pink candy and put it on his tongue, squeezing his eyes shut as small explosions occurred inside his mouth. It hurt, but he liked it, and when Mr. Everett offered him more, he took the whole bag.

Attendance was open on the computer, a plain white screen with a list of Mr. Everett's classes in a bar on the left-hand side. He would start with zero period—he could do that one without bothering his teacher for absences. It was rare that a student was late or absent from his honors class, and Alex could remember them all himself. But when he clicked on the link for attendance, a time-out message popped up on the screen; Mr. Everett needed to sign back in.

"Can you log me on?"

Mr. Everett was on the other side of the room, opening boxes of molecular module kits.

"It's just my last name, and the password is my last name and my room number, no spaces," he said.

The login redirected Alex to the system's home page: tabs for teachers, for administration, for enrollment. He clicked on TEACHERS and then found Mr. Everett and was finally back to where he'd started, zero period, honors science. He marked everyone present except for Sophia, who'd missed Monday for a student government field trip.

Excused, he marked beside the absence, not even considering for a moment marking her absence unexcused just because he could, just because she always did everything so perfectly.

When school let out, Alex ran all the way to Yesenia's. He wasn't supposed to see her alone anymore. Letty had told him to come straight home, and Carmen had changed her work hours so she could be there after school to make sure that Yesenia made it back to their apartment unharmed. But Alex went there anyway, and hid behind a wheelless camper van in the parking lot until Carmen got into her car and drove away.

The door was already open when he climbed the stairs.

"How was school?" he asked immediately, searching Yesenia's face.

"Fine."

She said it too fast to be believable. "Really?"

"Will you stop asking? You're not my dad."

Alex flashed on his own dad, hairy bare toes on the brake, hand trembling on the gearshift. "I saw Wes again this morning."

"Really?" Yesenia asked, her expression changing. "Cool."

"Maybe you can live with him."

Yesenia rolled her eyes and blew through puffed cheeks. "Would you stop already? I told you I'm fine."

They'd been breaking rules right and left to see each other, and all they did when they were together was argue. She pulled him down the hall, so the neighbors wouldn't see him and report his visit to her mother. Looking at him in the fluorescent lights of the living room, she scowled.

"You look awful."

"Thanks."

"No, really, you do."

He sat down on the couch, under the row of smiling Yesenias. The real Yesenia was not smiling. "I haven't really been sleeping."

"I don't think I'm the one you should be worried about."

"You aren't the first person to tell me that today." He leaned over to untie his shoe. The double-knotted laces had tangled; he yanked at them as he continued. "Mr. Everett cornered me before class. He asked what was going on with my project."

"What *is* going on?"

The laces on the first shoe wouldn't budge. He gave up and moved on to the second, which untied easily. He pulled off the shoe. "Nothing."

A sour smell emanated from his socked foot; Yesenia backed away from him. "Seriously? You were so excited about it. What's going on?"

Alex felt heat rise to his face, embarrassment and frustration both. "Do I really need to explain to you, of all people, what's going on?"

Yesenia crossed her arms and leaned closer, so close he could smell peppermint on her breath. "No, but you need to get it together." There was a long face-off, in which Yesenia waited for Alex to respond, to promise he would get it together and move on, and Alex said nothing. Finally, Yesenia stood up. "I think you should go home. Sleep, or work on your project or something. I don't want a zombie dropout for a boyfriend."

"Fine." Alex stood up to go, but the thought of leaving Yesenia when he'd just gotten there made him pause. "Do you want to come?" he asked. "You haven't even met my mom."

"I can't leave. I promised."

"I promised too, but I'm here."

Yesenia gave him a look that said: *Well, maybe you shouldn't be,* and Alex turned to go, snatching up the one shoe he'd managed to take off and marching to the door. If she wanted him to leave, he would leave. Outside he took the stairs two at a time, staggering awkwardly in only one shoe. Yesenia laughed, watching him struggle as she struggled, all day every day, with one leg longer than the other. But he was too mad to find it funny, just ran all the way home before ripping his muddy sock off in the parking lot and stumbling, out of breath, through the front door.

"Where've you been?" Letty asked, poking her head out of the kitchen. Luna was in front of the TV, as she was every day after school now. The house smelled like onions.

"Nowhere."

He filled a glass of water in the kitchen and carried it to his grandparents' room. Letty turned off the stove and followed him. He expected her to grill him, but instead she sat on the edge of the bed, eating chopped, blackened onions off the tip of a wooden spoon.

"Taste?" she asked, extending the spoon in his direction. He shook his head no. "You okay?"

Alex groaned. He wished people would stop asking. Setting the glass of water on the nightstand, he flopped facedown onto the bed. He was not okay, clearly. "Not really."

Rolling over, he looked up to where his mother sat, licking the spoon and waiting for him to elaborate. He didn't. "Is it about Wes?"

"No." He couldn't tell her about his fight with Yesenia—she would just take his girlfriend's side, and tell him he needed to get it together. But she wouldn't know what she was talking about.

"So what is it?"

It's my life, he thought, feeling overwhelmed by everything at once. Family, girlfriend, school: the three together felt like dry ice inside a bottle, about to burst. But it was more than his mother could handle, and so he told her only the least complicated, most pressing of the three. "I haven't even started my science project."

Letty set the spoon on the table, next to the water, and turned her attention to him. "What do you have to do?"

"That's what I need to figure out. The assignment is to design an experiment."

She looked at him with her eyebrows furrowed. "You've spent your entire life designing experiments. So what's the problem?"

Alex sighed. "The other kids have been working on their ideas for a year, and there's scholarship money at stake—not for this first round, but eventually."

His eyes wandered to the feathers, and Letty followed his gaze. "You miss your grandpa, huh?"

If his grandpa were here, he would open those drawers himself and unlock the mysteries of the feathers. But he'd left Alex alone, and it all felt too hard without him.

Letty moved closer to Alex on the bed, gently turning his head away from the file cabinets to look into her eyes. "I bet there isn't one thing you could ask him that you haven't already asked ten times."

Alex exhaled ruefully, remembering himself as a little boy, tugging on his grandfather's shirt, pestering him to explain flight paths and seasonal migration and juvenile bird identification for the hundredth time. "You're probably right."

"So if he were here, what would you ask him?"

Alex thought hard. There was only one thing he wanted to know. "I'd ask him what's so special about a feather."

"And what would he say?"

Alex pressed a hand into his heart. The missing hurt, but it felt good too. "He'd grab me by the ear and drag me over to look at his mosaic, and he'd ask me how I could possibly ask him that, and then I'd tell him I wasn't asking about art, I was asking about science, and he'd tell me to go look up keratin extraction and isotope signatures and I'd tell him I already had, five times at least."

Letty laughed. "That sounds about right. So what's so special about a feather?"

She'd gotten him to answer his own question. He sighed. "What's special is that it's a time stamp. A perfectly preserved record of where a bird has been, and when, and all the food and water and toxins it consumed."

"How do you find all that out?"

"I have no idea."

"Well, that's the first place to start, I think."

Alex sat up and riffled through the file folders, turning to his favorite color and then closing it from his mother's watching eyes. The note was still tucked among the feathers. They'd never talked about his grandparents' decision to stay in Mexico, and he had no idea whether she knew Enrique's flight had been premeditated.

"You don't think Grandpa would mind me using them?"

"He left them for you, didn't he? It's not like he thought you were going to become an artist."

They both smiled, remembering Alex's hopeless attempts at feather work. He closed the drawer and turned back to Letty. "Mom? I'm sorry—about what I said."

Letty stood up and grabbed her spoon, turning around and pressing it onto the top of his head.

"It's okay." Pausing, she looked out the window and then added: "Guess what? I found us a house. In Mission Heights."

"Really?" Alex didn't know how to feel about this news. On the one hand, he would officially belong at Mission Hills. On the other, he would be farther from Yesenia, and right when she needed him. "When are we moving?"

"This weekend."

"Wow."

"I know. It's sudden. But I think you'll like it." She got up, heading to the kitchen. "I'll call you when dinner's ready."

Alex lay back on the bed. He would rest for just one minute before starting to work on his project, he thought, but when Letty called him fifteen minutes later he was already deep asleep, pulled by exhaustion and relief into a dream in which Yesenia wore a headdress of black feathers and danced to the sound of an old man laughing. Alex danced around her, trying to pluck a feather, but when he finally got one, long and inky, the feather turned to tar and sealed his shivering lips closed.

3

Letty stood alone in her empty bedroom. It had taken all day, but together she and Sara had succeeded in clearing out the apartment, abandoning the furniture in a heap by the Dumpster and stuffing bags full of clothes, toys, and books into Sara's car. Sara had just driven off with the first load, leaving Alex and Luna to guard the second from Mrs. Starks, who sat in her lawn chair, looking on. Alex had already had to rescue his quilt from within Mrs. S's "shop," so he was on high alert. From the window Letty watched his diligence, Luna springing from box to box and Mrs. Starks standing up and sitting down and standing up again. Alex kept his eyes on both of them, pretending to play Star Wars with his sister and wielding a broomstick like a light saber any time Mrs. Starks got too close to the boxes.

Letty had told Alex and Luna she needed to do a final walk-through, but really she'd climbed the stairs to say good-bye. Besides a handful of nights she'd slept at Sara's or snuck out with Wes, she'd spent her entire life in this small bedroom, and traces of her were everywhere: fingerprints dotted the windows and the white paint, stains from shoes of every size crisscrossed the carpet under her feet. Walking to the window, she looked out at the same view she'd studied as a baby, looking over the bars of her crib. She didn't remember it, but her father loved to tell the story of coming to get her after a nap and finding her standing up and pointing at the planes. *Noisy birds,* she'd said as her father picked her up, and for the rest of her childhood, every time a particularly loud jet would rumble past, her mother or father would look up from whatever they were doing and repeat her observation: *noisy birds.*

She wondered what her parents were doing, right now, in Oro de Hidalgo. She had finally summoned the strength to open the letters. The first few were as she'd imagined—reminders of things that Letty had forgotten or never known. But in the more recent letters Maria Elena had started to write about her life in Mexico. She'd written that Enrique was working again, and that she had reconnected with one of her old high school friends, who now had thirty-six grandchildren. *I guess she decided to go for quantity,* her mother had written, as usual leaving what she really meant unsaid: none of them could hold a finger to Alex or Luna. She would write back to her mother after they were settled, she decided, and tell her parents about the move and Alex's and Luna's new schools. She hoped they would be proud.

With a final look at the runway, and the bay, and the birds she would forever think of as her father's, Letty made her way through the rest of the house, walking quickly through her parents' bedroom and the living room and lingering in the kitchen, where she opened and closed the refrigerator and every single cabinet, whisking dry beans and rice and pennies from the dirty Con-Tact paper her mother had so carefully laid down, all those years before.

Just as she'd pocketed the last coin, Letty heard footsteps on the stairs. It must be Luna, she thought—Alex would never leave the boxes unattended—but when she turned around, she saw Wes walking through the empty living room. He was wearing scrubs. A drawstring held up the loose blue pants; he'd tucked his shirt sloppily into the top.

"Wow," Wes said, taking in the empty space.

"We're moving."

"I can see that," he said, looking around. "I had no idea. You know, these are the kinds of things you're going to have to start telling me."

There was a confidence in the statement that hadn't been there when he'd called Flannigan's, and Letty wondered if he'd talked to Alex already, and what he'd said. "I was going to," Letty said. "It was kind of sudden."

"I guess so. When I told Alex I'd pick him up on Saturday he didn't mention he'd be posted in front of a pile of boxes."

So they had spoken. Alex didn't have a phone, which meant Wes had met up with him somewhere. As strict as she was trying to be with Alex after his late night with Yesenia, it was impossible to keep tabs on him all the time. She was working, and she still didn't have a car. Most of the time, she had no choice but to let him navigate the world alone.

Wes walked to the kitchen window and looked out. In the parking lot below, Alex faced off against Mrs. Starks, his broomstick twirling like a baton. "Where are you moving?"

"To Mission Heights."

Wes dropped one eyebrow, almost imperceptibly. She knew what he was thinking and also that he was trying to come up with a way to say it that didn't sound condescending. "How'd you swing that?"

"This guy I work with, Rick. He knew I was trying to get out of Bayshore, and a friend of his was looking for a caretaker."

"Sounds nice."

"It is. A little remote, though. I'm going to have to get a new car." She bit her tongue, hoping he wouldn't ask what had happened to her old one. It wasn't a story she was ready to tell. When he didn't, she added: "I've almost saved enough."

"Good for you."

Wes turned as if to leave, but instead he walked down the hall to her old bedroom. Letty followed him to the window, watching as he ran his fingertips along the sill. The cracked paint was still stained orange in a waxy ring where she'd burned pumpkin candles, her signal to Wes that she was awake, and waiting. From the top of the pedestrian bridge over the freeway he would see the light and come running, climbing a rope through her window and lying beside her, his sweaty heart pounding and neither of them speaking through the silent minutes, sure Maria Elena had heard. But she never did. Or she ignored it, loving Wes and trusting him completely. Letty had always wondered.

"Feels like forever ago, doesn't it?" she said.

"Not really."

With a fingernail she scraped at the orange wax, flicking it onto the floor. Next to hers, his forearms looked pink, sunburned and spotted. She remembered lying beside him, comparing their colors by moonlight, making up new words to describe them.

"Remember *vermocean*?"

The orange-ringed blue of his eyes.

He nodded. "My feet still hurt."

They'd come up with it the summer they'd challenged each other to a barefoot contest, and even now she remembered exactly the way he looked, stretched out on his front porch, feet propped up on the swing, a sunset of oranges and yellows spreading out from his pupils, bleeding into the blue of his irises. She'd still never seen anything like it. "*Vermocean*. Of all our words, that was my favorite."

"I liked *aquanude*."

As soon as he said it he looked away, and she knew he was remembering the night they'd invented it, hopping the fence to the junior high school pool and swimming naked, making up words to describe the color of their bare skin underwater.

"No," Letty disagreed. "Sounds like a sex-offending superhero."

Wes laughed and turned back to her, studying her face as if trying to compare the Letty of his memory to the Letty standing before him now. "You were so crazy," he said. "Remember that barbed wire? I don't know how you convinced me."

"I don't know either." It had caught on the frayed edges of her jean shorts, scraped a bloody line up her inner thigh, and yet she'd kept climbing, and convinced him to climb too. "I wasn't afraid of anything."

She marveled at the words, trying to remember what it had felt like to be that girl, breaking the law and baring her body to Wes, not to mention anyone who happened to walk by. Life had changed her. She was afraid of so much now, but even as she thought it she felt something shift, the great jaws of fear loosening, and in its place was a flicker of excitement, as if she were back in high school, with all the world still hers to conquer.

In the distance she saw Sara's car turn up Mile Road. It was time to rescue Alex from Mrs. Starks and pack up the final load. Reluctantly, she turned to go.

"You want to follow us over? You can see our new place, and take Alex from there."

Wes nodded, and Letty waited until he'd retreated down the stairs before she closed the door to her room, and then the door to her parents' room, and then locked the front door of Apartment 31C for the last time.

As soon as they'd unloaded Sara's car, Sara said good-bye, sweaty and late for a first date, and left them to manage the pile of boxes and bags on the front porch without her. Luna started to unpack her toys but deserted the task within minutes, spending the evening instead lining up her barn animals on the window seat and fashioning a fence out of screws and washers she pulled from the tiny drawers. Alex dragged his own bags into his bedroom and then tore through the remaining boxes in search of the telephone, which he carried down the hall and plugged into the jack by his bed. Letty and Wes listened to his hushed conversation with Yesenia as they carried labeled boxes into the house one at a time. Letty found herself moving quickly, her mind drifting back to their conversation at the Landing, and she realized she wanted to continue where they'd left off.

After they'd carried in the last box, Letty retrieved her new set of barware from above the refrigerator. It was a housewarming gift from Rick, left on the front porch with a note: *Make me a drink.* Letty had stuffed the note in her pocket before Wes could see. Lining up the strainer, jigger, and long, shiny bar spoon, she reached into the back of the cabinet for a jam jar labeled GINGER SYRUP. Rick had made it himself and brought it to the bar for one of his specials, and she'd snuck the not-quite-empty jar out of the bar at the end of one of her shifts. The syrup was thick and slow to pour. When she'd finally scooped it out, she added vodka and sparkling water, and then opened the freezer. Rick had filled it with Hoshizaki ice—cubes so expensive she thought they should have been made from something besides water. She could feel Wes's eyes on her as she shook the drinks, poured them into glasses, and squeezed in a wedge of lime.

"I've got to drive," he said, when Letty handed him one.

"There's less than an ounce of vodka." She sat down at the built-in kitchen table, taking a sip. The ginger was intense; she imagined it burning Rick's hands as he grated and peeled and pressed the spicy root.

Wes lifted the glass to his nose. "Smells good."

"Tastes good too."

From the opposite end of the hall, Alex's voice rose. For a second it sounded like he and Yesenia were arguing, but then he dropped his voice and began to whisper again. Letty heard the words *anything for you,* and she felt color rise to her cheeks, remembering her drunken attempt to teach Alex how to play hard-to-get. It hadn't worked.

Letty took another sip of her drink and nodded for Wes to sit across from her. "So how long have you been back in Mission Hills, anyway?"

Wes didn't answer. His expression had changed; he shook his head and turned away from her. Holding his untouched cocktail over the sink, he tipped the glass until ounce after precious ounce slipped down the drain. Letty had an urge to jump up and rescue the drink, but instead she gulped down her own and did nothing.

He handed the empty glass back to her.

"Listen," he said, letting out a huge, exhausted sigh. "I don't want to spend the rest of my life mad at you—I really don't. But I can't sit at your kitchen table and have a drink and make small talk. I'm not over what you did, Letty. Honestly, I don't know if I ever will be."

It had felt too good to be true, the nostalgic banter of those final moments in her old bedroom, and now here it was: the truth of how he felt. Letty set her empty glass on the table next to the one he'd handed back to her. Lipstick and fingerprints dirtied the glass she'd used; his was polished and clean.

"Look," she said. "If I could do it over again, I would. I promise you that." She stood up and carried both glasses to the sink. Warm water filled them and spilled out the tops. "But I was *eighteen,* Wes. And I loved you. I know it was wrong, but even tonight, when you walked into the apartment in those scrubs, for just a split second I thought that I was right to do it."

"You weren't right."

She set the glasses down on a dish towel to dry and turned back around. "Maybe not," she said, meeting his glare. "But I gave you your life. You can't argue with that."

"Which life?" he demanded. "Maybe it wasn't the life I wanted."

Letty blew out a loud puff of air, exasperated. "Do you even remember yourself in high school? It was exactly the life you wanted." She turned back to the sink. In the window over the faucet, the world was dark and close, leaves and branches and sky pressing in all around them. All of a sudden she felt claustrophobic. Opening the window as wide as it would go, she turned back around and continued: "Do you remember the first time we went out?"

Wes nodded, though the term *went out* was a bit of a stretch—what they'd really done was sneak out of a track banquet and up a fire escape with a miniature bottle of tequila Letty had nabbed from a passed-out neighbor the night before. One swig and tipsy, Wes had declared his future.

"You told me you'd be a bachelor for life, that there was no other way to live in the world and do the work you wanted to do. You said you wanted to die alone."

Wes rolled his eyes to the ceiling, shaking his head at his sixteen-year-old self. "Did I really say that? I'm surprised that wasn't the end of us, right there."

It sounded ridiculous now, but she'd loved that Wes. Smart, determined. So, so sure.

She shrugged. "You had plans."

"So did you," Wes reminded her. "I mean, didn't you think about—"

Letty's glare cut him off. "About what? About not having a baby at all?"

"It's a fair question."

It was fair, but it didn't feel fair now, not with the murmur of Alex in the other room. "It was too late when I found out."

Wes fiddled with the strings on his scrubs, pulling the bow tight and double-knotting it. He said nothing, but she knew he was considering what she'd said, playing back his life as he'd lived it: college, medical school, international work on four continents. Sara had Internet-stalked him when she found out he'd come back. He'd done well. In medical school at NYU he was elected to the Alpha Omega Alpha honor society, and he'd published an article in *The Journal of the American Medical Association* before he even turned thirty.

She crossed the kitchen and stepped into his line of vision. Wes swallowed hard and lifted one hand until his index finger rested on the underside of her chin, tentative, unmoving. Letty held his hand and moved it slowly, back and forth, a familiar caress. *My strange bird,* he used to call her, pretending to ruffle her feathers, and although it had annoyed her then, she craved it now, pressing his hand hard against her throat. "It wouldn't have been possible if you stayed," she whispered, "not any of it."

Her words brought Wes back to the present moment.

"Don't say that," he said, his face darkening. "It wasn't your decision to make. And there's no going back now, not ever."

"You want to go back? Really?" Sudden anger swelled inside her. "Take off those scrubs, then," she snapped. "Let's go back. *You* can give up college and medical school and watch *me* move across the country with a fat scholarship." Something in her had snapped, and even if she'd wanted to she wouldn't have been able to stop herself. She continued, a litany of all the things she'd missed, stuck at the Landing working three jobs while he was in college, and then medical school, and then flitting around the globe, saving lives. Mid-rant, she heard the scuffle of small feet and the door at the end of the hall slam shut.

"Stop it," Wes said, cutting her off. "I won't do this in front of them."

"Well, wake up, Wes—there's nowhere else to do it. They aren't going away. That's the thing about kids. They never fucking go away."

Wes clamped his hand over her mouth, stopping her from saying more. In the abrupt quiet she listened for Alex's voice, but he had stopped talking, and she knew by the absolute silence that her children had heard everything.

She started to cry. "I'm sorry," she whispered. "I'm so, so, so, so, so, so sorry."

He stood quietly while she cried, and when her breathing evened he walked her over to the kitchen table and helped her sit down. While she wiped her eyes he sat down across from her, his hands on the rough wood, palms facing up. Setting her hands next to his, they studied their palms in silence, as if reading what the future might hold.

After a long silence, she leaned forward and whispered, so that her children wouldn't overhear: "Why haven't you told him?"

Wes shrugged, resigned. "You're everything to him. What if he never forgives you? I can't take away the only parent he's ever had."

He was giving her more credit than she deserved, and she felt her eyes well again, thinking about Maria Elena and everything she'd done, and everything Letty should have done herself.

There were footsteps in the hallway, and when she looked up she saw Alex, clutching a file box full of feathers.

He wouldn't look at her.

"Ready?" Wes asked, and when Alex nodded he stood up to go. At the door he paused and turned back to Letty.

"Thanks for the drink," he said, his eyes on hers. There was a flicker there, if not of forgiveness then of acceptance, of moving on.

"Anytime."

With shaky knees she stood, walked to the door, and watched them go.

After they left, Letty stayed on the front porch, studying the deep grooves in the gravel where Wes's car had been. Inside she heard the quiet mutterings of Luna's play, instructions from one animal to another. She felt raw, as if her heart had been pulled out and examined and then shoved roughly back in her chest. Sliding down the handrail and onto the porch steps, she came face-to-face with the memory of Rick. They'd sat here—right here—the first night she'd seen the cottage. With a pang of longing and regret, she remembered her sudden kiss, and the apology that had led to a second kiss. She never should have kissed him, and especially not right now, when Wes had come back and she had the chance to make things right with the only person she'd ever really loved.

Just then, Luna wandered outside. She sat down and leaned her braided head against Letty's shoulder.

"Are they gone?"

"Yeah. They're gone."

Luna unfurled her closed fist, revealing two plastic cows, one big, one little, hidden inside.

"Mom?"

"Yeah?"

"Will my dad ever come back?"

Letty shook her head. "No. He won't."

"But you can't be sure, right? You didn't think Wes would come back."

"I'm sure."

Luna sank lower, her head falling into her mother's lap, and Letty was trying to think of a way to explain to her the certainty of what she said when her phone began to buzz in her pocket. The number that appeared in the caller ID box was international.

"Hello?"

"*Mija.*"

Letty felt her body flood with relief, as if just the sound of Maria Elena's voice across thousands of miles could set her world right. She took a deep breath and smiled. "Hi."

"Hi, baby."

It was her father too, and she imagined them crammed into a phone booth in the tiny zocalo, the single telephone line connecting the small village to the rest of the world.

"Hi, Dad."

"We haven't heard from you in a while—we were starting to worry."

It wasn't the first time they'd tried to reach her. In the past week there had been three missed calls while she was working, but Letty had no way to call them back.

"I'm fine, just busy," she said. "I was about to write." Luna pulled on her arm, wanting to talk, but she wasn't ready to hand over the phone. "You'll never guess where I'm standing."

"Where?"

"On the front porch of my new house. In Mission Heights."

Maria Elena gasped in surprise, and her father said exactly what she knew he would say: "You left my birds?"

"*You* left your birds," she corrected. "But Alex took your feathers."

She told them about Rick, and how he'd taught her to make drinks and found her the tiny, perfect cottage.

"But what about Wes?"

Letty's heart stopped. So Wes had written to Maria Elena. He'd called to ask for the address weeks ago but hadn't mentioned it again, and she had been hoping he'd forgotten. It was just like her mother to call up right now, and insert herself in the middle of it. But it was easier to ignore her mother from a distance, and so she did.

"Here," she said, thrusting the phone into her daughter's hands. "Talk to Luna."

Luna launched into an enthusiastic description of her new room, her new garden, her new school, her new teacher, and her new friends. Letty only half-listened as she thought about Wes, and tried to imagine Maria Elena's face when she'd read the letter he'd written. Letty was glad there were two thousand miles separating them in that moment.

"She's making my Christmas outfit!" Luna said to Letty, as she handed her back the phone. She twirled across the porch in her imaginary new dress.

For Christmas Eve—*nochebuena*—every year, her mother made Luna a dress and Alex a vest and tie, all of which they wore for their grandmother's famous party. The event, which was wholly unlike her mother in every way, had roots in Oro de Hidalgo and had, in its inception, involved her mother and all the Espinosa cousins in matching fur coats, a sight Letty could almost imagine now, having seen the family home. The preparation started in October with sweet tamales, which she would count and freeze, and by early December the house was a museum of manger scenes. The first few years Maria Elena had sent formal invitations to all her church friends, but for as long as Letty could remember everyone they'd ever met and many they had not had just appeared at the door uninvited. It would be strange to have Christmas without her mother's party; it was the only ritual she or her children had ever known.

"Send the dress to our new house," Letty said and waited until her mother found a pen and wrote down the address.

"What will you do for Christmas this year?" Maria Elena asked.

"I haven't thought about it. Maybe I'll have a party here."

"Seems like you have plenty of people to invite," her mother said, and Letty could imagine just the way she looked at her father across the booth, one eyebrow raised.

"Mom, stop," she said. And then, to change the subject: "Can you send the recipe for sweet tamales?"

"You know how to make them, raisins and pineapple and masa. A little *canela*. Cloves. That's it—but I'll send the recipe."

Maria Elena kept talking, but Letty was thinking about the party, about what she would cook and how she would decorate, given that most of her mother's boxes marked NAVIDAD she'd left for Mrs. Starks; there wasn't room in the cottage for more than the absolute necessities. When she tuned back in to Maria Elena's monologue, she realized her mother was no longer talking about the party—she was talking about her father's work. From what Letty could catch, the Galería de Arte Mexicano, Mexico City's first and still one of its best galleries, had bought a piece of Enrique's work and commissioned two more, along with a high-paying contract for feather restoration on a few of the pieces in its collection. Apparently, feathers were back in fashion.

"It's a lot of money," her mother finished. "Enough to fix the pool. And to fly you down for a visit too."

"Wow," Letty said, shocked. "That's a really big deal. You think you could actually fly us down?"

At this, Luna shrieked and launched herself from the porch, asking if they could leave today, or tomorrow at the latest.

"Not now," Letty said, shushing her, and Maria Elena sighed heavily into the phone.

"I miss them. Every day."

"I know you do. I'll get them passports."

There was a pause, and then her stiff, formal mother made a sound that could only have come from her lips being pressed up against the germ-infested receiver of the public phone. Letty laughed and blew back a kiss, and then there was the operator, asking for more money, and her mother saying good-bye through the plea.

"I love you," Letty said, and then the line went dead.

4

A package sat in the passenger seat, small and square and wrapped in brown paper and duct tape. Alex's name was scrawled across the top. He picked it up and shook it, then set it on his lap as Wes pulled out of the gravel driveway and onto the road.

"Aren't you going to open it?"

"If you want me to."

"Of course I do."

The duct tape tore the paper as he lifted the corner. Beneath the wrapping he saw the edge of a sleek white box, and then a picture of an iPhone. Ripping at the rest of the paper, he slid the box open and pulled out the phone. "This is for me?"

Wes nodded, smiling as his eyes moved between the road and the phone in Alex's hands. Alex had never even held an iPhone. A few of the kids at Cesar Chavez had flaunted theirs incessantly at recess, but he didn't hang out with any of those kids. He fumbled around the edges for the on switch, and Wes reached over and pressed the round button on the front. The black screen glowed to life. Though he'd never used a touch screen, Alex's fingers slid the lock open and then moved across the face of the phone as if he'd spent every day of his life on one, racing through the music and photo and camera icons and finally finding the

keypad. He wanted to call Yesenia immediately, and then his mother—
except he had no idea if she would approve.

"Did you ask my mom?"

"No," Wes said. "But she'll be fine with it. You know she doesn't like
you out in the world alone, and now she can reach you."

"But isn't it expensive?" he asked, anticipating Letty's line of questioning.

"You don't need to worry about it. I just added you to my plan."

There was something about this statement, casual and possessive
both, that made Alex's throat swell. He wanted to thank his father, but
he couldn't speak. Wes didn't expect him to; he reached for the radio
and turned the music up, filling the space where Alex's thank-you
should have been. At a streetlight, he glanced into the rearview mirror,
at the file box Alex had strapped into the backseat.

"What's in the box?"

Alex swallowed hard, gathering his voice. "My grandpa's feathers."

"Why'd you bring them?"

"I don't know." He'd grabbed them almost without thinking, feath-
ered armor to face his fighting parents. But now the fact that he had
them felt auspicious. "I'm working on a science project," he said. "I
thought maybe you could help me."

The light turned from red to green, and Wes started to drive again.
"What are you working on?"

Just as he'd explained to his mother, Alex told Wes about the complete world preserved inside each feather, clues to migration and diet
and water sources and a hundred other things.

"Isotope signatures."

"Exactly!" It was a thrill, that someone in his family had a block of
knowledge that mirrored his own. For the first time Alex didn't feel like
he'd been plucked from outer space and dropped into the Espinosa family. He could see exactly where he'd come from.

"The trouble with my idea," he said, "is that I need a mass spectrometer."

"That's all?" Wes glanced at him, a smile flickering at the edge of his
mouth. With a sudden pull at the wheel that sent Alex careening against

the passenger door, Wes made a U-turn. "I know where we can find one."

It took twenty minutes to drive to Stanford. Wes parked in the employee lot and led the way across campus. Though Alex had spent all his life within fifteen miles of the prestigious university, he'd never been there. He'd seen pictures, though, hundreds of postcards in gas stations and grocery stores, and walking down Palm Drive now, he was shocked at how completely the campus resembled itself. In his experience, this kind of thing was usually a letdown, the reality never as magnificent as the airbrushed advertisement—but Stanford was the opposite, everything even more perfect in real life than it was on paper. The arched buildings were symmetrical and grand, the palm trees spaced evenly, even the fronds splayed in a way that made Alex wonder if the gardener had arranged them. Not to mention the flowers, cardinal red, which must have been planted just that day, not a petal out of place.

Alex followed Wes through the quad and past Memorial Church, its mosaics glittering in the almost dark. Turning right, they walked until they got to a square building with a tile roof, its windows lit up. Wes led him through the main doors.

The lobby was plastered with posters. Wes stood in the center of the room, scanning the three-by-five-foot color printouts describing studies with titles like "The Age of the Rocky Mountains," "The Level of Arsenic in Ground Water in Bangladesh," and "Possible Increases in Severe Thunderstorms Due to Greenhouse Forcing." He scanned every poster in the lobby and made his way up and down two corridors before he found what he was looking for at the top of a flight of stairs: a paper relating the use of stable isotopes to determine the reproductive range of northern fur seals.

"They'll have one," Wes said, pointing to the closed lab door.

"How did you know where to find this? I thought you were a doctor."

"I am. But I've been working with a lot of scientists at my new job, so I know a little about the different labs on campus."

"What do you do exactly?" Alex asked, realizing he had no idea what his father did all day every day.

"I'm working on a team trying to improve the diagnosis of TB in HIV-infected patients," Wes said. "It's tricky, because HIV affects immune systems—so HIV patients don't respond consistently to basic skin tests. You get a lot of false negatives, and false positives too. So we're working on something new to use in low-resourced areas, where it isn't possible to run blood tests."

It sounded interesting, but Alex didn't like the sound of "low-resourced areas." He didn't think his father was talking about Bayshore. "Do you think you'll ever be just a regular doctor?"

Wes had his hand on the lab door, but he paused, thinking about Alex's question. "Maybe," he said. His Stanford ID dangled from the edge of his shirt, and he took it off, studying his own photo as if the answer to Alex's question might lie there. He stuffed it into his pocket and shrugged. "Who knows? I've got a few science projects of my own I'm working on. A proposal pending. We'll see where it takes me."

Alex remembered the grant his father had mentioned over their first dinner and felt a bloom of panic. *Where it takes me*—was that literal, or figurative? But before he had time to ask, Wes pushed the lab door open and introduced himself to a grad student huddled in front of a computer. He asked if he was part of the team working on the northern fur seals, and when the student nodded, Wes summarized Alex's science project and asked if it might be possible for him to see their mass spectrometer.

"Sure."

The graduate student led them across the room, to a spectacularly complicated machine. It looked like two big dishwashers put together at right angles, with an enormous silver cylinder attached to one and countless tubes connecting it all together. Any other high school student would have tolerated an explanation of a mass spectrometer for no more than three minutes, but Alex made clear within the first thirty seconds that he was not the typical high school student. He wanted to see, document, and understand every single step of creating an isotope signature, and the grad student took his time, explaining the machine as he would to a fellow scientist. Pulling his brand-new phone out of his pocket, Alex took pictures, starting with the chemical process of isolating keratin and ending with an inside-out exploration of how the machine combusted the keratin and used a magnet to determine the ratio of heavy to light isotopes.

"Wow," Alex said, when they had finished. "It's amazing."

"I felt the same way the first time I saw it," the grad student said. "You're lucky. I was almost thirty before I got to see one."

"I *am* lucky."

"I can't let you use it, because you aren't Stanford-affiliated. And the chemistry's pretty complicated. But maybe we could run a few samples for you."

Alex's face fell, a look of such disappointment it was like Santa had come back down the chimney to rip his Christmas presents right out of his hand.

Wes showed them his Stanford ID. He wasn't in Earth Sciences, he said, but maybe they'd make an exception, and the grad student handed him a business card for the director of the lab.

"You might as well ask," he said. "And if it doesn't work out, let me know how I can help."

"It has to work out," Alex said as they started back across the quad. "I don't want someone else running my experiment." He tried to imagine it, sitting at home, waiting for someone to call him with the results. "Could I at least be there? Just watch or something?"

"I'll do what I can." The business card pressed a rectangle against the thin material of Wes's scrubs, and Alex wanted to reach inside his pocket, pull it out, and dial the number right then and there. But it was almost nine, and a Saturday. Wes pressed the card deeper into his pocket, as though reading his son's mind. "I'll call him on Monday morning, first thing. I promise."

Alex sighed. "Okay."

They were quiet as they climbed into Wes's car. When they pulled out onto Palm Drive, Alex asked: "Do you think I should test a bird from every year?"

"I don't think so," Wes said. "I think you'd want to bin them, maybe

into five-year periods. You'd want ten to fifteen samples from every period, at least. That way you can determine if any differences you find are
random versus actual changes in the feathers over time."

Alex made the note in his book. Without looking up, he added: "You
can drop me off at Yesenia's."

"Don't you want to have dinner?"

"Not really." Alex felt his cheeks flush pink, embarrassed at his acci-
dental honesty. "I mean, I will, if you want to."

"I told you!" Wes said. "I knew there was no way you'd want to hang
out with your dad on a Saturday night."

"It's not that—" Alex started, but Wes cut him off.

"It's fine, really." He gave him a gentle pop to the temple. "I was just
messing with you, I promise. Go have fun."

Guiltily, Alex directed Wes to Yesenia's house, and when he pulled up
in front of her building, Alex jumped out.

"Hey," Wes said, calling him back. "How will you get home?"

"I'll get there."

"Are you sure?" Alex nodded, and Wes studied him. Alex could see
the uncertainty in his father's eyes. He had no idea what was and wasn't
allowed, and he wasn't going to call Letty to ask. Finally he dug a marker
out of the glove compartment and pushed Alex's sleeve up, writing his
phone number on his forearm. The ink was the same color as a tattoo.

"Save this in your phone," he said, "and call me if you need a ride.
No matter how late."

The light was on in Yesenia's bedroom. Alex could see it from the street,
and he thought about calling her on his new phone, but instead he took
the stairs two at a time and knocked on the door.

"Who's there?"

"It's me."

The door squeaked open. She was wearing a pair of pajama shorts
with yellow butterflies printed on them. They were short-short, and she
pulled them down self-consciously and adjusted a hooded sweatshirt
she wore over the top. "I thought you were moving."

"We already did. And then I went with Wes to a lab, and then we were going to go out to dinner but I wanted to see you instead." He pulled the phone out of his pocket. "Look."

"He gave you that?" Yesenia pulled him into her bedroom, closing and locking the door, even though her mother was at work. "Let me see."

He placed the phone on her unmade bed, and she moved it onto the pillow, so it sat between them like a third person. The face was blank and glossy, perfect. Alex had polished it on the way up the stairs. She pressed it on and scrolled through his empty contacts, then found the ringtones in the settings. She changed it to an electronic bird noise, nothing like any bird Alex had ever heard.

"I wish you had one too," he said. "We could FaceTime."

Yesenia slid the phone back across the pillow. "I don't think buying me an iPhone is exactly in my mom's budget."

Alex felt stupid for mentioning it. Carmen was doing everything she could for her daughter, but she never could have bought her a phone. He suddenly felt undeserving, and he pushed the phone deep into his pocket, out of sight, and rolled over on her bed, facing the ceiling. She scooted toward him, her stomach pushed up against his side.

"What did you do with Wes?" she asked.

Alex sighed, happy for the change of subject. He rolled over to face her. "We worked on my project."

"Yeah? What did you do?"

"He took me to a lab at Stanford. They have a mass spectrometer in the science building next to where he works. He's trying to get me permission to use it."

She took his hand in hers, pressing it under her shirt, on her stomach, up to her bra. "Use it to do what?"

It was significantly harder to explain with one hand reaching under her bra. "I'm working with isotope signatures," he started, but then his hands were around her back, pulling at her bra clasp, and he lost his train of thought.

She pushed his hands away.

"Hey, you started it," he said, struggling to hold on to her as she squirmed away and sat up.

"But you aren't capable of talking and touching at the same time," she said, and then: "Talk first. Touch after."

Alex sighed, sitting up and backing away from her, the distance clearing his mind. "The idea is that birds are what they drink. The water that birds drink while they're growing feathers stays in the feathers and doesn't change over time, so when you analyze them you can find out exactly where a bird has been and what it has consumed."

"Your grandpa would love it."

Alex went to the hall, where he'd left his box of feathers, and carried it back to the bed. Taking off the lid, he riffled through the folders. "I'm not sure he would," he said. "It's a destructive process. I don't think he'd like to see his feather collection destroyed, even if it was in the name of science."

Yesenia shook her head, disagreeing. "Wings, remember?"

Alex sucked in a quick breath. Until that moment, he'd forgotten: she'd been there the night he found the note, the night he learned his grandfather had left and wasn't coming back. He felt his chest contract the way it always did when he thought of his grandfather. Yesenia felt it too. Popping off the bed, she stood behind him, her arms wrapped around his waist. She was so short her head tucked underneath his arm without her having to bend down. "He didn't mean for you to take him literally."

They'd learned the Icarus myth in sixth grade, and he remembered it then, imagining a heavy set of wax-and-feather wings, jumping out the window and taking off toward the sun. "I know he didn't."

She reached out, her hands on his hands on the feathers. "So what are you looking for? I mean, what do you think you'll find?"

"I'm not sure yet. All I know is that I want to look for changes over time. I mean, anyone can go down to the shoreline and pluck a wing feather from an egret and put the feather through some fancy process to see where it traveled the year before. Not everyone can then hold the results up against feathers gathered from the same species in the same place in 2005 or 1995 or 1985."

It was the single thing that made his grandfather's collections so special, he'd decided: he had feathers from as far back as thirty years, all collected from the same location and all meticulously labeled.

"They go back that far?"

"Yep."

"That's amazing."

They were quiet as Yesenia pulled out the file folders and arranged them on the bed.

"You could look for toxins."

"I thought of that. But someone's probably got a whole lab full of soil samples that would prove or disprove any toxins much better than I ever could."

She was quiet, lining the feathers up end to end, a long red chain.

"You can really tell from the feather where a bird has been?"

"I think so."

He drew the shape of a continent on the table, as if this would make his explanation more clear, but she was looking out the window, into the night sky.

"So you could figure out where the birds are migrating. See if it's really true, what they are saying."

"About what?"

"About the planet heating up."

Climate change. It was a good idea—an amazing idea. Looking at her, he wondered, and not for the first time, who she would be at Mission Hills, as Mr. Everett's student. She'd be like any one of them only better, he thought, but instead she was at Bayshore High, filling in a coloring book full of planets and silent from boredom and fear.

He turned back to his notebook. "So the null hypothesis is that there is no change," he said. Opening a box, he scanned for something his grandfather would have found every year for thirty years. The Allen's hummingbird. His hummingbird feeders ensured a constant flow of red feathers. Flipping to the back of the box, he pulled out an envelope labeled SCARLET POPPY V744, ALLEN'S HUMMINGBIRD, JUNE 1995. "And the prediction is that if birds fly south to reach a particular temperature, they might not have to fly as far anymore."

"Exactly," Yesenia said. "But you'd have to run the experiment to see."

"If I win. I only run the whole experiment if I win."

She revealed two feathers she'd managed to smuggle into her fist, the exact color of the streak in her hair. She held one up behind each ear. "You'll win. How could you not win, with an assistant like me?"

"Hey, I might need those!" He reached for the feathers, but she leapt away, to one side of the room and then the other, and when he cornered her she crawled up on top of the bed and let herself be tackled. With one hand he took the feathers and with the other he held both her wrists. She winced in pain.

"I'm sorry," he said, letting go. Rolling away, he took both her hands in his and tried to lift the cuffs of her long-sleeved sweatshirt.

"Don't."

She pulled away from him.

"Let me see."

"It's nothing."

"Then let me see."

Holding her still, he peeled back the bandage until he saw what it covered: a large scrape surrounded by a circle of yellowish green scabs, the color of infection. It made him instantly sick, and his stomach lurched as he pressed the bandage back in place.

"You have to see a doctor," he said, remembering his own infection, but Yesenia shook her head fiercely and pulled away.

"See, that's why I didn't want to show you. I don't want you to worry. I don't want it to even exist!" Her voice was filled with exasperation, and her eyes were wet. "I just want it to be me and you, together," she whispered. "The way it was before."

The way it had been just moments before, she meant, before her pain had forced him to remember. She wanted him to forget, but how could he? She was so little, and Bayshore High was so big. He lay down on the bed and pulled her on top of him, held her there unmoving, tight. With his whole being he wanted to be with her, wanted to keep her safe.

And then all at once it hit him: he could get her into Mission Hills. He couldn't believe he hadn't thought of it before. He'd been so busy feeling guilty that he'd missed the obvious. And if she came to school with him he could protect her, every moment of every day.

Lifting her head off his chest, he looked into her eyes.

"I want you to come to Mission Hills with me."

"So do I. But you know I can't. My mom isn't like your mom."

But Carmen didn't have anything to do with it. He'd thought of another way.

"I can get you in."

She shook her head. "No, you can't."

"I can." He saw it all coming together, imagined himself and Yesenia racing to the school, logging on to the computer using Mr. Everett's password, and making her a new student profile. "We just need to say you live with me."

"But why would I live with you?"

"We could say you're my cousin. And you just moved here."

"Gross."

"It's not gross if you're not my girlfriend."

What classes would he give her? He wondered if it would be too obvious if they had all the same classes. Probably. But he didn't like the idea of letting her go off alone, even for an hour. The kids at Mission Hills might be learning, but they weren't any nicer and many of them were just as stupid. More, even. The more he thought about it, the more he realized she would have just as good a chance of getting bullied at Mission Hills as she did at Bayshore, with one difference: he would be there to protect her. She would have to have the same schedule, the same exact schedule he did.

Yesenia squirreled up higher on the bed so their foreheads aligned on the pillow.

"Not your girlfriend?" she asked. "Alex Espinosa, are you breaking up with me?"

I'm not breaking up with you, he thought. *I'm saving you.*

But instead he asked: "Are you in?"

Yesenia chewed on her lip, then took a deep breath and smiled.

"When do I start?"

5

The light from the west-facing window was only enough to see Luna's profile against her pillow. It was still early, but Alex had been gone for an hour at least, setting his own alarm and heating up the scrambled eggs Letty had left on a plate in the refrigerator the night before. She hadn't seen much of him since they'd moved in. Every day he stayed late at school to work on his project, and afterward he called her on his new cell phone to say he was taking the bus to Stanford, to see Wes—which Letty took to mean Bayshore, to see Yesenia, or at the very least a combination of the two.

She really should wake Luna, but she didn't want to, and she didn't want to go to work either. She'd picked up a co-worker's shifts the weekend before, which meant she'd been at the bar nine days straight, two of them with her daughter. Rick had spent most of the afternoons in the hallway with Luna, so she hadn't been alone, but she was still a distraction, climbing up onto his shoulders and sliding down his back and racing him to the escalator and back while Letty tried to concentrate on measuring with the jiggers that still felt awkward in her hands, looking up complicated recipes she'd not yet memorized. Now, she was tired. She wanted a break from the bar, and even more she wanted time to unpack and to explore her new treasure chest of a house. The owners hadn't emptied it, and every drawer contained a different surprise: embroidered dish towels in the kitchen and doll clothes in the closet and an entire medicine cabinet full of seashells. The tool-chest drawers in the living room were her favorites, though. Alongside the hammers and nails and screws of every size she'd found a collection of crystals, strings of dried flowers, and a heavy metal deity in the shape of an elephant. The elephant was on the windowsill now, light glinting off its golden back.

With a yawn, Luna stretched awake, wriggling across her mattress and climbing off. She staggered over to Letty's bed. Crawling in, she pressed her bony butt into Letty's soft stomach.

"I'm cold."

Letty wrapped her arm around her daughter and tucked the blanket under her chin. It was her favorite thing about their new room: the air that leaked around the closed window, which smelled of forest instead of jet fuel. She inhaled deeply, filling her lungs.

"Do you want to go to school today?"

"No." Luna parroted the answer out of habit, and in the quiet Letty could tell her daughter was considering her quick response, whether or not it was true anymore. Every day at dinner Luna added to the long list of things she loved about her teacher: the color of her hair (lemon sorbet, Luna called it), the way she read stories aloud, her crazy hat collection. Finally, she lifted her head off the pillow and turned to look at Letty. "Are you saying I can stay home?"

Letty dropped one eyebrow. "Don't think this is going to happen all the time," she said, and then grinned conspiratorially. "But if you want to, yes. Your grandma used to let me take a day off. Just one a year—if my grades were perfect—to help her make tamales. What do you say we find out where the backyard ends, and then you can help me get ready for our Christmas party?"

"We're having a Christmas party?"

It was too much good news at once. Luna sprang out of bed, jumping from Letty's mattress to her own and back again.

"Of course we are. Now put on something warm while I make us breakfast."

After big bowls of oatmeal with brown sugar (or brown sugar with

oatmeal, the way Luna made it), Letty called in sick, and then she dialed
the school secretary to report Luna's absence too. They put on the rain
boots they hadn't worn since they left the Landing and headed into the
woods. Letty wanted to know if there was a fence at the property line,
or if the forest rose unobstructed to the summit and then down the
other side, to the ocean. A step in front of Luna, she led the way through
a tangle of manzanitas and into the redwoods. Their boots padded
softly on the duff, and Luna kept popping off the trail and balancing on
one foot as if waiting to sink. But here, the ground was firm.

While they walked, Letty pulled her daughter forward with one
hand, firing off a hundred questions to keep her mind occupied and her
feet moving. It worked for a little while, Luna chatting away and following without complaint. But ten minutes later, Luna announced she
wanted to turn back. Her feet hurt, she said, and she was hungry. Again.
Already.

"Here."

Letty pulled a packet of gummi bears from her pocket and shook it
into Luna's cupped palms. She dumped them into her mouth.

"But I'm hungrier than this," Luna slurred through a mouth full of
the chewy animals.

"Well, we can't go back yet. We just started." Letty had seen miner's
lettuce already, and she realized then why she wanted to explore: there
were probably dozens, if not hundreds, of ingredients growing wild in
her backyard. She wanted to take inventory. Searching her mind for a
way to keep Luna on the trail, she said the first thing that came to her:
"We haven't even found the blackberries."

"Blackberries?" There wouldn't be blackberries this time of year, but
Luna didn't know this, and the idea of them kept her walking for an-
other five minutes, looking for the tangled brambles she knew from
Mrs. Puente's garden at the Landing.

"We're never going to find them," Luna said after a while, her voice
on the edge of a whine.

"Not if we give up we're not."

Luna groaned. She stopped walking and scrambled up a rock, so that she stood a good two heads taller than Letty. Her arms crossed, she planted her legs in a wide V. She wasn't moving.

"Come on, just a little farther."

"We already went a little farther."

"Just a little more."

Luna shook her head, braids spinning like blades.

"Let's pretend we're lost in the woods, and we have to find our next meal."

"I can't. I'll starve to death."

"Fine," Letty said, frustration bubbling up. It was supposed to be their perfect day together. "I'm going hiking. You stay here and starve to death."

"I will," Luna said. "Watch me."

As Letty watched, Luna collapsed dramatically, her head hanging off the rock and her eyes rolling back in her head, so that only the whites showed. Her tongue poked out the corner of her mouth.

Despite herself, Letty laughed. "Oh, don't die!" she wailed, and Luna started to laugh too, squirming out of her mother's faux-desperate grasp and rolling off the rock. Letty fell on top of her, pinning her down. In a tangled embrace, they laughed harder than the situation deserved, relieved not to be arguing on their one day off a year.

When they calmed down, Letty tried one final time: "Five more minutes. I promise. I'm looking for something."

"What?"

"Ingredients. Something edible."

Without a moment's hesitation, Luna sprang up.

"Where are you going?" Letty called out after her, but Luna was already gone, running down the path in the direction they'd come. Letty took off after her. "Hey—how can you run so fast when your feet hurt?"

As a response, Luna kicked off her boots and kept running. Letty stopped to pick them up and then sprinted after her. When she finally caught up, Luna lay flat on her back in the manicured rose garden separating the cottage from the main house. Her chest rose and fell under her sequined sweatshirt.

"Edible," she panted with a grin, pointing at the roses all around her. Letty smiled. She'd taught her daughter this, on the first morning in their new home. Rose petals, rose hips—the red fruit shriveled by the cold: all edible.

Letty flopped down on the ground beside her daughter.

"You're edible," she said, pretending to nibble her cheek. The sky was bright and clear; the last of the roses hung over them like paper cutouts, pressed against the blue.

They lay until their breath returned to normal, and then Letty disappeared around the back of the cottage, returning a few minutes later with a pair of gardening shears and a bucket. Letty trimmed rose petals from the bushes while Luna pulled the last of the pomegranates off the tree, and then they spent a messy morning at the kitchen table. With a book open on the counter, Letty followed the directions, making grenadine from scratch with the pomegranates and then dropping dandelions and pine needles into swing jars full of vodka. When they were done, they lined their creations up on the windowsill, the sunlight illuminating the dark purple grenadine and lighting up the plants suspended in liquid.

"Pretty."

"They are pretty. And they're going to be delicious too."

"Can I try?"

"This one you can," Letty said, pointing to the grenadine. "When it's ready."

"Why can't I have it now?"

"Because it's not ready. And besides, we have to make cookies."

They had lunch first, then made a batch of chocolate chip cookies, and Letty had just sent Luna outside to lick a nearly empty mixing bowl when she heard a car pull into the gravel driveway. Luna shrieked when she saw it, and Letty's first (irrational) thought was that her parents had returned; but when she ran out onto the porch it was Rick, climbing out of his Highlander. Luna jumped into his arms, trying to feed him a wet glob of batter from the tip of her sticky finger. He turned his head away, tickling her through his refusal.

"How did you know where we live?" she asked when he set her back down.

"A little bird told me."

Luna puzzled this over: "My grandpa?"

Rick wrinkled his brow and lifted his chin toward Letty, asking her to explain, but she just shrugged. As much time as they'd spent together in the past few months, she thought, there were still so many things he didn't know. Luna held his hand as he walked to the porch.

"I heard you were sick," he said.

Letty shook her head no. "Sick of Flannigan's."

She stepped inside, and Rick followed her, kicking off his shoes and lining them up by the front door, next to Luna's boots. "I know the feeling."

"Don't you work today?"

"Not until five. They asked me to come early to cover for you, but I told them I was busy."

"Busy doing what?"

"What does it look like?" he asked. "Checking on you."

She turned to hide a smile and walked to the kitchen, where she was greeted by the disaster on the table.

Rick followed her. "What's all this?"

"We were getting ready for Christmas."

"Already?"

"My mom always makes tamales and freezes them. I was going to do the same, but then I realized I don't really like tamales. So we made cookies instead. And drinks."

"That's not much of a Christmas dinner."

She'd had the same thought earlier, when they were baking, and it had given her an idea. She flashed him a sly grin. "Didn't I tell you? You're making dinner."

"They better be some good drinks, then."

He helped her carry the dirty dishes to the sink and then stood behind her as she turned on the water, his hands rubbing her shoulders for only a moment before Luna burst into the room. Stepping quickly away, Rick asked her to tell him about their morning, and he was still listening, sitting at the table with Luna on his lap, when Letty finished the dishes ten minutes later.

"Yum," he said, after she'd listed the ingredients in each bottle. "Please tell me you're planning to share?"

Luna wrinkled her nose.

"I'll think about it," she said, to which Rick started to tickle her and Luna shouted, *"Yes! Yes! Yes!,"* breathless when he finally stopped. "I will," she exhaled. "But they aren't ready. Mom said."

"Well, Mom's the boss," Rick said, winking at Letty and making room for Luna to wriggle away.

On her tiptoes she washed her sticky hands, letting them drip across the kitchen while Letty chased her down with a cloth. "What are we going to do now?"

"We're making a pie," Letty said, looking at Rick, who nodded at the suggestion. "Want to help?"

"I'm tired of cooking," Luna said.

"Well, you're on your own, then."

"But there's nothing to do." This had been her complaint since they moved in. Letty hadn't brought their old TV because there was no room for the oversize box, but also because she'd felt guilty, all these months, plopping her daughter down in front of the screen anytime she needed to do anything, or anytime she needed a break—which was a great majority of the time. Maria Elena had rarely let the kids watch TV, and she'd managed. But now, after spending an entire morning with her daughter and with Rick in her kitchen, Letty wished she had the option.

"How about this," she said. "If you can prove to me that you can entertain yourself without a TV, I'll look into getting one. For the *occasional* times when there really is nothing else to do. Which will be almost never."

Luna nodded solemnly and stuck out a hand to shake.

"Now get yourself outside. Build a fort. Look for birds. Something." The screen door opened and banged shut. "Stay where I can see you!" Letty called after her, but Luna had gone no farther than the bottom porch step, poking her fingers into the joint of earth and wood, where the pill bugs liked to gather. Letty turned back to the kitchen and started to collect the ingredients for a pie: apples, flour, butter, sugar, cinnamon, washing the mixing bowl while Rick washed his hands and opened the bag of flour. He was already dressed for work in his black button-down; the white flour clouded and drifted in dusty marks onto the black.

"Do you mind?" he asked, unbuttoning his shirt to reveal a white undershirt beneath it.

"Of course not." Letty said, but her heart raced, watching him disrobe in her kitchen. She remembered their first kiss, and their second, which had lasted long enough that she'd been late to pick up Luna—a mistake that had cost her fifteen dollars in fines. He hung the shirt on the edge of the bench and leaned over the cookbook. Poking out from the top of his T-shirt were the scripty letters of his tattoo.

"You don't seem like one to have a tattoo," she said, turning on the oven and leaning over the recipe beside him.

"I know," he said. "I've thought about having it removed, but I've had it so long. I can't really imagine myself without it."

"How long?"

"Since I was eighteen. So, almost twelve years, I guess."

Letty thought of the photo on Rick's driver's license while she handed him a peeler and a bag full of green apples.

"Are you going to tell me what it says?"

He pulled the neck of his undershirt down, so she could see the Latin; Letty stepped closer to read it. The ink was fuzzy at the edges, a shaky hand or cheap ink seeping into his skin, but she loved it anyway, the blue-green mystery painted across his body.

"I might," he said, lifting one eyebrow. "It depends."

Stepping toward her, he grabbed one of her hands and lifted it to his skin. With the lightest touch, he traced the words, translating them as he moved her fingertip across his body: *the origin of our identity is love.*

Just then Luna raced into the room. Letty dropped her hand, but not before Luna had seen, and she saw her daughter's cheeks bloom red as she ran into their bedroom and out again, a blanket in her hands. With the slam of the screen door, she was outside again.

Letty got to work on the crust. Drying the mixing bowl, she measured the flour, silently stirring in salt and cutting in butter, adding water a tablespoon at a time while Rick peeled apples in perfect circles beside her.

"So, what's the story?" she asked finally.

He sighed. "Do you really want to know?"

"I do." Setting down the peeler halfway through the last apple, he told her: there was a girl—a woman, really. He had met her working at his father's restaurant, just after his eighteenth birthday.

"I fell crazy for her," he said. "The way you only can when you're young, you know?"

"Oh, I know."

She regretted saying it. Rick looked at her and asked: "How old were you?"

"Sixteen when we got together. Eighteen when he went to college." With her hands she began to work the dough into a ball, waiting for Rick to continue, and when he didn't, she prodded: "Tell me about her."

"She was beautiful. Although sometimes I wonder if I saw her now, if I'd still think so."

Letty thought of Wes the afternoon he returned, his tangled hair streaked over one eye, his sun-spotted skin smooth. "You probably would."

"Maybe. But she was ten years older than me—the closing chef when I was managing. Not classically beautiful, but confident. She'd get naked under the fluorescent lights of the walk-in as easily as in the total dark of a hotel room, and the fact that she flaunted her body—God, I loved that. The girls at my school, they were all sticks, had their nails done every week and always looked like they were on their way to church, but Mel—that was her name—she was kind of sloppy. And loud, and fun. She made me fun, and funny, and daring, and romantic, and all these other things I didn't know I was before I met her. Thus the tattoo."

"You were a deep eighteen-year-old." Letty smiled, thinking of herself and Wes at that age, full of similar prophetic declarations.

"Something like that."

"We would have liked each other." The dough was dotted with flour, but it held together. From the cabinet she pulled a cutting board and floured it. "And then what happened?"

"And then she moved to Connecticut with her husband."

"Ouch."

There was a pause in the conversation, while Rick finished the final apple and dumped the peel into the trash.

"So why do you still have it? Why didn't you have it removed right then?"

"I don't know," Rick said, thoughtful. "I guess I just still thought it was true, even after what she'd done."

"It is true. And it's part of you," she said. "You should keep it."

She handed him a knife and watched him cut the apples into careful cubes. From where she stood she could see only the middle word: *amor.* Love.

"Did you ever see her again?"

Rick shook his head no. Letty flicked a wet blob of flour into the sink, her mind on Wes.

"I never thought I'd see Wes again either." It was a leap, from his scar to hers, and Rick nodded, following. "After the first few years, I stopped even imagining trying to explain."

"Explain what?" She'd said it on purpose, the need to purge greater than the desire to conceal her worst self, and before she could second-guess her decision, she heard the story pouring out of her. The unplanned pregnancy, the shock of it and Wes already gone, and how she'd meant to tell him and all the reasons she couldn't bring herself to do it, and then the shame, the horribleness that was her as a mother. "It was a stupid, awful, selfish decision. Now that I'm a parent—*really a parent*—I understand what I did to him. And it makes me sick."

"What do you mean—*really a parent?*"

"Oh, God, Rick, don't you remember me when we first met? I had no idea what I was doing." While he tossed the apples in sugar and cinnamon, she told him the second secret, the secret she couldn't even bring herself to tell Wes, the years and years she'd stood by as her mother raised her kids, missing everything that mattered. She hadn't told anyone, ever, and she felt it like a physical weight, lifting.

When she was done, Rick washed his hands and turned to her. "It makes sense, now. The first time I bought Luna a licorice rope, you acted like I was Houdini, escaping an underwater burial."

"It was practically the same thing," she said, and then, remembering: "Oh, my God, do you even remember that day?"

"*I am NOT fine!*" Rick mimicked, his fists banging his thighs in a spectacular impression of her daughter. Letty laughed so hard Rick had to hold her up, and when he finally let go, her eyes were watery.

"Seriously, Rick. I don't know what I would have done without you."

He reached out and wiped a tear away with his thumb. She backed up until she hit the counter, and he pressed himself onto her, the full length of his body against hers. Weakly, she tried to wriggle out from underneath him, but she couldn't and she didn't want to—so he was already kissing her, and she was kissing him back, heat in her body, when she finally succeeded in forcing herself to push him away.

"What's wrong?" He glanced out the front window, to where only Luna's feet were visible under a rosebush fort.

Letty sighed, trying to find the words. "I just don't want to mess this up."

"So you push me away?"

"I'm not," she said, but her flour handprints were still on his chest, white against white. "I'm just trying to keep you above the fray. At least until I can figure things out."

"It's way too late for that," he said. The flour flaked off his shirt and landed on his black socks. "Is it Wes?"

Letty nodded, then shook her head no. "I don't know."

"You have to know."

"But I don't."

Rick studied her face, looking for the truth. "Well, *I* know," he said and waited for her to ask what, but she didn't, too sure, all at once, what was coming.

"I'm falling in love with you," he whispered. The words hung there, unrequited. She looked out the door, trying to find Luna in the roses, and he took a step back before he continued. "But I'm not just going to sit around while you see if you can work it out with someone else. I won't be your backup, Letty."

"I don't want you to be my backup."

"So what do you want, then?"

What *did* she want? She didn't have an answer. All she knew was that everything good that had happened in her life in the last few months had happened because of Rick. If it weren't for him, she would still be stuck slinging crap drinks, making no money, and living in an abandoned apartment building at the Landing. But instead he'd walked into her life, seen her struggling and messy and incompetent, and somehow—impossibly, it seemed—fallen in love with her anyway.

She turned away from him and scanned the recipe, looking for something to hold on to, but the next direction was a dead end: *refrigerate for four hours.* Giving up, she thrust the bowl with the ball of dough into the refrigerator and slammed the door. Turning back to Rick, she placed her hand on his stomach, then the button of his jeans, pulling him toward her.

"I just want you," she said. "That's all I know. And I need you."

Rick sighed, his body relaxing under her touch. "What do you need?"

Standing close enough to feel his scratchy chin on the top of her head, her mind filled with all the things she needed and couldn't say. She needed him to teach her how to be with her children, how to distract and redirect and laugh; she needed him to teach her how to make drinks, how to set a goal and work toward it; more than anything, she needed him in her home, needed him to press her hands against his chest, needed to feel his heart beat under her hands, a slow, steady rhythm.

"I need you to come to my Christmas party," she said quietly. Rick looked at her hard, and Letty hoped he could see in her eyes everything else she needed and couldn't say. "I need you to cook dinner."

Rick's face was a jumble of indecision. Finally, he spoke, his voice rough with conflict: "Okay," he said quietly. "I'll be there."

Grabbing his shirt, he buttoned it quietly and slipped on his shoes. In the garden he said good-bye to Luna, who jumped into his arms, wrapping her legs around his waist and begging him to stay while Letty watched, wishing desperately she was six years old again and could do the same.

But she couldn't.

She was thirty-three, a woman and a mother, and all she could do was sit, silent, and watch him go.

6

He needed to borrow Mr. Everett's keys. As Alex worked on his project, he tracked his teacher's whereabouts in relation to his keys in relation to the eyes of everyone else in the class. But a week before school let out for winter break, he was still watching and waiting, no closer to achieving his goal.

Today the classroom was especially noisy and chaotic, students arguing over glue sticks and permanent markers as they put the finishing touches on their science posters. Alex had left his at home, the row of feathers he'd glued on still drying, and so he sat at his desk, his attention divided between a book on hummingbird migration and his cell phone. He was waiting for a text from Wes. Mr. Everett allowed cell phones (as long as they were used as tools of science, not tools of gossip or romance), so he didn't have to hide it, like he did in some of his other classes. Picking it up, he scrolled through the history of his texts with his father.

Their first exchanges were short and awkward: *Doing? Nothing.* And then two days of silence before: *Dinner? Yes.* They'd picked up, though, as his project had picked up. The first time Alex had sent his father a science question, Wes had responded with eight texts, two photos, and a link to a website for a lab at Purdue, and their exchange had continued, almost without pause, for days after. Once, Wes had even texted him in the middle of the night: *We need to talk about statistical significance*—and then *I'm sorry—I didn't realize the time!* to which Alex had replied: *I was awake! And thinking the same thing!*

He had just set down his phone and turned back to his book when the phone buzzed on the desk. It was the text he had been waiting for. Wes had located a scientist known for his isoscapes—maps that showed the stable isotope ratio of the water in every region on the planet—and had˙ sent Alex a link to the most recent map of the Americas. Alex clicked the link and zoomed in on the coast of California. He opened his notebook to check his own numbers—Wes had paid to have a few samples run, while he was waiting to see if they could get access to the lab.

"Yes," Alex said, when he saw the numbers matched. "Yes!"

Mr. Everett chuckled from where he stood behind him. Alex didn't know he'd been speaking aloud.

"Carry on, carry on," Mr. Everett said. "Don't mind me."

His teacher turned back to the bookshelf, a heavy-looking box in his arms and his keys clutched in his hands underneath. Setting the keys on the shelf, he began to empty the box, lining up a row of shining Erlenmeyer flasks before returning to his desk with the empty box.

He'd left his keys.

Alex stood up to go to the bathroom, swiping the key ring and walking immediately out the door.

As soon as the last bell rang he called Yesenia, and he kept calling until she got home from school and answered.

"I have them."

She didn't say *Finally!* Even though he knew she was thinking it. He was too. It had felt like forever, those weeks. He'd thought it would be easier, with everyone focused on their projects, but it was already the week before Christmas vacation—their big presentations would take place the next day.

"Where should I meet you?" she asked.

"At the top of the pedestrian bridge. At eleven?"

She agreed and they hung up. Full of nervous energy, he decided to cook something for his mother and sister and tore the kitchen apart looking for something he knew how to make. Settling on fried eggs and bacon and fruit salad, he made heaping plates before he realized he'd never cooked dinner for his mother, not once, and so instead of setting the table he dumped all three plates in the garbage, took out the trash, and lit ten matches in every room to mask the smell of cooking. Nothing could be out of the ordinary when Letty got home—he didn't want her to think for even one second that he was up to something.

But if Letty noticed the smell, she didn't say anything. She came home late with Chinese takeout and they ate from Styrofoam containers on the front porch, Letty exhausted but trying to ask Alex questions about his project, to prepare him for the next day. It wasn't necessary; Alex was prepared. He answered them all and then started his homework for his other classes while his mom put Luna to bed. Letty fell asleep mid-song, and Alex left the house right then, not wanting Yesenia to get to the bridge first and have to wait for him alone in the dark.

It took him over an hour to walk from his new house, though, and when he arrived she was already there, leaning against the wire cage. She wore all black—a good idea, he realized now, although he hadn't thought of it. He hadn't thought of it because until that very moment he hadn't thought of what they were doing as breaking the law. He wasn't hurting anything, wasn't stealing anything—just borrowing the keys and borrowing his teacher's password and borrowing his computer. Still, he knew it was probably illegal.

"Hi," Yesenia said, her face full of fear and excitement.

"Are you ready?" Alex asked.

"I think so."

"You don't have to come, you know." He'd been thinking this on the way over—that if anything about Operation Enroll Yesenia started to feel dangerous, he'd make her wait down the street.

"I want to, though."

They were quiet on the walk to school, apprehension growing with each step. Alex tried to calm himself by listing all the reasons they wouldn't get caught: it was the middle of the night, it was dark, and he had the key. He knew the password and knew exactly how the computer system worked. The whole thing would take ten minutes, at the most.

The lights were on in the art wing; through ten-foot windows Alex could see Mr. Mendoza, with his rolling trash can, moving through the ceramics studio. Alex was glad he was there—it meant the alarm wouldn't be set, if there was one. He hadn't thought of an alarm until that moment either, and the possibility made his heart beat faster—what else hadn't he thought of? He kept going, leading Yesenia around the side of the building, past the tables where he ate lunch every day and to the long, open-air halls of the science wing.

Yesenia stood guard at the end of the hall while Alex unlocked the door. With a nod of his head, he summoned her, and they slipped inside together. She clutched his waist hard as he felt his way to the front of the room from memory and reached underneath Mr. Everett's desk to push the power button on his desktop.

It took forever for the computer to turn on. The screen went from black to blue, and then there was a moment that stretched on indefinitely, when everything looked as it should but the cursor wouldn't move. When it finally did, Alex opened PowerSchool and clicked through the enrollment tab to create a new student profile: Yesenia Lopez-Vazquez, gender: female, age: 15, address: 7 Woodbridge Court; where he should have put her phone number, he made up a ten-digit number. The form was much longer than he'd expected, and required information he didn't have, including immunization records and dates. He entered a date beside each vaccine listed, at first trying to remember at what age he'd gotten certain shots and then, when that took too long, entering dates at random. Beneath the immunization records was a blank field in which to describe medical conditions. He looked at Yesenia for direction, and when she shook her head he wrote: *none*. Her profile complete, he was directed to choose her classes, and he entered his own spring schedule in order: first-period English to last-period gym. He'd already told her she'd have to wait in the library for zero period—it would be too risky to put her in honors science without prior consent from Mr. Everett.

She would start in January, the first day after break. No one would ask questions. They would walk from class to class and he would introduce her to everyone and tell his friends she'd just moved here and no one would wonder why or where she'd come from, because no one had ever wondered why or where he had come from. He was just there, and soon, she would be too. Finished, he pressed PRINT; the single sheet of paper slipped out the printer on the far wall. Alex retrieved it and handed it to Yesenia.

"That's it?" she whispered.

He nodded and closed himself out of PowerSchool. In the cold light of the computer screen, they made their way silently to the door, closing it firmly and locking it behind them.

They sprinted all the way back to Bayshore, Yesenia running as fast as she'd ever run in her life. When they reached the pedestrian bridge they were panting but full of adrenaline, their silence turning to loud laughter. They'd done it. Yesenia pressed her schedule flat against the wire fence of the bridge and read it in the pulsing light of the headlights passing below.

"Thank you," she said, but it was unnecessary; they had done it together.

"Are you tired?"

Yesenia shook her head no. There was no one waiting for her at home, and no one was awake to miss Alex either. Holding hands, they walked down the stairs and straight up Mile Road, past the Landing to the water.

It had been a long time since they'd been to the pier together, and the ocean air was colder than he remembered it, and damp. They sat down, and Alex peeled off his jacket and then, pausing, took off his shirt too. He spread the sweatshirt out on the pier and lay down on top of it.

"Aren't you cold?" Yesenia asked.

"I won't be." He reached out and grabbed her, pulling her down on top of him and covering them both with his jacket. He was warm but would be warmer if she would take her shirt off too, if they were skin against skin. She must have thought the same thing, because she pulled off layers of clothing until she was wearing only a bra before lying back down on top of him. She pressed her body against his.

"What's that?" Mr. Everett's keys were still in his pocket. He adjusted her until he could slip his hand inside his pocket and pull them out.

"I meant to put these back where I found them before we left."

"But what about the fingerprints?" she asked. "Better to destroy the evidence."

"You watch too much TV," he said and thought of Maria Elena, her disapproval hitting him hard and unexpected.

"I'm right, though." She nodded toward the bay.

Maybe she was. He didn't want to cause Mr. Everett the trouble of having to make new keys, but he wanted even less to get caught. Before he changed his mind, he sat up and threw them into the water, watching the surface until the ripples became waves and the keys had sunk to the bottom of the bay.

When he turned back to Yesenia, she was naked from the waist up. He was equal parts excited and terrified, to see her chest exposed in the moonlight. Her breasts and belly were perfect above the line of her black jeans, without the scars that crisscrossed her lower back and legs, and as much as he wanted to look at her, he wanted to cover her too, wanted to hide her away where no one but him could look at her body this way again, ever. He pulled her down and rolled over on top of her, kissing her hard while she worked at the button on his jeans. She'd never been so bold, but he didn't stop her, tried to follow her lead, pulling on the clasp of her pants for what seemed like an indefinite stretch of em-barrassment before she got his pants off and pulled her own off too.

They lay naked, then, for the first time. Their bare legs stuck out from underneath the jacket, his own long and pale and hairy, and hers short and dark and perfect only to him. He was shy all of a sudden, but his body wasn't, was in fact the opposite, bold and reaching toward her. He arched away, but she rolled him over on his back and pulled herself on top of him again, so there was nothing to do but let himself be pressed up against her belly.

She held his face and kissed him, softly, and he kissed her back, and he wanted to cry it was all so perfect, and he wanted to do what she expected him to do, but he also had no idea what that was. And he hoped it wasn't everything. He'd promised himself he wouldn't have sex, not only until he was married but until he wanted a baby, so that a child of his would never, not even for one moment, not even at conception, feel unwanted; but he would, if she wanted to, to show her there was nothing he wouldn't do for her.

She was squirming on top of him, rubbing herself against him in a wet, rhythmic way, and he couldn't tell if she was trying to get him inside her or trying to keep him out. She kissed his ear, and he opened his eyes and tried to think about the stars, about the birds, about his project, anything but the feel of her against him. He reached down, thinking there was maybe something he was supposed to do, something that might feel good to her, but when he touched her she rolled off, all at once, and took a breath.

"I'm sorry."

"Why? No, no, it's not that. It's not anything."

She was trying to say something else, he could tell. He hoped it wasn't that he was doing everything wrong, because he might be. He'd been thinking only about himself from the moment he saw her naked, and he should have been focused on her all along.

Finally she turned away from the sky and looked at him. "Do you want to?"

He didn't. But he would; for her, he would do anything. "Do you?"

She shook her head no, slowly. "I will, though."

He kissed her hard, relieved, but also curious, and still worried that maybe he'd done something wrong, something to turn her off.

"Is it God?" he asked.

She smiled big, and he saw Carmen in her face, the sly confidence at the dinner table, as if something had long ago been decided between mother and daughter and God.

"No," she said. "It's babies."

It made sense, that in this way they were the same: two unwanted children scared to create the next generation under similar circumstances. He kissed her again. "Let's wait," he said into Yesenia's mouth as she kissed him again: his lips, his cheek, his ear.

She pulled away just enough to look him in the eyes, her expression mischievous. "There are other things we can do, you know."

Alex's heart dropped as she dropped, her head disappearing underneath his jacket.

Alex wore a suit to school the next day. Yesenia had found it in the alley, along with a white shirt and lime green tie. He thought he'd be the only one dressed up, but he was wrong. The girls wore skirts and blouses or serious, high-necked dresses, and the only boy not wearing a suit was Jeremy, who was instead sporting a bow tie, suspenders, and an open white lab coat. It would take more than an eye-catching outfit for Jeremy to win, though; his project was one of the worst in the class.

Wes had picked Alex up and dropped him off that morning, his tri-fold presentation tucked safely in the trunk and sample feathers pressed into a glass frame. Alex expected his father to drop him off at the curb nearest the science wing, but instead Wes parked in the student lot and walked Alex all the way to class.

They were twenty minutes early, but already the classroom was crowded with students and parents and judges. The desks had been pushed to the center of the room to make space for tables that had been brought in and pushed against the classroom walls. Alex found his name and set his project down just as Miraya walked up with a box full of donuts. Alex took two, handing one to Wes, and together they ate apple fritters while setting up Alex's board. In the center was the title, which they'd come up with over a series of texts the weekend before, and which had gotten longer with each additional text: "Using Stable Isotope Signatures to Investigate the Effect of Climate Change on the Migration Patterns of Allen's Hummingbird." And below the title were the hypothesis and a photograph of his grandfather's file cabinet, open to the reds and showcasing his organization system. There was almost too much to fit onto the board—the description of the process of creating isotope signatures, photos of the mass spectrometer, and isoscapes of California and Mexico—in addition to the framed feathers, marked for where they would sample. The board was so crowded that Alex had had to print his expected results (*If my hypothesis is correct, feathers from earlier years will have a more southern signature*) in eight-point font and glue it to the very bottom right-hand corner, where he was now sure the judges would miss it.

But it was the best that he could do, and he was proud of it, and he could tell that Wes—who'd taken a quick tour of the room and given him a giant pat on the back upon his return—was proud too. Alex gave his father a hug good-bye and thanked him, and then he wandered the classroom himself, surveying the final presentations for the ideas he'd heard bits and pieces of over the last semester.

In the front of the room, a professional-looking poster was taped to the whiteboard. Julianna Skye's was the project everyone was talking about. Apparently she'd started a makeshift lab in her basement, trying to create a strain of algae high enough in oil content to be an economically feasible biofuel. An environmental lab had somehow gotten wind of the project (the other students said her dad ran the lab, but looking at the man in jeans and flip-flops who had accompanied her, it was hard to believe that was true) and had given her a budget and space to work. Already her results looked promising. It was an amazing idea, the kind of thing that not only made a great science project but, if successful, would make an actual, real-life contribution to the world. She would win for sure.

Which left just two more winners. Mr. Everett had invited half a dozen scientists from universities and labs all over the Bay Area, and they walked around with their clipboards, taking notes on a photocopied scoring sheet. In front of his own project, one of the judges snapped open the glass frame and picked up Alex's feathers one at a time. Alex wished he would put them down. His grandfather had taught him before he could walk exactly how to handle them, and it made him cringe to watch the man's fingers moving haphazardly against the barbs.

After an hour the judges left the room to confer, and a hush fell over the classroom. Alex had expected nervous chatter, but everyone went to his or her desk, pretending to read books or look through folders. No one made eye contact. Competition had been disallowed, and yet there was nothing but competition in that room. Too much was at stake.

Five minutes later the judges returned. They handed Mr. Everett a sealed envelope, and with more drama and flair than Alex thought necessary, his teacher sliced open the envelope and withdrew a sheet of paper.

"In no particular order, I present the winners. First." He paused here, and Alex, annoyed again at the exaggerated suspense, tapped his foot under his desk.

"Julianna Skye. 'Creating an Economically Feasible Algae Biofuel.'" Everyone clapped dutifully, and Alex thought, along with the rest of the class, that the results were clearly in order. Julianna's project was hands down the best. Without a pause, Mr. Everett announced the second winner: Sophia Joyce Chen, for her work on cholesterol and reductase inhibitors.

Mr. Everett stopped and looked around the room. There was only one remaining spot.

"Now I'm going to remind you all. Everyone's a winner here. Before Christmas break you will all divide up into teams, and every one of you will spend the next two months pouring yourselves into one of these projects as if it were your very own."

"Oh, come on!" Jeremy burst out, and then slapped a hand over his mouth. Jeremy couldn't really be hopeful, could he? But Alex was. He had a shot. His project was as good as any of the remaining projects, and he knew it.

"Fine." His teacher put the paper back in the envelope. His eyes moved slowly around the room until he found Alex, and then they stopped. "'Using Stable Isotope Signatures to Investigate the Effect of Climate Change on the Migration Patterns of Allen's Hummingbird.' Alex Espinosa—congratulations!"

He'd won. The rest of the class clapped in spite of themselves. He was the freshman, the underdog. There were hands on his shoulder, back slaps of congratulation. More than one person asked if they could be on his team, but it was all happening so fast, he couldn't keep track of who was speaking. His mind went to his father. All the hours they'd spent at the lab and in his office, the midnight texts, the printouts of maps and images and mathematical equations he'd brought over after work. Alex couldn't have done it without him, couldn't have done it if his father hadn't come back into his life right when he did.

They were packing up their presentations when Mr. Everett hit the lights. The room went still and quiet.

"Has anyone seen my keys? They've been missing since yesterday."

A chorus of muttered noes and shaking of heads.

"Weird."

Alex looked at the floor, breath held, heart stopped. The pause of his teacher surveying the room seemed to stretch on forever.

"I guess I'll have to make another set," Mr. Everett said finally. He turned the lights back on. "Another congratulations to the winners, and to the entire class for an impressive display of scientific thinking."

The classroom resumed its noisy motion, and Alex's heartbeat returned to its pounding.

That was it.

Mr. Everett had lost his keys, and would make another set.

Done and won and forgiven, all on one incredible day.

7

During the buildup to *nochebuena,* Letty tried over and over again to remember what she'd been thinking, hosting a party in which Wes and Rick would share a night together in the company of her best friend and children. But she hadn't meant for it to happen. She'd invited Rick and Alex had invited Wes, and by the time she realized it, it was too late to call the party off without ruining the holiday for Alex and Luna, and on this, their first Christmas without their grandparents. The party and her parents and Christmas were intertwined in their minds, the midnight extravaganza full of presents and people and dancing and food, all culminating in the happy hangover of exhaustion that was Christmas morning. The thought of just the three of them, alone in their teeny dollhouse cottage on Christmas Eve, was too much for even Letty to bear, so she shopped and cooked and decorated and answered a never-ending litany of questions about the food and drinks and music from Alex. He was almost as nervous as she was; for the first time, Letty would meet the mystery girl who occupied so much of her son's time.

Rick arrived at eight, his arms full of groceries. They hadn't spoken except in passing at work, and Letty could feel the tension between them as he handed her the bags and turned his attention to Luna, who yanked him down the hall to meet Alex.

"Luna talks about you all the time," Alex said, shaking his hand and then turning back to the dripping wet hair he was trying in vain to untangle.

"It's nice to meet you," Rick said while extracting Luna, who was attempting to scale his side.

Letty turned her toward the bedroom. "Go put your dress on."

It was too early to get dressed, but that was all Letty could think of to get her daughter to stop hanging on Rick. Luna listened for once, skipping off to her bedroom, and Letty followed Rick into the kitchen. "What are you making?"

"Linguini with clam sauce," he said, pulling out a large bag of clams, still in their shells. A downstairs neighbor had brought it to her mother's party every year, and when she moved out everyone had missed it, so Maria Elena had learned to make it herself. Luna must have told him, although Letty couldn't think of when he might have asked.

"Alex and Luna will be happy," Letty said. "They love it, even though they won't eat seafood any other day of the year."

Rick didn't meet her eyes as he moved to the sink and washed his hands, and Letty felt a bubbling anxiety, remembering what he'd said the last time he stood in her kitchen. *I won't be your backup.* He wasn't going to sit around and wait, and she wondered how much time she had to decide. Not much, she thought as she moved about the kitchen, shaking up a round of French 75s and stacking bottles of champagne in the refrigerator to top them off after everyone arrived.

As far away from her as possible in the tiny kitchen, Rick lined up cutting boards and chopped garlic and fresh parsley with a sharp knife.

"Do you need help?" Letty asked.

Rick shook his head no, not taking his eyes off the parsley, so she slipped out to check on Luna.

"Look!" Luna said when Letty walked into the bedroom. With her arms out to the sides she spun in circles, squealing as the lavender lace dress Maria Elena had sent twirled around her knees.

"It's beautiful," Letty said. "Let me do your hair."

Letty brushed her daughter's hair in long strokes while Luna ran her fingers over the lace and then along the back of the neckline, where the tag on a store-bought dress would be. Maria Elena had embroidered

Luna's name and the date, as she did every year, and this time she'd stitched the words *With Love, Nana* below the date in black thread. Luna traced the smooth words as Letty braided her daughter's hair into a crown, and when she was done they stood quiet in front of the mirror, admiring Luna's long dress and perfect plaits.

There was just one thing missing.

"Wait here," Letty said as she crossed to the closet, where she dug around on the top shelf until she found the other package her parents had sent. It contained Alex's and Luna's Christmas presents, as well as a letter from her mother and the most recent check Letty had sent, returned. Enrique continued to work, her mother had written—he'd even been contacted by a museum in Spain for a particularly complicated restoration. Attached to Letty's uncashed check was a Western Union claim number—Maria Elena had wired enough money to buy three plane tickets to Mexico. As a surprise, her father had drawn pretend plane tickets for Letty to stuff in Alex's and Luna's stockings. As nervous as Letty felt, she wished the tickets were real, and for tonight. Nothing sounded better than a quick escape.

"What is it?" Luna asked, tugging on her sleeve impatiently.

Letty stuffed the tickets out of sight and withdrew a bumpy envelope with Luna's name on it.

"This is from your grandpa, for Christmas," Letty said, handing it to her. "I think he would want you to have it now."

Luna tore the envelope open and gasped. On a delicate gold chain perched a miniature golden bird, no bigger than Luna's pinkie nail. A tiny sparkly eye winked up at her.

"A diamond eye," she said in awe.

The diamond wasn't real, of course, but Luna didn't need to know.

"Nana and Grandpa love you," Letty told her. "And they miss you."

"I wish they were here." Luna sighed.

Letty smiled as she fastened the necklace around her daughter's neck, thinking of tomorrow's presents, the plane tickets, and then she dressed herself quickly, passing over the long-sleeved gown her mother had sent in favor of a simple black cocktail dress with thin straps and a low back.

She'd already decided she would wear her hair in a high bun, and she took her time arranging the loose curls around the top and sides in a careful mess. When they were both ready, she and Luna spent the final hour dashing around the house, putting up strings of lights and hanging ornaments on a tabletop tree and lighting candles in the tin luminarias that stretched down the dark drive.

Wes arrived first, just after eleven. Luna had already started dancing, and was sweaty and out of breath when she opened the door. When Luna hugged him, her coiled hair came unpinned and flopped over one ear. Letty said hello quickly and then disappeared down the hall, grabbing a box of bobby pins and mixing two bubbly drinks in the kitchen. Rick didn't look up from his work.

Holding both drinks in one hand, Letty closed the door between the kitchen and the living room. The meeting of the two men was inevitable, but the longer she could put it off, she decided, the better.

"Merry Christmas," she said to Wes, exhaling heavily and handing him a drink. They clinked glasses, and Letty concentrated hard on taking slow sips, but the drink was too good and her stress level was too high. When she set the glass down on the windowsill, it was nearly empty.

"I love the lights."

Wes gestured to the wall of drawers, where they'd wrapped a string of colored lights from handle to handle to handle, up and down and across at random, giving the wall the look of an electric Jackson Pollock.

"That was Luna," she said, patting the window seat and beckoning her daughter.

Luna jumped up, and Alex sat beside her, checking his watch and then turning back to the dark road. Letty started on Luna's hair. The drink and the simple task relieved her tension. She took her time, unbraiding and rebraiding the tip before securing every last strand of hair with a pin. Wes stepped up beside her, one hand holding his drink, the other resting gently on Alex's shoulder, and Letty felt a rush of warmth, from the champagne cocktail or from the four of them there in the window, all together, waiting for the other guests to arrive. She imagined the look on Sara's face when she turned up the driveway and saw them, Luna and Alex in the foreground, Wes and Letty behind, arranged as if by an invisible hand into a perfect portrait of an American family.

Just as she'd put the last pin in Luna's hair, a car turned in to the driveway.

"Yesenia!" Luna screamed, jumping off the window seat. She raced out the door and across the gravel. Luna had made her brother's girlfriend a pipe cleaner, jingle bell, and silk rose wrist corsage at school, and while she slipped it onto Yesenia's wrist, a second car pulled up behind them. Luna ran over to hug Sara, pulling her up the stairs and beckoning Yesenia and her mother to follow.

They stepped into the living room all at once, and even though there were only seven of them, there was barely enough room for them all to stand. Letty pushed the furniture into the corners, and Luna jumped onto the window seat while Alex pressed in close to Yesenia, ostensibly to make room for other people. He slid his hand around her back with a comfort that made Letty's stomach turn.

Sara saw the look on Letty's face and stepped into her line of vision. "Back up, Mama Bear," she said. "I think it's time for a drink."

"It's time for *another* drink," Letty said, and Sara laughed.

They walked into the kitchen, where a steaming platter of linguini and clams sat on the table. Two salads and a glass filled with forks had been placed on the table beside it. Sara pinched a clam from the tray and popped it into her mouth.

"You made this?" Sara's expression was disbelieving.

"No way," Letty said. She called Rick's name, but he didn't answer, and so she poured a tray of drinks and followed Sara back into the living room. Just as she was about to go looking for Rick, Alex pulled her aside.

"Mom, this is Yesenia," he said. "And her mom, Carmen."

"I'm Letty," she said, offering Carmen a drink.

Carmen took a sip, a warm smile spreading across her round face. *"Gracias por invitarnos,"* she said as she squeezed her daughter's shoulder.

"Thank you for having us," Yesenia translated. "It's really nice to meet you."

Letty was surprised by her strong, sure voice, a mismatch with the girl's small body, and she watched as Alex took Yesenia's coat, leaning down and helping her out of her black jacket. He'd warned her about Yesenia's size, but in person the girl was even smaller than Letty had imagined. Her red velvet dress had a puffy skirt like Luna's—it had probably been made for a ten-year-old—and underneath the long skirt she could just see the tops of Yesenia's orthopedic shoes. But the dress was more flattering than it might have been. Studying it closely, Letty could see that Yesenia or Carmen had altered it, cutting a wide boat neck over her shoulders and tailoring the bodice so that it accentuated the curve of her chest.

When Letty looked back up, she realized that Carmen was watching her watch her daughter, her expression full of pride. *"Te ayudo?"* she asked, and Letty nodded.

In the kitchen they served dinner. Letty dished out the food while Carmen ran the plates into the living room. When everyone had been served, Letty carried the final two plates herself, one for her and one for Rick. But when she walked into the living room, he still wasn't there. Setting the plates down on the table, she looked back in the kitchen, and then walked down the short hall. The bathroom door stood ajar. She pushed it open, but found the small room empty. Where could he be? She thought of his flat, unresponsive face as he chopped garlic, and a flicker of panic bloomed inside her. Could he have finished cooking, set the dinner on the table, and left? Did he really think she'd invited him only to play chef? Her heart pounded at the thought, and she raced through both empty bedrooms before slipping through the living room and out the front door.

Rick sat in his Highlander, the engine off. Letty's relief was so great, and so unexpected, that it was all she could do to support her own weight as she walked across the gravel.

"Rick?" She opened the passenger door. "What're you doing out here?"

He'd changed. On the passenger seat his jeans and T-shirt were folded over his tennis shoes, a pile of hangers on top. Letty pushed the pile onto the floor and climbed inside the car, running one hand along the elbow of his suit jacket. He stared straight ahead, into the dark night.

"Hey," she tried again. "We're about to eat."

There was a rustle near the rose garden. Rick flicked his headlights on, but whatever it was had disappeared into the darkness; the garden was still and quiet. He cut the lights and turned to her.

"What am I doing here, Letty?" he asked quietly.

Letty took a long breath and exhaled. For the first time, she felt how close she was to losing him, and she shut her eyes against the feeling, swallowing hard. Silence rose like a wall between them, and she wanted to say something, but she couldn't think of what to say. The truth was, she had no idea what he was doing here; she only knew she didn't want him to leave.

"Look," Rick said finally. "You have a complicated situation in there. I'm not sure there's room for me."

"Of course there's room."

Her response came swift and certain, and he looked at her hard, as if trying to judge the accuracy of her rash statement. "Are you sure?"

Letty met his eyes. She knew the confirmation he sought, but she couldn't give it to him, not yet, not in the way he wanted. She just wasn't sure. Too much had happened too quickly. So she said the only thing she could think of to say. "I'm sure there's a hot plate of food with your name on it, and a seat for you beside me," she said, reaching for his hand. "Isn't that enough?"

Rick's gaze returned to the garden. After a long time, he nodded slowly, up and down and up again. "It's enough for tonight," he said.

But it wouldn't be enough for tomorrow. Tomorrow she would have to decide, he'd said without saying, and in the threat of his departure she felt an intense longing, wholly new, which she pushed away as she slipped out the door and walked around to the other side of the car. Opening his door, she took in his black suit, white shirt, and red silk tie. His dark hair smelled sweet, brushed back from his temples.

"Now, there's a Catholic," she said, pulling him out of the car.

"You sound like my mother."

Letty smiled. It was what Maria Elena always said, as if fashion and faith were somehow connected. But it wasn't about piety, she understood now; it was about respect. He'd dressed up for God and he'd dressed up for her, and she thought about how much her mother would like this Ricardo Lorenzo Moya, as she took his hand and pulled him up the steps and back into the house.

Wes's eyes followed them as they walked into the room. Everyone else was eating, plates balanced in their laps as they squeezed into the living room, but Wes's plate was still full. He'd been waiting. He lifted his glass now, as if to toast, but before he could get anyone's attention, Rick lifted his own glass and tapped it with a fork.

"To our hostess," Rick said, when everyone turned to look, "for a beautiful meal."

Letty was about to protest—the meal had been all him, after all—but he touched her lips with a soft fingertip, quieting her. He wouldn't take credit, not for any of it.

In the silence after the toast, Alex took a step into the center of the room. Letty looked up just in time to see Yesenia's hand drop from the small of his back. She had pushed him forward.

"I wanted to say something," he said, and everyone hushed, waiting. He looked nervous, standing in the middle of the crowded room, but when he glanced up and saw his father, his face broke into a smile.

"Yes!" Wes exclaimed, shooting forward and punching Alex on the shoulder. "Yes, yes, yes! I told you, didn't I?" He bounced around the room, whooping like a teenager, and Alex laughed, watching him.

"What?" Letty demanded. "What's going on?"

Wes stopped dancing, and Alex cleared his throat, running his hands over his rumpled dress shirt.

"I won," he said quietly.

"You what?" She couldn't believe he'd known, all this time, and hadn't said anything. The judging had been on the last day of school before Christmas break, and when he hadn't mentioned it, and then when he hadn't answered his father's calls, she'd assumed his project hadn't been chosen. But as she stood there, Alex beaming at her and then at his dad and then back at her again, she understood: this was a family announcement. He'd kept it from both of them, because he wanted to celebrate together.

"Are you serious?" she said. "That's amazing!"

"It's just the first step," he said and then grinned sheepishly. "But Mr. E said I'm the first freshman in his class to be lead scientist on a state entry. Ever."

"Of course you are!" Sara said. She'd slipped into the kitchen and returned with a second bottle of champagne, popping the top and refilling everyone's glasses. Into two empty glasses she poured an inch each for Alex and Yesenia, toasting them. "You know not one person in this room is surprised—but we're proud of you, Alex."

Letty nodded, lifting her glass. "We *are* proud of you."

Alex drank his champagne in one gulp and then turned the music all the way up, drowning the attention in noise. He'd somehow finished eating already, and he and Wes set down their plates and started to dance, a horribly awkward collection of elbows and shoulder bumps that Letty almost couldn't watch, but she had to watch, her love for her son expanding out of her heart and filling every corner of the small room. He'd done it. With Wes's help he'd won, and they were celebrating together. When the song was over, she saw Alex lean in to thank him. They were a team, and even if she didn't get any of the credit, Letty knew she was part of it too. She'd put him in that class, in that school; and now she'd moved into the district. He might have won with the help of his father, but she'd made it so that no one could take his victory away from him.

She ate slowly, leaning into Rick and watching the miniature dance floor fill up: first Alex and Wes, then Alex and Yesenia, then Carmen and Wes. Sara and Luna jumped in, Luna demanding to be spun until Sara fell onto the window seat, exhausted; then Luna clung to Alex's arm until he finally picked her up and continued where Sara had left off. Letty might have jumped in too, but just then Alex changed the music to something slow and, taking that as her cue to do the dishes, she ducked out of the room. When she turned around, she saw that

Carmen had followed her, her arms stacked high with the remaining plates.

"Thanks," Letty said, taking them.

Carmen gestured to the living room, where Alex leaned over Yesenia, their noses touching.

"No puedo verlos así." She couldn't watch them like that; at least that's what Letty thought she'd said.

"Me neither." Letty shuddered and closed the door, while Carmen set the dishes on the counter. A long strand of hair fell across Carmen's round face, and when she tucked it behind one ear in a quick, childish gesture, Letty realized just how young Carmen looked. Her skin was perfect, her face unlined even as she frowned.

"How old were you?" Letty asked, nodding toward the closed door, beyond which Yesenia danced.

"Catorce años," Carmen said, turning on the water. She pushed up her sleeves and added dish soap to the filling sink.

Letty frowned. Fourteen? Carmen couldn't have understood her question, she thought, and so she tried again: "When Yesenia was born? *¿Cuantos años tenías?"*

"Sí, catorce años," Carmen repeated. She met Letty's eyes briefly before submerging the stack of plates in the steaming water. Watching her, Letty tried to remembered herself at fourteen. She'd been a freshman at Mission Hills, a little girl alone at lunch, before she'd met Sara, before she'd met Wes, before she'd found her place in the completely foreign world she'd been dropped into.

"Wow," Letty said. "I was eighteen. And even then it felt impossible. My mom did everything."

A dark shadow passed over Carmen's face then, and Letty understood it had not been the same for her. She checked the door, to make sure it was closed.

"Es por eso que venimos aquí," she whispered, and Letty wished, as she often had, that her parents hadn't stopped speaking Spanish to her when she started kindergarten. It took complete focus to decode Carmen's words, and still she wasn't sure she understood.

"No entiendo," she said. "What do you mean?"

Carmen returned to the sink. The water was hot enough to scald her hands, and Letty saw the skin of her inner wrists pink as she moved them in and out of the water, reaching for one plate and then another.

"Estaban locos," she said finally, and then continued softly, her words in rhythm with the washing. Letty didn't catch every word, but she understood that Carmen's parents had been furious when she'd gotten pregnant. Falling down drunk the day she'd brought Yesenia home, her father had hurt the baby. *Casi se murió,* Letty heard: she almost died. But Carmen had taken her baby and run, wrapping tight the tiny, broken legs and riding two buses and a train to the border, where she'd crossed the river on foot. After that, she'd hitched rides all the way to Stanford Hospital, because someone had told her it was the best. The doctors there had saved her daughter's life.

"How did you even survive?" Letty asked, after she'd gotten over the shock of the completely normal-looking superhero standing in her kitchen. She remembered the empty road outside Tijuana, the casket-ridden fence; tried to imagine a fourteen-year-old torn up from birth, walking the road with a newborn. She couldn't. Her experience had been the extreme opposite, Maria Elena taking care of absolutely everything and leaving nothing for Letty to do. "How did you even feed yourself?"

The stack of clean plates dripped from the counter to the floor. Carmen glanced at the door again. She looked nervous.

"Trabajaba en el hospital," she whispered. A doctor had arranged for her to work the graveyard shift cleaning the hospital, and she had the same job still. She cleaned that hospital like it was the palace of the pope, she said, for saving her tiny baby.

Carmen stepped over the growing puddle on the floor and grabbed a dish towel, starting to dry. Letty had done nothing but listen, and she was suddenly embarrassed, standing in her own kitchen while Carmen did all the work. She found a second towel and grabbed the pile of utensils all at once, racing through the rest of the drying and putting the clean dishes away in the cabinets.

When everything was done, Carmen folded the dish towel and set it on the counter. She looked at the closed door and then back to Letty like she wanted to say something, but Letty understood without her having to say. Yesenia didn't know. Not any of it.

"You don't need to worry," she said. "I won't say anything."

"*Te lo agradesco,*" Carmen said and gave her a hug before pushing the kitchen door open.

In the living room, the music was still slow. Rick held Luna, twirling her like a baby, and Alex and Yesenia sat in the window seat. Color from the Christmas lights mottled their faces. Alex leaned down until his forehead touched Yesenia's, and they both closed their eyes at the same time.

Letty sighed. "What are we going to do about them?"

Carmen said nothing. There was nothing to say. Alex and Yesenia were happy, and in love, and if there was a time when either mother could have stopped it from happening, that time had long since passed.

Letty slipped down the hall and into the bathroom, wanting to avoid Rick and Wes for just a moment longer. In front of the mirror she took her time, applying lip gloss and adjusting her hair, and when she finally opened the door, Wes stood outside, leaning against the wall.

For a second she thought he was waiting for the bathroom, but when she stepped aside to let him through, he didn't move. He'd been waiting for her. In his hands were both their champagne glasses, refilled to the brim. She took a long sip and braced herself for whatever he'd come to say.

"I feel like you've been avoiding me all night," he said. He took a sip of his drink, and before she could think of how to respond, he pointed to a photo on the wall in front of him. "God, he was cute, wasn't he?"

It was a photograph of Alex as a toddler, drinking from one of Enrique's birdbaths. The bright blue sky and Alex's round face were reflected on the surface of the water, his joyful expression doubled, and in the background Letty laughed, head back, mouth open.

"He was," Letty said. "Hey—congrats on the win."

Wes shook his head. "It was all Alex."

"That's not what he says," Letty said. "For weeks I've been subjected to the intricacies of your brilliance over dinner."

"He gives me more credit than I deserve."

Letty took another sip of her drink. "Welcome to my life."

Wes looked at her curiously, waiting for her to explain, but instead she drank her champagne in one long gulp and, in a surge of alcohol-induced courage, pulled him into the bedroom.

"Sit down," she said, gesturing to the bed. She should have done this a long, long time ago. "I have something for you."

From the shoe box under the bed she retrieved a fat envelope. It was covered in dirty fingerprints, and Letty realized all at once how Alex had found his father. She pointed to the marks, but Wes saw only his name and address on the front, where she'd written it over a decade before. He took the envelope and ripped it open along the edge.

Inside was a collection of photographs from the first year of Alex's life. She'd put them in chronological order, with the date and a description written on the back of each one. For months after his birth she'd been meticulous, and she saw in her handwriting how much she meant to tell Wes—how she'd been trying, in her own impossible way, to explain. She hoped Wes saw it too.

He picked up the first one. It was a wrinkled mug shot of Alex in a blue and pink striped hat, taken in the hospital, just minutes after he was born. Even then, he looked exactly like his father. Wes turned the picture over, unable to look. On the back she'd written the time and place of his birth, his weight, and his Apgar scores.

"He was perfect," Wes said, and Letty didn't know if he was talking about the picture or about his scores, but she nodded, agreeing.

"He was."

Wes flipped the picture back over and held it just inches from his face, as if trying to catch a whiff of Alex's newborn smell.

"I miss him," he whispered. "At night I dream about him, six years old with skinned knees, crying, and then he becomes one of my patients, dying, and I wake up sweating. Every night a different age."

It made Letty feel sick, what she'd taken away from him, but there was nothing she could do, no way to bring back Alex at six, eight, ten, twelve. So instead she sat down beside Wes and started at the beginning, talking him quietly through each photograph. She told him about the way Alex had lunged at his first bite of rice cereal, about the fall after his first step, and how he didn't try again for another month. She told him everything she could remember, but there was so much she didn't know, and she wished Maria Elena had been there to fill in the gaps. Maria Elena knew everything.

When she finished, Wes put the photographs carefully back in the envelope and looked up, holding her gaze.

"Maybe we should try," he said quietly. "Maybe it's the best thing—for all of us."

From the living room, Christmas music drifted down the hall. She imagined a burning fire, a big tree in a big window, the kind of home and family she'd wanted as a child, long before she'd gone to Mission Hills, or met Wes, or had Alex. She'd loved Wes. It wasn't a far stretch to imagine that she could love him again. They could have a good life together. And it would be the right thing to do for Alex; it would make up, if only a little bit, for the landslide of wrongs she'd done throughout his short life.

But just then the music turned off, and when she looked up, Rick stood in the doorway, a sleeping Luna in his arms.

"I'm sorry," he said, startled. "I didn't mean to interrupt."

Luna slipped from his elbows to his forearms, and he jostled her up. Her head flopped back, mouth gaping open.

"You're not interrupting," Letty said, jumping up, and even though she didn't look at Wes, she could imagine the expression on his face—wounded, incredulous, confused. She pulled down the covers on Luna's bed, and when she turned back, neither Rick nor Wes had moved. The muscles in Rick's arms were taut under the weight of her daughter; on the bed, Wes sat with knuckles white, clutching the envelope of photos.

Oh, God, what was she doing? Looking at them both, she was reminded of her mother in Mexico, buried in feathers and glass and the weight of having to choose. Letty had to choose now too, and either way she would lose.

Taking Luna out of Rick's arms, she tucked her into bed and pulled the covers up tight. From the living room she heard Sara calling her, trying to say good-bye, and she looked at Rick, and then Wes, and then Rick again.

"I guess that's it," she said, finally, escaping into the hall. "I think this party's officially over."

They followed her onto the front porch, where she said good-bye to everyone at once. When the last car had pulled onto the main road, Alex kissed her cheek and went to bed, but Letty didn't want to go inside. The cold night air was numbing, and she sank down onto the steps.

Christmas morning was only a few hours away.

She had stockings to fill, presents to wrap. It would be no use to try to sleep now. Leaning against the railing, she took a long breath and closed her eyes, listening to the cars in the distance, and then to the barn owls, and then, for a long time after, the quiet.

8

Alex and Yesenia were still high on Christmas, draped in new clothes and shoes and backpacks, when they met at the top of the pedestrian bridge on January 5, the first day back at school. They would tell their mothers what they'd done after Yesenia was settled in and doing well, when it would be too late to pull her out. So for now, the secret was still theirs alone. Yesenia tried to hide her smile, just as Alex had tried to do on his first day at Mission Hills. But her happiness escaped her eyes, those deep black orbs taking in the sky and then Alex and then the sky again, and in her gaze he felt her joy envelop him and wondered if the sky could feel it too.

She looked beautiful. Carmen had bought her a fuzzy pink sweater for Christmas, tight in all the right places, a belt with a symbol of some fancy brand that Alex could never remember, and dark jeans long enough to cover up most of her orthopedic shoes. She'd fixed her hair the way Alex liked best, long and straight with the ends curled under and the red stripe in front held up by a diamond-studded pin, so that he could kiss her without getting a mouthful of hair. He kissed her now, and she smelled good, different—as if she'd guessed the perfume cloud at Mission Hills, though probably she'd just gotten something new in her stocking.

"Last kiss," Yesenia said. "At school I'm your cousin, remember?"

Alex frowned. "Only if anyone asks. We'll give it a few days, and if no one asks, I'm telling everyone you're my girlfriend. I don't want my friends hitting on you."

"They won't hit on me."

"You'll see," Alex said. "The guys here have this thing for pretty girls."

Yesenia smiled and took his hand, and they started the long walk to school. They talked about Christmas, Yesenia describing her gifts and the movie they'd seen, on Carmen's first Christmas off, ever; Alex told her about the ecstatic mayhem that had ensued when he and Luna had pulled the pretend plane tickets out of their stockings. As they got closer to the school, their conversation shifted to Mission Hills, and Alex told Yesenia everything he could think of: where he sat in Mr. Everett's class and the latest developments in his science project (he'd gone to the lab with his father three times over break) and who his greatest competition was and also that Mr. Everett disallowed competition; he told her what they had just finished reading in English and what they were about to start and about the kids in his classes, Nathan and Bobby and Sophia, who he'd already decided would be her best friend—they both liked salt water, wasn't that enough?—and about the piles of homework and the weight of the textbooks.

"You can share my locker," he said. "And I'll carry your books." It was the first thing he'd thought of when he hatched the "Yesenia takes Mission Hills" plan, that she would share his classes and he'd carry her books.

As they rounded the corner, Mission Hills came into view all at once, white and imposing, the sun like a spotlight above. Yesenia stopped walking and studied it without moving.

"Are you nervous?"

She shook her head no. "Not nervous." She smiled and squeezed his hand, then let it go quickly, remembering. "Just happy."

Alex slipped his forefinger into a belt loop of her jeans, holding her in a protective way. He was happy too. They'd done this big, brave thing, and they were safe now, and together, and they would be together every day of high school and then—well, every day after that too. Pull-

ing gently, he led her forward, up the long walk and columned staircase
and into the great front hall.

It was early. They had come for zero period—Yesenia was to wait in
the library—but the school was alive already, and Alex found himself
again surprised by the commotion. A group of Mr. Everett's students
leaned against the lockers, talking about their Christmas vacations in
loud, animated voices. He was about to say something to Yesenia, com-
ment on the earliness, the energy, that this was one of the first things
he'd noticed to be different about the school and did she?—but when
he looked at her he saw she was focused on something else: a man in a
suit walking briskly toward them. Mr. Daniels.

"Hello, Alex."

He was surprised the principal knew his name but also not—it was
no secret he was one of Mr. Everett's favorite students, and more than
one teacher at the school remembered his mother too. Alex didn't know
how long the principal had worked at the school, but he certainly
looked old enough to have known Letty as a student.

But Mr. Daniels wasn't looking at Alex; he was looking at Yesenia.
Standing just a few feet from her, he bent at the waist to study her beautiful, blushing face.

"You must be Yesenia Lopez-Vazquez," he said, nodding to a security
guard standing by the door, and for just a moment Alex thought they
were both part of some welcoming party, to let her know how happy
they all were to have her there, what great care they would take of her,
that they would never ever let happen to her what had happened at her
last school.

But there was nothing warm about the way they looked from one to
the other, principal to guard and back again, and with a sinking feeling
in his stomach Alex realized it was wrong, all wrong, and also that it was
too late: Mr. Daniels was walking away, Yesenia trailing behind. Alex
turned to follow, and the guard led them through the office and down
a long hall, to a closed door.

Mr. Daniels opened it.

Inside, a table. At the table, two uniformed police officers, waiting
for them.

Four

1

Letty followed a probation officer down a long, dark corridor. Behind them a heavy door clicked shut, and in front another stood tall and locked. The PO swiped an ID badge and the door opened, leading to another dark hall and then another. The clicking of the locks made her head spin; she wanted to sit down, but there was nowhere to sit and the PO kept walking. If she didn't keep up she'd be trapped between the doors indefinitely, unable to go forward or back. She concentrated on her steps, swallowed the bile that rose in her throat and mixed with the smell of sweat and soiled carpet, until the final door opened and she stepped into the light of the intake unit.

Outside the window, a police car pulled into a courtyard. A steel gate rolled down behind it, so that the car was contained on all sides before an officer opened the car door. The handcuffed boy who got out of the back wasn't Alex. Alex had been there hours already, hours that Letty had spent waiting in the lobby for permission to see him. She paused at the window, pulled in by the scene playing out in the courtyard—the boy was pressed up against the car now, an officer holding him in place with his knee—but the PO barked for her to keep walking, and she was led around a desk and along a row of thick glass cells. A fat teenager with buzzed hair lay on his back on a wooden bench, his flesh pressed up against the glass, and Letty thought of the animals at the zoo, thick-skinned hippos and rhinos and elephants lazing against the viewing windows. The boy didn't lift his head as she passed, but he tracked her just as any one of those animals would have, with neither interest nor self-consciousness. It wasn't his first time here.

They paused in front of another locked door; on the other side Letty stepped into a cavernous, horseshoe-shaped room with steep steps down like an amphitheater. At the bottom, lines of empty chairs faced a dark television screen. From a cluster of desks at the top, officers monitored the movements of everyone in the room. The PO pointed to a table in the corner and left her there as he went to knock on a row of doors. One at a time, boys in navy blue pants and matching T-shirts came out to get their shoes, then disappeared back inside to put them on. At one room the PO lingered, exchanging words with whoever was inside. Letty held her breath, expecting it to be Alex. But instead the PO yelled something about him declining to speak, and a man with a clipboard and a mental health badge turned and left the room.

They were coming out now. Shoes on, shirts tucked in, heads down. They walked with their hands behind their backs as if they were hand-cuffed, and it wasn't until the first one passed that Letty saw there was nothing actually holding their wrists together. It must have been re-quired, though, because when a boy in the middle of the line lifted a finger to scratch his collarbone, a PO shouted an order and his hand immediately flew back into place.

Some of the boys walked lazily, others stiffly. Watching, Letty could tell by the amount of fear in their eyes how long they'd been there, and whether or not they'd been there before. A boy with a swagger and loosely held hands swerved wide, as close to the officers as he dared before turning and walking down the steps to the chairs below. Behind the desk a black woman with short white hair called out after him: "You going to walk right by without giving me anything?" He turned at the sound of her voice and flashed a lopsided grin. "That's right, you'd bet-ter smile."

"I've known him since he was thirteen," the woman said, and it took a moment for Letty to realize she was talking to her. "I told him I'd come visit him on the outside—that he doesn't have to get locked up to see me."

The boy took his seat with the others and stared at the blank screen. From where Letty sat she could see only the back of his head, but she could tell by the way he held his shoulders that he was smiling, and for the first time since she'd received the call that morning, Letty felt the pressure in her chest ease. But then all at once there was Alex, the last of the long line of boys, his eyes angry and scared. Letty's stomach heaved. She covered her mouth and closed her eyes and didn't open them until he was seated at the table across from her. His chair scraped the linoleum as he pushed it in; she heard his clenched fists fall on the tabletop.

In the waiting room she'd thought of a million things she wanted to say, every variation of plea and accusation, but opening her eyes, she couldn't remember any of them. There was a rough patch on his forehead, a layer of skin missing, and Letty imagined him being pushed by an officer or a roommate against the cinder-block walls. The image made her stomach lurch all over again. She swallowed hard and forced herself to speak.

"How are you?" she asked, stupidly, and the row of boys below sniggered. Alex said nothing. He wouldn't look at her, and Letty felt her fear bubble suddenly into anger. She pushed her chair closer and whispered across the space between them.

"What were you thinking, Alex? You can't just go breaking into computer systems and enrolling kids in Mission Hills who don't belong there."

She felt the hypocrisy in her words even before Alex looked up, his glare challenging her, forcing her to remember. He'd stood by her side in Sara's kitchen as she'd filled out a phony lease, waited in line at the DMV to change her address to a zip code she couldn't afford even in her dreams. She'd modeled all of it for him, the rationalizing and the carefully calculated action. The only difference was that he'd gotten caught.

"There were security cameras in all the halls," she said. "They have everything on tape. Even if we had money to fight the charges, we'd never win."

Alex exhaled. His posture was defeated; he'd known before she said it that he didn't have a chance.

"Why are they charging me with burglary?" he asked. "I didn't take anything."

"It doesn't matter. You broke in with the intention to commit another crime. So it still counts as burglary."

"But I didn't break in!"

"Quiet!" From the corner a PO barked. Letty startled at the gruff reminder, but Alex didn't blink. Only hours in and he was used to it, a fact that made Letty want to take his hand and run. *He shouldn't be here,* she thought, *not Alex,* but behind the desk the door slammed shut again, the lock clicking loudly. They weren't going anywhere.

Alex leaned toward her, his voice low this time: "I didn't break in," he said again. "I had a key."

"Well, you weren't supposed to have a key."

At the bottom of the steps the group of boys stood as one and filed out the door. She watched them go, looking into their faces as they passed and trying to imagine each of their mothers sitting in her place. Would they think, as she did, that their boys didn't belong here? That they weren't like these other boys? Maybe. But most of the young men who walked past had the empty, wandering look of the motherless kids she'd grown up with at the Landing, kids whose mothers had overdosed or been locked up or otherwise couldn't be pressured to care. Alex *was* different in this way, just as she'd been different, and she knew from experience that it made the pain of screwing up more acute.

Only the white-haired woman behind the desk remained in the room. She stood up and moved to the chair farthest away from where they sat, an act filled with so much kindness Letty felt her eyes well. She clenched her teeth and waited for the feeling to pass before turning back to Alex.

"Why did you do it?" she whispered. "I don't understand. You see her every day after school."

Alex lifted his eyebrows in surprise. He thought he had been getting away with seeing Yesenia after school, but Letty had known. She just hadn't known what to do about it. He shrugged his shoulders but didn't say anything.

"You couldn't wait until three? Really? You had to risk all this?"

Alex lurched forward suddenly, shushing her in a way that sounded almost like a hiss. "Stop saying that. I didn't do it to see her."

"So why did you do it?"

Alex slouched back in his chair, all the effort it took to hold everything inside seeping out in one long exhale. "She was getting beat up, okay? And she wouldn't tell her mom, and I didn't know what else to do."

The words stunned Letty, even though she knew they shouldn't. Of course a girl like Yesenia wouldn't be safe at Bayshore High. No one was safe there; it was why she'd worked so hard to get Alex out.

"Why didn't you come to me?"

Alex met her eyes, and she remembered: he had come to her— begging and tormented, the morning after Wes returned. But she'd been so distracted she'd pushed it away, not understanding his urgency. "You did come to me. You fucking came to me, and I ignored you." The weight of it hit her all at once, and she folded forward onto the table, her cheek pressed against the smooth plastic. "God, I'm sorry. I'm so sorry."

"Stop it," Alex said. The harshness in his voice pulled her back to sitting. "I did this. I broke in and I enrolled Yesenia and"—he ran his finger over the scrape on his forehead, remembering—"I talked back to an officer." His eyes filled. Curling in his bottom lip, he bit down, trying to stop the tears that wouldn't be stopped. "I don't know what's happening to me."

Alex bent over onto the table, as Letty had done only a moment before. He was silent, but his chest rose and fell as the sadness overwhelmed him. Letty put both her hands on his shoulders.

"I miss my nana," he whispered, the words barely audible, and Letty remembered Luna on the back of the airport chair, wailing. Alex's voice was deeper, but the heartbreak was just the same.

"I miss her too," she sighed. "But we're okay. You're okay."

"I'm not."

"You *are*. You might have done something stupid, but you did it because you thought it was right. You did it for Yesenia."

Alex began to cry in earnest, not even trying to contain himself, and Letty glanced nervously around the room, thinking about what the others would do to her skinny, crying boy after she left. But the room was empty now. They were all out somewhere, in school or walking the grounds, and so she sat quietly and listened to him cry, stroking his back until all the tears were gone. Gently, she felt the back of his neck for temperature.

When she looked up, the white-haired woman stood beside her.

"Time's up, Mama."

Letty kissed the back of Alex's head and then reached for the hand the woman offered, allowing herself to be pulled up and led to the door. When she looked back, Alex sat tall in his chair, face wiped clean and hands behind his back, waiting for direction.

She paused at the door. "Do you want Wes to come? He wanted me to ask."

"You told him?"

"Of course I told him."

Alex shook his head no.

"Okay. I'll let him know."

"And, Mom? Tell him I'm sorry. And Carmen too. Tell her it was my idea—that it's all my fault we're in here. Will you tell her?"

Letty wanted to go back to him, to squeeze out the guilt and despair, to hold his head up high on his shoulders, but the door was already open, Letty being led through.

"I will," she said. "I love you, Alex. Remember."

The door slammed shut behind her, and Alex was gone.

Letty sat with Luna on the steps of Courtyard Terrace, waiting for Carmen to come home. In the parking lot, two girls drew hopscotch squares with fat chalk, and Luna wandered over every few minutes to see what they were doing, hopping once, twice, and then remembering. Guiltily, she raced back to her mother's side, slunk down on the steps, and waited, her lips in a thin, grim line.

It was late afternoon when Carmen finally came. The smile on her face as she climbed out of her car confirmed Letty's fear: she didn't know anything. Yesenia hadn't called. She hadn't given the police her mother's phone number—she probably hadn't even given them her name. Everyone was afraid of *la migra,* and from what she knew about Yesenia, Letty was sure she would do anything she could to protect her mother. Letty felt a fresh wave of nausea, thinking about Yesenia and Alex within the dark maze of locking doors, all alone.

When she saw the expression on Letty's face, Carmen's smile faded. She asked something loud and fear-filled in Spanish that Letty didn't catch, but someone in a nearby apartment heard. A head popped out of a doorway; Letty felt ears all around the crowded complex, straining to listen. She shook her head no—*not here*—and climbed the stairs to Carmen's apartment, waiting as she unlocked the door and pushed it open.

Inside the apartment, Yesenia was everywhere. Classwork framed on bookshelves, report cards taped to the refrigerator, photos smiling down from every wall—her absence was like a living, breathing thing, stealing the oxygen from underneath Letty's nose, and in the time it took her to walk from the front door to the living room, she felt herself dizzying from asphyxiation.

"*¿Dónde está mi hija?*"

Where was her daughter? Panic raised her voice.

Luna reached up, and Letty lifted her into her arms. Like a lemur, she clung to her mother's neck as she crossed the room and opened the window.

"They're in trouble."

Carmen's hands flew to her stomach, and Letty thought she was going to be sick, but then she saw her mime the round stomach of pregnancy.

Letty shook her head. "No. Not that. With the police."

"*La policía?*"

Disbelief warped Carmen's soft features into hard lines. It wasn't possible, her expression said. Yesenia wasn't that kind of kid. And neither was Alex. Letty set Luna down on the carpet, needing all her energy to explain. So many of the legal terms she barely knew in English, and it took more than one try to explain everything. They'd broken into the school in the middle of the night; they'd enrolled Yesenia in the computer system using Alex's address; it had all been recorded on the security cameras.

"It's a wobbler," Letty finished. "That's what the PO said. They could be charged with a misdemeanor or a felony, and just because it's recorded as a felony now doesn't mean it won't be lessened, or dropped altogether."

Letty couldn't tell if Carmen understood this last part, but she could tell she'd stopped trying. With great effort she walked to the couch, collapsing onto the lopsided cushions. Luna ran to her, crawling up onto the couch and covering Carmen like a blanket. It was too much, to learn the loss of her daughter with someone else's daughter in her arms, the touch of young skin, the smell of tangled hair, the steady, shallow breathing; she pulled a pillow over her face and began to cry. Luna's thin body shook as she squeezed Carmen tighter.

On the other side of the room, Letty stood at the window, watching clouds gather in the sky. It had been less than two weeks since her Christmas party, all of them toasting and together, but it felt like a lifetime ago. Everything had changed. Alex and Yesenia were locked up. Carmen didn't have the language skills or the documentation to even visit her daughter. Letty understood for the first time just how different their lives had been. All her life Letty had felt like an outsider, but Carmen *was* an outsider. The laws of the land that existed to keep Letty safe, to give her a chance at success—even if they didn't always work— these laws didn't apply to Carmen. She was beyond alone. She was invisible.

Letty pulled herself away from the window. The room was quiet, Luna's body still. Searching the bedroom, she found a blanket and brought it to the couch, wrapping it tightly around Carmen and extracting Luna from her arms.

She turned out the light.

"Call me if you need anything," Letty whispered as she turned to go. She scrawled her number on a piece of paper. "I'll bring her home. I promise."

Carmen turned over to face the wall, her assent barely audible.

All the lights were on at Letty's house, a tiny flame against a dark horizon. At first she thought she'd forgotten to turn them off, having left in a rush, but when she pulled Luna up the driveway she saw both Wes's and Rick's cars, parked side by side. She hadn't spoken to either one of them since the Christmas party, but when she got the call about Alex she'd called them both immediately, and now they were here. Before, it would have sent her into a panic, seeing their cars together, but she'd exhausted all her emotions visiting Alex, and then Carmen. Numbly, she followed Luna up the stairs.

The house smelled like ginger. Not the intense, sticky sweetness of Rick's ginger syrup, but something hot and wholesome. She smelled onions too, and carrots. In the kitchen Rick stirred a pot of soup; Wes sat at the table, blowing on the top of a shallow bowl and talking into his cell phone.

When Luna saw Rick she burst into tears. From the moment Letty had picked her up from school she'd sealed her lips in a straight line, holding on to her mother and then Carmen in a display of strength Letty hadn't recognized until she collapsed into Rick's arms. He lifted her up, pressing her face tight into his neck and rocking her in rhythm with his stirring.

"Shh, shh, shh, shh," he hushed. He pointed to Wes and then put a finger to his lips. "Wes will get him out."

"Are you sure?" she sob-whispered.

"I'm sure," Rick said, but when he looked at Letty she could tell he was not sure. He was just as scared as she was. Turning back to his soup, he dipped a finger in the pot, rubbing it on Luna's lips like orange lipstick. She licked it off, opening her mouth for more.

Letty sat down at the table. *Who are you talking to?* she mouthed.

Mr. Everett, Wes mouthed back. He was nodding slowly, tapping his spoon against his bowl. "I know," he said. Letty listened to Wes's half of the conversation. "He is, thank you," and "Yes, I'll tell her," and then, after a long silence, he confirmed something on Thursday and said good-bye.

With a sigh, he set down the phone.

"Wow," Rick said, filling three bowls of soup and then sitting down beside Wes. "That sounded intense."

"He feels terrible," Wes said wearily.

"Well, he should." It was Mr. Everett who had alerted the principal, when he'd realized that not only had his keys gone missing but his computer had gone from powered off to on in the dead of night.

"He never would have made the call if he'd known it was Alex," Wes said. "He would have taken care of it himself."

"That doesn't help us now."

"That's what I told him."

Rick placed a bowl of soup in front of Letty. Despite a full day of nausea and feeling like she would never be able to eat anything ever again, she lifted a spoonful of the steaming liquid to her lips. Traveling down, it warmed her mouth, her throat, her chest, and she took another spoonful, and then a third.

Wes picked up his bowl and drank the rest of his soup before continuing. "He'll talk to the principal, and he'll do everything he can to block an expulsion. He wanted me to tell you that. We have to be there on Thursday at eight A.M. for a meeting."

"Alex too?"

Wes nodded. There was a long pause, each of them counting the days until Thursday and trying to determine the likelihood Alex would be released by then.

"He'll be out," Letty said, trying to sound more confident than she felt. "By law he has to be in front of a judge within seventy-two hours."

Letty glanced up at Rick, who squeezed Luna and nodded. He would pick her up in the morning and take her to school. Letty didn't even have to ask. She felt a flood of relief as Rick stood to refill Luna's bowl, and then Wes's.

"Thanks," Wes said. He took the soup and met Rick's eyes, and Letty felt something pass between the two men that hadn't been there at Christmas. Whether they had talked about her before she'd arrived she didn't know, but what she did know was this: none of it mattered anymore.

2

It felt like being inside a movie Maria Elena wouldn't let him watch. The dark, winding corridors, the armed escorts, the bored, lecturing judge. *Statistics say you'll offend again,* he said: *don't.* The way the judge said it, Alex knew he didn't actually care if he did or if he didn't. The judge was simply reading a script, saying the things that were expected of him, and Alex did the same, *Yes, Your Honor, yes, Your Honor, I understand, Your Honor.* In the gallery, Letty sat on her hands, the muscles in her jaw clenched. From across the room Alex could almost feel the dull ache in her jaw growing as she willed herself to keep her mouth closed.

When it was over, and the next court date was set, Letty burst through the low, swinging door and grabbed Alex by the hand. His probation officer wanted a word, but Letty dragged him toward the exit.

"You can say whatever you want to say under the clear blue sky," she told him, and both Alex and the officer had to skip to keep up, barely making it into the elevator before she pressed the button to close the doors.

The outside light shocked Alex's dilated eyes. There hadn't been a window anywhere in the entire unit; in bed at night, he had lain on his back, blowing a current of air over his upper lip and imagining a breeze. To calm himself he'd recited the birds in alphabetical order, and now here they were to greet him: a hungry band of rock doves, the incessant knock of a woodpecker in a tall tree. He watched a red-rumped house finch dance around a scraggly nest as the officer reviewed the terms of his release.

When he asked if they had any questions, Letty demanded Alex's backpack.

"He's a straight-A student," she said, and even though it wasn't true anymore—he'd been suspended for five days, and would likely be expelled—he felt a tiny glimmer of hope, that the mistake he'd made, as enormous as it was, might not be the end of life as he knew it.

"They'll have it at intake," the officer said, guiding them back through the main building. "You have to sign for his release."

At the desk, Alex took the mesh bag they handed him. It smelled like Yesenia's perfume, and his stomach lurched, remembering them pressed together in the back of the police car, her long hair fluttering wildly in the blast of the heater and Yesenia unable to push it from her face, her wrists locked behind her back. She'd been pulled from the car first, and if she'd tried to turn around, to wave or whisper, Alex hadn't seen it. Watching her being led into the girls' unit, he'd folded in half and heaved onto the hard plastic floor.

With relief, he watched his mother retrieve a change of clothes from her oversize purse. He couldn't have survived putting the Yesenia-perfumed clothes back on. She thrust them into his hands and nodded to the bathroom.

"Go change," she said. "I'll fill this out."

When he returned, Letty was wearing his backpack. She'd stuck his release forms into the round outside pocket, where the water bottle should have gone.

"Ready?" she asked and turned to walk away, but Alex shook his head no.

"I want to see Yesenia."

Her name stuck in the back of his throat, a great ball of sadness that made it hard to swallow, and even harder to breathe.

The young woman behind the desk didn't look up from her computer. "You talking about that little girl came in with you?"

Alex watched his mother's eyebrows lift. He stepped forward to respond, before his mother could.

"Yesenia Lopez-Vazquez," he said. "Can I see her? Do you know when she's going to court?"

"I know everything," the woman said. She adjusted her badge and pulled a nail file from a drawer, still not looking up. "But unless you're her papa, I can't tell you anything."

Letty made a noise of exasperation. She'd spent the past seventy-two hours calling everyone she could think of, she'd told Alex, but hadn't gotten any further than this. Now she put both hands on the woman's desk, demanding. "Look," she said. "It's a public courthouse. No one can stop us from sitting there all day long."

"You go sit there, then," the woman said. Her eyes darted to the guard by the door, a glance that said something specific and nothing good. He whistled low, and she nodded. "You go ahead and sit, sit, sit."

"What? What happened to her?" Everything he'd been trying not to think about hit Alex at once; the girls behind these walls, most of them locked up for violence, and Yesenia among them. Anger and frustration propelled him toward the desk, his face so close he could smell the grease in the woman's hair. In one swift motion, Letty pulled him back. When he looked up there was genuine fear in her eyes, and he thought about what the judge had said about him reoffending. From the moment he'd been arrested he'd felt like a different person. The worst had already happened. There was no reason to try to be good ever again.

Letty looked at him hard, as if searching for the Alex she knew. He stepped back and closed his eyes, trying to calm himself.

"I'm sorry," he said softly. "I apologize."

The woman looked up then, surprised, and she might have said something, if another PO hadn't stepped out of the storage room just then. Alex recognized her from his unit—she'd been working the desk when Letty came to visit, and she held his mother's gaze as she led Alex swiftly to the door.

"She isn't here anymore," she said quietly. She pushed the door open and stepped outside. "I'm sorry. ICE came for her days ago."

*   *   *

Alex didn't even have to ask her. Letty ran so fast to the parking lot that he struggled to keep up. Clicking Rick's car unlocked, she jumped in and backed out even before Alex had closed the passenger door, one eye on the rearview mirror and the other on Alex's phone. She'd looked up the address for the Immigration and Customs Enforcement office in San Francisco and was trying to find directions as she pulled out onto the road.

The street around the courthouse was clogged, food trucks lining up on the curb and pedestrians crossing the traffic for snacks. Letty wove in and out of the lanes without ever taking her eyes off the directions.

"Where is she?" Alex asked. Letty's urgency made him start to panic. "What's happening?"

She thrust the phone into his hands and accelerated onto the freeway. "Look up immigration attorneys," she said. "We need one today."

"But we don't have any money."

"We have money." Unless his mother had won the lottery in the three days he'd been locked up, that wasn't true, but Alex didn't argue. It *was* true that they were at that very moment driving a new-model Highlander and would go home to their house in Mission Heights. They might not have money, but they were now the kind of people who could find it in an emergency. And this was an emergency.

Alex typed *immigration attorney SF* into the search field. "There are millions in San Francisco." He held up the phone while Letty scanned the list.

"Try the first and keep going until you find someone available now."

Before he could dial, the phone began to vibrate in his hand. He didn't recognize the number. "Someone's calling."

Letty nodded, and Alex accepted the call, holding it up to her ear.

"Hello?" A noise came through the phone, loud and high-pitched, that Alex could hear all the way from where he sat. "Hello?" his mother said, louder. "Hello? Who is this?"

She grabbed the phone and pressed it harder into her ear, so that whatever it was the person said next Alex couldn't hear.

"Slow down," Letty said, and then she said something in Spanish, and Alex knew it was Carmen.

He shook Letty's shoulder. "What's happening?"

Letty swatted his hand away, a look of complete concentration on her face. She was in the fast lane, but they were slowing down. Honking cars passed her on the right. Without looking over her shoulder she changed lanes, one and two and then three, slowing until she sat idling on the gravel shoulder. She said something else in Spanish that Alex couldn't understand, and then hung up the phone.

Leaning her head onto the steering wheel, she set off her own horn, but she didn't lift her head.

Alex pulled her back.

"Tell me what's happening. What's going on?"

"Yesenia called Carmen."

A flood of joy was replaced almost immediately by fear. "How is she? Where is she?"

Letty exhaled, long and slow.

"I have no idea how she is," she said finally. "She's in Virginia."

He'd taken a horrific situation and made it exponentially worse. Instead of being bullied, Yesenia had been picked up by *la migra*. All the way back to their house, Alex fought the urge to throw himself out the car door and into oncoming traffic. He'd done this to her; it was one hundred percent his fault. Through a silent dinner he tortured himself by thinking about all the things he should have done instead: he should have made her tell her mother what was happening to her; he should have told Letty, or Wes, or Mr. Everett. He should have insisted they move back to the Landing, so that he could go to school at Bayshore High with her. He tried to imagine himself walking through the low-ceilinged, dirty halls of the cinder-block buildings, Yesenia's protector. But he'd loved his science class almost as much as he loved Yesenia. As much as he wanted to help her, he'd never seriously considered giving up his education.

And now Yesenia was gone, and he'd lost it anyway.

*　*　*

At seven the next morning, Wes knocked on the door. He was wearing a suit and tie. Alex had rarely seen him in anything but scrubs, and it made him even more nervous, the care his father had taken to prepare himself for their meeting with Principal Daniels. Avoiding his father's eyes, Alex tucked in the too-small white shirt he hadn't worn since the last day of eighth grade and ducked around his embrace, sinking into the backseat of Wes's car.

He stared out the window as Wes drove them all to Mission Hills and parked in front of the school. The first bell had already rung, and Alex kept his head down as he led his parents through the halls to the principal's office, afraid to see anyone he knew.

In the office, Letty signed in and the secretary ushered them into the waiting room. Alex was surprised to hear Mr. Everett's voice. He should have been in class, but instead he'd left his students to work alone. *Jeremy's lead scientist this hour,* Alex pictured him saying as he walked out the door. Sadness lodged in his throat as he imagined all the other kids in the classroom, hard at work on their projects without him.

The door to the principal's office was cracked open; his parents sat side by side on the bench in the waiting room, but Alex got as close as he could to the door without being seen.

His teacher was pleading. Before he could make out any of the words, he could hear it in his voice. Alex leaned closer, listening.

"It's an expellable offense," Mr. Daniels said. "More than one, actually. Theft, breaking and entering, tampering with data. I just don't see how I can *not* expel him, politically."

"What do you mean *politically?* This isn't about politics. It's about a kid's future. A good kid."

"I believe you," Mr. Daniels said. "But I've been fielding calls from concerned parents all week—and most of them are parents of kids in your honors class."

"Mrs. Burke."

Mrs. Burke was Rachel's mom. Rachel's project on processing style and standardized test scores had won fourth place. If Alex were eliminated, Rachel would compete in his place. Of course Mrs. Burke would be "concerned."

"She wasn't the only one."

There was a rustling of papers, as if Mr. Daniels was looking for his call log, but Mr. Everett stopped him. "You don't need to tell me the others. Ahmed, Chen, Coker—although Jeremy didn't have a chance, and he knows it."

There was a long silence, punctuated by a sigh and then Mr. Daniels's voice. "I'll be honest with you. I don't want to expel him. But the kid has broken the law. He needs to understand the consequences of his action. If I'm going to recommend to the panel he not be expelled, I need to come up with another way to make him suffer."

"There's something else you can do."

Alex's stomach dropped, waiting, as Mr. Daniels waited, for Mr. Everett to continue. Finally, he spoke.

"Force him to withdraw his project from the science fair. Believe me, he'll feel the pain. And the parents who are pressuring you will back off."

Alex stood stunned, his knees weak, unable to believe the words he'd just heard. How could Mr. Everett do this to him? He'd rather be home-schooled and continue to work on his project than withdraw. It was the only thing left for him to care about. Inside the office, the conversation continued, something about additional punishment—a suspension, community service hours, tutoring—and then Mr. Everett walked out.

Without thinking, Alex started to run. Mr. Everett called after him, but he kept running, out the office door, down the hall, through the quad, and all the way to the gym before Mr. Everett caught up with him. He was yelling Alex's name over and over, and when Alex wouldn't stop Mr. Everett grabbed hold of his white collar and pushed him against the wall. He held him there with both hands on his shoulders, and Alex didn't realize he was crying until he felt his teacher's breath on his wet face.

"Jesus, Alex. Stop."

Alex wiped his face, embarrassed. He knew he was overreacting. But it wasn't just the science project; it was everything.

"Get off me," he said, pushing Mr. Everett away. He ducked behind a fire escape, wedging himself between the wall and a metal ladder, away from the curious eyes of the passing students.

Mr. Everett joined him in the shadow of the ladder. "Hey—I'm sorry."

Alex shrugged. "I don't even care about the stupid science project," he said.

But his teacher shook his head. "Yes, you do," he said quietly. "I *know* you, Alex. You'd probably rather be expelled than withdraw your project."

Alex lifted his eyes, studying his teacher. "Then why did you do it?"

Mr. Everett reached around and pulled something out of his pocket. He handed it to Alex. "Because I got this in the mail yesterday."

Alex accepted the folded sheet of paper and opened it slowly. It was water-spotted, like Mr. Everett had carried it through the rain. The ink had bled in messy splotches across the paper.

But Alex could still read it. It was a letter from the board of the state science fair, dated the day before. *We regret to inform you,* it started, and Alex skimmed the polite nothingness that followed until he got to the heart of the matter. *Alex Espinosa, lead scientist*—Alex's heart skipped a beat at the title he'd been given—*has been disqualified from competition.*

"What?" Alex asked. "Why?"

Mr. Everett pointed to the bottom. *The above referenced project has been disqualified for the use of illegally gathered wild bird feathers.*

"I should have thought of it," Mr. Everett said. "It's illegal to so much as pick up a feather from the sidewalk. The Migratory Bird Treaty Act of 1918."

Alex stood in shock as the information sank in. He crumpled the paper into a ball and stuffed it back inside his pocket. He couldn't look at Mr. Everett.

"I'm so sorry." Gently, Mr. Everett touched his shoulder, but Alex wouldn't look at him. "And not just for this. I never would have reported anything if I'd known then what I know now."

Alex remained silent.

"I hope you believe me," he continued. "I'm trying to make things right, and to keep you from being expelled. I only suggested it to Mr. Daniels because it had already been taken away from you."

It had already been taken away.

All the work, all the hours with his father—Alex felt a wave of guilt and sadness, for letting him down. How could he tell Wes? Everything they'd worked for, gone. The midnight texts, the breakthroughs. There he'd been, going through life like he was special, like he might even win, and now it had been taken away from him, before he'd even started.

He thought of Yesenia in Virginia somewhere, locked up, pictured barbed wire and cement floors and hundreds of kids cowering under foil-lined blankets, the images of detention centers he'd pulled up on his phone haunting him.

All her life she'd been working hard, acting like it mattered. But it hadn't. Her life had been taken away too, and long before she'd started.

3

Letty sat on the window seat, her cell phone still warm in her lap. Her right ear burned from the long call, and she pressed it against the cool glass, looking at the porch and the winter-bleak rose garden beyond.

Wes had called. He'd just gotten off the phone with the district attorney's office, and in a breathless rush had told her the news: the DA had dropped the case. After their meeting with the principal, Mr. Daniels had decided not to press charges, and even though the state could have taken the case anyway, in the end they had decided not to, citing the school as a reluctant victim and the lack of any real harm caused.

It was good news—as good as any Letty could have hoped to receive. Alex would have a clean criminal record. Sitting in the early-afternoon sunlight, she felt a flood of relief, followed almost immediately by dread. Alex wouldn't care about his reprieve from the criminal justice system. If anything, it would make him feel worse. Yesenia was still gone.

Letty glanced at her watch. It was almost noon. Rick would be there soon, to take them to meet with Carmen and an immigration attorney. If she wanted to tell him the news before she left, she would have to do it now.

Standing up, she walked down the hall and gently knocked on the door. When Alex didn't respond, she tried to push the door open, but for the first time, it was locked. She knocked harder.

"Alex?"

No response. Racking her brain, she tried to remember the last time she'd checked on him. Had it been before she'd taken Luna to school? Or after? Either way it had been hours.

"Alex?" She pressed her ear to the door but heard nothing. "Alex! Open up."

Finally, the door cracked open. Letty made out one bloodshot eye in the darkness.

Alex was drunk.

The smell hit her first. Sharp and stale, a scent she associated with bloated bar mats and poorly cleaned spills. She pushed the door in so hard it knocked Alex to the floor, his body stretching the whole length of the room. He didn't try to get up. Crouching beside him, Letty shook him hard.

"Get up!" she yelled. At the foot of the bed, a bottle of tequila leaked in a dark pool onto the bedspread. She grabbed it, but not before it was almost empty. There was no way to tell how much he'd had to drink. But by the way he lay there, unmoving, his neck twisting at an angle that would have been painful if he hadn't numbed his body to the point of near unconsciousness, she could tell it had been way, way, way too much. With both hands under his armpits, she pulled him up to sitting and leaned him against the bed frame.

"What were you thinking?" she demanded.

His eyes tried to track hers but ended up somewhere around her ear, his head weaving back and forth on a weak neck. He mumbled something unintelligible. Reaching for the empty bottle, he held it up, studying it the way he'd studied the beakers in the orange glow of the porch light, all those months ago. Letty's heart stopped completely in her chest. She'd done this; she'd introduced him to alcohol as oblivion. Letty had the urge to stick her finger down his throat, to bring it all up and out of him right there on the floor, but instead she went into the kitchen and returned with a glass of water, pressing it to his lips.

"Drink," she said. He pulled the water in, a slow sip, his eyes rolling back in his head. When he gave up and slumped over, Letty ripped the glass away from his mouth and threw the water in his face.

He startled, his eyes wide, water dripping from his lashes.

"Wake up!" She shook his shoulders. "Oh, my God, Alex, you could kill yourself, drinking like this."

Something passed over her son's face, and Letty could tell her warning was something he'd already thought of, and something of which he was not completely afraid. Numbly, she went back to the kitchen for a second glass of water, and when she returned he pulled himself onto the bed, his back straight. He drank the water slowly, and when he was finished, Letty dried his face with a towel.

"I'm sorry," she said. "You scared me."

Alex nodded. She'd wiped the water away, but his eyes were still full. She sat down next to him, wishing he were ten and she could pull him into her arms and make it all go away, the way Maria Elena could always make it all go away when she was that age, everything from mean jokes to skinned knees. This was much bigger than that, and Alex was too old to be comforted anyway, she thought, but then she felt his head fall onto her shoulder, and heard the loud release of a shudder-sigh.

She wrapped an arm around his back and pulled him closer.

"You okay?"

Alex lifted his shoulders and let them fall.

"The charges were dropped."

When he still didn't say anything, Letty leaned away, tilting his face up so that she could read his expression. If he'd understood the consequences of what she'd said, he made no sign. His eyes held a combination of defeat and exhaustion, and looking at him, she was transported back in time, looking at herself in the mirror, watching her body change and every future she'd ever dreamed for herself falling away. Then, and for years after, she'd worn the same empty expression Alex wore now.

She sighed heavily. "Alex?"

It was a long time before he responded. "Yeah."

"I want to tell you something. And I want you to listen."

He nodded into her shoulder.

"You made a mistake. One fucking enormous, stupid mistake."

A sound like a hiccup crossed with a laugh escaped from Alex's mouth, and it made Letty hopeful, that one bad word could still make her son squirm. She squeezed him tighter.

"Did you hear what I said? *One* mistake."

"One fucking enormous, stupid mistake," Alex whispered.

"Exactly. That's all." She pulled away so that she could tilt his chin to look at her. "Now get over it. Buck up and fix it, and if you can't fix it, keep going anyway. It's the only way to live."

Alex sighed. It wasn't that easy, his collapsed body said, and she wanted to tell him she understood—but she couldn't, because the mistake that had derailed her had been him. She remembered telling her mother she was pregnant, remembered how Maria Elena had brought her breakfast in bed the next day and remembered also how she hadn't gotten out of bed for a week. It wasn't her mother's fault. Maria Elena had loved Letty the only way she knew how, with impeccable care and unending generosity. But she'd never made her buck up and get over it, and Letty wondered if her life would be different now if her mother had.

Standing up, she pulled Alex to his feet. He wore the same clothes he'd worn to the meeting the day before, his shoes still on. Letty kneeled down to retie the laces.

"Brush your hair," she said. "We're going to meet with an immigration attorney."

"Me?" Alex wobbled on his feet. "I can't go."

From the kitchen she grabbed a mixing bowl and handed it to him. Now that he was standing, his face was an unnatural shade of yellow.

"You're going," she said, and when he groaned she grabbed both his shoulders roughly, trying to make him understand. It wasn't just one meeting. It was everything.

He looked at her, surprised, and she was surprised too. She sounded like Maria Elena demanding ironed shirts, but this time it was Letty, and she was demanding something much more important: that he care about his own life.

Shaking, Alex doubled over and heaved pure tequila into the bowl.

*   *   *

Ten minutes later, Letty led a still-reluctant Alex to Rick's idling car. He was wearing a fresh T-shirt, and she had sprayed and brushed his hair, but he walked in a crooked line and clutched the mixing bowl to his chest as he stumbled down the stairs. Rick opened his mouth to say something, but Letty silenced him with her eyes, opening the back door and helping Alex inside.

"Hey," she said, climbing into the passenger seat. She leaned over, inhaling Rick's cooking-oil scent. He was wearing his white chef's coat, and Letty remembered he had class that morning. "Thanks for picking us up," she said. "It means a lot to me."

Wes was working; Sara had done all the research to find the best attorney, but now she was at a conference, and wouldn't be back for a week. When Letty called Rick to ask him for a ride, he'd said yes without hesitation—but now he turned away from her gratitude, and in a voice quiet enough that Alex wouldn't be able to hear, said: "You need to know, Letty—I'm not doing this for you. I'm doing it for Yesenia. And for Carmen, and Alex, and Luna."

His words knocked the wind out of her. For days he'd answered all her calls on the first ring, and if he hadn't been exactly affectionate, he hadn't been cold either. But now, in their first semi-alone moment, he'd made himself clear. She'd waited too long. Sinking deeper into the seat, she thought about the day after Christmas, when she'd spent the entire morning with her phone in her lap, flipping it open and snapping it shut, over and over again. The decision whether to call Rick or Wes felt strangely like choosing between her two children, and though she knew in her heart who she craved, it didn't seem like she'd earned the right to listen to her heart. She needed to do what was right for her family, and since she didn't know what that was, she hadn't called either of them. At work the next day, she'd waited nervously for Rick to arrive, but her manager said he'd taken the week off, and instead of calling to ask why, she'd agreed to cover his shifts, pocketing the extra cash like a Christmas present.

Now, it was too late.

"We need to talk," she managed, her regret almost thick enough to trap the words in her throat.

"We do," he said with a sigh. "But now's not the time."

He was right. The tragedy of their near-connection-turned-miss was nothing compared to the tragedy of Yesenia, sent three thousand miles away from her mother, and as much as she wanted to curl up in Rick's cooking-oil scent and unwind her knotted web of insecurities, Letty knew that he was right. Now wasn't the time. Now was about Yesenia.

Rick turned the radio up, and Letty looked out the window, watching the trees thin out and then disappear altogether as they drove from Mission Hills to Bayshore and then, with Carmen sitting numbly in the seat next to Alex, all the way to San Francisco.

The four of them sat in a line, crammed inside a small office on the fifth floor of a nondescript building. Letty sat beside the only window. Across the street she could see the ICE detention center, the parking lot fenced with hurricane wire and a row of white, unmarked buses, waiting. The attorney—KATE MARTIN, the nameplate on her desk read—saw Letty looking, and pointed to where an armed officer led a middle-aged man onto a bus.

"It's the reason I chose this office," she said. "So I wouldn't forget."

The reminder appeared to be too much for Carmen. She covered her mouth with her hand, and Rick stood up to close the blinds. Alex glared at Kate as if she was personally responsible for the handcuffed man in the parking lot below.

Letty wished she would hurry up and tell them what they needed to do. It was too much, being crowded into that tiny office with Alex's guilt and Carmen's fear and Rick's focus, but the young attorney wasn't in any hurry. With her dark, serious eyes moving steadily down the row, from Letty to Rick to Carmen to Alex, she spoke with as much passion as if Yesenia had been her own family member. Rick leaned into Carmen's ear and translated every word.

"The truth is," she said, after explaining in the simplest terms possible what had happened to Yesenia, "it isn't supposed to happen like this. Probation officers are only supposed to call ICE on perpetrators of violent crimes. But I've seen a kid face deportation after stealing a junk bike, so I can't say it surprises me. Especially in Mission Hills."

"But why is she in Virginia?" Alex blurted. "Is she going to be deported?"

Carmen closed her eyes against the word, rocking gently back and forth in her seat. Watching her sway, it was easy to imagine her with Yesenia in her arms, easy to imagine the warmth and strength of Carmen as a mother. Letty felt sick, thinking about Carmen sitting alone in her apartment now, waiting for Yesenia to call. She'd been cleared to call her mother, but only twice a week, and every time she called she said she was fine. But Carmen had told Letty she was not fine. The fear in her voice came through loud and clear from across the country. She didn't understand where she was, or why she was there; all she wanted was to come home.

As an answer to his question, Kate lined up her paperwork on the desk, pointing to the words *unaccompanied minor* written in red.

"Yesenia wouldn't give her mother's name," she said. "Which is common. Kids don't want their parents to get in trouble with immigration, especially when they're the ones who have done something wrong. So the Office of Refugee Resettlement got involved, and she was sent to Virginia, which just happened to be where they had a bed for a nonviolent fifteen-year-old girl with a pending felony charge."

Letty watched as each of them reacted in their own way to Kate's explanation: Rick's sigh, Carmen's crumpled shoulders, Alex's fear. *It doesn't matter that Yesenia is with nonviolent offenders,* Letty saw him thinking. There was nowhere in the world Yesenia would be safe without him.

As they listened, Kate went on and on, talking about why the Office of Refugee Resettlement existed, explaining that immigrant kids alone in this country were some of the most vulnerable to predators, and that ORR was created to keep them out of the hands of the wrong people. Letty shook her head wildly at this, silently begging the attorney not to go into detail about these "wrong people"—or what they might want

with Yesenia. Alex was beyond terrified already; anything else might put
him over the edge.

Rick must have had the same thought, because he interrupted Kate
before she could continue.

"Look at us," he said. In his lap he pulled each finger until it popped,
barely containing his frustration. "How can you say she's alone? She isn't
even close to alone."

"*I* know she isn't." Kate shook her head and looked Rick straight in
the eye. "I'm on your side, remember? I'm here to help you get Yesenia
home."

The room was suddenly hot. Kate walked to the window and pulled
the blinds, sliding the window open as far as it would go. The gray San
Francisco day seeped through the screen, and Rick looked up at the
ceiling for a long moment, gathering himself.

"I'm sorry," he said. "I know you are."

Kate looked out the window. Below, an unmarked bus pulled forward, its brake lights glowing red. The windows were tinted. Men,
women, children, babies; anyone could be on that bus, going anywhere.
No one would ever know. "It's okay," she said, her eyes on the parking
lot. "I can't even imagine what you're going through."

Sighing, she made her way back to the other side of the desk and
pulled a packet of paperwork from the printer. She handed it to Carmen. Carmen, who hadn't spoken a word since they'd entered the office, looked at her wide-eyed. Yesenia needed a sponsor, Kate said
matter-of-factly. She would have the best chance of coming home
quickly if her mother sponsored her. Men, family friends—she dis-
missed Rick with a quick look—were tricky. It would be a much longer,
harder process if anyone but Carmen came forward.

The expression on Carmen's face was one of pure panic. She'd spent
her entire life hiding from anything official, and now she was being
asked to fill out a stack of paperwork and present herself to be fingerprinted. And that was only half of it. In addition to everything she had
to lose here, Letty knew what would be waiting for her if she were returned to Mexico.

"What about me?" Letty asked, and Alex turned to her with a hopeful expression, full of love and a gratitude so intense it almost knocked her flat.

"They wouldn't release her to you," Kate said, shaking her head. "Alex is her coconspirator. Unless there's another family member, it really should be Carmen."

The four of them sat in silence. The only thing worse than Yesenia being taken away was the idea of Carmen being deported. Letty imagined Yesenia returning home to find her mother gone, and knowing it was her fault. It couldn't happen. Did this attorney understand what she was asking Carmen to do? But as if she could read Letty's mind, Kate came around the desk and kneeled in front of Carmen.

"Look," she said. "I know this must be terrifying. But ORR isn't an enforcement agency. They won't come after you."

Terrifying didn't begin to express it, Carmen's face said.

"How do you know they won't?" Rick asked. "Even if ORR's not an enforcement agency, what's to say they won't just turn her over to ICE?"

Kate sighed. "Nothing's to say, honestly. It would be unethical for me to sit here and promise you anything. But I can say that in my *ten years* doing this, I've never seen it happen."

Alex looked relieved. Given his short life span, ten years was enough certainty for him. But Letty and Rick knew better. His mother flashed him a look, and he glanced at Carmen, who kept her eyes steadily on the floor. It wasn't enough for her either.

Placing the paperwork in Carmen's hands, Kate stood up. There was nothing else she could do. "Just bring it back when it's complete."

With that she started to the door, but Alex rose suddenly, cutting her off. "Once she comes home," he asked slowly, looking again out the window and struggling to find the words, "will she be free?"

Letty felt a collective inhale at the question. He was so grown-up, and also still such a boy. *Just say yes*—the mother in her silently begged—but Kate was too much a professional to tell lies, even to ease his pain. Yesenia would never be truly free again. She was on the books now. They might get her a reprieve, but any victory they managed to obtain in court would only be temporary.

"She's not going back to Juvenile Hall," Kate said finally, meeting

Alex's steady gaze. "If that's what you mean. But her case won't go away. We'll ask for relief under DACA—Deferred Action for Childhood Arrivals—but even if it's granted she'll have to reapply every two years. And hope that nothing changes."

"What do you mean by that—*nothing changes*?" Alex asked.

"DACA is an executive order," Kate explained. "Not a law. Which means it can be revoked at any time. We elect a new president? It's gone."

As the meaning of the words sank in, Letty watched the tentative hopefulness drain from Alex's face. Seeing him ghostly white and quivering, Letty remembered just how recently he'd been laid out drunk on the floor. She should have brought the bowl, she thought as he dropped back into his chair and clutched his stomach.

"I don't understand how this could be happening," he moaned softly. "It isn't right. She was practically born here."

Practically. Yesenia's entire future hinged on that one word, and Letty knew it, and Alex knew it, and Carmen and Rick knew it, but there was nothing any of them could do about it. Threading an arm underneath his shoulders, Rick pulled Alex to standing, guiding him gently out the door. Carmen followed them, the weight of the papers—and all they'd just heard—slowing her steps.

Pausing at the door, Letty asked: "How long will it take to bring her home?"

Kate thought for a moment, counting something silently on her fingers. "I don't really have any control over when children are released," she said. "But if you fill out the paperwork today, I can start working on it. And we'll hope for the best."

"Thanks."

Letty felt Kate's eyes on them all the way to the elevator, and then again as they walked the sidewalk below her office window, all the way to Rick's car. Sara had done a good job finding her, Letty thought. She was smart and she cared, even if she couldn't completely understand. But who could understand, really? What had happened was beyond comprehension.

In front of Rick's car they all paused, unsure of what to do. It was a long way back to Bayshore, and when the paperwork was complete, they would need to turn it back in to Kate. From the glove compartment, Rick grabbed a pen and opened the back, gesturing for Carmen to spread the paperwork on the flat surface. The live scan office was right down the street. They would fill out the forms here, and then get her fingerprinted and turn them back in. Letty calculated the time in her head. They should be able to finish it all before they had to pick Luna up from school.

But before Carmen could take the pen Rick offered, Alex grabbed it.

"I'm not sure you should do this," he said. His expression was torn—as much as he wanted Yesenia home, he didn't want to endanger Carmen, didn't want another casualty on his conscience.

Carmen reached for the pen, but Alex backed away, keeping it just out of her reach. They moved in circles across the parking lot.

"Please." His voice broke, desperation in his eyes and throat. "There has to be another way. She wouldn't want you to do this."

Carmen dropped her hand and stood perfectly still. *"Es mi hija,"* she whispered.

Her words stopped Alex's frantic dance. Yesenia was her daughter. And he had no right to say what her daughter would or wouldn't want, or to try to stop her from helping. Carmen would do anything for Yesenia, her fierce eyes said. No matter the consequences.

Alex handed her the pen.

"I'm sorry," he whispered. "This is all my fault. Everything."

Carmen studied Alex, and Letty held her breath, waiting for a glimmer of forgiveness: a nod, a turn of a lip, a word. But Carmen said nothing, just took the pen and turned away from him, and it was Rick who stepped forward, his arm around Alex's shoulders, pulling him close. From where she stood, Letty couldn't hear the words Rick spoke softly into his ear, could see only Alex's head shake vigorously, *no, no, no, no*. With his whole body he fought against Rick, but Rick just held him still, and after a long time, Alex closed his eyes and leaned back against him, surrendering.

"¿Me ayudas?" Carmen asked. She held the pen up to Letty. Her face was a mask of indecision, and confusion, and fear, emotions Letty un-

derstood intimately. But for the first time, watching Rick hold Alex tight in the background, Letty felt her own indecision leave her.

She knew exactly what she wanted.

"Of course," she said, taking the pen from Carmen and sighing deeply. "Let's get Yesenia home."

4

Alex sat through class for an entire week with his eyes on the clock. Every day after school he walked the familiar path back to the Landing, all the way to Building C and then north through the marsh, to the fence that surrounded the airport. Leaning against the wire, he kept his eyes on the sky, watching planes arrive from every direction. Soon, Yesenia would be inside one, flying east to west, escorted by a uniformed officer whose plane ticket—along with Yesenia's—Rick had had to cover.

Alex ditched last period on Friday and went straight to his post by the water, pulling up the hood on his jacket and tying the strings in a tight knot under his chin, so that only a small circle of his face showed. It was cold. The hard ground cracked and broke apart under the weight of his footsteps. When he got to the fence he made a pad of dry grass to lie on and used his backpack as a pillow.

The queue on the runway was long. As a little boy he'd liked Fridays best, sitting by his grandfather while he worked and they invented the weekend adventures of the people inside the planes, earning points for the most creative or outrageous stories. He tried to do it now—imagining picnics in Yellowstone and a night at the New York City Opera, but his heart wasn't in it. The fun with his grandfather had always been in secretly believing that all of it could be his life someday, and as much as his mother had insisted that he not give up, that he keep going, the future felt different now, fuzzy and unreachable. The stack of books underneath his head, whose sharp corners and thick spines had once felt like a direct path forward, now felt like nothing but a heavy weight.

There was a loud rustle in the grass, just a few feet from where he lay. He sat up, expecting a jackrabbit or maybe even a fox, but instead he saw Wes striding through the marsh. Alex was surprised to see him. He hadn't told anyone where he'd been spending his afternoons.

"How did you know I was here?"

"I tried school first," Wes said. Alex waited for the reprimand, but Wes said nothing more, just pulled him to standing.

"Come on," he said. There was urgency in his voice. "Yesenia's plane lands in an hour."

Everyone was there when they arrived—Rick and Letty and Carmen and Luna, waiting at the bottom of the escalator. They nodded hello but said nothing, all of them too scared to speak. The attorney had called when Yesenia was already in the air, but it still felt like anything could happen. The plane could crash. Or be rerouted, or immigration could change their mind and handcuff her again upon arrival.

And then, suddenly, there she was at the top of the escalator, floating down. Alex bolted away from the crowd, unable to stop himself, sprinting up the downward-moving escalator, tripping over suitcases and high heels and handbags until he reached her. He had climbed halfway up the escalator, his shins scraping against the sharp metal steps hard enough to tear the fabric of his pants, and he could feel a thin line of blood trickling down his leg as he threw his arms around her. But the pain was nothing. All that mattered was Yesenia—home, in his arms, her smile eclipsing everything. She disappeared into his chest, let him hold her all the way to the bottom, where she pulled away and fell into her mother's arms.

Carmen cried great, bucketing tears of relief. Wiping her face, she showered her daughter with questions Alex couldn't understand, and Yesenia nodded vigorously, her back as straight as Alex had ever seen it. *I'm okay*, she said, over and over again, but Alex could tell Carmen didn't believe it, and he didn't believe it either. But her answer never wavered, and finally Yesenia peeled away from her mother, hugging Luna and Letty and Wes and Rick in a line. Never taking her eyes off her daughter, Carmen signed the forms the escort held, her tears blurring her signature at the bottom of each page. When she was done, and Yesenia had officially been returned to her custody, Carmen held Yesenia's hand and led her through the maze of parking lots, where they climbed into their cars and caravanned to Courtyard Terrace.

Alex worried that Carmen would want to be alone with her daughter, but she was too grateful for everyone's help to turn them away. All week, in an incredible display of optimism, she had been planning her daughter's welcome home feast. While Yesenia showered and changed, Carmen poured drinks and set the table and slid a tray of enchiladas into the oven.

Carmen had just closed the oven door when Yesenia came out of her room, wet hair brushed into a messy knot and smelling exquisitely like herself, shampoo and baby powder and strawberry lip gloss. She kissed her mother, leaving a shiny spot on her cheek.

"How long until dinner?" she asked, looking at the clock. It was only four.

"*Una hora,*" Carmen replied, setting the timer on the stove for one hour.

Yesenia turned to Alex. "Want to walk to the water?"

Carmen looked worried, as Alex imagined she would look from now on, whenever Yesenia wanted to do anything, or was out of her sight for even one moment. But she didn't object. When Alex nodded, Yesenia kissed Carmen again and told her in Spanish they'd be back before dinner.

Alex followed Yesenia down the stairs and into the marsh. The frozen paths were empty, but still she looked around as she walked, nervous, as if an immigration officer could be lurking in any one of the surrounding bushes. The change was so complete that it was hard to remember her as she'd been the night they'd met on the pedestrian bridge, brave and determined, her eyes full of excitement.

In silence they turned onto the pier, where in summer they had sat together barefoot, their toes lazing in the water. It was too cold for that now. Huddling as close to her as possible, Alex watched each breath leave Yesenia's mouth in a frozen puff of air.

"Are you okay?" he asked finally.

She nodded slowly, then shivered.

"Are you sure?"

She pulled her eyes away from the water and looked at him. "It was the longest week of my life."

"Two hundred and seventy-one hours, fifteen minutes." He'd done the math in the airport, as he'd waited for her to appear at the top of the escalator. "For me too."

Grabbing both her hands, he tucked them under his shirt, pressing them against his stomach to warm them. Yesenia looked past the Landing to the airport, and then past the airport to something only she could see, her eyes glazing over and then snapping shut.

Alex's stomach turned, trying to imagine what she had been through. "Was it awful?"

She sighed. "It wasn't any worse than Juvenile Hall," she said. "Just a bunch of kids that didn't want to be there, fighting because they were bored."

He turned her chin to him, studying her face for marks, and then pushed up both her sleeves.

"I'm fine," Yesenia said, and then she lifted her hand to run her fingers over the pale patch of skin on Alex's forehead, the mark from when the PO had held him roughly against a wall. The scab had shrunk and fallen off, but the scar had not yet faded. "Better than you."

"It's nothing," he said quickly, pulling the hood of his jacket up to cover it.

Yesenia raised her eyebrows. She'd tried to tell him the same thing once. Maybe if he had listened, if he had believed she could take care of herself, none of this would have happened. He turned away from her, stricken by guilt, but she pulled him closer and swung a leg over his lap.

Straddling him, she leaned forward until her forehead pressed against his. He could feel her breathing on the fuzz of his upper lip. They were quiet for a long time, looking at each other.

"What are you thinking?" she asked finally.

The words sprang out before he'd even had a chance to consider them. "I'm thinking we should get married."

Yesenia rolled her eyes up to the sky, shaking her head. "Alex Espinosa, you're just trying to get in my pants."

"I am *not*," he said, embarrassed, but Yesenia smiled, letting out a tiny, swallowing laugh. It was good, magic, to hear her laugh, to know that she still had it in her to make fun of him.

"You're not even sixteen," she said. "It's probably not even legal."

"I'm almost sixteen. And it would solve everything."

"Everything except that we'd be married. Ask me again when you have a college degree and a diamond ring."

It stung a little, that she acted like it would be such a bad thing, being married to him, when all he wanted was to spend the rest of his life with her, to make it so that no one could take her away from him ever again. But she didn't give him a chance to mope, pulling him in and kissing his ear and neck and cheek and chin, making her way from shoulder to fingertip. He let her, remembering Yesenia in every kiss, her smell, her touch, her breath, her taste. When she made it back to his lips, he jerked away, another idea coming to him.

"Or maybe Wes could adopt you. Or Rick."

Yesenia pulled away. She gazed in the direction of her apartment, where Carmen was likely checking the temperature of the enchiladas, setting out forks and napkins, arranging flowers in a vase. Yesenia didn't want to be anywhere but there.

"I'm sorry," he said, regretting his words. "It was a stupid thing to say."

Yesenia shook her head, batting away his apology. Sliding off him, she turned to the water, looking out across the bay to where the lights of San Francisco glittered in the gray sky.

"Where would they send me?" she wondered quietly. "I don't even know anyone in Mexico."

"They won't send you anywhere," Alex said. "I won't let it happen."

His words drifted between them, a fragile string of lies, not strong enough for either of them to hold on to. Alex was powerless. If they'd ever believed otherwise, they knew the truth now. But still he couldn't stop himself. He kept going, painting a picture of her life like he wanted to believe it would be.

"You'll stay with your mom," he said. "You'll apply to private school, and my dad will pay for it, and when you graduate you'll be offered scholarships to all the best schools in the country, and we'll write letters every day and see each other on holidays, and after we graduate I'll get down on my knee with a diamond as big as a star."

Yesenia sighed, going along with it. "And we'll have babies," she whispered. A tear escaped from the corner of her eye; Alex wiped it away with his thumb. "A little girl. And we'll name her Maria Carmencita, and she'll grow up in a good neighborhood with good schools, and she'll never know any of this."

Alex nodded, feeling his own eyes well.

"Maybe," she said after a time, but she knew, and Alex knew, that the future was the thing that had been taken from her. In two weeks she would have to appear in front of a judge. Her attorney would argue relief under DACA, and it would likely be granted. But it would only be temporary. Everything she worked for, from here on out, could be taken away at any moment. He looked at her, expecting tears, expecting unraveling, but for the first time since she'd left the house, she didn't look sad or afraid. She looked determined. She looked like the Yesenia he remembered, her strength a constant surprise.

"I love you, Alex Espinosa," she said suddenly, kissing him.

"I love you too," he said.

And together they stood, hand in hand, and started the long walk home.

5

It was dusk when they finally left Carmen's. Yesenia walked them out to their cars, but Carmen hung behind, grabbing Alex as he tried to pass. Letty watched her place her hands on his shoulders. She couldn't hear what Carmen said, but her whispered words caused his chest to fill with air, and then he let out a long, heavy sigh. He had been forgiven. It would take longer for Alex to forgive himself, but Carmen had done what she could. Letty thanked her as she said good-bye, and Carmen hugged her quickly before ducking back inside. They had been reassured again and again that ICE wasn't looking for Carmen; but it would be a long, long time before any of them believed it.

Rick drove Letty and Luna, Wes drove Alex; so twenty minutes later, it was all five of them who climbed the front steps of the dark cottage. Letty sank immediately onto the window seat. The intensity of waiting had been eclipsed by the intensity of the reunion, and she was beyond exhausted. With her eyes closed, she listened to the sounds of Rick getting Luna ready for bed, the sounds of Wes and Alex making a snack in the kitchen. Footsteps padded down the hall and then approached; when she opened her eyes she saw Wes, sunk silently into the chair across from her.

"Hey," Letty said, sitting up.

"Hey," Wes said. In his hands was a crumpled piece of paper that Letty recognized immediately. "He showed me the letter."

"Awful, isn't it?"

Wes nodded. "Just exactly what he didn't need right now."

"I know," Letty agreed. "And it isn't like Mr. E not to think of it. Swept up in the brilliance of the idea, that's what he told me."

"It *was* brilliant."

"*He's* brilliant," she said, looking off toward Alex's room.

Wes followed her gaze down the hall, and then glanced out the window, to where the dark trees arched through the cold night. He had something to tell her. Letty recognized his expression. It was the same look—elation underneath uncertainty and sadness—he'd worn when he'd come to tell her he'd gotten into Columbia.

"What's up?" she asked, when he didn't say anything.

He bit his lower lip. "I have an opportunity," he said slowly. Drawing his eyes away from the window, he looked at Letty. "I wasn't going to take it. When I first got the call I almost said no right away, but then I thought about it, and I thought it might actually be good for everyone. For Alex, especially."

"What is it?" Letty asked.

"It's a grant from the World Health Organization. Our team has been studying improved diagnostics for TB in HIV patients, and the grant is to go to South Africa. We'd be building capacity—mentoring and training local doctors—so they can better diagnose and treat their own patients."

Letty listened, wondering how any of this could possibly be good for Alex. But Wes continued, answering her question before she could ask: "I thought Alex could come with me. We could pull him in May, right before the science fair, and he could spend all summer working as my assistant."

Was he really asking her to let Alex, her only son, spend four months in South Africa—without her? Her heart screamed a resounding *no* as she tallied up the myriad dangers he could encounter, from plane crashes to political violence to infectious disease. But Wes held her gaze, and Letty knew he was right. It would be good for Alex. He wouldn't have to suffer through the state science fair, and it would give him time to bond with Wes. Not to mention the huge head start it would give him in designing a science project for the following year's competition.

"And at the end of the summer," she asked, "Alex would come back?"

Wes nodded.

"But you wouldn't."

His eyes flitted away from hers, and he shook his head no. "I wouldn't."

Letty thought about Wes at the Christmas party, his hands full of photos. His wanting to be with her had been a product of the holiday spirit and too much champagne, she saw now, nothing more. Wes had a life to live. And his life didn't include Letty—it had never included Letty, which was why she'd let him go in the first place, all those years before.

Just then, Alex walked into the room. He'd changed into flannel pajama pants and a T-shirt, and he sat down on the second chair, next to his father. Letty could tell from his expression that he already knew.

"So what do you think?" Letty asked.

"What do *you* think?" Alex's loyalty lay with her, and it made her heart swell, to feel his dedication, even after everything she'd done.

"I think it sounds exciting."

Relief flooded Alex's face. "Me too. But not for the whole summer. I was thinking maybe just a month."

"Right. Because more than a month away from your *mother* would be way too much."

Alex turned red, grinning guiltily. He'd just gotten Yesenia back. Letty was a little surprised he was considering being away from her at all. But she was glad. They were still so young.

Wes stood up to go. "Thanks, Letty."

Letty nodded, standing up to hug him before watching Alex walk his father to the car. Wes had him by a few inches still, but Alex's shoulders had broadened. They had the same build, the same step, the same hair. Someday soon, from the back, she wouldn't be able to tell them apart.

In the hall she heard Luna's soft feet. Turning away from the window, Letty watched as her daughter appeared in the doorway. Rick had put her in a summer nightgown, but he'd found kneesocks and pulled a sweater over her head.

"Ready for bed?"

Luna shook her head and skipped across the room, jumping up onto the window seat. "I don't want to go to bed."

"She's tired," Rick said, and Letty wondered about the conversation that had led to the kneesock-nightgown-sweater ensemble.

"I am *not* tired," Luna said.

Letty looked at Rick, her eyebrows raised, and Rick moved his chin up and down almost imperceptibly, the motion too subtle for Luna to see.

"Thanks for getting her ready," Letty said. "And I know Carmen already thanked you, but thank you again for paying for Yesenia's ticket. It was a really big deal."

Rick shrugged. In his jacket pocket he felt around for his keys. "You know I was happy to do it."

"I know you were," she said. She'd been trying to find the right time, and now, watching him prepare to leave, she knew she didn't have another minute to wait. Bolting from the room, she grabbed an envelope from her closet.

Rick stood by the door when she returned, looking at her curiously.

"I would have bought Yesenia's ticket myself," she said, swallowing hard. "But I was saving for something else."

Rick took the envelope and slowly opened it. From inside, he pulled a plane ticket. SFO to Morelia and back, April 6–16.

"It's your spring break," she said nervously. The tickets were nonrefundable. "I was hoping you'd come with us—to meet my parents."

Suddenly understanding what was happening, Luna sprang off the window seat and snatched the tickets. If she'd been tired before, she wasn't anymore. On one foot she hopped all around the room, waving the tickets in the air above her head. She'd had a similar reaction on Christmas morning, when she learned they were going to visit her grandparents.

"You're coming with us!" she screamed, hanging off Rick's waist, and Letty watched Rick's expression progress from shock to understanding as Luna dragged him to the window seat, sprang onto his lap, and launched into a detailed description of the Espinosa family home. Luna had heard all the same bedtime stories Letty heard as a child, and she told Rick about the lemon groves and the swimming pool and the feather mosaics in the attic and the festivals in the town square.

When she finally stopped talking, Letty sat down next to them, burrowing her hand underneath Rick's knee, where Luna couldn't see it, and squeezing gently. "Will you come?"

Rick paused, a hint of a smile on his face. Then he nodded. "I will."

Letty exhaled, feeling her body relax fully for the first time since Alex had gotten in trouble. Her head leaning into Rick's shoulder, she pulled Luna against her chest. "I'm sorry it took me so long."

"It's okay," he whispered, his lips pressed against Letty's ear. "You're worth the wait." Then, reaching out to smooth Luna's wild hair, he added: "All of you."

Alex walked into the room then, the screen door banging shut behind him, and Luna jumped down, grabbing his hand and pulling him toward the already crowded window seat. Letty and Rick moved to the end to make room, and Alex flopped down beside them, his head in his mother's lap. Luna dove onto the pile. Alex yelped and tickled her, and Letty tickled Alex, and Rick held on to the window frame to keep them all from falling.

When they'd settled in, Luna lifted her head off the cushion and looked her brother in the eyes.

"Alex?"

"Yeah?"

She looked worried, and Letty wondered if she'd overheard them talking about South Africa. Luna wouldn't want her brother to be gone for a month.

But she hadn't. Dropping her head onto Alex's chest, she asked: "Is Yesenia home to stay?"

Alex's eyes flicked up to meet Letty's, and suddenly Letty flashed on Alex as a little boy, sitting on his grandfather's lap at the Landing. She'd come home between shifts to change and found them by the window, watching the long-empty winter sky flood with bright white gulls. *Are they home to stay?* Alex had asked, the birds' incessant squawking drowning out the loneliness in his six-year-old voice. But her father shook his head no, and then there was Maria Elena behind them, reciting from St. Francis's sermon to the birds. *It is God who made you noble among all creatures, making your home in the thin, pure air.*

Letty remembered feeling a connection to the birds then, en route from one minimum-wage job to another: God had given them nothing. But now, the heaviness of Alex's thoughts in her lap, she realized she'd gotten it all wrong. The birds had been given everything they needed. A home in the thin, pure air: a moment of weightlessness, a reprieve from the gravity of life.

Alex sighed and kissed his sister softly on the nose.

"She's home," he said simply, and maybe he remembered his grandmother's words too, because he added, so quietly Letty almost couldn't hear: "Wherever she is, she's home."

It was enough for Luna. Sighing contentedly, she closed her eyes, and Alex turned to look out the window.

There was a big, dark world out there.

But from where they sat, underneath the soft living room light, Alex couldn't see any of it. He could see only his reflection—and next to him Luna, and Letty, and Rick—the four of them piled together on the too-small window seat.

Letty's eyes met Alex's in the glass. "She's home."

Alex nodded. "Us too."

Rick squeezed Letty's hand, a comforting pressure, and Letty kissed the top of Alex's curly head.

He was right.

Like birds in flight, they were here, and they were home.

ACKNOWLEDGMENTS

They say book two is hard. Whether or not this is true I don't know, but I *believed* it to be true, and so this book was hard for me. *Really* hard. Which means I never would have finished it if it weren't for a number of people who stepped in to revive both me and the book at our darkest hours.

First, Tasha Blaine, who appeared just as I'd almost given up and in record time was able to show me exactly what wasn't working and why. I tore the heart out of this novel and rewrote almost every single page, and I never would have had the confidence, strength, or vision to accomplish that without Tasha answering every call. On a sunny afternoon in Boston we sat in the Public Gardens and outlined the entire backstory, and I, full of joy, remember thinking—*what's so hard about this?* Tasha, I plan to write all future books with you, whether you like it or not.

My agent, Sally Wofford-Girand, is truly my rock, and I am just starting to understand how unbelievably lucky I am to have her as an agent, editor, and friend. Sam Fox and everyone at Union Literary make working with her even more of a dream.

For the second time I have had the great fortune of being published by Ballantine. I am grateful to Jennifer Smith, Jennifer Hershey, Kim Hovey, and Libby McGuire, who believed in this book when it was barely readable, saw the potential in the pages, and didn't stop pushing until I'd written the novel they knew I could write.

When I hired Maria Wessman-Conroy, just after I sold *The Language of Flowers,* I told her I needed someone to help with my kids—except I wanted to be with them every single second—and also that sometimes just the thought of clearing the breakfast dishes made me feel so over-whelmed I had to go lie down. My whole life had just been turned up-side down, and I didn't know what I needed. But Maria did. I needed her to love me and to love my children, and she did that, every single moment of every single day, for three years and on book tours across six countries. I couldn't have done any of it without her, and I will always be indebted to her for her transformational love and care during an in-credibly intense time. I am also grateful to Kasey Reinitz, who sup-ported our family with dedication and grace under pressure through the hardest year of my revisions, and to Emily Grelle, whose thoughtful, poetic spirit and deep knowledge of language made every sentence of this book better. If I manage to write a third book this decade, Emily will be the one to thank!

There is a moment in writing every book that feels almost divine or otherworldly. In writing *We Never Asked for Wings,* that moment oc-curred at an event in San Luis Obispo, when I met Gabriela Sepúlveda. Strong, funny, smart, and a survivor, Gabby made real to me everything I was trying to write about and told me to keep going. I might not have, though, if I hadn't had Nancy Gutierrez and Maritza Cervantes work-ing relentlessly to correct my Spanish and geography and Mexican card games, and later Ara Jauregui, Sandra Martinez, Mayra Morales, and Maria Rendon-Garcia, who gave the manuscript a final read and gave me the courage to send it out into the world.

To write this book I had to learn about all kinds of things I didn't know: science (Allison Shultz, a PhD candidate at Harvard, taught me about feathers and, at the exact right moment in my plot development, e-mailed to make sure I knew that it was illegal to gather wild bird feathers; Noah Diffenbaugh, my brother-in-law and a Stanford climate scientist, explained isotope signatures and helped me revise the chal-lenging opening chapters in the final hour before the book went to be typeset); immigration (Marisa Cianciarulo and Hayley Upshaw helped me make sense of immigration laws that make almost no sense at all); medicine (Kathryn Stephenson and Reagan Schaplow helped me figure out exactly who Wes was); and bartending (Gabrielle Dion and my brother, Mark Botill, both extraordinary bartenders, opened up my eyes to the past, present, and future of the cocktail). I am grateful to all these extraordinary individuals who gave freely of their time and expertise, and also to Adan Gutierrez-Gallegos, who let me borrow the tattoo right off his chest, with its beautiful phrase that inspired Rick's character.

For giving me a room of my own when I needed it most, I would like to thank everyone at the Grand Del Mar and at Mt. Madonna Center, in particular my mother-in-law, Sarada Diffenbaugh, and my father-in-law, Dayanand Diffenbaugh, who makes the very best chai west of the Indian Ocean. For nurturing my children and giving me the mental and emotional (and physical!) space to write, I would like to thank Ken Fleming, Melinda Vasquez, Amy Moylan, Lucia Castiñeira, Noelle Danian, Megan Gage, Kirsten Fried, Lissa McDermott, Dawn Calvert, Jan Mongkolkasetarin, and Holly and Rebekah Wilson. For reading early drafts and giving me kind, honest feedback: Rachel McIntire, Angela Booker, Polly Diffenbaugh, Heather Kirkpatrick, Mary Sullivan Walsh, Talaya Delaney, Barbara Tomash, Ed Vasquez, Liz George, and Jim Botill. For long walks and fantastic talks I would like to thank my dear friend Jennifer Jacoby; most of the major epiphanies I had about this book occurred running around Fresh Pond with Jen, through rain and sleet and snow.

It took me four years and many sleepless nights to find the right title, and in the end it was my childhood friend David Jones who came up with the phrase that became *We Never Asked for Wings*. I can never thank him enough for capturing so well the themes and emotions in this story in a single line.

Finally, I am most grateful of all to my husband, PK Diffenbaugh, the love of my life, and to my children, Donovan, Tre'von, Graciela, and Miles, who had to live with me as I wrote this book. At one point, in the middle of a particularly hard chapter, my seven-year-old daughter said: "I don't want to be a writer anymore, because when you are a writer and your book isn't going well, you are in a really bad mood!" Which is of course true, and also heartbreaking. I can only say I'm sorry, and I hope you won't remember me as I was while writing book two. I've heard that writing book three is pure joy the entire time—I don't know if it's true, but I believe it!

2015